She had learned to
survive in a new land.
Now she must make the most
important choice of all ...

RAVES FOR *PRAIRIE BOUQUET*

"Williams brings her characters to life with a notable attention to detail."

—Booklist

"VINTAGE JEANNE WILLIAMS—told with flair and always with an integral, moving love story as part of the bargain."

—Rocky Mountain News

"AN ENGAGING, WELL-TOLD STORY."

—Amarillo News (TX)

"PAGE-TURNING READING!"

—The Roundup Quarterly

AWARD-WINNING AUTHOR JEANNE WILLIAMS has written over fifty novels, including the *New York Times* bestseller *The Cave Dreamers*. A former president of the Western Writers of America, the Kansas-born author currently resides in Portal, Arizona.

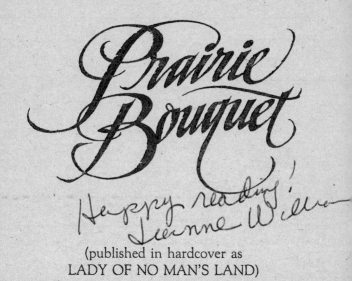

Happy reading!
Jeanne Williams

(published in hardcover as
LADY OF NO MAN'S LAND)

JEANNE
WILLIAMS

ST. MARTIN'S PAPERBACKS

St. Martin's Paperbacks titles are available at quantity discounts for sales promotions, premiums or fund raising. Special books or book excerpts can also be created to fit specific needs. For information write to special sales manager, St. Martin's Press, 175 Fifth Avenue, New York, N.Y. 10010.

Prairie Bouquet was originally published in hardcover under the title *Lady of No Man's Land*.

PRAIRIE BOUQUET

Copyright © 1988 by Jeanne Williams.

All rights reserved. No part of this book may be used or reproduced in any manner whatsoever without written permission except in the case of brief quotations embodied in critical articles or reviews. For information address St. Martin's Press, 175 Fifth Avenue, New York, N.Y. 10010.

Library of Congress Catalog Card Number: 88-11603

ISBN: 0-312-92146-2

Printed in the United States of America

St. Martin's Press hardcover edition published 1988
St. Martin's Paperbacks edition/February 1991

10 9 8 7 6 5 4 3 2 1

For my sister and brother, Lewis and Naomi,
who shared with me a Kansas childhood.

For my children, Kristin and Michael,
whose great-great-grandparents settled the prairies.

And for my grandsons, David and Jason.

Author's Note

My imagination was fired when I first learned, from reading *Calico Chronicle* by Betty J. Mills, that "sewing women" traveled the frontier, staying with customers for two or three months while making their year's clothing. My family on both sides were Kansas and No Man's Land pioneers, so I decided to have Kirsten follow the old wagon-freighting trails from Dodge City to Texas.

I was thinking along these lines when Dr. Kenneth Davis of Texas Tech University in Lubbock, Texas, took me to visit the Ranching Heritage Center in that city. This is a fascinating collection of actual ranch dwellings from the earliest times, authentically furnished. When we entered the magnificent Barton House and went up the stairs, I stared in amazement at a small, neat, cheerful room with a single bed, rocking chair, and sewing machine in front of the window. The sewing woman's domain! But a large intricate structure of wires totally bewildered me. A birdcage? A superior mouse trap? Ken astutely declared it a dress form, and so in this book, we have Milady.

It was also Ken who told me what Kirsten discovers: "Look to the sky for beauty." I owe him warm thanks for taking photos of the wagons and houses and escorting me around the center, which would be of great interest to anyone interested in the history of the plains. JoDee Kite, a graduate student of Dr. Davis's, very kindly sent me material on the Barton House and other information. And the Southwest Collection, under the direction of Dr. David Murrah, himself a distinguished writer and historian, is a treasure trove of plains history, especially of ranching. Thanks also to Preston Lewis, Harriet, Scott, and Melissa, who showed me such gracious hospitality.

My father grew up on a homestead near Dodge City, and I taped and wrote down his recollections, which proved invaluable. He knew old Ben Hodges, the former outlaw, in Dodge, and it is on Ben's reality that my Blue Martin is patterned. My cousin, Alice Shook, of Beaver, Oklahoma, sent me some interesting information and clippings. I am grateful for the efforts of my cousins-in-some-degree, Julia and Maude Elliott of Hartford, Kansas, for tracing our family history and sending me a copy.

Of course, it takes information from many books to create the background for a novel like this. The ones I list will be of interest to you if you enjoy Kirsten's adventures.

Trails South by C. Robert Haywood is a fascinating history of the wagon freighting between Dodge City and the Texas Panhandle. He details the road ranches, stage stops, the salty men who patronized them, and the emerging towns. If you've enjoyed my book, get Haywood's and follow the route again and in greater detail. John Erickson's *Through Time and the Valley* (Austin, Texas: Shoal Creek, 1978) covers part of the Canadian River in a modern ride through old country.

The Kiowa legends and Grandmother Spider's lullaby come from the beautifully illustrated *Kiowa Voices* by Maurice Boyd (Fort Worth, Texas: Texas Christian University Press, 1983).

Two books by Harry Chrisman give the flavor of the Neutral Strip: *Lost Trails of the Cimarron* (Denver, Colorado: Sage Books, 1961) and *Fifty Years on the Owl Hoot Trail*, edited from a manuscript by Jim Herron, first sheriff of No Man's Land (Chicago, Illinois: Swallow Press, 1969). *Panhandle Pioneer* by Donald E. Green (Norman, Oklahoma: University of Oklahoma Press, 1979) also tells much about those days. Ranching life and the disastrous blizzards are described in *C. C. Slaughter* by David Murrah (Austin, Texas: University of Texas Press, 1981); *The Espuela Land and Cattle Company* by William Curry Holden (Austin, Texas: Texas State Historical Association, 1970); *The LS Brand* by Dulcie Sullivan (Austin, Texas: University of Texas Press, 1968); *6,000 Miles of Fence* by Cordelia Sloan Duke and Joe B. Frantz (Austin, Texas: University of Texas Press, 1961), and *Between Sun and Sod* by Willie Newbury Lewis (College Station, Texas: Texas A&M University Press, 1976). My favorite book on Kirsten's first home in America is *Queen of Cowtowns: Dodge City* by Stanley Vestal (Lincoln, Nebraska: University of Nebraska Press, 1952).

The Prairie World by David F. Costello (New York: Crowell,

1975), and *Natural Kansas* by Joseph T. Collins (Lawrence, Kansas: University Press of Kansas, 1985) give wonderful accounts of the creatures of the plains and the changing seasons.

Good accounts of daily life on the frontier, stressing women's experiences, are C. L. Sonnichsen's *From Rattlesnakes to Road Agents* (Fort Worth, Texas: Texas Christian University Press, 1985); *Interwoven* by Sallie Reynolds Matthews (Austin, Texas: University of Texas Press, 1958); and *The Sod House Frontier* by Everett Dick (Lincoln, Nebraska: Johnsen Publishing Co., 1954). Much of the detail of frontier fashion and sewing came from the earlier mentioned *Calico Chronicle* by Betty J. Mills (Lubbock, Texas: Texas Tech Press, 1985).

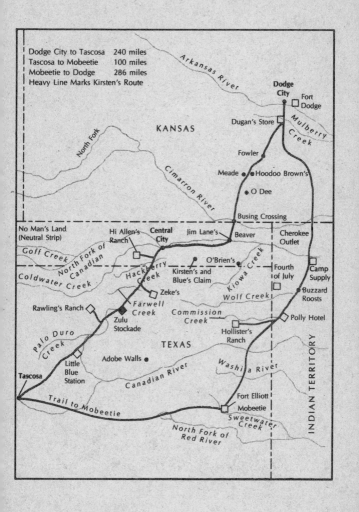

Dodge City to Tascosa   240 miles
Tascosa to Mobeetie   100 miles
Mobeetie to Dodge   286 miles
Heavy Line Marks Kirsten's Route

Arkansas River

Dodge City
Fort Dodge

Dugan's Store
Mulberry Creek

KANSAS

North Fork

Cimarron River

Fowler

Meade
Hoodoo Brown's

O Dee

Busing Crossing

No Man's Land
(Neutral Strip)

Hi Allen's Ranch
Central City
Jim Lane's
Beaver
Cherokee Outlet

Goff Creek
North Fork of Canadian
Hackberry Creek
O'Brien's
Kiowa Creek
Fourth of July
Camp Supply

Coldwater Creek
Kirsten's and Blue's Claim

Zeke's
Wolf Creek
Buzzard Roosts

Rawling's Ranch
Farwell Creek
Commission Creek
Polly Hotel

Zulu Stockade

Palo Duro Creek
TEXAS
Hollister's Ranch

Little Blue Station
Adobe Walls
Washita River

Tascosa
Canadian River
Fort Elliott
Mobeetie

Trail to Mobeetie
Sweetwater Creek

North Fork of Red River

INDIAN TERRITORY

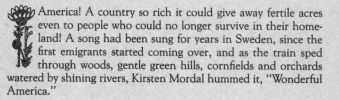 America! A country so rich it could give away fertile acres even to people who could no longer survive in their homeland! A song had been sung for years in Sweden, since the first emigrants started coming over, and as the train sped through woods, gentle green hills, cornfields and orchards watered by shining rivers, Kirsten Mordal hummed it, "Wonderful America."

> *When it rains the poultry falls,*
> *Ducks and chickens pour down.*
> *Geese all fried, prepared to eat,*
> *The fork is in the drumstick!*

Kirsten had seized that promise for herself and her younger sister, Lucia, who looked like a blond angel except for a scatter of freckles on her slightly uptilted nose. Kirsten's hair was darker, the color of autumn sedges with sun on them, and instead of Lucia's blue eyes, she had dark-lashed gray ones. Two years older than her fifteen-year-old sister, Kirsten had always looked after her, and she worried now to see how thin and weary Lucia was.

That would change, Kirsten assured herself. In America, everything would be different. It must be, for there was no going back. After Grandfather Nils died that winter, Kirsten had taken counsel with Sexton Carl, the schoolmaster returned from some years in America, who taught all the children English, since, he sadly predicted, many of them would have to emigrate. He told her that though the eastern and middle parts of the vast country were filled, there was still land in the West to be had almost free. Kirsten loved their village, the mountains, woods and serene lake, and Herr Lynnken, who owned the fields their grandfather had plowed, might out of charity have given them work on one of his farms, but Kirsten wanted something better than that, both for herself and Lucia.

So that spring of 1884, she had sold their cow, horses, furniture and, oh so sorrowfully, even the centuries-old family wedding crown to pay for their journey. The ancient carved chest wedged between their seats held their few clothes wrapped carefully around grandfather's fiddle; the big family Bible that contained the record of generations of the marryings, buryings and births of Mordals; a red satin wedding belt with silver plates showing the wedding at Cana; a stiff-legged wooden Dalarna horse, paint dimmed by many small hands; packets of wildflower seeds; and the bridegroom shirts every young girl began to sew years before she would marry. There had been almost no young men in the village. They had gone to America or to the cities for work.

Lucia had been very quiet all that day. Small wonder. After the foul, crowded steerage of the ship, the emigrant train had at first been a welcome relief, though since its passengers paid such low fares, it was shunted onto sidings to make way for every other kind of train. At least it was possible to get off when the train stopped or to get some exercise by going to the water filter and making tea on the nearby stove. They had rented a bed board and straw cushions for the staggering sum of two and a half dollars, so they could stretch out at night—though this family car was always noisy with crying babies or restless children and an amazing babble of many languages, for everyone had come from another country. It was impossible to wash more than perfunctorily. The smell of odorous foods and humans was as bad as that of the toilet at the end of the car. Lucia had always been frail. Six days on the train had exhausted her.

Kirsten squeezed her sister's hand. "We'll be in Kansas soon, darling; I'll find some kind of work till we can homestead. Which will you have wear your bridegroom's shirt, a handsome cowboy or a rich farmer?"

Lucia tried to smile but her cheeks were flushed and her blue eyes had a glassy look. "You're two years older than I am, Kirsten. You'll be the first to wear the wedding belt. I wish Grandfather could play at the wedding." She sprang up hastily and rushed to the toilet. When she returned, she was pallid, except for the scarlet patches on her cheeks.

"Do—do you suppose I could lie down, Kirsten?"

Fear gripped Kirsten, but she put the board and cushions in place and said cheeringly, "Of course you can, dear. It was so rackety last night that no one could have got much sleep." She unlaced her sister's shoes and covered her with a shawl. There was an empty seat next to theirs, and Kirsten took it, watching Lucia with dread knotting her own stomach.

This was more than weariness. Lucia was ill. Thinking back, Kirsten remembered that her sister had eaten almost nothing last night or today. Maybe some tea would help. Waiting her turn in the line at the stove, Kirsten made the tea and, gently raising Lucia, encouraged her to sip it slowly.

Oh, if only they were in Dodge City, their destination, where Lucia could rest and eat properly, where there must be a doctor! All that interminable night, the sick girl tossed and murmured. Kirsten, sitting up, drowsed now and then, but her mounting fear kept her from really sleeping. Two people had died on the voyage and many had fallen seriously ill. What if Lucia, who always got any childhood ailment twice as hard as Kirsten, had contracted something dangerous?

Every hour or so, Kirsten made tea and coaxed Lucia into drinking it, but the fever seemed to increase, and when morning came, when the train at last huffed to a stop at a depot with the sign DODGE CITY, Kirsten needed the help of the conductor to get her sister off the train.

"She looks bad," muttered the sparse-moustached man. "Better get her to a doctor. I'll have the newsboy get your trunk."

Kirsten's bones seemed to dissolve in fear. This wasn't the way it was supposed to be, their journey's end: Lucia burning with delirious fever, the broad treeless street with its frame buildings that looked as if a strong wind could blow them away. The enormity of what she had done, of what she had brought them to, overwhelmed Kirsten. She stood cradling her sister's head as Lucia huddled on the bench. A number of other travelers got off here, but they walked off with people who were meeting them, stowing their belongings into wagons or carriages.

Whoops and raucous music came from the south side of the tracks, which ran through the middle of town. Horses, carriages and wagons were hitched all along the main street and several side ones. A long line of ox-drawn wagons rumbled out of town, while men on horseback—cowboys, they must be—herded a great mass of cattle, all colors, with long curving horns, toward large wooden pens. Kirsten felt that she and Lucia had been set adrift in a world that was utterly strange and desperately glanced around for something familiar.

As the train chugged jerkily on its way, idlers who had come to watch it wandered off, a few casting curious looks at the sisters. Only a quietly dressed woman of middle age was left. Lucia needed a doctor, but first of all Kirsten must find a place for them to stay. Maybe she could work at one of the hotels in return for food and lodging. They had very little money. Summoning all her courage, she was starting across the street when the gray-gowned woman approached.

"You girls need a home?" She smiled, but her lips were thin and her piercing black eyes had a peculiar glint, which Kirsten took for sympathy. She turned eagerly.

"Kind madam, if I can work—"

The woman gave an incredulous glance. "Now green as you look, how would you know what I am? Don't worry, honey, you'll work." Raising her voice, she called briskly. "Jimbo!"

A stoop-shouldered giant lumbered from behind the depot. He had wide blue eyes and unwrinkled skin, though his brown hair was sprinkled with white. At a word from the woman, he scooped up Lucia and strode across the tracks.

"Jimbo'll come back for your trunk." The stranger slipped her arm through Kirsten's.

Her gratitude tainted by an uneasy sense of having been almost taken prisoner, Kirsten saw the big man entering a building with an ornately lettered sign above it: SELINA'S PALACE. "I'm Selina," the woman said, holding the door open for Kirsten. "What's your name, dear?"

Kirsten couldn't answer, stunned as she was at the sumptuous but terrifying room. Above a long, high counter was a life-size painting of a naked woman in the embrace of a man shaped like a goat from the waist down. Card games were going on at several polished tables, and the room was thick with cigar smoke and perfume. But what sent hot blood to Kirsten's face and made the back of her neck prickle with horror were the filmily robed women who sat drinking with men or hovering around the card-players.

Drawing away from Selina, Kirsten said. "I—to work here, it is not possible."

Selina smiled coaxingly. "It's good money."

"No."

"What about your sister?" As Kirsten shot an anguished glance toward Lucia's limp body, doll-like in the big man's arms, Selina's voice gentled. "There's nowhere else in Dodge where you can earn enough to keep her and buy her medicine."

That shook Kirsten. She hesitated. But just then a man pulled a woman into his lap and ran his hands inside her low-cut gown. To be touched like that by men she didn't know? She had danced at the village feasts, but never had she been alone with a man, never had she been kissed. This was horrible! She couldn't do it, not even for Lucia. There had to be another way.

Backing hastily away from Selina, Kirsten called to Jimbo. "My sister, let me have her!"

He glanced at Selina, who might have argued further had not a big man who'd been laughing and drinking with a woman risen from a sofa and stridden forward. He had thick, wavy red-gold hair, and his eyes, of such dark green that they seemed almost black, searched Kirsten's before he gave her a reassuring smile.

"I'll take the lady, Jimbo," he said, taking Lucia as easily as if she'd been a child.

"Now, see here, O'Brien," began Selina.

"Sure, and if you can't see these colleens aren't for you, 'Lina, you better close down." His tone moved Selina quickly out of his way. Kirsten hastened to open the door, and then to keep up with him.

"Little money we have. Do you know, sir, a work I can do?"

"We won't worry about that till your sister's better." He had a slow, easy way of speaking that in itself would have been comforting, even if his smile hadn't flashed so cheeringly. "You've come from over the ocean?"

"From Sweden."

"Well, my folks came from Ireland in the Famine. This is a rough country in some ways, but a grand place for starting over." He grinned at her. "My name's Patrick O'Brien. What's yours?"

She told him and was explaining about Lucia's illness, when he turned into the doorway of a white-painted frame building.

"Minnie!" O'Brien shouted as they stood in the small foyer. "Got some roomers for you!"

A large, freckled woman with ropelike blond curls pulled up at the back of her head bustled in from a crowded dining room.

"What's the matter with that one?" she demanded, peering at Lucia, whose head nestled in the curve of O'Brien's shoulder.

"Worn out from the long journey, I expect. Come on, Minnie, she needs a bed."

"Who's going to pay for it?"

"I will," said the big man impatiently.

Minnie grunted. "Don't see how you have two bits left after the way you've been carrying on. All right, I guess they can have the little room at the back."

Kirsten stepped forward. "Please, Madam Minnie, I will work to pay." They weren't beggars!

Minnie's bosom swelled. "Now see here, my girl, if you think I'm a madam—"

"Pete's sake, Minnie!" growled O'Brien. "Miss Mordal's just being polite. She's only come over from Sweden. Where's that room?"

Minnie swished down the hall and opened a door. O'Brien gently placed Lucia on a bed that was hollowed in the middle before he turned to a dark, shriveled little man who had a peculiar way of walking, shuffling along in scuffed, rundown boots.

O'Brien got out a worn leather wallet and handed a bill to the older man. "Blue, get the doctor, will you? And then fetch the ladies' trunk from the depot. Minnie, I'll pay you for a week and settle the rest next time I'm in town."

"Whenever that may be," she sniffed.

"I will pay with work!" Kirsten insisted.

"I admire your spunk," O'Brien said. "But your sister may need medicine and doctoring, which can cost an arm and a leg before you know it." At her frightened stare, he chuckled and patted her hand. "Not a real arm and leg, Miss Mordal, that's just a way of speaking. Look, supposing I lend you some money? You can pay me back next time I'm in town, or if it's burning a hole in your pocket, Minnie can tell you how to send it by the stage."

A burning pocket? Even when she knew the words, would she ever understand what these Americans were saying? Before she could argue, O'Brien cleaned his wallet of green paper bills and weighted them with two coins the color of his hair before he gave Minnie a hug and chucked her under the chin.

"You be good to these colleens, Minnie. You weren't always the fine figger of a woman you are now. Just suppose when you were these girls' age you'd found yourself in another country? They need something to eat and—"

Minnie freed herself with an exasperated laugh. "You and your blarney, O'Brien! All right, I'll do what I can."

He bussed her soundly on the cheek. "That's my lady! And now I'll just see what Bridget can fix that's light and tasty."

"Just so you don't keep her from fixing dinner," Minnie warned with a resigned sigh. "I'll make some willow tea. That's good for fever."

Once alone, Kirsten took off Lucia's shoes and gently undressed her down to her shift and a single petticoat. Lucia's skin, like Kirsten's, had always been translucent, but its rose-petal softness, scorched by illness, felt dry and fragile. Battling the fear that gripped her when she saw how wasted Lucia's once shapely arms and shoulders looked, Kirsten smoothed her sister's hair, quieting a protesting whimper by saying, "We can rest now, Lucia. Rest till you're all better. We'll have nice food now, maybe even fresh milk and—and we have a *friend!*"

A rap sounded at the door. Before Kirsten could move, Minnie flowed into the room like a wave of which her large bosom was the crest. Pale lavender eyes flicked between the sisters. She swept to the bed with a switching of the cloth draped between whatever it was that fashionable ladies wore to make a gown stick out behind and set down a tea tray. Stubby but well-kept fingers felt for Lucia's pulse. Curls bounced as she shook her head and spoke in a husky voice.

"Skin and bone. But we'll get some good rich broth down her and this tea should cool her off." Sitting on the edge of the bed, she cradled Lucia's head as if she had done this a hundred times and urged a cup of hot tea through parched lips.

"You are kind," Kirsten ventured, and stopped as she wondered how to address this rather formidable woman.

"Just call me Minnie, child. Well, I've got to see to dinner, but O'Brien will be back to cosset you, and mind you eat, too, my girl. You don't have much more flesh on you than this poor little mite."

All the white-haired doctor could say was that Lucia needed rest and nourishing, soft food. "And you, my dear, could do with those," he added kindly. When Kirsten reached for O'Brien's money, he shook his head. "There's no charge. Send for me if there's any change for the worse."

O'Brien came in with a tray that wafted tantalizing odors through the room. "You'll have a care for the colleens, Doc?" he urged.

"Of course I will," said the doctor a bit testily. "But the young lady's body will have to mend itself, and not even you can rush it." He gave Kirsten a nod and departed.

O'Brien set down the tray and made a comical grimace after the doctor. "Sawbones are all alike. Want to make things sound dismal so you'll think they're the good God himself if you get well." He took the lid off a tureen. "This nice potato soup'll do your sister more good than he can, I'll be bound!" He perched awkwardly on the edge of the bed, but his hands were deftly gentle as he lifted Lucia. "You aim the spoon, colleen. We'll get a little down her, and then you can eat before we give her a tad more."

"Here, darling," said Kirsten in Swedish. "Potato soup, your favorite! Take a swallow."

Eyelids fluttering, Lucia obeyed. After a few small spoonfuls, her eyes opened. "Good," she said, and smiled faintly.

"That's the spirit," encouraged O'Brien. Lucia's wondering glance moved up to him and he smoothed her hair back. "Ay, mavourneen, when you're thriving again, 'tis many a lad's heart you'll break!"

Lucia snuggled closer against him as if entrusting all her cares to him, and Kirsten, aching with weariness, couldn't keep from thinking how heavenly it would be to rest like this in his protective arms. Perhaps her face showed something of that, for O'Brien's eyes, meeting hers, widened for a second, kindling with a—well, a *male*—look before he said, "Your turn now, colleen, there's rice pudding and Bridget fixed you a pot of tea."

"You would like some?"

Merriment danced in those ocean-green eyes. "I haven't drunk tea in fifteen years, but pour ahead, miss, I reckon it won't corrode my innards."

Pleased to do him even such a small service, she carefully filled a cup and passed it to him. He still cradled Lucia, whose fair hair rested on his dark-brown shirt. She looked entirely relaxed, as if sensing she'd found a haven. Surely now that she could sleep soundly and have nourishing food, she'd quickly improve.

Heartened by that thought, Kirsten filled a bowl with fragrant soup. Though she wasn't too hungry at first, the third warming swallow made her ravenous. She had to exert control to keep from gulping, and even so, when she finished, O'Brien watched her with such sympathy that she colored.

"We could not eat well on the train."

"No," he said. "But that's over. Food here in the West isn't always the finest, but there's usually plenty of it. Might be your sister could fancy a bit more of the soup, but you'd best save the pudding till later. A little at a time fairly often's generally the best way to feed sick folk."

His voice had a musical lilt that Kirsten loved, though it made her words more difficult for her to understand. He spoke slowly, though, so she caught the gist of what he intended, and that was pure kindness and concern, as revivifying in its special way as the strengthening food and drink.

Kirsten coaxed Lucia to take perhaps a half cup of soup before the younger girl sleepily turned away, her arm going around O'Brien as she had used to cuddle against Grandfather Nils. Again, Kirsten couldn't keep from wishing she could do that, and to hide such a shameless impulse, she helped herself to rice pudding sweetened with plump raisins, careful this time to ply her spoon with decorum.

O'Brien said regretfully, "I'd like to stay around till your sister's better, but my wagon's loaded with freight I must haul to Camp Supply before the quartermaster sends me to the devil. You'll be all right here, though, with Minnie and Bridget."

With incredible tenderness, he eased the sick girl to the pillow and was drawing the sheet up to her chin when Minnie came in. "Blessed if you don't make a pretty good nursemaid," she joked. "But you better be on your way if you're going to fight fleas at Dugan's road ranch tonight."

"Yep, I've got to rustle." Once again, he took Kirsten's hands in his. Warmth and strength—and something more, something wild and new, inexpressibly sweet—coursed through her veins.

"Don't know when I'll get back to Dodge, Miss Kirsten, but I'll see you one of these days. I sure hope your sister gets well real quick."

If only he weren't leaving! Kirsten felt as if he were the person she'd been searching for without knowing it, someone without whom life would never be as rich and exciting. But they had been so lucky to meet him at all, that she blessed that circumstance and managed a smile. "Thank you, sir, for—for everything."

"Call me O'Brien." Lines radiated from the corners of his eyes and crinkled when he smiled. His long face had a carved jaw that made a surprise of the fleeting dimple. "Everyone does, unless they're naming me something a good deal worse."

"Travel well," she said earnestly.

"Do my best if those durn mules will cooperate. If they see any water, durned if they don't stick down their heads and try to drown."

Minnie snorted. "There's no telling with you, O'Brien, if you'll be back or if you'll get yourself killed down there in No Man's Land."

"Oh, I reckon it's safer than Dodge and a sight healthier." He sobered and shook Kirsten's hand. "Good luck, colleen."

He nodded and moved out the door, while Minnie turned with a shrugging smile. "Bet he gave you all the cash he had. That's O'Brien for you and why he'll never get ahead, though that little freight line of his makes good money. What he needs is a woman to settle him down, but that big Irisher, he loves them all." She looked critically at Lucia. "Got a better color now, not so feverish. Now, dearie, you have a good rest, too. The world always seems better after you've eaten and slept." She gave Kirsten a pat on the shoulder and swayed out with a rustle of petticoats.

When Lucia got well, this would all seem an adventure! They might have to work for Minnie or people like her for a while, but America was a boundless country where people could do almost anything they dared. Look at O'Brien with his own business, though his parents had been starved out of Ireland. She and Lucia would take up land, and comfort each other for the loss of their village and familiar ways. Someday they'd marry and have families for whom they could bake Christmas breads and cookies, to whom they could tell the old stories. Now they were off that smelly, crowded train, Lucia just *had* to get better.

Kirsten got Lucia into a nightgown, took off her own stale garments, and had to empty the wash basin several times before she had sponged off the journey's filth with tepid water from the pitcher. How wonderful to be clean! Putting on her change of underthings, she lay on the edge of the bed, intending to rest for a few minutes, but she sank into a heavy drowse from which she didn't waken till dusk shrouded the room.

After she got another cup of willow tea down Lucia, Kirsten went in search of Minnie to ask what she could do to earn their keep. O'Brien's money was a wonderful surety, but she wouldn't touch it unless she had to, and she intended to return it with a little extra.

Minnie gave her a look of approval. "You know, Kirsty, I think you'll do all right here. You must be tired and Lord knows you're worried about your sister, but you're ready to pitch in and work rather than use up what O'Brien left. The woman who was helping me caught herself a husband last week, so I can sure use you. Like to start with the dishes?"

Blue helped, still wearing his old gray hat, which was tipped back to show his graying, kinky hair. Hobbling between cupboards and rinsing bowl, he dried every plate, utensil and crusted pan that Kirsten washed, piles and piles of them.

"You—work already all the day," she protested, but he laughed, and his soot-colored eyes glowed.

"Pleasure to be with a nice pretty young lady."

He asked where she had come from, obviously trying to use simple words and go slowly, and before she knew it, she was pouring out her story in labored English. How Grandfather Nils, a tough old soldier who had helped give Napoleon his first defeat at Leipzig, had raised his orphaned granddaughters, who'd missed their parents as much as they did food. But even when they went to bed with only water in their stomachs and a little of the pithy, tasteless bark bread that was the starvation food eaten by peasants from ancient times, Grandfather had told them stories first and played his fiddle till they went to sleep. It must have been a way to hearten himself, too, playing the tunes with which he had accompanied the life of the village, from christening celebration to wedding and grave ale, holidays and feasts. As Nils played, perhaps he saw his wife again, the fair young maid with whom he stayed out one long-past Mid-summer night, saw his daughter crowned with candles as Lucia Bride, and his sons, both dead before him, one lost in a storm, the other consumed by fever, riding in the cavalcade that rollicked from farm to farm on St. Stephen's Day.

Through hard work he had managed to buy cows again after those worst years, and a team. He had fallen dead that spring as he ploughed the fields he had tilled since boyhood but never owned.

"Only the rich can own land in Sweden, Blue," Kirsten explained. "The rest are lucky to keep enough of their crops to eat. A song you can hear in any village goes:

Jeanne Williams

> *It's too bad America,*
> *That wonderful America,*
> *Should be so far away.*

Suddenly overcome, she turned her face away to hide her tears, feeling that America, her dreams of it, were still far away, though she was here in body. Could she ever forget the shimmering lake and forested mountains with snowy peaks jutting into the sky? Could any dwelling be home except the old log house with the great birch by the door, the rooms with furnishings made, carved and used by countless generations? No more. No more. The cow sold—Silke, with her sweet moist breath—the geese and chickens and Mork and Moln, Grandfather's team, who had pulled the plough so faithfully. So that they would not be separated, Kirsten had sold them cheap to a neighbor she knew was kind to his animals, but she had felt guilty of betrayal when he led them away and the horses looked back at her inquiringly . . .

Blue patted her soapy hand. "Sure, you'll miss them big lakes and mountains and forests. No way you won't, 'specially in western Kansas. But you want to farm, and you're white, so you'll do fine—better than me."

She frowned in puzzlement. He gave a soft, wry little laugh, accompanied by a hitch of one scrawny shoulder. "I was born a day's ride from here, Miss Kirsty. No towns, no roads, no farms—just grass, an ocean of it, changing colors when the wind blew. It fed herds of buffalo that spread farther 'n your eye can reach, and buffalo fed us. The herds are gone now and the grass is going." He shook his head. "It changed so fast! Twelve—thirteen years ago, there were still lots of buffalo. My people—I'm part Kiowa—ranged over the whole western part of this state and Indian Territory and lots of Texas. They're penned up now on a reservation—that's a mingy piece of land the government gives Indians after stealing what was theirs." She shrank from the bitterness in his tone, from the realization that there could be wrongs even in America, wonderful America. "You left your country, Miss Kirsty," Blue went on. "My country left me—or, truth to tell, it's been ruined."

"You—you don't like farming?" Kirsten faltered. From Sexton Carl's lessons, she vaguely knew red-skinned people had once roamed America, but she hadn't realized they were still here, that the fulfillment of Chinese and Europeans' hope to farm their own land meant ploughing the seas of grass into croplands, and replacing free-ranging animals and people with tame ones.

"No," said Blue. "I don't like farming. I like how it was. But never mind that now, Miss Kirsty! We've earned us a hunk of pie."

2

Lucia seemed to improve. She drank thirstily, though she couldn't eat anything heavier than soup, and sometimes she recognized Kirsten, though she never asked where they were. She only smiled and weakly put out her hand. Kirsten gripped it as if she could force her own health and energy into the wasting body, and talked to her, though she doubted Lucia heard much, telling her about the good farm they would have, how their flower seeds would bloom, and how they'd plant a family tree by the door. Blue stayed with Lucia when Kirsten was making beds, sweeping, dusting, emptying chamber pots—which Blue called thunder mugs—in the outdoor privy, or peeling potatoes and doing dishes.

"Now you stop flying about for the shake of a lamb's tail," Bridget Malone would scold, proffering milk and a cookie or buttered biscuit. "The work will keep, macushla, but you may not if you don't get some flesh on those bones."

Bridget, the red-haired, middle-aged widow of one of the Irish laborers who had helped bring the Santa Fe Railroad into town in 1872, did most of the baking and cooking, and took the laundry home. Harried as she was by incessant toil and her flock of growing children, whom she left in the charge of the eldest, twelve-year-old Annie, Bridget had a joke and a gap-toothed grin for all the lodgers, saved tidbits for Kirsten, and, without being asked, brewed tea and made soup for Lucia.

"Don't ye be after learning my brogue, colleen!" she warned Kirsten. "Now ben't it a marvel ye can read the squiggly cussed words! It's beyond me, but maybe my Annie and the other tykes—" She wiped her sweating brow and rolled out a pie crust with expert twirls of the rolling pin. "I declare, I get so homesick for green that I'd go back to Kilkenny if 'twas only me. But the young'uns, they'll have a chance here, and that's what my poor Mike wanted."

Kirsten was glad that Minnie didn't consider her English good enough for her to work at the hotel desk or take food orders, but she concentrated on learning her new language as swiftly as she could—though she despaired at the welter of accents, and much of what she heard was incorrect. Each day was a battle to get through, even without her fear for Lucia, and she sometimes sobbed with relief when she closed their door after the supper dishes were done and she could stop trying to speak and understand this alien language.

If O'Brien were here, it wouldn't be so hard. She clung to the memory of his smile, his deep reassuring voice. O'Brien, Kirsten was sure, could handle anything and laugh while doing it. According to Blue, O'Brien had been a bull whacker on the Santa Fe Trail, served as an Army scout, and had recently gone into freighting to earn money to stock the small ranch he had started down in the stretch of land that lay west of the Cherokee Outlet in between Kansas and Texas.

"Neutral Strip or No Man's Land. Whatever you call it, there's no law and no legal way to claim land," Blue explained. "But you can bet that hasn't kept some big cattle companies from moving in, including some foreign-owned ones. They fatten cattle on public grass but are mighty quick to hang anyone who takes a cow of theirs. And do they hate farmers! Want to keep them out, but they've got no right to do it."

"We came to homestead," Kirsten said. "Oh Blue, won't there be some left for us?"

"Why, there's sure to be, Miss Kirsty." He smiled. "Course you could marry someone who already has a ranch or farm."

Kirsten blushed because she had immediately thought of O'Brien. Would he be back in Dodge soon? She hoped so. She had looked so awful before, gaunt, exhausted from travel and fear. She was still thin, but she was clean, her hair was neat, and color softly tinted her cheeks. She didn't want O'Brien to treat her like one of the women in Selina's, but she burned for him to see her as something other than a destitute ragamuffin.

That night, as Kirsten was sitting beside her sister, trying to puzzle out a newspaper article on why people in Dodge had a right to drink whiskey, even though it was against Kansas law, Lucia opened her eyes and smiled. "Kirsten, I'm thirsty."

"There's buttermilk right here, darling." Kirsten supported her sister while she drank, then eased her to the pillow. "Could you eat something? A little chicken broth?"

Lucia's childishly full lips drew down in distaste. "No broth. Mother's making Lucia cakes—can't you smell them? I'll have some of those."

Coldness gripped Kirsten, sealing her throat so that she had to swallow before she could say lightly, "It's a long time till Saint Lucia's Day, dear." *And a long way from where we wore the crown of light and took blessings through the parish with a host of star boys and trolls following along.*

Lucia caught her hand. "What a tease you are, Kirsten! Why, you have on the crown, though you're too old for it! The candles shine so brightly!" She listened and laughed. "Grandfather's playing his fiddle. And I hear the star boys coming, and Lucia maidens. Have I been sick, Kirsten? Is that why you're Lucia Bride instead of me?"

"No, love, no! You're our Lucia light."

Lucia fell silent. She still gripped Kirsten's hand, though her long, brown eyelashes rested on her pale cheeks. Kirsten went to the kitchen to make the fever-quenching tea. When she returned, her sister was dead.

It could not have been painful or frightening. Lucia smiled faintly, as if she had slipped into the procession that danced to Nils's music. Mercifully, death had rapt her back to her own country, to happy times.

People were kind. Hotel patrons donated money for a nice coffin, and Blue helped find a burial place, for Kirsten couldn't bear to put Lucia into the dreary graveyard. There was a big honey locust on a small knoll above the Arkansas River, and this was where a young girl from Dalarna was placed under the prairie soil, the bridegroom's shirt she had embroidered folded beside her, the heirloom wedding belt, their only treasure, around her slender waist, the Dala horse she'd played with in her hands.

When Blue saw, he nodded. "Kiowa do that, too. Bury nice things with their folks. Who knows but what they use 'em?"

Blue waited after Minnie, Bridget and a few hotel residents

who'd attended the funeral had gone back to town. He stood far enough away so that Kirsten could cry and talk to Lucia without his hearing, close enough to be seen, to let her know she was not alone. She leaned against the tree so different from the great birch that had guarded their home, and wept the tears that she hadn't been able to loose before, huddling by the raw earth, mourning for the youth and sweetness so tragically blasted, for all the beloved past.

Prairie flowers had been trampled by Blue as he dug the grave and by the minister's team that had hauled the coffin. Just so had Lucia been crushed before she came to full bloom, before she'd found the man who would wear that fine linen shirt she'd made with such care. Would she still be alive if they'd stayed in Sweden? Had Kirsten, trying to better their lives, taken Lucia's? It was an unbearable thought.

When she could weep no more, Kirsten got out the packet of flower seeds brought here in the family Bible. She crumbled the silty earth and planted the seeds, carried water up to them from the river in a tin pitcher she had brought for the task.

Let them grow, Father. Let her have at least some of the flowers she knew . . .

Kirsten wanted to give up and throw herself on the grave, but she was too young and strong to die so easily. Wild with grief, pervaded with guilt, she realized that she was truly alone in the world, a stranger in an unknown land. But in that extremity, determination steeled her, the will that had brought her to America, the dream she cherished even more now, since it was all she had. She would walk back to the town, sleep in the bed she had shared with Lucia, and work the next day and the days after that. She was alive and so she had to live.

The only presence Lucia, Grandfather Nils, or their parents could have now on this earth would be through her. She would sink roots in this land, send them deep to nourishment, deep so they could withstand the scouring winds.

Some man, someday, would wear the wedding shirt she'd sewn, and there would be a little girl as sweet and quick as Lucia, a son to play Grandfather Nils's fiddle. With a wave of longing, Kirsten thought of O'Brien, then straightened her shoulders. A husband would come later. So did dreams. To make them come true, to live through this pain, now she must work.

* * *

Work she did, but every day she walked to the river and watered the seeds as she talked to her sister, the only time she permitted herself to think in Swedish, though it was still most often the language of her dreams. When she dreamed about her daily life, the people's mouths moved but she couldn't distinguish their words.

The haying would be over now in the village—if there was hay. God willing there had been to feed the cattle and horses through the winter. But this year, Nils would not play for the feast. Kirsten sighed as she stripped a bed that looked as if more than one cowboy had forgotten to take off his spurs before collapsing on it.

They didn't have feast days here. When the minister who had buried Lucia had questioned Kirsten about her religion, he had seemed to think Lutherans were some kind of Swedish Catholic and had urged her to repent her sins and be saved. Kirsten had never been overly devout—she and Lucia used to giggle at the dignified old gentleman in a tall silk hat and long coattails who represented God on the church wall—but it would have been a great solace to kneel in the old church now and pray for strength and grace as countless kinfolk of hers had done. If Lucia could only rest in that churchyard by the iron crosses marking Nils's grave and their parents'—

Kirsten gave herself a shake and carried the sheets into the hall. When was Minnie going to pay her? She had worked two weeks now since her sister's death and surely had helped enough even before to have paid their board and room. Her heart went into her throat when she thought of asking about her wages. Minnie had a way about her that intimidated even the boldest drummers and a cold stare that could freeze a drunken soldier or cowboy in midwhoop. Bridget got paid every week. Blue only got his tiny cubby by the kitchen, food, and a little money for tobacco. His shirt had almost fallen off him a few days before, and Minnie, with a great show of generosity, had given him money for a new one.

Was that how Minnie intended to use her? Slow anger burned in Kirsten at the thought of working these grueling weeks for nothing. Minnie had taken them in, and for that she was grateful, but she would never get ahead if she let the woman take advantage of her.

As soon as she had made the scarred bed and rinsed the chamber pot, she went to the kitchen, where she found Minnie ordering Bridget to put plenty of dumplings in the chicken stew to make it stretch further.

"Excuse, Minnie," Kirsten said, fighting to keep her voice even, neither shrill nor pleading. She didn't think it proper to broach the subject before other people. "We talk one minute?"

"Have you cleaned all the rooms?"

"Not all."

"Do it. Then we'll see what's on your mind."

"Minnie, we see now."

The big woman flushed. Bridget smothered a cough that might have been a chuckle. Without flinching, Kirsten met those sharp lavender eyes. It wasn't entirely the money. For Minnie to act like this tarnished Kirsten's bright hopes of America, the faith that hard work counted. Bridget had told her she worked faster and better than anyone Minnie had ever hired; she deserved her wage. "I want to talk now," she repeated firmly.

"Oh, all right, come along then!" Minnie stalked through the dining room to the foyer and posed at the desk. "I suppose you want your pay. I call that dratted ungrateful! Here I took you and your sister in, not knowing but what she had something contagious! Gave you the day off for her funeral and passed the hat for her coffin! Not to mention bothering with a dumb Swede who can't speak the language." She leaned forward, biting off her words. "You ought to be obliged to me, young lady."

"I—obliged, Minnie, but I work hard. To beds and chamber pots, I am not the English speaking."

In spite of her annoyance, Minnie smothered a grin before she argued, "I been training you—"

Kirsten shook her head and smiled a little. "I make beds, do dishes since I am little."

Minnie struggled for a moment. Grudging respect showed in her eyes. "I suppose you'll walk out of here if I don't pay you."

"Yes."

Minnie shook her head but studied Kirsten shrewdly. "Since you've found your tongue, you can start waiting tables. You're too pretty to waste on jobs I can get some ugly old hag to do."

Kirsten inwardly flinched at the prospect of serving the bewildering assembly, mostly men, who took meals at the hotel, but she said pleasantly, "I am paid more, yes?"

"It's not as hard as the work you're doing," sniffed Minnie. "I should think you'd be glad to get out of dumping thunder mugs and washing dishes till bedtime."

Nodding across the street at the town's best hotel, Kirsten said, "Maybe I see what the Dodge House pay."

"Damn it to hell, they got billiards and a bar! They don't need you!" Minnie's eyes narrowed before she laughed. "All right. Fifty cents a day and you get to keep your tips. What with board and room, you can't do better, and that's my last word." She looked disparagingly at Kirsten's black dress. "You need a few pretty dresses."

"I wear black for my sister. One year."

Minnie pulled a face, then said slyly, "If I buy you a uniform—"

"Black it must be." Kirsten met the hard lavender stare till Minnie shook her head.

"Well, with a ruffly white apron and that ripe blond hair and big gray eyes, black may be all right—sort of stylish and high-toned. I have a sewing machine. I'll pay for the material if you make the dress—and be sure it fits."

"A sewing machine?" Kirsten frowned. "What is that, Minnie?"

"Now if you've never seen one, you'll think it's a miracle," Minnie said expansively. "I'll have Blue put it in your room, and when you're finished with your work, I'll show you how to run it."

A machine that sewed! Filled with eager curiosity, Kirsten hurried to finish the rooms. Minnie proudly demonstrated how the Family Gem, clamped to a table, could do single or double stitches with amazing swiftness, evenly spaced and perfect. "Of course," Minnie admitted, "there's still lots of handwork, but this cuts the labor to a fraction. Ready to try it?"

Such a magic? Kirsten could scarcely wait. "Oh, yes!"

It took her a while, practicing on scraps, to learn to guide the cloth while she turned the wheel with her other hand. "While you're getting the hang of it," suggested Minnie, "you might do the skirt seams, parts that won't show if you swerve a bit. Now let's see if we can fold one of my Butterick patterns to fit you. But first—" She reached into her reticule and counted ten dollar bills into Kirsten's hand. "There's your fifty cents for the twenty days you've been here. I'll pay you again next week."

Kirsten gazed at the riches that could join the lonely silver coins she kept in her chest along with O'Brien's money, which she wouldn't have to touch. "Thank you, Minnie."

"Don't mention it." Minnie shrugged good-naturedly. "You're

not as helpless as O'Brien was scared you'd be. You can sew the rest of the afternoon and start waiting tables tonight. Bridget's got a neighbor who can take over your old job."

It was nearing sunset when Kirsten rose, for the first time felt the crick in her shoulder, and stretched like a cat. Fresh energy flowed through her as, swaying, she rotated her shoulders, flexed her legs and reached high as if to catch all the promise of America, where there seemed to be no end of things to be achieved if one did reach.

She caught up the soon-to-be dress and whirled with it as with a dancing partner. Just a few hours ago she had cut it from the black bengaline, heavy silk with a cross-ribbed weave, Minnie had purchased, and already the skirt seams were finished and the sides of the bodice stitched! After work tonight, she'd gather the skirt by hand to make sure the fullness was evenly distributed and perhaps work the buttonholes. Kirsten had always taken pride in her sewing. Now, with most of the drudgery taken over by the machine, she could lavish attention on the finer details.

Kirsten smoothed her hair and put on the ruffled white apron Minnie had located. Concentrating on her sewing had kept her from dreading the ordeal of serving people that night, and now she was too pleased with her accomplishment, too delighted with the miracle of the Family Gem, to get very nervous. If she couldn't understand someone, Bridget or Minnie could translate. She confronted her image in the discolored mirror and thought, *I look different. That color in my cheeks makes my eyes shine, and though the bones show in my face, I don't look like a starved cat, the way I did when O'Brien met me. I look like an American—a woman who can do things.* If he saw her now, maybe he wouldn't just feel sorry for her. Maybe he'd—well, maybe he'd see she was a woman, not the desperate waif he'd pitied.

"Macushla," counseled Bridget as Kirsten set the tables, "remember two things and you'll do fine. Smile and keep their coffee cups full."

That proved excellent advice, though several cowboys gazed at her in such wide-eyed admiration that Kirsten blushed, which only made them blush, too, and order the first thing she suggested. If she didn't catch what was said the first time, the men were happy to repeat themselves, since it kept her with them longer—and some sat ordering more pie or coffee till waiting friends hustled them out. One middle-aged rancher had his wife with him, but otherwise the patrons were men of all sorts, from drummers to well-dressed men who exuded power and were identified by Bridget or Blue as bankers, railroad executives, land magnates, or one of the influential thirty-four members of the Western Kansas Cattle Growers' Association.

"Among 'em, they own half a million head of cattle," said Blue. "And they run most of them cows on the Cherokee Outlet over in Indian Territory and in No Man's Land or the Neutral Strip which is public land though the Cherokees reckon it's part of their outlet to their western hunting grounds. Anyhow, ranchers act like their rules and regulations are the law and they want to keep out homesteaders pretty near as much as south Texas cows with ticks."

Since she planned to be one of those unwelcome homesteaders, Kirsten served the ranchers with concealed trepidation, but they saw no threat in the pretty young foreigner who filled their coffee cups with a dazzling smile and remembered who had ordered what. They tipped almost as generously as the cowboys, the men they hired, and long before closing time, Kirsten had to empty a spill of silver and a few dollar bills into a jar Bridget gave her.

"Huh!" said Minnie, caught between gratification at having every table filled and a virulent attack of her chronic close-fistedness. "By rights, *you* should pay *me* for the chance to feather your nest. But I was right. You do look high-toned in that black and with your accent—shucks, I'm going to raise prices!"

Kirsten laughed. "And you'll pay me more?"

"You're learning our ways too fast," Minnie said. "Don't be greedy." When Kirsten's eyes wandered across the street to the Dodge House, Minnie sighed. "Listen, if business stays this good once folks get used to you, I'll raise your wages. But Lord knows, with all those tips—" She muttered her way to the cashbox.

One man sat alone in the far corner. Kirsten couldn't guess his profession, and neither Bridget nor Blue had seen him before he checked into the hotel that day. His gray suit was precisely tailored to fit broad, almost barrel, shoulders, his black shoes gleamed, his snowy shirt had minute tucks across the front, and he wore a stickpin that looked like a dark diamond. There was a hint of bulldog to his jaw, a look of strength in the flat planes of his ruddy, squarish face. His eyes were the gray of a frozen lake, but the most startling thing about him was his thick, silver hair—even in Kirsten's inexperienced assessment, he couldn't have been much past thirty.

After his meal of steak, gravy, and mashed potatoes, he asked if there was fresh fruit; when told there wasn't, he declined pie and sipped coffee as he scanned the stack of newspapers he'd brought in. Throughout, he treated Kirsten with such polite indifference that she felt a trifle piqued. He spared not a glance to those waiting for tables, and apparently he was a stranger because no one gave him any rowdy encouragement to move.

He left without a word or a glance. "Bet he left a dandy tip." Bridget's grin showed all the gap between her teeth as Kirsten carried back a tray of empty dishes.

Kirsten shook her head. "Not a cent."

Blue and Bridget looked dumbfounded before Bridget's hazel eyes flashed. "Did the spalpeen try to take advantage of you and get mad because you put him in his place?"

"No. He was polite."

"Polite, the divil! Him all got up in that fancy rig and won't leave a working colleen a dime!"

"Yeah," Blue agreed. "That black diamond had to cost him enough to buy all of Front Street. I calls it mingy-stingy!"

Kirsten had to laugh at her friends' indignation. "He paid for his meal. A thief he is not."

Blue curled his lip. "Give me a train robber any day over a durned tightwad!"

Kirsten was tired at closing time. She had cleaned all morning, sewed all afternoon, and waited tables that night, but she felt triumphant. Not once had she needed a translator. She had been pleasant and efficient. And she had five dollars in tips, as much she earned for one week of stripping dirty sheets and dumping chamber pots.

Too thrilled and excited to sleep, she began gauging the skirt, running needle and thread through the gathered material. Why not make bodice and skirt separate? Together, they'd make a dress, but tops always wore out faster than skirts, and when she was out of mourning, she could make a white waist, perhaps even a blue one, and easily extend her wardrobe.

Out of mourning? She thought of Lucia and her needle wavered. How could she be—yes, happy, when Lucia was only two weeks buried? Her eyes brimmed with tears and grief seized her.

She wept but she could almost hear Grandfather Nils speaking as he had after their parents died.

Cry when you must, but laugh as soon as you can, my girls, never think it's wrong to be happy. The best way to honor your parents isn't by mourning at their graves but in making lives they'd be proud of, good and useful. Laugh all you may, for it strengthens the heart. Somehow she thought that was the kind of advice O'Brien would give, too.

Kirsten purged herself of the upwelling desolation, washed her eyes with cold water, and went back to her stitching. A narrow ruffle would look nice around the wrists, collar and hem and could be made from pieced scraps. The fabric, a corded mixture of cotton and silk, was the best Kirsten had ever had, and she treated it almost with reverence. With proper care, it could be what Bridget called "Sunday best" for years.

By the time the gathers were stitched securely and two buttonholes were worked, Kirsten's eyelids were drooping. Carefully draping the pieces over the chair, Kirsten stroked the Family Gem as if it were a friendly genie, ready to labor at the touch of her hand.

"If you were mine," she told it, "I could make my living. You'd be all I'd need." She caught in a breath of delighted realization. Why, it was possible she had enough to pay for such a machine!

That would be her first investment. With it, she could earn her way anywhere there was sewing to be done, and that was practically everywhere. Such a skill would combine splendidly with homesteading, providing she had enough customers.

As she prepared for bed, her head buzzed at the prospect. How she wished O'Brien would come to town so she could discuss her idea with him! Of course, that was far from the only reason she longed to see him. He'd been her first friend in America, and in a way he represented the country to her, all her dreams of it. In order not to mourn fruitlessly for Lucia or the loss of her own country, Kirsten had fixed her mind on O'Brien each night when she went to bed, going over every motion he'd made, every word he'd said, and especially his deep, reassuring voice and the way his dark-green eyes had rested on her. Tonight, though, as she conjured up his face, the silver-haired man intruded and would not be banished, just as he'd dominated his corner in spite of those waiting for it.

Was she that upset because he hadn't tipped her? Kirsten chuckled sleepily at the absurd idea before a shock jarred through her. He hadn't chatted with her, or admired her as the others obviously had, even the married rancher with his wife along. But Kirsten now remembered that every time she had glanced his way as she hurried from table to table, he had been watching her. His gaze had immediately dropped back to his paper and she'd been too busy to connect the visual encounters until now.

What difference does it make? she chided. I'll probably never see him again. Just a stranger passing through. She called up O'Brien's smile, nestled against it, and soon was asleep.

3

Kirsten was up before dawn next morning, humming as the Family Gem purred along seams it would have taken her ten times as long to do by hand. The ruffles would be the last touch, and she was eager to get to them. When, reluctantly, she went to the kitchen for a quick breakfast before the dining room opened, Blue was bursting with news.

"Hey, Miss Kirsty, guess who didn't tip you last night? None other than Ash Bowden!"

"Who is he?"

Blue's jaw dropped. "Well, course you wouldn't know. Cattle, railroads, land, mining, he's made a fortune in each—lost a few, too, lands on his feet and takes off on some new trail afore anyone else sees there's money in it."

"He is on a new trail here?"

"That's the story. He's part of a big Chicago concern and acting for a big Scottish syndicate, too. The word is they'll back him to do just about anything he thinks will make them money." He dropped his voice. "Here he is, first one for breakfast and ten minutes early."

"Drat him," muttered Bridget, who was just slipping pans of biscuits into the oven. "He'll wait till it's ready, that's all."

"I will pour his coffee," Kirsten said, finishing her oatmeal and rising.

"A sight more than he deserves," Blue grumped.

"My job it is." Kirsten shrugged and along with her apron put on a smile that was polite but not warm. She mixed Borden's condensed milk, poured it in a dozen small pitchers, and brought one to Bowden's corner table along with the coffee pot.

"Good morning, sir. Will you coffee have?"

His mouth twitched. "I will coffee have, thank you, miss. If there was no fresh fruit last night, I assume there is none today."

"We have ham or steak or sausage, eggs, biscuits and fried potatoes."

"Strange. I smell none of them cooking."

"They will be ready at seven."

"So I must wait?"

"Oatmeal I can bring."

He made a face that intensified the slightly bulldoggish features. "Don't bother. I'll have steak with all the fat trimmed, two eggs fried on one side only with no more grease than it takes to keep them from sticking, and three biscuits if they're light and fluffy, none if they're sodden." He raised an inquiring silver eyebrow. "Do you understand this well enough to express my wishes to the cook?"

"Bridget's biscuits are very nice," Kirsten said indignantly.

He laughed for the first time and was suddenly quite handsome with that dominating jaw relaxed. "And if I'm so particular I would do well not to travel? Indeed, I would, miss, but business requires sacrifice." He drained his cup and held it out while she refilled it. "Very well, serve me at the earliest possible moment and till then kindly don't hover around me." He got a sheaf of what looked like maps out of a leather case and was immediately absorbed in them.

Cheeks burning, Kirsten longed to kick him for his brusqueness. He needn't worry, she wouldn't go near him except when it was necessary! Bridget almost exploded at the instructions. "That's the way of the skinflints, confound 'em! Always holler for special treatment. I've a good mind to fry his blamed eggs hard as a rock in that grease I was about to use for soap making!"

Kirsten had set the tables the night before, and sugar, salt and pepper were already in place. Now, ignoring Ash Bowden, she put out the milk pitchers and, as patrons came in, began to take orders. She took satisfaction in setting perfectly done eggs, lean steak and feathery golden biscuits in front of Bowden at exactly five minutes after seven.

"Ah," he said, putting aside his maps. "That looks appetizing."

Remembering what many in Sweden would give for the scraps thrown out here, Kirsten said, "If you were hungry, sir, you would be glad for the grease and fat you don't want now to flavor your

27

bread and root soup." That was not the way to speak to customers and she colored furiously. "Sir, that I should not say."

"But you think it."

She wouldn't lie, even if it meant losing her job. "I know it, sir."

"I never expect apologies for the truth," he said, and fixed his attention on his plate.

Again, he left no tip and he took his dinner elsewhere, but that evening he was back in possession of the corner, with more papers and maps. Kirsten said not one unnecessary word to him, though she was civil, smiled, and kept his coffee cup filled. When she went to clear his table, a gold coin like those O'Brien had left with her lay beside his plate.

"He must drop it," she told Bridget and Blue, showing it. "Blue, will you take it to his room, please?"

"You'd ought to keep it," Blue said. "What's five dollars to the likes of Ash Bowden?"

"I can't."

Blue's wrinkles deepened in a smile. "I reckon you can't, not you, Miss Kirsty." He hobbled off while Kirsten cleaned the tables and made them ready for morning.

"Would you believe it?" he said disgustedly. "Thanked me cool as a cucumber and didn't send you a red cent!"

"Maybe that is why he is rich," Kirsten grinned. "It doesn't matter." She clinked her heavy apron pocket and gave Blue a quarter. "For the errand, Blue. I can appreciate if he does not."

She insisted he keep it and hurried to her room where the Family Gem, her magic helper, waited with her dress. That afternoon Bridget had helped her fit the bodice, positioning the slender metal stays so that the top fitted snugly without binding under the arms. That was the most difficult part. If she finished sewing the stays in place tonight, in the morning she could finish the lining and start the ruffles!

Promptly at seven, Ash Bowden took his usual position and placed the same order, this time without cautions or useless inquiries about fruit. "The colored man said you found my gold piece last night, miss."

"Yes, sir, I did."

"Most waitresses would think it a sign of the patron's satisfaction with the service."

"I couldn't think that, sir, not when—" She broke off.

He laughed, and again it made him attractive. "When I left no tip before? But why weren't you angry enough to pocket it and think it served me right? Especially when, as you so forcefully told me, I don't value my fortunate condition?"

"I do not steal."

He gave her a shrewd, carefully evaluating scrutiny before he smiled. "I admire your probity, miss, though it will be no asset in building up a bank account. However, the gold was for you. Rather than bother with dimes and quarters, I prefer, on occasion, to leave a substantial sum with those whose service impresses me."

He set the gold coin beside his plate. Kirsten had never forgotten those horrifying moments in Selina's when she had seen men buying women. "Sir, too much that is. I cannot take it."

Again his eyes swept over her, and she couldn't tell whether he was annoyed or amused. "All right, will you be kind enough to tell me what is acceptable?" Though the most expensive dinner was seventy-five cents, patrons left a lot more quarters than dimes or nickels.

"If you left a quarter, sir, for your three meals, that would be seventy-five cents."

He replaced the gold piece with a silver dollar. "Let's say this takes us through tonight's dinner." He turned to his papers, dismissing her so completely that she felt a bit annoyed, though she assured herself that at least he wasn't trying to lure her into sin.

Minnie happened to be in the kitchen when Kirsten told Bridget about the puzzling encounter. "You turned down a five-dollar gold piece from a rich man who wasn't even drunk?" she demanded. "And after the way you made me pay you wages on top of board and room? You'll wind up poor or a millionaire, and right this minute I'll be doggoned if I can guess which!"

Kirsten had to chuckle at Minnie's indignation. "I don't like to be poor and don't know how to be rich, Minnie. I just want enough."

"Enough!" Minnie raised her hands to heaven. "What in the world is that?"

"Good food. A roof, clothing." Kirsten paused, shaken by a surge of longing for the log house in the birches between the mountains and the lake, before she thought of O'Brien. "I want a home, Minnie, to live with a man I love who will love me, too."

"I wish you luck with that," Minnie scoffed, but her usually hard eyes misted. "But if you're going to homestead, you'll need a husband for the heavy work, same as you'll need a mule or horse or ox."

"Boy howdy!" whistled Blue as Bridget and Kirsten laughed. "No wonder you never got married, Minnie!"

"After watching Pa drink himself to death on money Ma and I earned scrubbing miners' clothes, I figured I'd do better on my own. Sure, running a business alone is tough, but not as tough as having some Dandy Dan to trip over."

"My Sean was a good man," objected Bridget. "Never bespoke me a cross word, handed over his pay and let me decide if he could afford a dram."

"That's right. He was good, hard-working and honest, but could he leave you anything to live on?"

Bridget's mouth quivered and she daubed at her eyes. "Sure and we neither of us ever thought he'd leave me, not young as he was. Whisht, 'twas a cruel day entirely!"

"Better a good dead one than a no-account live one," Minnie said by way of rough comfort before she turned back to Kirsten. "Don't get in a rush, Kirsty, for that home. Save money first for the things you'll need, for I'll tell you flat—it's little cash you'll get in your fingers once you go to farming."

"You'll never see a homesteader's wife in here for a meal, macushla," nodded Bridget. "Most of the poor pitiful creatures don't get to town for years on end or even have a neighbor close enough to natter with."

"That'd be the hardest thing on you, Bridget," Blue teased affectionately.

"I'll be a homesteader," said Kirsten. "A poor, pitiful creature, no! I didn't come here for that."

"That's the way, Miss Kirsty." Blue applauded as she went to pour more coffee.

She had spoken boldly and her determination had not wavered, but it would have been foolish to ignore such warnings. All too well, she knew crops could fail and she wanted a cow and chickens and yes—she smiled to remember Minnie's comparison—a mule or a horse. But a husband most of all—let it be O'Brien!

Her heart smote her. In her haste to finish the dress, she hadn't visited her sister's grave for two days. This afternoon, instead of sewing ruffles, she must do that. And now that she had money, she'd go to the blacksmith and see if he could fashion a wrought-iron fence to enclose and protect the grave. Blue had scavenged up a solid piece of mahogany and carved it with Lucia's name, wreathed with roses and doves, and her birth and death dates. No matter how much money she had, Kirsten wouldn't replace it, not as long as he lived, for it was made with love.

Another thing she must do was return O'Brien's money. As soon as she was free for a few hours before noon, she borrowed paper and pencil from Minnie and labored over a note. She couldn't bear to write down that Lucia was dead. After much thought, she had only a few lines to tuck into the small packet she'd made for the money.

> Dear Mr. O'Brien:
> I have not needed your money but you were most kind to lend it and help me. Thank you. I hope you are well.
> Kirsten Mordal

It was not at all what she wanted to say. To this first American friend she wanted to pour out her feelings, her success as a waitress, her amazement at the Family Gem, but she couldn't do that unless she was sure he'd be interested. She delivered the packet to the stage office, where she was told with a laugh that, yes, certainly, they knew where O'Brien lived, and the missive would safely await him at the Kiowa Creek way station, where mail was left for the surrounding area.

That afternoon she watered the seeds at Lucia's grave and, sitting beneath the honey locust, told her sister, in their own language, about the sewing machine and of how, in her new work, she was beginning to understand much more of what Americans said, and how generous they were.

"They're big, like this country, Lucia. And, oh, these prairies roll out of sight in all directions! The sky rests on the grasslands with nothing between, no forests or mountains. But the sky is so blue, little sister! A bright shining, and when clouds build up, people hope it will rain. There can be terrible storms with winds that knock down houses and carry animals through the air, and in winter, Blue says there are ice storms, just the kind trolls would send. At home we had so much water, so many rivers and lakes, that it's hard to believe crops and even animals and people die here from lack of water."

Gazing across the boundless spread of the plains, Kirsten tried to say clearly what she felt about this country. "It's—open. Wide. No fences, no walls. I love that, but it's a little frightening, as if the wind might whirl you right off the earth into the sky." She laughed at this fancy and then sobered.

This was not the kind of place Lucia could have liked. She needed a sense of shelter and coziness. Tears filled Kirsten's eyes. She could speak no longer, but buried her face in her arms and sobbed. *Dear little sister, whose bridegroom was death, would you be alive if I hadn't brought you here? Or is it destined anyway, the time we must die?*

She had no answers, but as she walked back to town, she thought the ache that was always deep in her heart even when she laughed would never really vanish till she held a girl child in her arms, one she could love as she had loved Lucia.

Ash Bowden's table went to others that night, nor was he at breakfast, though Minnie said his luggage was still in his room, except for a small satchel. Kirsten sewed the final ruffles on her sleeves that afternoon, washed her hair, scrubbed herself pink in the round zinc tub, and put on fresh undergarments before donning her creation, which she had decided to make without a bustle. She thought bustles grotesque, and anyway, she would always have been bumping it into patrons when she tried to maneuver in the crowded dining room. By holding the unsatisfactory mirror at different angles, she could see the dress fitted well and was becoming. The small ruffles gave it, she thought, a touch of elegance. Her hair wasn't completely dry when she braided it so she made the coils looser than usual and approved of the effect, for it softened her face and made it seem fuller.

Bridget fingered the bengaline. "Good enough for Queen Victoria her own self," she admired. "And look at those buttonholes and the ruffles! 'Tis a real gift ye have, macushla."

Blue's eyes spoke for him, but he said softly, "You look just beautiful, Miss Kirsty. What I'm hopin' to see you wear before too long, though, is a white bride dress."

"Don't give her notions," Minnie reprimanded. "We're getting twice the customers we had before Kirsty started waiting tables." She examined the finishing with a critical eye, and at last, after circling Kirsten, gave a nod. "Well done. The ruffles sure add style. I've got a length of velvet I've been afraid to butcher. Sewing's not my strong point, even with the machine. Like to make the dress, Kirsty? I'd pay you a dollar and a half."

"You don't use the machine, Minnie?"

"Not much. I've run up aprons and plain skirts and petticoats."

"You would sell it to me?"

After a moment's surprise, Minnie shrugged. "Reckon I would if you've got six dollars."

"I make your dress. Then I owe four and one-half dollars." Kirsten mentally calculated what she had left after paying for the iron fence. "I can pay you two dollars now, you keep my wages five days, and all is paid."

"Makes my head ache!" grimaced Blue.

Minnie gave Kirsten a thoughtful look. "If I'm not careful, you'll wind up with the hotel! But I was sorry I'd bought the dratted thing when I found out it didn't do the wonders it was supposed to."

"Oh, it does them!" Kirsten defended, as if Minnie were disparaging a friend.

"For you, maybe. All right, Kirsty. Make my dress, give me the cash, and end of the week, the contraption's yours."

Kirsten couldn't keep from giving Minnie a hug. "Thank you, Minnie! When you need sewing done, I will give to you a special price."

"I bet," grinned Minnie reluctantly. "Get on your apron. Someone just came in."

As she entered the dining room, Kirsten glanced involuntarily at Ash Bowden's table. He wasn't there, and though she stayed busy the whole evening, she found herself regretting that he hadn't seen her dress, even though she doubted that he'd mention it. He clearly didn't miss much. That small disappointment subsided, though, when she went to her room and caressed the Family Gem.

"You're almost mine," she told it. "And we'll make dozens and dozens of dresses for all kinds of women in all parts of their lives, whether they're courting, or marrying, carrying a baby, or burying. You are going to help me earn what I need to homestead, we'll stitch away if crops fail. With you, I can earn my own way."

A heady feeling. If she could just tell O'Brien! Someday, if he'd let her take the measure of those wide shoulders, that strongly columned neck, she'd make him a fine tucked shirt like those Ash Bowden wore. When he got his money, surely she'd hear from him. Wouldn't he have to be proud of her? Rejecting Ash Bowden's quizzical face, she summoned up O'Brien's, her nightly ritual and, smiling at him, drifted into the best and deepest sleep she'd had since she decided to sell everything to come to America.

Next day, between meals, Kirsten and Minnie pored through *Harper's Bazaar* for ideas with which to alter or embellish Minnie's McCall and Butterick patterns. "I'm a long way from slender," sighed Minnie, "but let's try to make me look that way. Maybe this pointed basque—"

Kirsten studied the tight-fitting bodice and shook her head. "Minnie, for you this better is." She pointed to a princess sheath. "You will slimmer look if the waist is loose. And," she added delicately, "this way you are not likely to have to take out the stitches; that is hard on velvet."

"You may be right. That's a plain line, but with plenty of passamenterie—that's trim, Kirsty, braid, gimp, tinsel and the like—and a stylish bustle, it would look dressy enough."

"The fabric *is* the beauty," Kirsten said. "With purple velvet, Minnie, you don't need trimming. But if we could find some handsome buttons, they'd make a long, narrow line down the front that would slim you." At Minnie's dubious frown, Kirsten laughed. "Please try it, Minnie. If you don't like the way it makes you look, I promise to sew on all the fancy work you want."

"Fair enough," Minnie consented. "I have some nice jet buttons with crystal centers. Think they'd do?"

"If they're not too big."

The rest of Kirsten's free time that day went to designing and fitting a pattern for the princess front, incorporating it with the pattern featuring the bustle that Minnie would not give up, and cutting out the garment with infinite care for the rich, soft fabric that felt like a kitten's fur.

This dress had to be near perfect, for Kirsten was determined that it would justify her advice and taste. She basted and fitted, in spite of Minnie's complaints, till she was satisfied with the effect. Only then did she confirm her basting stitches with the Family Gem, which would soon be her very own. So absorbed was she with her creation that when, at each meal, she saw that Ash Bowden wasn't there, the little twinge of disappointment faded more quickly each time. Sarah Taylor, a graying, buxom friend of

Bridget's who had taken over the cleaning, said his belongings were still in his room, so he'd be back sometime, unless he met with disaster. The person she really longed to see was O'Brien. When she'd asked Blue how long it took to drive a wagon to Camp Supply, he'd given her a knowing smile. "Good mules like O'Brien's make about two and a half miles an hour, and it's a hundred miles to Camp Supply, but don't start holding your breath, Miss Kirsty. Mules and oxen have to graze. Eight days to the camp's pretty fair time, and of course he may go on south before he swings back to Dodge." Blue winked. "If O'Brien ever gets hitched to double harness, there'll be a lot of sad ladies—and not such ladies—all the way from Dodge to Tascosa and Mobeetie down in Texas." At Kirsten's dismayed look, Blue grinned reassuringly. "None of 'em pretty as you, though. He's sure going to be surprised when he sees you."

"I did look terrible," Kirsten agreed dolefully. Why would he want to see her when he must know all too many attractive, seductive women? He'd felt sorry for her, and from all she heard, it was his nature instinctively to help anyone who needed it. All the same, she kept track of the days.

On the seventeenth day, she was laying the tables for the next meal when the door opened. She glanced up and almost dropped some plates. O'Brien stood in the door, bright hair rimmed with light, eyes the green-black of the deepest waters. At the sight of her he laughed in delight, crossed in a long stride, took the plates from her and set them down before he captured her hands.

"Colleen! Roses in your cheeks, enough flesh so you don't look like a stray kitten! It's a pure pleasure to set eyes on you, though I ought to scold you for sending my money straight back!" His smile dimmed, but the strength of his hands buoyed her. "Blue told me about your little sister. I'm sorry, Kirsty girl."

His words brought back, in an overwhelming rush, those terrible days of mingled hope and fear while Lucia was slipping out of this new world she'd never had a chance to know. Eyes brimming, Kirsten tried to speak and choked.

In an instant, O'Brien was holding her close, stroking her hair, patting her shoulder, as no one had done since Grandfather Nils died. "There, colleen, cry it out." His heart beat strong and steady beneath her cheek. "Of course 'tis a shame your sister died and

35

she so young and like a flower. You'll always miss her, but someday you'll remember the happy times you had more than the sorrow, and then it'll be like she's just off in another part of the country. But sure, for a long time, you'll grieve."

To him she could voice that haunting guilt. "O'Brien, she—still alive she might be if I hadn't decided to come here."

"No one but God knows about that, Kirsty." It seemed natural for him to call her that. "Who's to say if you'd stayed put and half-starved instead of trying for a better life, that she wouldn't have been carried off by some piddling sickness that wouldn't faze a healthy person?"

"But I decided for her."

"You did your best, all anyone can do." He held her while she sobbed out her dammed-up feelings. When she drew away, snuffling and embarrassed, he extended a big red handkerchief.

"Tell you what, Kirsty," he said as she wiped her eyes and was forced to blow her nose, "I brought a load of bones back—that's buffalo bones; they're worth money. Just sold 'em, and need to get rid of some of the money. Why don't we go to the vaudeville show and—" At her shocked face, he looked abashed and tugged at his ear. "No, sure that wouldn't be fitting." He brightened. "But let me take you to eat tonight at the Dodge House and you can tell me everything you've been doing."

"I must work. Besides, Minnie cannot like your dining at the competition."

"Leave Minnie to me," he said confidently. "I've got a bottle of her favorite peach brandy. For that, she'll be glad to take over for you. I'll talk to her right now."

4

"Brandy and blarney!" Minnie said as Kirsten left on O'Brien's arm. "Now listen, Kirsty, I can stand your having a meal at the Dodge House, but don't you let them talk you into going to work for them."

"I won't, Minnie," Kirsten assured her, turning to give her employer a hug. "Thank you."

"Thank O'Brien," sniffed Minnie. "Giving me the brandy before he says what he wants and when I hold back a bit, he makes me feel like a dadburned slave driver."

"You should thank me for giving you a chance to be generous," O'Brien laughed, giving Minnie a hearty smack on the edge of her ear. "Laying up treasures in heaven you be and—"

"Oh, go on with you!" Shaking her head, Minnie pushed them out the door.

This was Kirsten's favorite dream, being with O'Brien. The reality made her breathe fully and deeply as she would in the high mountains. Her heart was racing, the familiar buildings of Front Street etched suddenly sharp and clear as if she saw them for the first time. A hawk wheeled toward the sun and her spirit rose with it, exalted, joyful.

O'Brien, too, gazed after the hawk, then smiled down at her. She was tall for a woman, but her head just reached his shoulder. "It's a grand country, colleen, and sure, you've got the heart for it. Blue tells me you're going to conquer the West with your needle."

"Not my needle! With my sewing machine. Have you seen one, O'Brien?"

"Not that I recollect, but such contraptions aren't much in my line." He added hastily, "I'd admire to see yours, though."

"Do you have something that needs mending?"

"Might. I just wear things till I can't poke an arm or leg in 'em and then toss them away."

She shook her head, aghast, stopped, and surveyed him critically while he fidgeted like a small boy. "The elbows, almost out of your shirt they are, and the collar needs turning," she decreed. "After we dine, I'll fix it."

"Sure, Kirsty, 'tis an old rag and not worth your trouble. It's not more work that you're needing but a little enjoyment." As they came up the steps of the two-storey white frame hotel with its columned portico, several loungers called out greetings to O'Brien. He cheerily responded but didn't stop, which made Kirsten amusedly suspect that he didn't want to introduce her to his acquaintances.

"I'd enjoy mending for you," she said. "You can borrow a shirt from Blue and watch me."

"Stubborn as you are pretty," he groaned, but his eyes twinkled as he drew out her chair and seated her with a flourish. "All right, Kirsty, you can save my shirt and show off your newfangled machine, but first we're going to have the best food between Kansas City and San Francisco!"

Intimidated by the linen tablecloth, china, and silver, bemused by the array of unfamiliar dishes on the bill of fare, Kirsten said, "Please, O'Brien, you order for me. But the lemon tart, could I have it for dessert?"

"Anything your heart desires," he said expansively, and smiled at the middle-aged waitress. "And how does this day find you, Mrs. Gardiner, and those two fine twins of yours?"

"All well, O'Brien." The tired face lightened with a smile and the woman said to Kirsten, "He's a rascal, my dear, but a nice one. I can tell you that he's usually in our billiard room or bar, not the restaurant."

"I'm here tonight," said O'Brien righteously. "Maybe, Mrs. Gardiner, you'd be kind enough to recommend what we should have."

She dimpled, looking years younger. "Well, O'Brien, that depends on whether you're flush or almost broke."

" 'Tis rich I am at the moment," he chuckled.

"Then better you spend on good food rather than bad whiskey. The spiced oysters and celery would be nice to start. Then perhaps broiled ham or porterhouse steak with mushrooms. Peas creamed with onions. And folks who've had them in both places say our Saratoga potato chips are as good as those they make at fancy Saratoga Springs resorts. The mince pie with rum jelly is absolutely scrumptious."

O'Brien raised an eyebrow. "Sound good to you, Kirsty? With lemon tart? I'll have the mince pie and you can sample it." She nodded, dazzled by foods that made Bridget's cooking, good as it was, seem very plain. "And, Mrs. Gardiner," O'Brien concluded, "might there be some champagne punch?"

"You?" she asked, eyes going round. "You, O'Brien? Champagne punch?"

"Indeed, that's what I'm asking," he said serenely.

"Wait till I tell Johnny in the bar." Mrs. Gardiner stifled a giggle. "He'll fix your punch, O'Brien, but you'll never hear the last of it."

She was off, skirts swishing with renewed energy. Kirsten, just wanting to hear O'Brien's deep, rippling voice, determined to store up and remember every precious moment, sighed with vast contentment and said, "Tell me about your trip to Camp Supply, O'Brien. Tell me about all those roads you take."

"Well, now, it was just an ordinary run, but at Hoodoo Brown's road ranch, I happened on to Temple Houston—that's old Sam Houston's son. Dresses fit to kill but can outshoot most gunfighters—and I reckon that I taught him some finer points of poker. Then down at Jim Lane's on the Beaver River—"

Kirsten hung on every word, but he broke off when Mrs. Gardiner returned with a crystal decanter, oysters and a platter of relishes. He filled their glasses and touched the rim of his to hers.

"Here's to the future, Kirsty. May all your dreams of America come true."

Just being with him was her best dream. In his open-handed fashion, he'd asked her out tonight to give her a treat, but at least he was seeing her a lot differently than at their first meeting. Maybe someday, even though he knew so many women, he might possibly, conceivably, come to care for her in a special way. Anyway, she could dream.

"Here's to your future," she told him. "All your trails, smooth may they run."

"Oh, I don't mind the rough, as long as they're interesting." He downed his punch like water, while Kirsten sipped hers, not sure that she liked the bubbles but determined to savor the drink because O'Brien had ordered it as a celebration. The bubbles *were* nice, she decided after her third or fourth cautious swallow. They entered her blood and swirled effervescently, turning her head pleasantly light and dizzy as if she'd been spinning in a dance.

The food was delicious. She especially liked the thin-sliced, crisp-fried potatoes and tangy lemon tart. Mrs. Gardiner, smiling benevolently, didn't rush them, but kept their cups filled with coffee till Kirsten noticed with a start that all the other patrons were gone. Knowing how tired her own feet were at the end of a day's serving tables, she said urgently to O'Brien, "We must leave now so Mrs. Gardiner can. And I still want to fix your shirt."

"So I'll appreciate your sewing machine?" he teased. His eyes looked black except where the chandeliers struck glints of jade, and he studied Kirsten with a sort of puzzlement. "I invited you out to give you a change, Kirsty, but I don't know when I've had a better time. 'Tis a grand conversationalist you are." His grin broadened. "Or I should say, a fine listener."

"You listened to me, too," Kirsten laughed. "Will—will you be in town long?"

Motioning for the check, he shook his head regretfully. "Got to haul a load of lumber to a rancher on Wolf Creek. He's got a bride coming from St. Louis soon as he builds a house, so he's all of an itch to get it done. But I'll be back, colleen, of that you may be sure. Maybe I can take you to the Firemen's Christmas ball. That's the fanciest doin's in Dodge, and we can watch even if we can't dance."

"But O'Brien, you should dance," she protested.

"I'll wait till you can." His tone deepened. Their eyes met, and something in his made her catch her breath, turned her more deliciously light-headed than the champagne. "I'd like real well, Kirsty, to be the first man you dance with in America."

The dizziness became rosy fire glowing in her, till she felt it must surely be visible. "I would like that, too, O'Brien."

"Kirsty—" Mrs. Gardiner returned with his change. He praised the dinner and left a silver dollar by his plate. As he pulled back Kirsten's chair, she could tell he'd changed his mind about whatever he'd started to say and felt a stab of disappointment, though she knew it was much too soon, even in America, even if she hadn't been in mourning, for a man to begin to woo a woman.

She guessed, too, that it was to protect her reputation that he stood chatting with Blue in the open door while she turned his collar and patched his shirt.

"Doggone if that's not pretty work," he said with gratifying wonder when she handed him the shirt. "Looks like new—can't even see the stitches! Well, Kirsty, I'll show this off to my married friends and tell them about Minnie's dress and I bet their wives'll be wanting you to make them up some high-falutin' duds."

"That will be fine, if they come to town so I can fit them," Kirsten said. She gave him her hand. "Thank you, O'Brien. This evening was—oh, it was the most wonderful evening of my life!"

Should she have said that? But it was true. Her other happy memories were those of a child—and she was a child no longer. He brushed a light kiss across the tip of her nose.

"Wait till we dance," he promised, laughing. "Blue, keep an eye out for this young lady. She's pretty special."

"Reckon we know that, O'Brien," said Blue, and went after him with a chuckle.

Too excited to sleep, Kirsten worked on Minnie's dress while she lived over every minute she'd had that day with O'Brien, especially those hushed times when his eyes said much more than his lips. She warned herself that he was impulsive. Maybe he behaved this way with any woman he chanced to be with, but she couldn't quite believe that, especially when he'd obviously bridled his tongue.

Next time he came . . . Dreaming ahead to that, dreaming back over the last hours, Kirsten at last made ready for bed and drifted into sleep, smiling at O'Brien, remembering a song from her homeland.

So night and day and day and night are yours and only yours.
Oh will the time yet come, love, when day and night are ours?

She dared to hope it would, for wasn't she in America, the land where dreams came true?

The ornamental fence was finished that week and the blacksmith obligingly helped Blue mortar it in place. The smith had worked lilies into the grilles, and Kirsten drew comfort from the artistry. Anyone who passed the grave could tell it belonged to someone beloved and remembered. As she stood by it, Kirsten closed her eyes and saw Lucia robed in white for Saint Lucia's Day, the time of the winter solstice, a crown of candles lighting the morning dimness as she handed out crunchy Lucia cakes before joining the procession that carried Lucia's blessing to all the parish folk, even to the beasts. "Lucia light! Shortest day and longest night . . ."

Oh, indeed, Lucia's day had been short. Kirsten bowed her head, gripping the fence. *Lucia, Lucia!*

"Ah," said a voice so close beside her that she jumped and retreated. "If you have such love for a sister, Kirsten Mordal, how would you love a man?"

Though he was not a tall man, Ash Bowden standing close blotted out everything else. The silty earth softened footfalls, but to have come up so silently, he must have made an effort. As startled by his question as by his presence, Kirsten could only stare at him. It was broad day, and they were near the town, yet her pulse quickened as it would at danger.

His gray eyes, usually so chill, shone as if they had absorbed the sunlight. He smiled in the way that eased the thrust of his jaw. "Why don't you answer me, Kirsten? You could always say it's none of my business."

"It *is* none of your business." As if snapping a paralysis, Kirsten found her tongue. "And, sir, it is not right—not proper—that you call me by my first name."

His mouth tucked down. "I had thought better of you than that you put timid stock in formalities, but very well, Miss Mordal, I stand rebuked."

"How do you know my name?"

"I make it my business to know about—people who interest me." That she could interest such a man was both flattering and disturbing. He gave her a cool smile. "I'll wager you can't answer my question anyway. Some lad in your Swedish village may have made your heart beat faster, but if I can judge a woman's eyes, you're well nigh as innocent as when you were born."

"Sir, this is—it is—" She broke off, unable to think of the right English words.

"Not proper?" he suggested. "Believe me, Miss Mordal, I intend no disrespect. If I apologize abjectly, will you allow me to escort you into town?"

A bay horse waited in the road, "hitched" by its reins trailed in front of him. A squashy leather satchel was tied with a bedroll behind the cantle. Bowden had been where there were no hotels.

"You have a horse," said Kirsten. "Why should you walk?"

"I could put you up in the saddle in front of me, but however romantic that sounds, it's damnably uncomfortable for all parties, including the horse. If you've no violent objection, I'll stroll along with you."

It seemed childish to argue further, though as they walked toward town, Kirsten was so uncomfortably aware of his gaze that she tried to dispel the tension mounting between them. "You have been gone almost two weeks," she said.

"So you noticed." He gave a pleased laugh and she colored. "A mightily uncomfortable time it's been, too, stopping at way stations where the food was scorched and the bedding full of vermin. But I've seen enough of No Man's Land to be sure it's what I'm looking for."

"No Man's Land?" That was where O'Brien lived. "Did you pass by Kiowa Creek?"

"Would that I had, but I got there so late I spent one of the most miserable nights of my life in a dugout with six men who stank to high heaven. The smell wasn't the worst part, though. I had to spend a long time in a cold creek to get rid of all the small beasties that staked out claims on my person." He gave her a side glance as thorough as it was fleeting. "No, I didn't happen onto Patrick O'Brien, the part-time rancher, part-time freighter, who succored you and your sister. You doubtless feel grateful to him."

"Yes. Kind he was."

Bowden laughed. "Any man of his type would have done the same. Given away his last dime on impulse. Easy come, easy go."

"He worked hard for the money he lent me."

"Of course. And he'll always have to because he uses his back, not his brain."

"He uses his heart," retorted Kirsten. "He didn't watch me as a cat does a mouse for several days before he offered to help. He didn't set tests to see if I was honest, or creep up behind me, or ask wrong questions!"

"From what Minnie says, he didn't have time for such interesting pursuits. Did you know that he's getting married?"

Kirsten's heart plummeted like a stone. "Married?" she whispered. "But he was here last week, and—and—"

"Said nothing?" Bowden gave a flick of his hand. "It seems a sudden decision. Lorena Meadows was engaged to his best friend, Jack Stuart, who got shot by rustlers. Stuart was scarcely buried when the young lady's family announced that she'll be marrying O'Brien. Some think he loved her all the time but held back because of Stuart. She's said to be a beautiful woman, and very sweet to boot."

Trying to quell the sick feeling in the pit of her stomach, Kirsten said, "O'Brien deserves that. I hope they will be happy."

"Do you? Don't you hope, just a little, that things may not run so well between them, and he'll remember a lovely Swedish girl who's very grateful to him?"

Kirsten's cheeks blazed. "You—you—" She searched for the worst American curse she'd heard. "You go to hell in a hand basket!"

Back stiff, she marched down Front Street ahead of him, avoiding the water-filled whiskey barrels ranged outside the buildings for fire protection. When she reached her room, she fell on the bed and cried. What a fool she'd been! Dreaming of O'Brien, going to sleep with thoughts of him, comforting herself with the memory of his smile! To him, she had just been a waif, someone to feel sorry for and lift to her feet with an encouraging pat before going back to the woman he'd marry.

It was all her fault, this crushing disappointment. He hadn't said anything, not really. But the way he'd looked at her when he swept her off to dine at the Dodge House, the way his voice had deepened as he said that when she was out of mourning, he'd teach her how Americans danced. . . . Oh, she was foolish! He charmed as naturally as he breathed! Kirsten's thoughts ticked back. But hadn't he been drinking and heaven knew what else with one of Selina's women? So he *could* notice females other than Lorena, even if he'd been in love with her for ages.

Well? Would you want him to pay you money to do whatever men do and then yearn after his sweetheart?

Kirsten angrily jerked herself up, splashed cold water in the basin, and cupped her eyes with it. It hurt, but it was well she knew the truth before she was completely besotted with fantasies. She owed O'Brien a debt she'd repay if ever she could, she was bound to wish him joy, him and his bride, and there must be no more lulling herself to sleep with imagining that she traced with her fingers the planes of his face, the hard muscles of his throat, that his mouth came down on hers . . .

She gave herself a shake and began to tidy herself for work. No. She must never dream that again. When he entered her mind, she must add Lorena, conquer the flood of envy, and try to bless them both. That would not be easy. Praise be for work, something to keep the mind too busy to dwell on dark-green eyes and fiery hair, to make her body so tired that rest would come.

Humiliation flamed in her at knowing that Bowden guessed her secret. Why had he gone to so much trouble to find out about her? Whatever she did, she wouldn't give him any further chance to read her feelings. Was he simply cruel? Did it amuse him to expose people and watch their struggle to cover themselves against his expressionless stare? She wouldn't give him that satisfaction.

Steeling herself, she tied on a fresh apron and went to the kitchen. *Smile, and keep their coffee cups filled.*

Kirsten had become adept at refusing invitations from cowboys, ranchers, the occasional farmer with money enough to eat at Minnie's, and officers and soldiers from the post five miles from town. They invited her to the Lady Gay vaudeville theater, to dances and horse races and even to church. When a leading merchant asked her to a party at the Fire Company and she declined, saying that she was in mourning for her sister, Minnie overheard and, when they were out of earshot, exploded.

"I'd give my eyeteeth to get asked to an affair at the Company Hall! They've got a Brussels carpet and a library, all the latest magazines and papers, and only the most important men are asked to join. Pride of Dodge City, the company is. You don't appreciate your luck."

"Mr. Finister is nice," Kirsten said. "But Bridget tells me his wife died last year and he looks for another. He is old enough to be my father and—"

"He's going bald!" Minnie finished. "The things a girl will overlook for a head of handsome hair and a white-toothed grin! Well, Miss Picky, if you'd rather wait tables than marry well, it's no skin off my nose."

Most of the men respected Kirsten's excuse for shunning entertainment, though a few continued to suggest new amusements. The truth was that though she did indeed mourn Lucia and would have felt guilty to seek pleasure this soon beyond what she found in her sewing, Kirsten couldn't banish O'Brien from her thoughts and, in an orgy of self-pity, shed tears at a vision of herself growing old still faithful to a man who would never know she loved him. In some embroideries on this theme, she nursed him through a dread disease Lorena shrank from and then nobly stepped out of their lives.

The problem with these bittersweet morbidities was that she was young, healthy, and eager for life. She wanted a man to wear her bridegroom's shirt and hold her in his arms. She wanted children, a small Lucia to love. All that would have to wait, though, till she mastered this feeling for O'Brien.

Ash Bowden made no mention of their afternoon's encounter as she waited on him that evening, but when she briskly refilled his cup a third time and was hurrying away, he said, "Miss Mordal?"

"Yes, sir?"

"I am insulted by that professional smile." His tone was soft. "Give me an honest glower, and welcome, but I don't want pretense from you."

It felt good to let the smile fade and give him a withering stare, except that he didn't wither, but chuckled. "Amazing what temper does for your coloring, my Swedish ice maiden." His eyes caught and held hers as compellingly as if he had seized her hands and a sort of lightning flashed through her veins.

"Will you have dessert, sir?"

"Not unless there is fresh, sweet fruit."

She had to laugh at that. "I'm afraid you'll have to wait a long time for that, Mr. Bowden."

"I can wait. This may surprise you, but I'm used to doing without when I can't have what I want. That whets my appetite all the more."

"You have always gotten what you want?"

His smile died. She could tell he was swept back to something he didn't want to remember. With a slight movement of his broad shoulders he gave her an ironic look. "Let's say I have since I was grown. Long enough to form the habit. Fill my cup once more, Miss Mordal, and then you may ignore me the rest of the evening."

Next day she gave Minnie her final fitting and finished the handwork by sitting up till midnight. She might as well work. Denied the familiar ritual of invoking O'Brien as she fell asleep, she had to stay up till she drowsed off in her chair from weariness, and when she lay down, sleep fled as imagined Lorenas haunted her.

Sweet and pretty, Bowden had said. But was she small or plump, fair or dark? What had made O'Brien love her instead of—

Stop it! Turning over for the dozenth time, Kirsten tried to block out the taunting phantasms with different visions, banished Ash Bowden's face which came uninvited, and at last found one she could hold. A house—it changed from log to white-painted frame to stone. What it was made of didn't matter, but it was shaded by a great tree, and beyond a big garden, fruit trees were weighted down with apples and pears. A bronze and green rooster strutted among his diligently pecking hens, and a cow the color of rich cream grazed beside a stream.

O'Brien was lost to her, but she could have this dream. Entering the house, she put the Mordal Bible on the mantel of the fireplace, placed the old chest under a window with a bouquet of flowers on top, pulled up a rocker before the cheerful fire. By the other window gleamed the Family Gem, which had helped pay for the cupboard of delftware and shining copper and pewter, the four-poster bed in the second room with a marble-topped dresser and big etched mirror. The house, though, seemed to cry out for O'Brien, so she went outside and down to the orchard, walked among the trees and at last selected the ripest, reddest apple. As she savored its smell and crispness, the dream deepened into sleep.

Delighted with her gown, Minnie displayed it to Bridget and Blue, turning slowly so they could admire every detail. "Now that's style, Minnie." Bridget's tone was so wistful that Kirsten was jarred into considering the position of this woman who'd been so kind to her. Every cent Bridget earned went for rent and to feed and clothe four children. She had no money for a pretty dress or any other self-indulgence. Her wages were twice Kirsten's, but she got no tips.

Well, Kirsten decided, Bridget shall have a dress, as nice as I can make it.

Preening in the hall mirror, Minnie said, "You were right about the buttons and the princess line, Kirsty. I do look slimmer. Guess I'll have to start going to church so's I can show it off. There are a few other seamstresses in town, but you're more than that, you're a—well, doggone it, you're an *artist!*"

"With the machine—"

"Drat the machine! I couldn't make anything like this with twenty of them." Minnie checked herself. "Mind now, you'll still make more working for me and getting those good tips, but in your spare time, you could do right well. Only the other day down at the mercantile, I heard the banker's wife saying she'd buy some of the new challis Mr. Wright just got in if she could have it made up nice. I could drop a word in Mr. Wright's ear."

"Thank you, Minnie," said Kirsten. "Why don't you show Mr. Wright your dress? If he likes it, he can tell customers about me. But it will be a week before I can make anything."

"Need a rest?" Minnie nodded and again surveyed herself approvingly. "You've been at it day and night for three weeks. Time you had a change."

Kirsten had planned to visit Wright, Beverley & Company's mercantile establishment that afternoon. When she got there, the owner, Bob Wright, and a number of other men were arguing over who'd win the November election for President that autumn of 1884, so she had plenty of time to study all the dress material while she tried to understand something of the accusations supporters of Republican James Blaine and Democrat Grover Cleveland were hurling at each other's candidates. Blaine, it seemed, had been corrupt while Speaker of the House, and Cleveland had fathered a child by a woman he hadn't married.

Dismayed at these revelations, Kirsten assured herself that such behavior couldn't be common in American politics and chose a soft gauze-like wool and silk grenadine of golden-brown that would flatter Bridget's hair and bring out the color of her eyes. With thread and some dark brown braid, the purchase took all of Kirsten's small hoard, but with the machine and the expensive fence paid for, her savings would quickly start mounting. There was no use spending her time on a cheap dress. This would probably be the best garment Bridget would ever own and Kirsten vowed to make it special.

The problem was how to fit it without arousing suspicions. Kirsten invented an aunt back in Sweden with Bridget's dimensions and asked Bridget whether she would model the pattern and dress Kirsten was sewing for that imaginary lady. Bridget was glad to oblige, and before she went to bed that night, Kirsten had the dress cut out. She had just time to sink down in the rocker of her dream house before she fell asleep.

* * *

Since his disclosure of O'Brien's impending marriage, Kirsten waited on Ash Bowden expeditiously and, taking him at his word, didn't smile unless he smiled first at her. Then it was impossible not to respond. That morning, he was smiling.

"Miss Mordal," he said as soon as he'd had his breakfast, "since your arrival in Dodge, you've done nothing but work. Don't you want to have a look around your new country?"

Of course she wanted to! Hadn't one of her best O'Brien dreams been of riding with him over all the unclaimed land between here and the settled parts of Texas till they came to just the right place for her homestead?

"I have no way to go," she said. "Besides, in the day I have no more, ever, than three hours off."

"This day is all free." At her wondering stare, he laughed. "I've talked to Minnie. She agrees you've earned a little vacation. I've rented a buggy. Take off your apron and let's go."

"Go ahead, dear," Minnie said. "I can take over for one day and you need a little fun."

Kirsten hesitated. A drive through America, a look at what lay beyond the town? She burned to go. Ash Bowden could anger her, but he also made her feel completely alive. "Why do you invite me?" she asked flatly.

"Because I want to be with you. Why else?"

"Then I had better not go."

He made an impatient sound. "Be reasonable, Miss Mordal. Of course I want your company. But you're not obligated to me in any way. I won't presume that we're keeping company." His mouth quirked on one side. "I know all too well you'd only come to see more of this country."

"You—often I do not like the things you say."

"Have no fear. I promise to drop any subject you don't wish to discuss and act with total circumspection—that means I'll behave." His eyes coaxed laughingly. "Don't be timid, Miss Mordal. We can each have what we want—or some of it. Forget about tomorrow and tomorrow and tomorrow. Take off your apron and come with me."

She took a deep breath and the blood in her veins seemed to dance as she ran back to the kitchen and hung up the apron. Bridget blew her a kiss. "Have a grand day, macushla."

Not a hint of envy. Kirsten was glad she was making that dress. She blew back the kiss, smoothed her hair and went outside. Bowden waited to hand her into the gleaming black buggy with gold plush upholstery before he climbed up and took the reins of the matched bay team. Except that it wasn't O'Brien at her side, she felt caught up in a fairy tale, in all her dreams of America, as the team clip-clopped smartly down Front Street and turned sharply south on Bridge Street. An ancient cottonwood stood on the south bank of the Arkansas River.

"Dodge is built right on the wheel ruts of the old Santa Fe Trail, which used to bring goods from St. Louis to what was then Mexico," Bowden said as he paid the toll for using the bridge. "That tree was a landmark in those days. It's the last one you'll see for a good many miles."

It was late September now, and cattle that had to be trailed north to Wyoming and Montana had already passed through, but herds were still coming in from the Texas Panhandle, the Indian Territory and No Man's Land, so there were several cowboy camps along the road from which the men sallied in to revel in the town's assortment of pleasures. For several miles beyond the river, sand from flooding or blowing had shaped rolling hills, some tufted with grass, others ready to shift with a strong wind.

When the buggy had passed the last camp and they faced prairie that stretched vast and limitless as the broad blue sky, Bowden slowed the team. "Welcome, Kirsten Mordal," he said softly, and he smiled, gazing on the horizon as if he, too, had a dream. "Welcome to America."

Her throat was tight and her eyes blurred, but she drank in the air like wine and could not keep from lifting her arms as if to embrace all that lay before her. "It is so *big!*"

"It is, and it gets bigger. We're headed for Mulberry Creek, ten miles from here. Thirteen miles beyond it, the road forks, with the Military Road running easterly to Camp Supply over in Indian Territory and south to Mobeetie and Fort Elliott, two hundred eighty-six miles all told. The Jones and Plummer Trail stays west and misses Camp Supply before it runs to Mobeetie or turns off to Tascosa."

"Tascosa? How far is that?"

"About two hundred and forty miles." At her stunned look, he chuckled. "Sounds mighty far, doesn't it? In miles and days it is. A freighter who makes it from Dodge to Tascosa in eighteen days has had a good run. But you've got to look at this region as a huge triangle with Dodge at the top, Tascosa and Mobeetie with Fort Elliott at the southern corners. In fact, it's called the Triangle. Prime buffalo range. Up to about seven years ago, hide hunters sold hundreds of thousands of hides in these towns. Generally blew all their money before they went back on the plains. Tougher lot than cowboys ever thought of being."

Kirsten remembered something Blue had told her. "That was when the Indians finally had to stay on reservations, when the buffalo were gone?"

"Yes. General Sheridan was all for the hide hunters. Said when the Indians' 'commissary'—the buffalo herds—was destroyed, they'd have to submit. Of course, the hunters made such a clean sweep that they put themselves out of business, though there's a good trade in hauling buffalo bones to be sold for fertilizer and buttons. You can still find big piles of bones where a herd was slaughtered in just a few hours."

Kirsten looked at the short, thick, bluish grass spreading away from the broad wagon ruts. "I wish I could have seen a buffalo," she said wistfully.

"Oh, you may. There are still a few around, and Colonel Charles Goodnight's protecting a small herd on his ranch down in Palo Duro Canyon. Anyhow, before the hide boom ended, cattle started trailing to Dodge, which became the railhead in 1872. That boom's about over."

"But Blue told me that more than three hundred thousand head of cattle came through Dodge this year, over a hundred big herds!"

"They did, but things are happening fast in No Man's Land. Cattlemen started running stock there when the Western Trail was laid out in 1876 to give cattlemen a way of moving Texas cattle north that would protect other cattle from their ticks. Wasn't long, of course, till there were ranches, though legally no one can own land till the government rules on whether it's part of the Cherokee Outlet, as the Cherokees claim, that connects their Nation to Western hunting grounds, or if it's going to be opened to homesteading. Some squatters have already settled, but once the lands are surveyed and opened, grangers will swarm in and fence their claims, and that'll be the end of trail herding."

"You seem sure the land will open."

Bowden smiled. "I have good information that it won't be long till the secretary of the interior hands down an opinion that the Cherokee Outlet ends at the hundredth meridian. I intend to be in a position to take full advantage of that."

"How?"

"I'm going to build a city." He said it as casually as if proposing to draw a picture, before his voice deepened. "Not a hide town, not a cow town, but a capital for the heart of the Triangle."

"Who'll come there?"

"Merchants with vision, people wanting a new start, all those who're going to pour in as soon as the Strip opens."

"What if they don't come to your town?"

"They will. What other place can promise good schools and a university, a hospital, an opera house and the best stores in five hundred miles?"

Such plans took Kirsten's breath away. "You can do this?"

"With the backing of my partners."

A cloud of billowing dust approached till part of it solidified into mules hauling wagons that creaked and groaned as if the rough track was shaking them to bits. With some difficulty, Bowden drove the team up the ruts and to the side, where they could wait till the freighters passed in a cloud of profanity as thick as the dust.

"Their time's running out, too," said Bowden. "When the railroad builds through my city, there'll be no need for freighting, except just from the track to ranches and small towns."

They traveled now across a flat plain with a kind of grass growing on it that changed color as the wind rippled it, dull brownish-gold when bent one way, soft rose as it swayed back. "Buffalo grass," Bowden said, following her gaze. "This will always be good cattle country. For my friends of the Scottish syndicate, I'll put together a ranch."

"The biggest one in America?" Kirsten couldn't resist asking.

"Of course," he said good-naturedly. "I never bother with second-best." His eyes rested for only a second on her mouth, but that look sent a shock through Kirsten, of warning mixed with anticipation, followed quickly by shame.

How could he make her feel that way when it was O'Brien she loved? No, it was O'Brien she must *not* love—although she did. They drove on in silence.

5

In spite of her distress, Kirsten gradually lost herself in the immensity of the plains. White and purple asters rose on long stalks, drifts of goldenrod grew alongside the road, and brilliant sunflowers spangled the grass. Ash told her that the spires rising from clumps of long, dagger-pointed leaves were yuccas. Prickly-pear cactus she already knew. It was one of the few plants that survived around Dodge.

After miles with no sign of mankind except the road, she mistrusted her eyes when she saw a straggle of earthen walls and structures before them. "A. H. Dugan's road ranch," Bowden said. "Dugan makes a good thing of charging twenty-five cents a bucket for watering teams from his well when the creek's low, providing corrals and feed for stock, and meals and accommodations, such as they are, in that sodhouse, for humans. I think you'll prefer the lunch Bridget put up for us."

Kirsten frowned. "You were so sure I would come?"

"My dear," he said lightly, "in spite of your high principles, I think you're human. For the six weeks you've been in Dodge, you've done nothing but work, sleep as little as possible, and visit your sister's grave."

"I've enjoyed sewing." At his incredulous stare, she tried to explain. "The machine, it does the tedious work. I like to think of ways to make a dress match the person." When he still looked dubious, she said defiantly, "You like to make towns. I like to make dresses!"

He held up a surrendering hand. "If you're that addicted to sewing, Miss Mordal, there must be a way to make it profitable. Let me ponder it."

They passed the house, a few outbuildings, and the corrals, all made of blocks of earth. A stagecoach and several wagons were drawn up outside, and from within came loud voices and hooting laughter. The creek was low, flowing between high banks, but no trees had managed to take root along it, except for small willows that were turning orange and yellow.

"It's hard to credit now," said Bowden, halting the team on a slope bright with flowers, "but this creek often floods the bottom-lands and even has whitecaps swirling on the crests. A cowboy drowned here a few years ago, and Dugan told me that wagons and stages may set at his place two days waiting for the water to go down. But usually it's a safe crossing and there's no quicksand."

From the storage box behind the seat, he produced a basket and two blankets. "If you'll lay out our banquet, I'll water and grain the horses." While he unhitched the team and led them to the crossing, Kirsten spread the blankets; on a dish towel she found in the basket she arranged all the good things Bridget had packed for them: rolls, butter, pickles sweet and sour, ham, fried chicken, spicy-smelling gingerbread, wedges of dried peach pie and a jar of buttermilk.

"It is a feast," said Bowden, sitting down cross-legged, which somewhat dispelled his usual dignity. "It would be perfect if only there were—"

"Fresh fruit," Kirsten finished, laughing and filling their cups. "As important as that is to you, I'm surprised you came out here."

"This is where the opportunities are." He saluted her with his glass and took a swallow that left a white moustache above his upper lip. "The challenges." Again, those frost-gray eyes touched her in a way that, in spite of his disarming appearance, made her compellingly aware of his leashed male energy. "You must like challenges, too, Kirsten Mordal, to face a strange country and in little more than a month be launched in your own business."

The way he said it was a challenge, one Kirsten was not pre-pared to answer. "Challenges?" She shrugged. "I have only done what seemed necessary."

He laughed outright. "Then may I say that your ideas of neces-sity are far from ordinary? In your shoes, many a young woman would marry the first man who asked her and let him take care of her."

"No one has asked me." Kirsten was immediately sorry she'd let that slip, but before she could rectify it, he said, "That's because you don't give them the chance. I've watched you a good many evenings, and the faces of men when you come near. You don't want a husband."

None I can have, she thought with a pang. How blissful it would be to sit like this with O'Brien! But that could never happen again. It was wicked, but she wished he had at least kissed her, held her as a lover, not a kindly rescuer.

Something of her feelings must have shown. Bowden's eyes veiled and his tone was suddenly harsh. "No doubt you fancy yourself in love with that big Irishman. You don't know your luck, that another woman got him. He couldn't hold on to a dollar if it was glued to him."

"No sin it is to be generous!"

"It is if it stints those a man's supposed to provide for, but never mind that now, Miss Mordal." His mouth twisted in mockery. For himself? For her? "When one can't have love, I assure you that success is the best substitute. You should stop wasting your energy in waiting tables and become a *modiste.*"

"What is that?"

"An exclusive, expensive dressmaker and designer."

Kirsten had to laugh. "Me? I haven't studied anywhere. The fashions to me are new—"

He smiled. "Minnie showed off her velvet. You performed the miracle of slimming her and avoiding the dreadful fripperies I'll be bound she wanted. That dress you're wearing is elegant simplicity. You have taste. You can sew. All you need is courage."

It was Kirsten's turn to laugh. The sheer impudence of his advice shocked while it intrigued her. "Minnie would call it brass."

"They're often much the same. Don't ignore the fact that though some Americans look down on poor emigrants, they look up to those who give themselves airs. Your accent is charming."

"I still don't see—"

"Miss Mordal, I'm offering you a partnership. I'll pay the rent for a house where you can live and set up shop, buy any equipment you need, round you up customers till your fame spreads." As she stared, amazed, he made a sweeping motion. "In short, I'll supply the money while you invest your skills."

"Why would you do this?"

"Shall we say I admire enterprise?"

She eyed him skeptically. "All right," he chuckled. "I admire you. But I swear I have no evil designs. There would be locks on your doors and you would have the key."

"There could be papers, all legal and correct? I could pay you interest?"

"Indeed you would." His eyes twinkled, almost warm. "A whole percent above the going rate if that will make you happy."

"The going rate would make me happy enough." Kirsten felt dazed as she let sweet, moist gingerbread dissolve in her mouth. Her gaze followed the brown road as it wound out of sight, luring her.

Somewhere south, somewhere in that mysterious No Man's Land, there must be a woman's place, the land she would homestead. But before she settled, she wanted to travel the region, seek out the best available location, simply become acquainted with her new world.

"There are ranches between here and Tascosa and Mobeetie? Army posts?"

"Sure. Some big ranches."

"There are women on the ranches?"

"At most of them, I'd guess."

Taking a deep breath, Kirsten plunged. "What I would like to do is get a wagon and travel around your Triangle, stop where people needed sewing done, and move on to the next place. A wonderful way it would be to get to know the land."

Bowden seemed unable to speak for a moment. When he did, his tone was scathing. "A wonderful way to get stuck, sink in quicksand, drown, or freeze in a blizzard!"

"I do not think your winters are worse than we had in Sweden, and I drove our horses there." As he stared at her, Kirsten smiled demurely. "Didn't you just say that all I needed was courage?"

"That's not the same as foolhardiness."

"Roads run all the way. I can't get lost."

"You could in a storm."

"In a storm, I won't travel."

"That shows you don't know about weather here or the distances between shelter," he snorted. "People have frozen to death within a hundred yards of their own doors. But crossing all those creeks and rivers, that's your worst hazard."

"In my wagon I will have food and a bed," she said more tranquilly than she felt. He was raising problems she hadn't really considered, but she was loath to abandon the idea, which, apart from the risks, seemed increasingly appealing. She couldn't afford to journey around the region for pleasure or curiosity's sake, but if she could do it and earn her way, what an adventure! "I can wait till the water goes down," she said airily.

Bowden groaned. "I take back my offer. God forbid I lend you the money for suicide."

"I don't need your money, sir," Kirsten said with a lift of her chin. "I will save, and when a wagon and team is for sale cheap—"

"A cheap wagon and team could be your death."

"I'll make sure they're not *too* cheap. Blue will help me."

"That pathetic old derelict!"

"He knows about horses."

"He should. Stole enough of them before he was given the choice of being hanged or hamstrung."

"Hamstrung?"

"They cut the tendons at the back of his legs." At the horror on her face, Bowden added roughly, "Go prowling around No Man's Land and you'll see a lot worse than that."

Kirsten set her jaw. "If I'm going to live there, I need to know what happens."

Tossing away half his pie as if his appetite had vanished, Bowden got to his feet. "I think this drive was a mistake. I'd better get you back to town before, in your urge to explore, you strike out over the prairie on foot."

Stung, Kirsten began to repack the basket while he hitched up the team. He wouldn't ask her for another ride, so as they rolled along, she savored the crisp air, the unbounded ocean of grass. She would always miss her lake, pine trees and mountain, but what gripped her about these plains was their openness to heaven, the way, like America, they seemed to have no limits.

The buggy was nearing the sand dunes when Bowden cast her an appraising glance. "Have you had an attack of sanity, Miss Mordal? Seen that a shop in town would be infinitely preferable to nomadic seamstressing?"

She didn't understand all the words but she knew what he meant. "When I have the money, I will buy a wagon."

He said nothing more till he helped her out of the buggy in front of the hotel and, formally, he thanked her for her company. "I must thank you," Kirsten said. "You have given me a wonderful idea." She smiled into his dismayed eyes and quickly ran inside.

* * *

She was in time to work that evening, and in between duties, she told Bridget, Blue, and Minnie about her excursion, but not about Bowden's offer or her own plan. Minnie wouldn't be thrilled at losing a waitress who brought in extra customers, and anyway it would take a long, long time, even with good tips and sewing, to buy a team and wagon.

Briefly she had considered traveling by stagecoach and hiring someone from the way stations to drive her to ranches in the vicinity, but what she had seen of stages leaving town packed with passengers often neither clean nor sober made her discard that notion at once. That was no way to see the country, in a cloud of dust, squeezed in like a sardine, rattling along as fast as the driver could exhort his mules or horses to go.

It would be hard to wait. Now that she saw the possibility, she longed to start at once, but she would have to be patient. In spite of Bowden's low opinion of her judgment, she had no intention of beginning with a ramshackle outfit that could indeed bring disaster.

Bowden had not claimed his table. He was doubtless angry with her. However that was, she was grateful for the glimpse he had given her of her new country and flattered that he had told her his bold plans. With Bowden, one didn't speak of dreams but of carefully worked-out strategies. Was his confidence infectious? If she hadn't heard him talk of a city where none existed, would she have hit on a way to make a living while she learned the region?

She had to admire Bowden, but felt she must be on guard. However hard it was for her to believe he was attracted to her, his behavior demonstrated that this was so, though their argument might have cured him. It was undeniably duller without him, though; he dominated the room so that always she was conscious of him.

She carried a tray to the kitchen. When she returned, he was in his place. He ordered as if nothing unusual had passed between them, as if she were, in fact, simply a person whose function was to bring him food. As he rose to leave, however, he produced a document from his leather case.

"Study this overnight, Miss Mordal. If it's agreeable, you may sign it and have your money."

Before she fully understood, he was gone. Sign? Money? He must have decided to finance her venture! Burning to read the paper as she made the round of the patrons with coffee and brought dessert to the latest diners, she sighed with relief when the last cowboy gave up trying to blandish her and departed. As soon as she had cleared the tables, she picked up the paper with quivering fingers.

In legal verbiage, it said that Kirsten Mordal, upon receiving a business loan of five hundred dollars, agreed to repay the total, including interest at two percent, within one year. Should the said Miss Mordal default, her business assets would become the property of the creditor, Ash Bowden.

The sum took Kirsten's breath away. Surely she wouldn't need that much! Swift computations told her that if she worked every day of the year for Minnie, she'd only earn $182.50, though her tips were more than double that. More computations. At $10 for interest, she would have to pay back $42.50 a month.

Impossible, even if she saved a considerable sum the payment-free first year. Chagrin tasting metallic in her mouth, Kirsten wondered whether Bowden was taunting her, trying to shock her into abandoning her idea. She started to crumple the vellum, then thought better of it.

Before she resigned herself to at least a year more of waitressing, she should find out what an outfit would cost and then negotiate with Bowden. Now that she was possessed by the lure of the broad horizon and constantly tormented by the thought of O'Brien's marriage, the town and hotel cramped her. With or without Bowden's help, she would go as soon as she could.

That night she worked on Bridget's dress, smiling as she imagined her friend's delighted surprise, at the same time planning to ask Blue to find out what he could about a suitable wagon, perhaps light enough to be drawn by one horse. When she went to bed and O'Brien's eyes laughed at her, she clenched her hands at the pain that shot through her. *I can't dream about you anymore,* she told him. *But may you be happy, you and your Lorena.* With all her will, she pictured again that vast caparison of grass lit with brilliant flowers and set herself in the midst of it with her wagon and Family Gem.

* * *

Bowden raised a quizzical eyebrow as she brought his breakfast coffee. "Well, Miss Mordal? Is the agreement legal enough to suit you?"

"It seems correct, but I'm afraid I can't pay the money back within a year. I'm going to ask Blue to look for a good used wagon and a strong, gentle horse. Maybe he can find them for a few hundred dollars."

Bowden's eyes glinted. "I will lend you whatever you need for your start, my dear, and payments can be spread over another year or two if you prefer, though if you charge what you should, there'd be no need. What I will not do is lend you one cent for a broken-down wagon and nag."

Kirsten scowled. "If I borrow the money, it's mine. You have no right to tell me what I must buy."

"No right, perhaps, but I can certainly refuse the loan."

Frustration swelled in her, crested, and overflowed. "Games you play with me!" she blurted, inverting her speech as she still did when she was upset. "Keep your money, and I will do as I—as I *damn* well please!" Expecting a lightning bolt for her profanity, she stalked to the kitchen, glad now that she hadn't confided in anyone, not even Bridget, about the proffered loan.

Disappointment ate at her, though. She served Bowden's food with the fixed, bright smile he detested and, with her eyes, dared him to object. His mouth slanted down at one edge and he regarded her with a tolerance that made her want to scream. Hateful creature, trying to run her life! It would take a long time to save what she needed, but at least she could spend her own money any way she pleased.

She tried to convince herself this was better, in the break between breakfast and noon while she worked on the lining of Bridget's dress, but she still smarted with resentment, heartily wishing that Bowden hadn't tantalized her with the prospect if he was going to be so impossibly overbearing.

Brooding darkly over this, she jumped and let her seam run crooked at a knock on her door. "One moment," she called, giving the seam a rueful glance.

She opened the door, smothered a cry, and gripped the doorknob for support. O'Brien stood there, hair catching all the light in that dark hall.

"Kirsty!" Her hands were lost and warmed in his big strong brown ones. For a moment she forgot Lorena, gazing up into his eyes till his smile died and he released her, quickly stepping back. "I'd like to talk to you, Kirsty. Reckon we would visit awhile this afternoon?"

She shouldn't, but she would have risked her hope of heaven to be with him. "I get off work about two."

"Fine. Would you like to go riding? I can get a sidesaddle at the livery stable."

"I'm not a good rider, O'Brien. A few times only I rode one of Grandfather's team bareback."

"Time you learned, then. I brought some horses up to sell, and one of them's a sweet-tempered little mare that'll make you think you're in a rocking chair." He laughed at Kirsten's doubtful look and gave her hand a squeeze. "I smelled Bridget's raisin pie baking. Reckon you could cut me an extra big piece for dinner?"

He left then to attend to business. Kirsten went back to her sewing, but the lining kept showing O'Brien's face. She mustn't feel this way; he belonged to another woman. Yet she did, and just for today, just for a few hours out of all their lives, she would savor being with him, the bittersweet joy.

At Bridget's urging, after O'Brien had worked through steak and potatoes, Kirsten took him almost half of one of the delicious-smelling pies, oozing with plump raisins and spicy sauce, crust golden with melted sugar. She was glad Ash Bowden wasn't there. How cynically he would have noted the tremor of her hands, her flushed cheeks and shining eyes. Simply being near O'Brien heightened her senses, limned objects so clearly that she seemed to see them for the first time, made the good smells of food penetrate so that she felt ravenous, turned her fingers sensitive to everything they touched. It wouldn't, she thought, take much to make her happy. If she could wait on him like this every day, talk with him and fill her eyes. Even as she regretted she couldn't have that much, a wave of longing made her realize that wouldn't be enough; in the end it would be torture. No, since he was Lorena's, better not to stare through thick glass at what couldn't be hers. But she would share with him this one bright afternoon.

* * *

As soon as she had cleared the tables and set them for that night, she took off her apron, fluffed her hair a bit around her face where the braids had loosened, and got her shawl, before meeting O'Brien in the foyer.

"Know something, Kirsty?" he grinned. "Your hair's a match for Honey's mane and tail. Come and meet her."

A buckskin mare stood hitched to the rail beside a chestnut gelding, and though the comparison had slightly piqued her, Kirsten had to admit that though the mare's mane and tail were coarser, they were the exact color of her own hair, a rich brown-yellow. Kirsten stroked the white blaze on Honey's forehead, and caressed the muscular neck and shoulder, offering dried apple slices. Honey accepted these neatly, her soft muzzle brushing Kirsten's hand.

"She's lady-broke," O'Brien said. "I'd have kept her for Lorena, but she's got a favorite horse." Kirsten was glad he couldn't see her face as he helped her perch on the saddle with one knee hooked over the horn jutting to one side. "That's my big news," he said, mounting. "I'm getting married, Kirsty. My best friend got killed and I'd promised to look after Lorena if anything ever happened to him. She—well, she's not strong like you, Kirsty. Her folks aren't good to her. She needs a husband."

Don't I? Kirsten wailed inwardly. *Don't I need you, too?*

She swallowed hard. It seemed she wasn't to have even these few hours free of Lorena. "I—I hope you'll be happy, O'Brien."

He didn't answer that but said rather grimly, "Kirsty, one thing I've got to do while I'm in town is get material for Lorena's wedding dress and find someone to make it. From what I hear, you could figure out something really special, and, well—it would mean a lot to her."

Dizzied for a moment, Kirsten gripped the saddlehorn, smothered an outraged cry and fought to get herself under control. Why shouldn't he ask her? She should be flattered that he'd entrust the task to her. But oh, oh, how savagely it hurt!

There was, thank goodness, a valid excuse. "The gown needs fitting. You must find someone who lives close enough to do that."

"Mrs. Meadows has arthritis in her hands so bad that she can't sew, and to tell the truth, she wouldn't do it anyway. Lorena can mend but she's not much of a seamstress. That's why I said I'd get the dress. They gave me all the measurements." The dashed look on his face touched Kirsten in spite of her rebellion. "Won't that work?" he asked plaintively.

Kirsten squared her shoulders. Always, she would owe this man for befriending her. Instead of shrinking away, she should be glad to be able to do him a favor. "I'll do my best. Maybe I can find someone almost the same size who'll let me fit the dress on her."

"I'd bet you could each wear each other's clothes, though Lorena's a tad shorter and plumper."

That really was too much, serving as a model for Lorena's bride gown, but there was nothing for it but to say woodenly, "If that's true, it will be easier."

They were passing Lucia's grave. "Mighty handsome fence you put around it," O'Brien said. "And that's a nice marker."

"Blue carved it." Kirsten's gaze was caught by the sight of a green clump freshly planted at the foot of the mound. "Now who—" Breaking off, she turned to O'Brien, who reddened.

"Thought she'd ought to have a rosebush. Bob Wright has a couple in his yard. He let me dig up this one."

How glad Kirsten was she hadn't refused to do the dress! "Thank you, O'Brien," she said through tears. "So good you have been to me, I can never make it up."

"Sure, you can." His big hand reached over and with gentle awkwardness smudged away her tears. "You're going to help me pick out the material for the prettiest bride dress there ever was, and you're going to make it. No way I can pay you enough for that!"

It *would* be a dazzling gown, Kirsten resolved, the most lovely garment she could conceive. "I won't take pay for it," she said. "It is a gift. Because you are kind. Because you were my first friend here in America."

"Hold on, Kirsty! I can't let you do that."

She firmed her jaw. "Making the dress is a gift or I don't do it."

"Now look here, Kirsty—"

"I mean it, O'Brien."

After a moment, his broad shoulders moved in a shrug. "I'll get even some way. All right now, this sewing business, how does that fit in with homesteading?"

"Oh, O'Brien, they fit like hand and mitten!" she cried and burst forth with the advantages. She concluded with her plan to journey around sewing as she surveyed No Man's Land for that perfect place that would be her home. "How much do you think a wagon and team will cost, O'Brien?" she asked. "Ash Bowden says I'll need five hundred dollars, and when I didn't want to borrow that much—"

"Bowden offered to lend it?" O'Brien's tawny eyebrows lifted.

"Not after I wouldn't take that much. Do you know Mr. Bowden?"

"Heard of him. Can't say I'm tickled he's decided to take a hand down in the Neutral Strip. Be the ruination of the country to have a big city that'll draw in the kind of people who'll want everything all tame and civilized." O'Brien looked grave. "It's none of my business, Kirsty, but you've got no family and you're new here. Why would Bowden lend you money?"

Kirsten blushed and concentrated on patting Honey's neck. "He knows I sew well, but of course a business like mine would be small to him. I—I think he just wants to be able to tell me what to do."

"And why would he want to do that?"

"I don't know and it doesn't matter," Kirsten flashed. "I told him to keep his money. But," she added with a sigh, "I would so love to start now!"

The horses' hooves kicked up puffs of fine dust as they rode north. Veils of cloud streamed from the sun and a wedge of geese called high overhead. "Hold the reins up more," suggested O'Brien. "Honey's not sure what you want. A firm hand won't hurt her and she'd rather know you're in charge."

Honey responded by carrying her head more proudly and refining her pace. O'Brien lifted his battered tan hat and reflectively rubbed above his ear. "Reckon there's no use my telling you about quicksand and floods and—"

"Blizzards," Kirsten grimaced.

"Outlaws, too, but they're not likely to give you any trouble. Listen, Kirsty, if you're set on this, why don't you take Blue with you? He's a good hand with horses, knows the country, and I bet he'd jump at the chance."

"I can't pay him, not at first."

"He doesn't get anything now but his board and a little tobacco money. The ranches where you'd stop won't begrudge him a bunk and grub, and most likely he could help the cook."

"It would be good to have him along," Kirsten agreed. "I won't talk to him about it yet, though. I think it is for a year at least that I must save."

"Maybe not." At her startled glance, O'Brien furrowed his brow. "Let me ask around some. Could be there's a sound used spring wagon for sale."

"But the money!"

"My credit's good and I'll back yours."

"The horses—"

"Do you like Honey?"

"Why, yes. Gentle she is but proud-spirited."

"I brought her to sell. She's as good in harness as with a saddle, and I've got another mare, Stockings, who's just a little darker with four white legs."

"But I can't pay you for one mare, much less two!"

"I'll make you a deal," went on O'Brien sunnily. "Forty dollars for the pair, paid inside a year. Shucks, Kirsty, for me it's like putting money in the bank."

"You will take interest?"

"If you make Lorena's dress, that's better than interest." As Kirsten hesitated, tempted, but frightened of going into debt, he gave her a challenging grin. "You took a big chance to come to America, Kirsty. Don't get cold feet now."

It would be wonderful to have his horses, a blessing to travel in a wagon he'd helped her find. She took a deep breath and smiled. "All right, O'Brien. Find me a good cheap wagon and I will be in business!"

6

The next afternoon, Kirsten was studying the pattern she and O'Brien had selected that morning, along with shimmering ivory satin, yards of Chantilly lace, and taffeta for the lining. But she was making slow work of it, for her eyes kept blurring. In spite of all her brave resolves, every stitch she took on this dress was going to hurt. There was no way she could keep from yearning to wear it, though if she could have married O'Brien, she'd have gladly done so barefoot and in her shimmy. The ironic fact was that adding three inches to the length of the dress and tucking in the waist by two inches would make it fit her, which was at least convenient. Bridget had helped adjust the pattern. Now Kirsten simply had to set her teeth and start.

Carefully arranging and pinning the pattern parts to conserve the expensive fabric, Kirsten, angry at the tears she had to keep blinking away, was almost through cutting when a smart *rat-a-tat* came at the door, followed by Blue's eager voice. "Kirsty! Come have a look at what's out in front!"

Could O'Brien have found a wagon this soon? Maybe he'd just brought the horses. Kirsten's hands so trembled with excitement that it was folly to try to finish the painstaking task. Putting down the shears, she ran up the hall and outside, halting on the boardwalk in disbelieving delight.

What a beautiful wagon! The wheels, the running gear and the base on which the box rested were crimson, and the box, gleaming a lustrous dark green, was striped with crimson and bright yellow with scrolling and curlicues in the same colors. It was hitched to Honey and a mare a shade darker with four white stockings.

"Like it?" O'Brien's eyes danced as he stroked Honey's shoulder. "Thimble skein axles, hickory wheels, standards and tongue double-braced, box clamped with iron, twenty coats of paint and varnish. See, the gearing's set high to clear water unless it's so deep you shouldn't get into it anyway. Think it'll do?"

Rendered speechless by the lump in her throat, Kirsten ventured to caress the resplendent surface. The cushioned spring seat, also brilliantly painted, had room for two. "It—it's beautiful!" she said at last. "But O'Brien, it must cost a fortune!"

"It's yours for eighty dollars," he grinned. "The farmer who ordered it went broke and moved back East. It's too small for freighting, so it could set around a good spell before it found a buyer. Jim Carson, who owns the livery, wants ten dollars now and the rest, plus interest, within the year. He'll throw in the harness which is used but in good shape."

"That's sure a fine bargain, Miss Kirsty," said Blue, chuckling. "Prettiest little wagon I ever did see."

Kirsten's head spun, but she managed to add the forty dollars for the horses to the price of the wagon. If she worked a few more weeks for Minnie, she could pay the livery owner ten dollars and still have some cash for supplies. That would leave her owing one hundred and ten dollars for the outfit.

The thought of that large a debt twisted her stomach, but it was so much less than what Bowden had made her think she'd need that hopeful relief mixed with her caution. She hadn't thought about what to charge for her work, but certainly she should add a reasonable amount for traveling to a patron, and the flair she had for judging what was becoming lifted her out of the ordinary rank of seamstresses. She should be able to earn enough to pay for her traveling business in the agreed time, and when she was ready to homestead, a wagon and team would be very useful.

She met O'Brien's eyes and pain suffused her. How could he watch her with such proud interest when he was going to marry another woman? If Kirsten had thought he truly loved Lorena, it would have been easier to accept, but she was certain that the last time he'd been in town, that night at the Dodge House, he'd begun to see her as more than the foreign waif he'd befriended. But there was his promise to a dead friend, and already she knew that O'Brien, however impetuous he was, would staunchly keep his word. Only why, *why* did he think Lorena couldn't manage without him?

Fighting down her rebellion, Kirsten patted the star on Honey's forehead and scratched Stockings behind an ear. "Thank you, O'Brien. Again, you are my good friend. I'll go talk to Mr. Carson now."

"Why not drive up in style?" O'Brien suggested. Before she could protest, he helped her up the step attached to the running gear and into the wagon, handing her the reins.

"You come, too," she urged. "Blue, want to come along?" Both squeezed on the seat—O'Brien so close to her that she felt the warmth of his body and smelled his masculine odor with its aroma of horses and leather. She wheeled the team, thrilling to their ready response to her voice and use of the reins. As they rolled up Front Street, she couldn't have been happier with a golden chariot. If only O'Brien could always be with her, she would have been too joyful for any mortal woman to bear.

She signed an agreement with portly, black-whiskered Jim Carson and insisted on doing the same with O'Brien. Carson, a bachelor, offered to take care of the horses till she was ready to travel if she would sew buttons on his clothes and mend them.

"I'll come and see you every day," she told the horses, with farewell pats.

"And I'll curry you till you shine like harvest moonbeams," Blue murmured, tending to the harness as if there was no question about whose job it was.

"That's a job you can have from now on, if you want it, Blue," Kirsten said. As his dark eyes widened, she said, "I can't pay you, just food and pocket money, but if you'd like to travel with me, help me find a place to homestead when I'm old enough—"

Blue's lips quivered. "You mean that, Miss Kirsty?"

"Sure's you're born," she laughed, using one of his phrases. "You know the country, Blue, and I'd like company."

Moisture showed at the deeply creased edges of his eyes. "Never thought to get out on the plains again, reckoned I'd just have to shuffle around Dodge the rest of my life." His thin chest expanded and he gave his old hat a rakish tilt. "I can't walk fast, but I can sure drive a team and can still use a gun." His voice gathered strength. "Hell's bells, Miss Kirsty, I could be right handy!"

"I know you can," she assured him. "Maybe you could start by figuring out some kind of covering for the wagon. It *must* rain sometime."

"When it does, you'll wish it would quit," warned O'Brien. "Weather out here's got no sense, not civilized at all."

Blue nodded and squinted at Kirsten. "You told Minnie yet?"

"No." That was a chore Kirsten wished she could avoid, but now she'd bought the wagon, she must talk to Minnie at once.

"She'll give you an earful," Blue shrugged. "You've been good for business. But let her blow off steam and she'll come around."

Actually, Minnie took it better than Kirsten expected. After an indignant blast labeling Kirsten an ingrate and completely daft to think of roaming No Man's Land, Minnie tried to wheedle Kirsten into staying till spring, offering to double her wages.

"With tips, you'd be making more than you can gypsying around," Minnie argued. "And you could sew, too."

"I want to see the country," Kirsten explained. "And Minnie, you will understand, it will make me so proud to own my own business."

Minnie's lavender eyes softened and she seemed to be thinking back. "Yes, child, that is a good feeling. Not that you won't have many a headache you'd miss by working for someone else." She sighed, pinning up a stray curl. "I knew I was bound to lose you soon or late the minute I saw that dress you made for yourself. But if you get a crawful of flooding creeks and dusty roads, you can always work for me till you dream up some new craziness."

"Thank you, Minnie," Kirsten said demurely. "It's all right then that I work two weeks more?"

"As long as you want. I won't have any trouble getting someone to wait tables but there's no one going to take your place." Minnie enfolded Kirsten in her plump arms. "I hope you get as famous and rich as those fancy dressmakers in Paris, dear, and find a good homestead, and someday there'll be just the right man to go with it!"

Did Minnie guess about O'Brien? Quelling a stab of pain, Kirsten returned the older woman's hug. "It's wonderful to have my business, Minnie, and I owe that to your letting me use the Family Gem."

"You owe it to your gumption," Minnie corrected. "America's full of chances, but a person still has to hustle and take them. Speaking of which, it's time to put on our aprons. Folks'll be coming in any minute now." She eyed Kirsten curiously. "What's Ash Bowden going to think about this?"

"I hope he won't tell me," Kirsten shot back, and hurried to tidy herself. As she glanced at the face in the blotched mirror, cheeks flushed and eyes shining, she hugged herself and made a pirouette. "You own a wagon and a team and a sewing machine!" she sang, enjoying the almost rhyme before a glimpse of the bridal satin on the bed struck her like a sluice of ice water.

Just being with O'Brien again had made her know that the way she felt wasn't simply gratitude to the man who'd helped her in her distress. She hadn't falsely idealized him in those weeks when she'd embraced and held the image of him to comfort her in her loneliness and grief for Lucia. He was as handsome and kind and vibrantly masculine as she'd remembered, the only man of the many she'd met in Dodge who called to the depths of her being.

What was it Ash Bowden said? If you couldn't have love, success was the best substitute? She didn't care about success in the grand way Bowden meant it, but a business of her own, a home and farm someday—these were possible, and after starving winters in Sweden, she would be grateful and not taint what she could achieve by moaning after what was denied. She'd make Lorena's bride gown, wish the couple well, and get on with her own life, yes, she would. But though she tied her apron in a jaunty bow and held her head high as she left her room, Kirsten had to brush away tears and stop for a moment to swallow hard and summon a smile before she entered the dining room.

O'Brien was seated in Bowden's corner. She almost told him another man usually sat there but decided against it. Bowden didn't own that spot, after all, and might not even come in.

"Well, I see Minnie didn't scalp you," O'Brien teased as she poured his coffee.

"She was nice after the first explosion," Kirsten said.

"Good. Just as soon not have her mad at me for finding you wheels to roll away on." His thick, red-gold hair was so close that Kirsten had to battle an urge to touch it, smooth her fingers through it to the muscular back of his neck. "How soon can you finish Lorena's dress?"

Heart constricting, it was a moment before Kirsten trusted her voice. He hadn't the least idea what he was expecting of her; yet he had every right to expect it, and if she could help it, he'd never guess her feelings. At least now she had his respect. "I'll finish it before I leave Dodge. Shall I send it to you by stage?"

"Reckon that'd be best." He frowned and added reluctantly, "You could bring it yourself and stay for the wedding if you'd like to show all the ladies how well you can sew. Bet you'd get a passel of customers."

Use the dress that was breaking her heart for business advantage? "Thank you." Kirsten, with great effort, kept her tone civil. "But I'll need to be working all I can to pay off the wagon and team."

"Oh, I won't prove that stern a creditor, my dear." Kirsten whirled in confusion as Bowden's voice came from behind her. He had silently taken a chair at the next table. He smiled carelessly at O'Brien and rose, extending a hand. "We haven't met, sir, but allow me to extend congratulations and fervent wishes that your marriage will be blissful. I'm Ash Bowden."

O'Brien's tawnily bleached eyebrows drew together, but he shook hands and gave his name. "Thanks for your good wishes, Mr. Bowden," he said. "But how in the name of all that's wonderful did you get to be this young lady's creditor?"

Bowden's strong teeth flashed. "Simple enough. I bought her note from Jim Carson, who was mightily pleased to get all his cash right now."

"Why would you do that?" asked O'Brien flatly.

"Now why do you suppose?" Bowden's words were silken but his eyes were chill. "I admire Miss Mordal's enterprise and felt she didn't need the pressure of owing money to Mr. Carson."

"I guess I can't see why it's less pressure owing it to you."

Bowden's pugnacious jaw hardened before he smiled in a way that was far more menacing. "It's a matter of indifference to me whether she pays in a year, ten years, or never. However, sir, I would suggest that my dealings with Miss Mordal are none of your business."

The laughter was gone from O'Brien's eyes. "I'd reckon they are, Bowden. I'm her friend and she's new to this country."

"I, also, am her friend but I haven't accused you of devious reasons for selling her a good team on credit." Bowden turned to Kirsten. "What do you say, my dear? Nothing's changed except that now you owe me instead of Jim Carson."

It was a change she didn't like, but she couldn't bear to withdraw from the bargain and lose the wagon, even if that were legally possible. The tension between the two men almost hummed. It wouldn't take much to start open conflict. She'd tell Bowden later that she didn't appreciate his high-handedness.

"I want the wagon," she said. "I will pay you, Mr. Bowden. Now, if you'll sit down, I'll pour your coffee and take your order."

So far as she could notice, the two had no further exchanges, but the atmosphere around them was so charged that Kirsten felt a wave of relief when O'Brien finished his second piece of chess pie and came over to pay.

"I'll be on my way early in the morning," he said. "But I'll see you at breakfast." His eyes searched hers. "Is it really all right, Kirsty? You won't feel like Bowden's got a hold on you because he has that note?"

That was, in fact, how she did feel, but she didn't want to worry O'Brien. "It's just money I have to pay to someone," she shrugged.

"Well, be careful around him. He's sure got his eye on you." O'Brien hesitated. "Bowden's left a trail of women behind him."

"I won't be one of them."

O'Brien chuckled. "You're so different from anyone he's known that he might even break down and propose."

"I'm not interested in that, either."

O'Brien gave her a quizzical look. "Sure, colleen, 'twill be a pitiful waste if you don't find a husband. Don't get so wound up in being your own boss that you miss what God made you a woman for."

I've missed you, Kirsten thought. *Maybe someday, sometime, I can love somebody else, but right now I don't believe it.* But oh, how she longed for a family, a loving home like the one she'd lost, with a little daughter in whom she could again cherish Lucia!

"There's plenty of time," she said to the man whom she loved and who would soon take a bride. "First I will travel around in my wagon and find a wonderful place to live."

O'Brien flinched. Something flamed deep in his eyes before he pressed her hand. "You'll do that—and just about anything you set your mind to, Kirsty."

Except have you. She told him good night without meeting his gaze and went to pour coffee for a table of officers in from the post. When Ash Bowden rose to go, he only smiled at her, but there was such a proprietary air about him that she passionately wished he wasn't the holder of her note; at the same time, she wondered how, with just a glance, he could make her feel besieged.

As O'Brien prepared to leave next morning, he took Kirsten's hands in his and gave them a hearty squeeze. "You're welcome at our place anytime you want to stop," he told. "Folks at Kiowa Creek Station can tell you how to find us. I'll try to drum up some business for you, and say, Kirsty, blizzards can come up fast, so don't travel more than you have to in the winter, and pay attention to Blue."

"We'll be careful." She felt as if she had no strength and would fall if he took his hands away. The muscles of her face were so rigid that it seemed they must crack as she smiled. "I wish you a beautiful wedding and that you'll have all happiness and good fortune. Please tell Miss Meadows that."

"I will. Lord knows she deserves some happiness, she's had a damned hard time." For a moment, bleak determination hardened his face. "I sure appreciate your making her dress."

"I'll do my best," Kirsten said in a strangled voice. "And I'll pack it very carefully so it won't wrinkle."

Why didn't he go? Quickly, before she broke into tears? "So long for now, Kirsty." He hesitated as if finding it hard to choose his next words before he gave her at least a hint of his old flashing smile. "Next time we meet, you'll be a woman with her own business!"

She nodded mutely and was glad he strode away before she lost all control and screamed at him. It didn't calm her to turn and see that Ash Bowden was in his corner, watching her with an unreadable expression. She had to steel her nerves to wait on him, but he made no reference to her debt or to O'Brien.

"So, Kirsten Mordal," he said when he had ordered, a strange little smile hovering on his lips. "How does it feel to have a good part of what you want?"

He must have known that at that moment it tasted like dust, but Kirsten tossed back her head and steadily met his gaze. "It feels good. And it's going to feel better."

He raised his cup in salute. "I believe you. Now try to believe me. When one stops yearning after what can't be had, it's amazing how satisfactory life can be. Don't wear blinders, my dear."

"I won't," she said. "I'm going to look all over No Man's Land for the best place to live, so you may be sure I'll keep my eyes wide open."

"And your mind closed?"

"I don't know what you mean."

"I think you do. But I'll save you a prime lot in my city for when you find out homesteading's not as marvelous as you think."

"I don't want a city lot."

His eyes rested on the pulse in her throat and she felt dangerously exposed. "That's a stupid remark, but I won't hold it against you."

Realizing that she couldn't win a passage of words with him, she said, "I have to give Bridget your order," and quickly walked away, though there was no eluding his soft laughter.

The wedding dress taunted her every time she entered her room. The sooner it was finished and on the stage, the better for her peace of mind, so she put Bridget's gown aside and devoted every possible moment to fashioning the satin and lace into a garment fit for a fairytale princess. Though she shed some tears, especially when Bridget helped her try on a part, she was entranced with her creation and, yes, *almost* wished that she could see Lorena wear it and hear the admiring comments.

O'Brien had ruled against the exaggerated bustle presently in style, so Kirsten had altered the pattern to allow the skirt to flow gracefully over a modest padding. The overskirt, swept up with bows, was lace over satin, as was the bodice, which pointed in front and cut so that softly draped folds of satin revealed the shoulders. The sleeves, puffed at the top, fitted closely down to the elbow, where they became a froth of lace. The veil was lace fitted to a pearl-sewn satin cap. It was a timeless dress that brides could wear for generations, and that thought made Kirsten sadly recall the family wedding crown, sold for passage to America, and the silver-plaqued and red satin belt that Lucia had worn for death, not for an earthly bridegroom. Before Kirsten left, she must buy candles and ask Bridget to burn them at Lucia's grave on her birthday and at Christmas, though if Lucia's gentle spirit found its way to earth, it would surely visit the graveyard in their village in company with all the other beloved ghosts. It grieved Kirsten to know that she would never go back, but after a half-sweet, half-bitter reverie, she fixed her thoughts on what seemed a miracle—that she would soon be driving, in her own handsome wagon, through the country where she would one day have a home, one no Herr Lynkken could take away from her.

Every day she seized a few minutes to go and see Honey and Stockings, bearing treats saved from her meals or scraps left by patrons. Honey loved dried apples, while Stockings was partial to cornbread. Blue took them for a ride every day, and they were so inseparable that the unsaddled one stayed close to the one Blue rode; once they cleared the rowdy turmoil of Front Street, he could slip off the halter and let the unridden horse run free. He curried and brushed them till they shone satiny as the wedding dress, but to get them used to her, Kirsten brushed them, too, talking to them softly.

"You're the smartest, gentlest, prettiest horses in the world," she crooned, burnishing Honey's flank as the mare turned to regard her with large, intelligent eyes. "We're going to travel all over Bowden's Triangle together. The wagon won't be too heavy for the both of you, and I'll be sure you have plenty of grain. You won't be sorry O'Brien sold you to me."

Honey nuzzled her as if in agreement, and Stockings whinnied as if wanting attention, so Kirsten brushed her, too, before she hurried back to work on what she had come to think of as the Dress. Jim Carson, perhaps feeling a little guilty for selling Kirsten's note without discussing it with her, had procured, at no charge, a perfect cover for the wagon, a hard-topped roof that had survived a runaway crash that wrecked the bottom of a Fort Dodge ambulance. The roof had canvas curtains that could be rolled up or tightly fastened down to suit the weather, and Blue had built a platform along one side of the wagon to hold the long horsehair cushion from a discarded lounge, Minnie's gift. That would be Kirsten's bed when it was necessary to camp overnight. There was storage underneath, and Blue had made braces to hold in place Kirsten's trunk and the padded, covered box he'd designed to protect the Family Gem from dust and jolting. Of course there was a feed box and one for supplies. Bridget had contributed a braided rag rug.

Scarcely able to believe it was really hers, that soon, her small, traveling home—and *business*, too—would be carrying her over the prairies, Kirsten smoothed the lustrous finish and hoped Grandfather Nils and all her loved ones could see it and be glad for her, and proud. That forced her to admit that she couldn't have done this had Lucia been alive. Her timid little sister would have been terrified of venturing out on the plains, going around to strangers.

I wanted her to have a good life, Kirsten thought with blinding clarity and agonized regret. *But it wasn't the life she'd have chosen. She belonged in the village. It was I who dreamed of "wonderful America." I came here for myself. Lucia, Lucia!*

She bowed her face against the wagon and sobbed. A hand fell on her shoulder. Slipping from under it, she turned to confront Ash Bowden.

"Tears, Miss Kirsten?" His mouth slanted down at one corner. "I confess that I expected disillusionment within a few months but right now I should think you'd be ecstatic. Is something wrong with the wagon?"

"No! It's wonderful, exactly right. But—" Her voice choked off.

"I hope you're not crying over that scapegrace Irishman."

"I'm not, but I will if I want to!"

"Ah, then," he said, his tone quickening with compunction, "it must be you're thinking of someone who can't travel with you, someone whose journeys are done."

How could a man, often so harsh and sardonic, sound as if he understood? "I—I just realized that Lucia would never have belonged here. But I made her come!"

He took Kirsten by the upper arms and held her firmly. "All right. That's something you have to live with. Memories like that are the price of life, of surviving when others fall. No one can make a sign on your forehead and give you absolution. But you're alive and you must live your life."

Those hard, straight words put steel in her, and she straightened, moving away from Bowden's hands. She would mourn Lucia, she would probably always feel some guilt, but she could not be sorry she had come to America.

Bowden, watching her, gave an approving nod. "That's better," he said, eyes on her like a physical caress. His face changed and he left her.

7

The bride gown was indeed lovely. When Kirsten modeled it for the last time, Bridget and Minnie oohed and aahed over it, and Blue gave an indrawn whistle. Kirsten was glad none of them knew that almost as many tears as stitches had gone into the making. Blue cadged a big box at the mercantile, and Minnie unearthed some hoarded tissue paper.

Kirsten hadn't intended to add a note, but in the end, it seemed churlish not to, so she borrowed a sheet of paper from Minnie and wrote: "Miss Meadows—I hope you like the dress and that you'll have a lovely wedding and a very happy life." As she signed her name she fiercely scrubbed away tears that *would* come. She'd almost surely meet Lorena one day, but she hoped that it wouldn't be till she'd made some kind of peace with that marriage —and would she, could she, ever do that?

The day she dispatched the dress, there was a letter for her at the stage office from a rancher's wife, Amanda Allen. O'Brien had told her how beautifully Kirsten sewed, and Amanda, her sister, and she herself, needed a year's garments made and would be much obliged if Kirsten could do it.

"Hi Allen's about the most prosperous cattleman in No Man's Land," Blue said, when Kirsten consulted him. "Good place to start, Miss Kirsty. His headquarters is on Hackberry Creek maybe ten miles from the Hardesty road ranch—say, one hundred and fifty miles from here. You say we can leave in a week? Then we'd ought to be at their ranch easy before the middle of November."

Kirsten wrote the Allens to that effect, and then, with what would surely be the most difficult commission of her sewing career off on the stage, Kirsten returned thankfully to Bridget's dress. How good it was to create without mixed feelings! When she had

Bridget try on the golden-brown garment for its last fitting, she wistfully smoothed the bodice that made her look quite slender.

" 'Tis lucky your aunt is, macushla. Sure, any woman would love this dress!"

"You'd better," Kirsten laughed. "It's yours."

Bridget gaped. "But—but your aunt—"

"I don't have one. I made her up so I could fit the gown to you."

"Macushla!" Bridget hugged her until she was breathless, shedding joyful tears, but then she stepped back, shaking her head. "No. I can't take it. All your work and the material and fixings, too!" She sighed and fumbled at the buttons. "I know you owe for your wagon and team. You just put this over in the mercantile and—"

"I'll do no such thing!" Kirsten caught her friend's work-roughened hands. "There's a way to pay me, Bridget, something I can't trust anyone else to see to."

"What's that?" asked Bridget between hope and dubiety.

"It's the custom in our village to burn candles on our loved ones' graves on their birthday and at Christmas. I'll be too far away to come back, Bridget, but I—I can't bear to think Lucia won't have her candles on St. Lucia's Day, which is her birthday, December thirteenth, or for Christmas. If you would—"

"To be sure and I will!" Bridget gathered Kirsten to her and patted her shoulder. "And I'll keep out the weeds and water the flowers if it's dry next summer. I'd want to do that anyway. The dress, sure, 'tis too much!"

"I made it for you," Kirsten insisted. "If you won't take it, I'll put it in one of those missionary boxes they send to clothe the heathens."

Bridget wrapped her arms defensively about the bodice. "No! If you're that daft, I'll be for keeping it! But mind, 'tis myself will buy the candles for your little sister."

Kirsten assented and followed Bridget as, calling on Minnie and Blue, she rushed off to exhibit her gown. They both gazed, thunderstruck.

"Is that you, Bridget?" whistled Blue.

"Makes you a different woman," Minnie said with a trace of envy as she fingered the material. "Sets off your eyes and hair, and I sure didn't know you had such a nice figure." She frowned slightly. "I hope this won't give you ideas, Bridget. It sure makes you look like a lady, but you're a widow with children to support."

"And don't I know that?" returned Bridget pertly. "That's true, God knows, and I'm not about to throw up a good job—but now when I get a chance, sure and I can be a pretty woman in a pretty dress!" Dimpling, she whirled in a curtsy, gave Kirsten another hug, and floated off to show her children how grand their mother looked.

Annie! thought Kirsten, reminded of the carrot-haired, big-eyed twelve-year-old, so early burdened with caring for a small brother and sisters. *Bless her, she'll get a dress for Christmas. I can make it on the road and send it back by stage.* She smiled at herself a bit wryly. If she meant to make a living, she couldn't keep giving away clothes, but money couldn't bring the warm pleasure that Bridget's joy had—why, the dress had brought up her shoulders and chin, given a sprightly grace to her walk. She looked years younger, and like a *woman,* not a kitchen drudge. It was close to magic.

But no magic, no dress, could free O'Brien from what he had promised his dead friend. The bright flush of Kirsten's exhilaration faded, but she took herself to the mercantile and found some pale green calico strewn with tiny flowers of many colors. Trimmed with darker green braid, it could be a best dress till Annie handed it down to her sister. The child was straight as a board and looked as if she'd stay that way, so repeated fittings wouldn't be essential. Kirsten would just make a wide hem and bodice seams that could be let out and she'd get Annie's measurements by saying she wanted to make up a girl's sample dress to show her customers. She had two more days to work for Minnie —only two more days!—and would get the dress cut out first, since that would be difficult to manage on the prairie.

Kirsten had little to pack. For the comfort of something familiar, she had kept the Mordal Bible on her dresser. As she put it in the trunk, she ached to see the ruffled, finely embroidered bridegroom's shirt that was wrapped around Grandfather Nils's violin. Would it fit O'Brien? She couldn't resist gently placing the violin on the bed and holding up the shirt, stretching the arms to match an imaginary O'Brien. It was certainly long enough. The tail dangled below her hips, and how had she known that the man she'd want to marry would have such broad shoulders?

Sighing, she again wrapped it carefully around the violin. Would either be used? Oh, the violin would; if she never married, if there was no hope of a child who could play it, she'd eventually give it to someone who could make it sing again. It would be a crime to leave it silent in a world that needed all the music it could get. But the shirt—she didn't think she could ever love anyone but O'Brien, and she couldn't marry, not even for the home and family she craved, unless she loved her husband.

It only took a few minutes to add her clothing and sewing supplies, including a few patterns and copies of *Harper's Bazaar* and the *Delineator* she'd bought, which had illustrations of the current fashions back East and in London and Paris. She couldn't afford to carry a lot of material, but she had invested in various colors of thread, braid, buttons, and hooks and eyes. On top she placed Annie's cut-out dress so she could get to it easily when they stopped for any length of time. Blue had devised a way to brace the folding table so it would hold the machine, and a box would make a seat.

She had made herself two bonnets, both black, one of material from her ruffled dress, the other of woven wool for winter. Putting on her shawl, she tied the bows of the lighter-weight bonnet beneath her chin and took a last look in the spotted mirror before her gaze swept around the little room in a leave-taking and summing up.

This had been her first dwelling place in America, her place of refuge after hours of waiting tables and straining to understand peculiar accents. Lucia had died in that bed. Often, Kirsten had cried herself to sleep on that lumpy pillow. But this was also where she'd made beautiful dresses with the amazing Family Gem, where she'd launched what she hoped to make a successful business. Of all her memories of the room, though, the most vivid were of O'Brien, carrying Lucia in his arms, bringing food, standing there as he had when, the last time, she had known he was going to marry Lorena.

All the memories of this room weren't sad, but she was glad to leave it, glad to venture out on the broad plains and get to know this land she had chosen. Hearing steps in the hall, she called, "I'm ready, Blue!" and swung open the door.

"So eager?" Ash Bowden watched her with mocking regret before he glanced around the room and grimaced. "No wonder you think camping out will be an improvement! That trunk is all you have?"

"Blue loaded the Family Gem earlier."

Eyes as silver as his hair in the poorly lit room, Bowden looked at her in a way that made her move swiftly out the door. He laughed and swung the trunk lightly to his shoulder. "Running from me?"

"I'm ready to go so I'm going," she retorted.

"Just so. But we'll meet along the trails. And if you get tired of the gypsy life, my dear, don't be too proud to let me put up the money for a shop in whatever town best suits you."

"After I pay back the note you bought from Jim Carson, I don't intend to ever owe you anything again."

Sorrowfully, he shook his head. "You'll never find a more lenient creditor. Why do you feel that way?"

"You make me—nervous."

At that, he threw back his head and roared. "Well, that's a start, I trust."

Kirsten wanted to throw a withering stare over her shoulder, but to her cost she knew he didn't wither easily. She escaped outside and gasped.

Everyone in Dodge seemed thronged around the wagon. Restaurant patrons, Bob Wright from Wright, Beverley's Mercantile, Jim Carson, Mrs. Gardiner from the Dodge House, Bridget's brood with young Annie as their shepherdess, even Jimbo and Selina. And what was that advancing down Front Street, bell clanging as they dragged the hose cart, but the Fire Company, in their long-handled red flannel union suits! Behind them marched the Dodge City Cowboy Band in blue flannel shirts, chaps, fancy boots and spurs and white Stetsons, each hatband stamped with the brand of one of the sponsoring ranches. Instruments flashing in the early sunlight, they burst into a thunder of drums that drowned out the fire bell before bugles sounded and the band soared into "The Star-Spangled Banner."

"Is—is it a holiday?" Kirsten whispered to Bowden.

Looking none too pleased, he didn't answer till he'd handed her trunk up to Blue. "It seems they've come to give you a big send-off." As her jaw dropped, he smiled reluctantly. "You're the kind of person a town like this takes to its heart. You're pretty, you're alone in the world, and you've got gumption."

"Gumption?"

"Courage."

"I'm not brave. I only want to see America."

"Well then, you'd better be on your way." He waited till she'd embraced Minnie and Bridget, promising to be careful, and then helped her up the step onto the seat next to Blue, whose chest puffed out as he held the reins and soothed the mares, who fidgeted at the ear-splitting music.

Bowden held her hand for a moment, then turned it over and deliberately kissed the palm. His warm lips and breath sent a tingling up her arm. As it vibrated through her, he stepped back and raised his hand. "Fare you well, Kirsten Mordal."

He turned abruptly and went up the street as Blue started the team. Fire Company ahead, band following, cheered by the people who lined the street, they turned to the bridge, and on this day, Kirsten paid no toll. The wagon rolled across the river while the crowd cheered; the band stopped at the north bank, playing till the wagon disappeared among the sand dunes.

Tears coursed down Kirsten's cheeks. "Oh, Blue!" she said, when she could speak. "America *is* just as wonderful as the song!"

"Hope it always will be for you, Miss Kirsty." She remembered, with a pang, that for him America hadn't been kind, but he smiled at her as he lifted the reins. "Well now, Honey, Stockings, let's see if we can make it to Crooked Creek tonight!"

Dug three or four feet deep into the sand by the hooves of millions of cattle and thousands of heavily laden wagons and thirty feet wide in places, the trail stretched like an invitation to the future on this day of brilliant sun with just enough briskness to quicken the blood. As they left the sand dunes for the bluestem grasslands, which slowly yielded to rippling buffalo grass turning rosy-brown again after greening with the fall rains, her heart swelled as if to encompass the high plains and the sweep of sky, and she felt as if she'd been drinking O'Brien's champagne, without judicious pauses.

"Can you believe it, Blue?" she asked softly, spreading her arms. "All this country! And with this good team and wagon, we can travel anywhere!"

"Anywhere a sane person would want to," he said drily, but his black eyes shone. "Know somethin', Miss Kirsty? I had some high old times when I was a young buck and used to swagger down

Front Street like I owned it, but I'd reckon this is sure the happiest day of my life."

She didn't have to search for the best time of her American life; it was that magical evening when O'Brien had taken her to the Dodge House, but it was no use harking back to that. "It is a marvelous day," she agreed, and they smiled at each other with great content.

The wagon had good springs and the cushions helped, but of course it lacked the comfort of the buggy in which Ash Bowden had driven her this same route only three weeks ago. Had it been that short a time since she'd struck on the idea of traveling around to her customers? It seemed like months and years since she'd come to Dodge City, but in fact they'd arrived in mid-July and it was now late October. Since she had no one with whom to speak her language or recall the village, that life seemed more and more dreamlike. She didn't want to forget the traditions; she would plant a family tree beside her door, save the last sheaf of the harvested grain to feed the beasts and wild birds on Christmas Eve, serve steaming glögg, made with wine and spices, and X-shaped saffron buns on St. Lucia's Day. All these things she would do, but she would learn the American feasts and keep them, too, especially the Fourth of July, the birthday of her new country.

At noon, passing Dugan's road ranch, where a stage and freighters were stopped, Blue drove along Mulberry Creek to some good grass. He watered the horses and hobbled them to graze while Kirsten made coffee and spread out the fried chicken, corn muffins, pickles and plum cake that Bridget had packed for them.

"It's ten miles to the next sure water, where a spring-fed stream runs into Crooked Creek," said Blue, stretching. "We can make it before dark if we don't stop too long now."

Treating Stockings and Honey to dried apples, Kirsten stroked them, liking the feel of the strong muscles under their smooth hides. "Will that push the horses too much?"

"Not today. They've been eating themselves fat and sassy at the livery. But most times, we'll let them graze several hours at noon." He grinned at her. "Don't worry, Miss Kirsty. I know horses. Folks used to say the ones I stole were delivered in prime condition, better'n when I sneaked 'em out of the pasture."

Wild geese called overhead, winging south in a wedge like

stitches in the sky. The flowers had withered except for some orange mallow, but there were fresh green rosettes of what Blue said were hairy pinweed and verbena, while silver beardgrass and other plants contrasted with the prevailing rose-browns of buffalo grass. A flock of white-crowned sparrows flitted in the willows, which were shedding their last yellow leaves, and a meadowlark, with a melodious whistle, winged up from the grass.

"It's funny about birds," Blue said. "Some crows fly south, but others stay the winter and it's the same for shrikes. And speaking of traveling, I reckon we'd better."

They camped on the east bank of Crooked Creek that night, immediately setting the pot of beans that had soaked all day to cook on a fire of cow chips encouraged with twists of dry grass. The coffee went on the other side. As soon as Blue took off their harness, Honey and Stockings had a good roll in the sand, munched their ration of grain, and started grazing. It would take the beans several hours to cook, so after she and Blue had amassed a good supply of buffalo chips, which Blue called "prairie coal," Kirsten opened her chest to get out her bedding. Seeing Grandfather Nils's violin, she suddenly wanted to touch the mellow wood and unwrapped it from the wedding shirt.

"What's that you've got, Miss Kirsty?" Blue moved to the wagon as quickly as his shuffle would permit, eyes lighting up, and gave a long, soft whistle. "That's some fiddle! Bring it from the old country?"

"It was my grandfather's." Kirsten swallowed to ease the lump in her throat. "I wish I knew someone who could play it."

"You're lookin' at him," said Blue. "First time I got locked up, the deputy sheriff fiddled to pass the time. I was just a kid. He taught me to play—reckon he hoped it might keep me from gettin' into more mischief. It didn't, but I sure like bowin' out a tune. Course I'm rusty. A drunk busted up my fiddle several years ago and there was no way I could get enough money to buy another."

"Oh, Blue!" Kirsten's delight mixed with vexation as she handed him the violin and bow. "If I'd only known you could play!"

"Well, you know now, and it'll sure cheer the evenings." His brown hands lovingly touched the satiny wood. "If you can hum some of your grandpa's tunes, I ought to be able to pick 'em up."

"That'll be wonderful! But I want to hear American songs, too."

"You will," he promised and began to experiment while Kirsten spread her pallet on the long bench, thinking how snug the canvas curtains made the back of the wagon, and set a basin of spring water near the fire to heat so she could wash herself before going to bed.

Blue put down the violin long enough to show Kirsten how to make sourdough biscuits. These, baked to a perfect gold-brown in the cast-iron Dutch oven, were feathery light inside, crunchy outside, and so good with their tangy flavor that Kirsten ate as many as Blue. When they had sopped up the last of the thick bean soup from their tin plates, it only took a few minutes to wash dishes, and then they settled back with steaming coffee while Blue played dance tunes that made Kirsten's feet keep time, tunes like the wind sweeping the plains, some with the trill of birds, others lonesome as a night without a moon.

Coyotes yipped their shrill, laughing staccato, neighbors on the prairie. Kirsten kept the fire fed, glad not only for its warmth but for the friendly glow. She wasn't afraid, but it was strange to be out like this, far from any dwelling. Wonderful, though, to see the stars spangled across the sky, to recognize the North Star, guide of travelers through the ages, including her Viking forebears; to locate the Big and Little Dippers; to trace Orion astride the heavens.

Blue put down the violin, flexing his cramped fingers, and sighed in vast contentment as he sipped his coffee. "That's a mighty fine fiddle of your grandpa's, Miss Kirsty. Sure glad you brought it across the water. Can you give me some of your grandpa's tunes?"

Kirsten began shyly with Grandfather Nils's favorite, "The Blessed Day," a hymn sung in a special way by Dalarna folk; then hummed the tune with which the women of her family had long called their cows in the summer meadows. Gay little snatches of children's rhymes and the words that made her ache for O'Brien: "So night and day, and day and night, are yours and only yours . . ."

His days and nights belonged now to Lorena. There was not an hour of loving, not a minute, that he could rightfully give another woman. Foolish, if not wicked, to cherish the memory of the few times they'd been together, yet Kirsten couldn't help it, and bitterness left a dryness in her mouth.

He *had* seen her differently that second time. He'd meant it when he said he wanted to be the first man she danced with in America. If his friend hadn't died, if O'Brien hadn't promised to look after Lorena, if— Longing for him swept through her, shaking her as a storm bends a young tree. She had made his bride a beautiful dress; long, long ago, stitching the bridegroom's shirt, she had dreamed of the laughing, handsome man who would one day wear it. Now it seemed that no man would, for she couldn't imagine loving anyone except O'Brien. Each time she sewed a bride gown, would her heart shrivel a little more because it wasn't hers?

No! She might not marry, but she had her business and friends and she was in America. She hadn't come here to flounder in despair, spoil what she could reach by yearning for what was forbidden. Throwing back her head, she gazed up at the stars, drank in the night wind, and changed the words of the song sung so wistfully in Sweden.

> *It's so grand America, wonderful America,*
> *It's so grand America is here, right here!*

Blue picked up the violin and they went through the whole song, laughing together as they finished. "Lord love you, Miss Kirsty," Blue said. "I hope America never disappoints you."

"People may. America—never!"

His mouth tugged down, but he nodded. He handed the violin to Kirsten, who put it carefully in the chest, and got his bedroll out of the wagon. As he spread it on the grass, light glimmered on a double-barreled shotgun. "Just an old muzzle loader," he told Kirsten apologetically. "But it'll keep us in prairie chickens and antelope."

Those fleet, graceful creatures that seemed to float over the plain? "Blue! You won't kill an antelope? Please, not unless we're starving!"

He pushed back his battered hat and scratched his ear. "Reckon I can't if'n you feel like that," he said resignedly. "But we sure are goin' to get tired of rabbit and prairie hen. Get a good sleep, Miss Kirsty. We'll make Hoodoo Brown's tomorrow."

It felt good to wash off the dust of the trail, unbraid and brush her hair while watching the stars from the wagon seat, and then slip between her blankets. In summer, it would be delicious to have the curtains rolled all the way up, but she was grateful now for the shelter.

The journey had begun. She had launched her venture. Ash Bowden wasn't the only one, probably, who thought her addled to fare around to customers rather than establish herself in town, but she glowed with pride in Honey and Stockings and the marvelous wagon that held everything she needed to earn her living anywhere she stopped. Reveling in that, when O'Brien's face rose before her, she told him: *I love you. I always will. But I won't cry after you, or hold you in my thoughts while I go to sleep. Don't plague me, O'Brien, please. . . .*

She fixed her mind on the wild geese, and the cranes she'd seen later in the day, making their way south. By the time they passed her again going north with the summer, she, too, would have traveled many miles, had adventures, made all kinds of clothes for all kinds of people. And maybe then it wouldn't hurt so much, that O'Brien was Lorena's. In spite of her weariness and stern resolutions, it was a long time before Kirsten slept.

The two soddies, corrals, and outbuildings of Hoodoo Brown's road ranch were located near a spring overlooking a valley north of Crooked Creek. A freighting outfit had already taken over the accommodations in the soddie where the family lived, but plump, rosy-cheeked Mrs. Brown, twin girls of perhaps six peeking around her skirts, welcomed Kirsten eagerly, wanting all the news of Dodge, where the Browns had lived while George—Mrs. Brown did *not* call her husband Hoodoo—ran a saloon there.

"Close enough to the river to cut whiskey with that good silty water," he laughed. Leather-skinned, bewhiskered and with hooded eyes, Brown looked to be about forty. "Danged if it's not good to see you out on the trail again, Blue. You better eat with us tonight. Buffalo steak."

"Buffalo!" Blue snorted. "Hoodoo, you must sure of been drinking your own whiskey and shot a cow."

"Nope," said Hoodoo, unruffled. "We're getting some new neighbors who'd never seen a buffalo so I got together a little hunt last week. Took us a lot of ridin' but we did find a couple."

The meat was tough and stringy, but the gravy helped, and

there was fresh-baked bread and, since Mrs. Brown kept chickens, the luxury of egg custard to go with dried-peach pie. Some of the freighters bolted their food and, with whiskey purchased from the store, withdrew to their quarters, but several lingered to hear Hoodoo's tales or steal glances at Kirsten.

After seeing considerable action as a Union soldier, young George had drifted west, freighting with ox teams, scouting for the Army, trail-herding cattle, cutting railroad ties and then hunting buffalo for their meat and hides.

"I was freighting to Dodge when I camped here one night, and it was so cold, with nothing much to burn, that I decided someone ought to put in a road ranch. So I built the soddies, stocked the store on credit, and we've been here ever since."

"Almost ever since, Hoodoo," said a grizzled older freighter with a chuckle. "You made pretty fast tracks out of here when old Dull Knife and his Cheyenne came through on their way north after bustin' off their reservation down in Indian Territory in the fall of 1878."

Hands on her hips, Mrs. Brown gave the freighter an indignant glare. "George was worried about his family, and didn't he have a right to be? That poor man scalped right on the trail and ten folks killed south of the Arkansas River? Just as soon as George had us safe in Dodge, didn't he take a wagon and all by himself go back down the trail to bring in the body of John Tuttle's black cook?"

Vindicated, Hoodoo groomed his moustache and said, "It was a lot worse in Nebraska. Dull Knife's young men killed forty-three people, kidnapped some boys and ravished women. Course the government was crazy in the first place, trying to keep Northern Cheyenne in country they hated, where they sickened and died."

Why, this had happened only seven years ago! "The Cheyenne," Kirsten asked. "What became of them?"

"Little Wolf's band went on north, but Dull Knife surrendered at Fort Robinson, Nebraska—reckoned they'd be allowed to go to their old home," said Hoodoo. "Instead they were locked up till they'd promise to go back to Indian Territory. They broke out in January, and must have been over a third of them killed. Guess the rest got to the Sioux reservation. Old Dull Knife died up there a couple of years ago."

"You sound kind of sorry for him," growled the freighter.

"Maybe," shrugged Hoodoo. "But I sure wasn't ready to make any of 'em a gift of my hair, such as it is." He turned to Kirsten with a smile. "Never thought I'd live to see the day when a young lady could jaunter all over this country with a sewing machine and not have to worry about losing that pretty hair."

"Do you have a pattern book?" Mrs. Brown asked wistfully. "Sometimes one of the settler's wives gets to come here for the mail and to buy at the store, but they're even further behind on the fashions than I am."

Kirsten brought in her *Delineator* and *Harper's Bazaar*. For the next few hours, while the men debated whether or not No Man's Land would be opened for settlement, Kirsten and Mrs. Brown sat near the kerosene lamp and discussed the styles. The road rancher's wife kept leafing back to an amber cut-velvet trimmed in moiré taffeta with a side-draped polonaise, a looped-up overskirt. "I never saw a prettier gown," she sighed, and then shut the book with a good-natured grimace. "I don't know where I'd ever wear anything that elegant, though. Still, it was a treat to look, Miss Mordal."

"I'm glad you enjoyed it," Kirsten said, rising. "Thank you for the good supper."

"Be sure to stop when you're back this way," Mrs. Brown urged. "I want to hear all the news and how you did with your sewing. If you want breakfast in the morning, there'll be fresh eggs."

"That sounds good," Kirsten nodded.

Hoodoo escorted her out with a lantern. "That dress my wife liked," he said. "Any way you could make it for her?"

"I'm sure I could if I had the material and her measurements."

He rubbed his chin. "I'd kind of like it to be a surprise." He brightened. "Would it work to measure one of her dresses instead of her?"

Kirsten thought a moment. "I suppose it would if you stuffed the dress where she—uh—fills it."

He chuckled. "Reckon I can manage that, and if you'd make a list of the fixin's, I can get them next time I go to Dodge for supplies. I can send the stuff by stage to the Hardesty Ranch, the nearest stage stop, if you're going to be at Hi Allen's for a while, and when you're finished, you can stage it back. Ten dollars sound fair with your supper, breakfast and hay for the horses thrown in?"

"More than fair," Kirsten agreed. That day at the long midday stop, she'd worked on young Annie's gown. It was beginning to look as if she wouldn't have any wasted time. Thinking of Mrs. Brown's delighted surprise when she got the unexpected and luxurious gift, Kirsten thought what a pleasure it was going to be to make a living at something that would mean so much to the isolated women of these wide plains. Kirsten patted the Family Gem and murmured, "My good helper, you're going to make a lot of women happy!" That was a gratifying prospect, even if she was fated to make bride gowns but never wear one. But she was too young, too much in love with O'Brien, to believe, no matter what Ash Bowden said, that success was any substitute for living with the one you loved.

8

Beyond the Marts' road ranch at Odee, they traveled through drifted red sandhills, some skewered in place by sage and yucca, others still shifting till no plant could take root. It was hard going for the horses and there was nothing for them to graze on. Only in great necessity, said Blue, would they eat sage, though antelope loved it. After Odee, it was fifteen miles to water at the Cimarron crossing, variously known as Hines' Crossing for the road ranch on the north bank, or Busing Crossing, or Miles City for the store and post office to the south. The Cimarron River ran between hills cradling a valley of good grass, and an immense prairie-dog village covered acres of the northern flats. A number of the yellowish little creatures sat erect on their mounds, giving sharp, rapid barks.

"Guards, they be," smiled Blue. "One out of every bunch is always on duty. This kind may sleep in their burrows during really cold weather, but they don't stay there all winter like the whitetailed ones you find up in the Rockies."

He drove past the soddies and corrals of the Hines' road ranch, for he had shot several prairie chickens that day, and they were going to cook their own meal. Halting at the sandy, slow-moving but wide river, he said, "No Man's Land's right across the Cimarron. Unless you'd rather stop over by Busing's store, we might as well camp this side and cross in the morning, when the team's fresh. Low as the river is now, we shouldn't have any trouble, but that sand is real miry and sure sucks at a critter's hoofs."

No Man's Land. With a sense of destiny, Kirsten gazed south. Where in that unclaimed region would she make her home? Where was Kiowa Creek, where O'Brien lived? O'Brien and Lorena? That thought hurt, and Kirsten shut it out. Dreaming of

O'Brien had been her great delight and solace for so long that it was hard to root out, but he could never enter her thoughts now without Lorena intruding—no, not intruding. She belonged with him; it was Kirsten who did not. Yet still he was always at the back of her mind, always present in her heart. Even if, by an act of will, she could change that, she wasn't sure she would.

"Let's wait till morning to cross," she said, and while the horses savored their grain, she helped Blue brush them free of the red dust that had turned them into sorrels.

Blue played the violin that night. He hadn't finished the plaintive notes of "Colorado Trail," when half a dozen freighters drifted down from the road ranch and took off their hats to Kirsten.

"Mind if we listen, ma'am?" asked a barrel-shaped man with fierce black whiskers.

"You're very welcome," Kirsten said. They exchanged names, and then she asked, "Would you like coffee?"

"Much obliged, ma'am," he said, holding up a jug. "But we got our own refreshment."

One of his companions took the jug. "Beg your pardon, ma'am, we didn't know there was a lady down here. I'll stick this snake juice under your bed, Bart, and borrow the coffee pot and some cups from Hines."

"I want a drink," growled the black-whiskered one.

"Then go have it with the bedbugs," shrugged the younger man.

Bart stood scowling, undecided. "You know 'Sourwood Mountain'?" he demanded.

Blue grinned and swept his bow across the strings. Bart cut a caper, remarkably light on his feet for so big a man, and sat down by his friends. He next called for "Blue Juniata." The freighter who had confiscated his jug was returning with coffee and cups, when a light bobbed from the store across the Cimarron and halted on what must have been the riverbank. In the yellow glow, Kirsten could make out seven or eight shadowy figures settling down around what had to be a lantern. Blue ended one of his wind songs, cupped his hands and shouted to his new audience.

"Any tune you folks would like?"

" 'Battle Hymn of the Republic,' " someone called back.

Bart curled his lip. "That'll be Captain Busing from the store.

Well, go ahead and play it if you can, mister, but then how's about a real song, like 'Bonnie Blue Flag'?"

"I don't play that one," said Blue, "seeing as how my daddy was a slave till he run off to the Kiowas. If you want a real treat, maybe Miss Kirsty would sing a song that helped bring her to America."

Willingness to be a peacemaker overcame Kirsten's shyness, and after the martial music of "The Battle Hymn," to Blue's accompaniment she sang "Wonderful America." When she finished there was fervent applause from both sides of the river, though on the south bank they must have been barely able to hear her.

Bart smoothed his bushy whiskers. "Guess this is a pretty good country in spite of damnyankees," he allowed. "My folks got burned off their croft in the Highlands of Scotland, land they'd farmed for hundreds of years, to make room for sheep. Came here with nothing, but now they've got a good farm in Missouri. How about a freighting song, maybe that one that ends up, 'Root hog or die'?"

That was one both banks joined in on, and there were many more before Blue set the violin in his lap and rubbed his fingers. "If we're goin' to travel tomorrow, that better be all, but it sure was fun."

"Music's good for people," said Bart, and he handed Blue a bag of tobacco. "Sure was a better evenin' than swilling whiskey and playing cards. Thanks to the both of you, and ma'am, I sure hope you find everything you want in America."

His big hand swallowed hers in a hearty shake. His companions shook hands or nodded, wishing her and Blue a good journey before they disappeared into the night. A chorus of thanks floated from the south side. By the time the lantern had flickered its way back to the store, Kirsten and Blue had made down their beds.

Since their wagon was lightly loaded and the river was low, they crossed the muddy Cimarron next morning without real difficulty, though Honey and Stockings had to pull hard to move the wheels through the mire. "After a big rain, the Cimarron's a killer," said Blue. "I've seen it churning three hundred yards wide, brick-red, and sucking down anything it got ahold of."

"I will be happy never to see that," said Kirsten. As they passed the store and the sodhouse beside it, a gray-haired, gaunt woman ran out, apron flapping, holding a pie so hot that steam rose through the latticed top crust.

"Can you put this in something?" the woman asked. "I'm Mrs.

Busing, and the captain and I just have to thank you for the music last night."

Thanking her, Kirsten scooped the pie into the Dutch oven, hoping the giver couldn't see that it had torn apart, though it would taste just as good. As they rolled on, the storekeeper's wife called after them, "Next time, stop on our side!"

"We will," Kirsten waved back. "It's so strange to me," she said to Blue above the rumble of the wheels. "When one meets people for a first time, they act like old neighbors."

"In this part of the country, anyone who's not plumb ornery or crawlin' with graybacks *is* a neighbor," Blue said with a chuckle. "You can bet it won't be long till everyone on the way to Tascosa and on to Mobeetie, Camp Supply, and back to Dodge, have heard all about a pretty young sewing lady who's making the grand tour in her wagon. News spreads out from the road ranches to dugouts and big ranches a hundred miles away." He called to the horses. "Git along there, Stockings, Honey! We've made it to No Man's Land!"

When they camped that night, Blue's fingers were too stiff from the night before to play the violin, so they watched the stars. He pointed to the Pleiades halfway up the eastern sky. "Kiowas call those the Star Girls." With a pang, Kirsten remembered how Lucia, dying, had seen the star boys who paraded on her saint's day.

"Is there a story?" Kirsten asked.

"Always got to be a story." She filled his cup by way of encouragement, and he settled against the wagon wheel. "Once ten little girls were playing that one of them was a bear that chased the others when they were picking grapes and plums. It wasn't long till the bear-girl was scratching and biting too deep for fun, and her sister noticed that hair was growing between her fingers, which had turned into claws. This girl ran away and hid while her sister turned into a monster bear that tore up and ate their playmates and then ran to the village and killed everyone there, though it was wounded with many arrows. It found the sister and made her hunt rabbits for the bear's food and carry wood to warm the tepee.

"One day the slave sister met some young men who said they'd help her escape. One put her up behind him on his horse, and they galloped as hard as they could. The bear monster came after them, across canyons and rivers and mountains and plains, till the horses gave out and they had to go on foot. The bear chased them far, far to the north, till they were too worn out to go on. They stopped at a rock to make a last fight against the monster. Then that rock said, 'You climb on top of me and maybe I can help you.' They didn't see how it could, but there was sure nothing else they could do, so they crowded onto that rock. Well, it grew wider and higher and by the time the bear got there, they were out of its reach. She clawed at the rock, though, and left big scars, till at last her claws all broke off. It could still bite, so the rock put the girl and six young men up in the sky to be safe."

"But if six were men, why call them Star Girls?"

"I'm just telling you the story," Blue shrugged. "But that rock is Devil's Tower up in Wyoming and my people say hunters found some great big bear claws scattered around the bottom."

"Did you grow up with the Kiowas?"

"Partly. My mother died when I was a tyke, and my pa left the Kiowas then and went to freighting on the Santa Fe Trail for Alexander Majors. Time I was ten or 'leven I was ridin' the jerkline, but I remembered my mother's people. When I was big enough to strike off on my own, I found them. Hunted buffalo, went on raids against the Pawnees, ranged down to Texas and back to the Smokey Hill country in Kansas. Took me a wife. But when she died havin' our baby, I heard about the war, and for my pa's sake I joined up with the Union. Went to cowboyin' after the war, and from there it's an easy road to rustlin', Miss Kirsty."

"Why, Blue?"

"Ranchers let most of their hands go after the fall cow work and don't hire again till spring. Leaves an awful lot of men ridin' the grubline, stayin' a few days at one ranch, then ridin' on to the next. Quite a few of the boys figger it don't hurt to chouse a few head of cattle up some canyon and come back that winter to hole up and eat beef."

"Why," said Kirsten, aghast, "that's not fair! A man must eat the whole year, not just when a rancher needs him!"

"That's what some of the hands reckoned a few years ago in the Texas Panhandle. Bunch of 'em went on strike for better wages in April of '83 when they were needed bad for spring roundup. They got fired, and after that they couldn't get a job in this part of the country. Some drifted to other ranges, but others stayed and stole cows. No way a cowboy can win over a cowman unless he turns into one himself—which lots did, till the Cattle Growers' Association made a rule that no cowboy working for any of them could have his own brand." Blue smothered a yawn. "World's never been fair, Miss Kirsty, that's the truth of it."

"But in America—"

"When folks get rich in America, I reckon they act like rich folks anyplace—want to hang on to all they got and grab more." Blue pondered and then laughed. "Guess what America does is give a bunch more people a chance to get ahead, but it sure don't change human nature."

"But every man can vote here, Blue, not just the well-to-do. And all the free land—"

One of the horses whinnied and was answered by an animal out in the night. Kirsten broke off, startled. Blue pushed himself to his feet with all the speed he could and caught up his shotgun, which leaned against the wagon wheel. It was only then that she detected muted sounds beyond the dimmest reach of their fire's light.

"Put down that shotgun, nigger." The darkest shadows coalesced into the solid massiveness of a stranger who moved into the light with a menace that alarmed Kirsten more than the glint of rifles and guns carried by his followers, perhaps a dozen men, who moved close enough to be distinguished from the night but not near enough to reveal faces.

The leader carried no weapon, but his thick hands looked as if they could strangle an ox. A fringe of sandy hair bristled around his broad, flat-featured face, but he was clean-shaven beneath the nose and to the edge of his jaws and chin. He was the first man Kirsten had met in America who didn't take off his hat to her.

"Who might you be, young woman?" he asked, advancing after Blue reluctantly leaned his shotgun back against the wagon. "Where did you come from? Where are you headed?"

Kirsten's heart thudded, but she was angry at the way he'd spoken to Blue and moved into their camp with guns. "Are you an officer of the law?" she demanded.

Black eyes sunk deep in fat gouged into her. "We're the law in No Man's Land, miss, and I'll ask the questions. What's your business here?"

Kirsten was frightened, but her temper was up. "I do not think you can ask such questions."

Blue said, "Miss Kirsty, it's true they got no right, but they got the guns."

That brought home to her that he'd suffer the results, too, if she defied the intruders. Reluctantly, she said, "I'm Kirsten Mordal and this is Blue Martin. We're on our way from Dodge City to Mr. Hiram Allen's ranch, where I will sew for the family."

"*Sew?*"

"My machine is in the wagon."

"Hank," the big man ordered, "hop up and have a look."

Kirsten seethed as a rawboned man clambered into her wagon and peered under the seat and long bench, even opened the trunk, but there was nothing she could do. If she provoked the gang, Blue would try to protect her, and though they probably wouldn't really hurt her, she feared they would have no scruples about him.

"She's got a sewing machine and pattern books, Gus," said the one named Hank, coming down from the wagon. "No sign of Randall."

The heavy man took a step toward Kirsten. A wave of physical dread swept through her. It took an effort of will to stand her ground as he asked harshly, "You see a dark young jasper yesterday or today? Might be riding a roan with a Bar L brand, could be afoot, most likely wounded?"

"Some freighters and stages we have met," said Kirsten, inverting words as she still did when upset. "No men by themselves."

He grunted and turned to the others. "Probably holed up with some of his thievin' friends. Wish we had dogs to track him, but it looks like we'll have to dig him out." Spinning with amazing swiftness to confront Kirsten, he said in his grating way, "We're hunting Bob Randall—dark, good-looking, maybe twenty years old. If you run into him, don't give him any help or you'll be responsible to the Committee."

"What has Randall done?" The huge bully terrified Kirsten, but she was determined not to show it. "And what is this Committee?"

Laughter came from the shadowy armed men. "We're the Committee," said their chief. "I'm August Kelman. We're cleaning out the rustlers and no-goods. Bob Randall butchered one of my cows and he's going to hang for it."

Kirsten couldn't believe her ears. "Hang a man for a cow? You —you cannot!"

Kelman laughed. "Who'll stop us? You just mind your own business, young lady, and we'll take care of ours."

His bulk merged with the darkness. In a few minutes the sound of their footfalls receded and then there was the rasp of leather and metal as, some distance away, they mounted. Kirsten stared at Blue.

"Do they mean it? Can—can they really hang this Randall?"

"Can if they catch him." Blue sighed and shook his head. "Look, Miss Kirsty, you got all these ideas about America, and some ways it is a wonderful country. But it ain't Glory Land, and folks can be just as mean and nasty as they are anywhere, 'specially where there's no law to rein 'em in." He touched her shoulder awkwardly. "Don't fret too much about Randall. More'n likely he's made for the Indian Nations and I don't think this pack of coyotes have enough guts to hunt him over there."

Retiring in subdued silence, Kirsten hoped that he was right. The odor of Hank's sweat, tobacco, and whiskey soured the wagon, and she rolled up the curtains till the prairie wind carried his stench away.

Sickened and grieved by this first true evil she'd found in her chosen country, Kirsten kept seeing and hearing Kelman. At last she blotted him out by calling up O'Brien's face. If he'd been in camp, Kelman would never have dared act as he had.

A new worry buzzed in her head. If Kelman and his Committee had set themselves up as judge, jury and executioner in No Man's Land, where did that leave decent people like O'Brien? It was a long time before she slept, and then her rest was broken by dreams where Kelman or his shadows advanced on her and she couldn't scream to alert O'Brien, whose back was turned, nor could she run or fight. She could only wait, paralyzed, while Kelman showed small white teeth and reached for her. . . .

Thick, heavy fingers grasped her. Breath trapped the cry in her throat. Kirsten woke sitting up, only gradually seeing that she was alone, that she had been dreaming. It was that gray time between night and dawn when shapes have mass but no details. Shivering in the chill, she was settling back in her blankets, when she heard a sound by the wagon and someone said in an urgent whisper,

"Ma'am, I'm sure sorry to bother you but I'm hungry and on foot. If you'd give me something to eat, I'd be mightily obliged."

Blue was up with his shotgun before the first words were out of the young man's mouth. Hardly more than a boy, this stranger was dark and slight, and even in the faint light, though he was unshaven and tousled, his smile was reckless and winning.

"You're Bob Randall," Kirsten said.

"I am, and the Committee's after me." His smile flashed. "If they find out you fed me, you can always say I held a gun on you."

Blue said sharply, "Don't even joke about that, young fella."

"We'll give you food," Kirsten said. "But what can you do without a horse?"

"If I'm lucky, maybe I can make it to a friend's place, get another horse and light out for New Mexico." He swayed, catching hold of the wagon, and now it was light enough for Kirsten to see a dark stain where his blue shirt showed beneath his sheepskin vest.

"You're hurt!"

"Doesn't say much for their shooting that that's all I am." His cocky grin ended in a grimace and he glanced at Blue. "The bullet's still in there. I wasn't going to pester you folks with it but since you know who I am and that I'm hit, I'd be beholden if you could dig it out."

"Let's have a look at it," Blue said. Kirsten built up the fire and helped soak the shirt loose from the wound, then scrubbed out as much as she could of the telltale stiffness. "Wish we had some whiskey for you," Blue said as he probed with the small blade of his knife. "There, I hit the doggone thing, but gettin' it out is somethin' else. I don't think Miss Kirsty would mind if you cuss."

"Thanks, but I reckon I can stand it without that."

He did, gripping the wagon with his other hand, jaw rigid. Sweat rose on his brow and upper lip. By the time Blue extracted the bullet, Kirsten's stomach was roiling, but she washed the reopened wound and dressed it with arnica salve, one of the several medicaments she had in the chest, and made a pad and from a clean pillowcase a bandage to hold it in place.

"Why don't you crawl in my bedroll while we get breakfast?" Blue suggested. "My guess is you didn't sleep much last night."

"Use my bed in the wagon," Kirsten urged. "That way you'll be more out of sight in case anyone comes along."

"From the sign I found where they left their horses, the Committee's already been here."

"Last night." Kirsten controlled a shudder. "I hope we never see any of them again."

"Doubt if you'll be that lucky. They're all over this part of the Strip like blowflies on a carcass. I don't want to get you in trouble."

"No one'll come along so early." Kirsten fervently hoped she was right. "Get some rest." She made biscuits while Blue fried side meat and made gravy. "Blue," she whispered. "We should hide him in the wagon till he's well enough to strike off for his friend's."

Blue's sooty eyes didn't blink but he said quietly, "That bunch of Kelman's might come back, Miss Kirsty."

Her insides twisted at the thought, but it was worse to imagine the exhausted young man trying to escape on foot if Kelman picked up his trail. "We have to help him, Blue."

Blue studied her. At last, he nodded. "I guess we do. A man's life for a cow's isn't much of a swap. We'll pull the front curtains when we see anyone coming. Randall's young and full of ginger. Now the bullet's out, won't take him long to get feisty."

When his breakfast was ready, Kirsten took it to him. He slept with his sun-browned face partly hidden by his arm, thick black hair waving across his forehead. So young to be on the run for his life! He hadn't fleshed out yet to match his bones.

"Mr. Randall," she said softly.

He jerked up, wincing, relaxed as he saw her. "Sorry to be a nuisance, ma'am. You should have just hollered at me."

"You need to rest." She set down his plate and handed him a mug of coffee laced with condensed milk. He fell ravenously upon the meat and biscuits. "You must travel with us," she said firmly. "You can stay behind the curtains, and sleep all you can till you're strong again."

The eager relief in his eyes faded and he shook his head. "Ma'am, thank you, but I can't do that. No telling what Kelman would do if he caught you helping me."

"Did you butcher his cow?"

"I did, and I wish I hadn't. Stringiest, toughest meat I ever tried to chew." He pulled such a face that in spite of the gravity of the situation, Kirsten had to smile. "You see, I worked for Kelman last summer, and part of our deal was that when he laid me off in the fall, he'd give me a beef to get me through the winter. When he paid me off this month, Gus had plumb forgot that beef. So I took it."

"Then you really didn't steal."

"Not to my way of thinking, but that wouldn't cut any ice with a court, which we don't have."

"This Committee, what is it?"

"Vigilantes." At her puzzled look, he explained. "Because there isn't any law in the Strip, Kelman's got together this bunch that deal out what they call justice. They've hanged a few men and run a lot more off."

"And no one stops them?"

"Folks out here are scattered around and mind their own business. Besides, I'll have to say the men Gus hanged weren't much loss. You go eat your breakfast, ma'am, before these good biscuits cool off."

He got down from the wagon for his second mug of coffee and almost collapsed by the fire. "I'm a little swimmy-headed," he apologized.

"You lost a fair amount of blood," Blue said. "Miss Kirsty and me've already talked it over. You're stayin' with us till you get your legs back."

Bob Randall glanced at Kirsten, saw the determination in her face, and grinned. "I'll take you up on that today, since I sure am wobbly as a fresh-dropped calf, but when we cross the Beaver, I'll head up the river to my buddy's."

"Let's wait and see how you feel," Kirsten said and urged him to have the last of the biscuits and gravy.

"Best food I ever tasted," he said. "Of course, after they shot my horse, I didn't count much on ever eating another meal." He got back in the wagon, and by the time they were ready to travel, he was sound asleep. Kirsten pulled down the front curtain and prayed that they wouldn't meet Kelman again.

During the long noon stop Bob Randall ate heartily and talked to Kirsten as she worked on Annie's dress.

"You're a brave young lady," he said, eyes warm with admiration. "Coming all the way from Sweden and now doing this. Miz Allen is real nice. You'll like sewing for her."

"You know the Allens?"

"Miss Kirsty," he grinned, "everybody in the Neutral Strip knows everybody else—at least by reputation."

"Would Mr. Allen lend you a horse?"

Randall's jaw dropped. "Hi Allen's a good man, but in a case like mine, he'd just naturally have to side with Kelman. No, Miss Kirsty, I'll be obliged if you'll let me cross the river with you in the morning, and then I'll get out a few miles down the trail."

To avoid the people at Jim Lane's road ranch on what was called the Beaver River, though it was really the north fork of the Canadian, they drove off the trail a mile or so and camped near the river in good grass. Blue didn't play the violin that night for fear of attracting company, but they had a pleasant visit, and Randall seemed much recovered, joking and watching Kirsten with an intent delight that embarrassed her. She liked him. If it weren't for O'Brien—But there was O'Brien, hopeless as her love was, and she had no heart for any other man.

Randall had left his bedroll and saddle on his dead horse, too hotly pursued to carry anything, so Kirsten got out their extra blankets for his bedroll; he spread it a little way from Blue's and then came to Kirsten, who was still in the wagon.

"It was worth getting shot to meet you, Miss Kirsty. I never will forget you. Hope someday I have a chance to pay you and Blue back."

He was an orphan, he had told her, with no close kin. Touched, Kirsten pressed his work-calloused hand. "We've been glad to have you with us, Mr. Randall. And you mustn't leave till you're sure you're able."

Briefly, he held her hand in both of his. "Right now," he said, with a twinkle in his eyes, "I feel like I could fly clear to Dodge. Sleep tight, Miss Kirsty, and God bless you."

When they woke up next morning, he was gone.

9

A train of eight ox-pulled wagons was crossing the Beaver when Blue and Kirsten reached it, so they drew off to one side and waited while the drivers cursed, cajoled and encouraged their animals through the water and up the bank. Kirsten returned to the topic of Randall's disappearance.

"Why did he leave in the night? He said yesterday he'd stay with us till after we crossed the river."

"Reckon he didn't want to argufy with you, Miss Kirsty," said Blue. "And of course he's safer travelin' by night than day."

"He didn't even take any food," she worried.

"Well, he ate good yesterday, and it's only ten miles to his friend's place. Look, Miss Kirsty, he knew the longer he hid with us, the more likely he was to get us in trouble. Shucks, he's well along to his friend's by now. He'll hole up a few days and then hightail it for the border."

"What border?"

"He said New Mexico," Blue shrugged, "but he's also got his choice of Kansas, Indian Territory, Texas and Colorado. Great country this Strip is for a man on the run. Well, now them oxen have the mud stamped down good, let's see if we can get across."

The horses had to pull hard, but they crossed with no real problems. The wider, more heavily worn trail ran south to Mobeetie and Fort Elliott, but Blue swung the horses west on the fork that followed the river valley. They soon struck deep sand. "Good thing we don't have much of a load," Blue said as the wheels sank in. Even so, the horses had to labor. Kirsten got down to walk, easing them that much, but it was the worst traveling they'd had. They'd inched along perhaps two miles when they met twelve mules straining to haul one big, heavily laden wagon.

"Double-teaming," Blue told Kirsten above the racket. "They've left one wagon and'll take all the mules back for it after they get this'n through."

Sure enough, three hours later as they were getting out of the sand, they saw a wagon at the side of the trail. Since the horses were tired, they stopped longer than usual, and Kirsten made considerable progress with Annie's green gown, glad to concentrate on her work so she wouldn't be so anxious about Bob Randall. With any luck, he should be at his friend's by now, and she hoped with all her heart that he was.

They crossed the river next day and stayed on high ground, skirting the north bank through gentle hills. "We'd ought to make the Hardesty Ranch tonight," said Blue. "And from there it's just one more day to the Allens' Hi-A spread. Be glad to stop journeying for a spell, Miss Kirsty?"

She sighed. "I liked the traveling, Blue, till we met August Kelman."

"Now don't you let him ruin things for you," Blue scolded. "He's a stinker right enough, but he won't be plaguing you at Hi Allen's."

At their noon halt, Blue unhitched on the flats and led the horses down to drink, and Kirsten followed to wash off the red dust of the trail. Blue halted so abruptly that she almost ran into him, then froze as around the bend of the river she glimpsed what he had seen.

A man dangled from a limb of a cottonwood tree that was shedding its last yellowed leaves. He had dark hair, wore a blue shirt, and something was pinned to his chest. His face—the purpled protruding tongue—

Kirsten cried out. Everything whirled and her knees turned to water. "Don't look," Blue said, turning her around, putting the horses' halters in her limp fingers. "Go water the horses down that other direction, Miss Kirsty. I'll take care of this poor kid."

Stumbling ahead of the horses, Kirsten thought numbly, *He didn't get to his friend's. When did they catch him? Would he have had a better chance if he'd stayed with us?*

Through a blur of tears, she watched the horses drink, then took them up the bank and hobbled them. Blue, she saw, was making his way up at another point, dragging more than carrying the body. Kirsten got a clean sheet from her chest and went to join Blue, who had set to work with the shovel they carried to dig themselves out of sand. Fortunately, the sandy earth yielded easily to the shovel. He had wrapped Bob Randall's vest around his head and upper body. Kirsten spread the sheet on the ground.

"Let me do that for a while," she urged Blue. His hamstrung legs had little strength, and the task was making him pant.

He gave her an angry look. "Now God forbid you ever dig a grave, honey-girl, and you sure won't do it while I'm around! Go back to the wagon."

"No. I—I can at least stay here." After what had been done to that young body, there seemed to be no use in washing it, but she smoothed the black hair that showed above the sheepskin and wept for a boy who would never be a man, never laugh or eat or sleep again or feel the sun on his face.

When Blue had finished the grave, he helped Kirsten wrap Bob Randall in the sheet. Together they carried him to the trench and gently placed him in it. Kirsten wailed at the sound of the earth hitting his body.

Straightening, Blue said, "Go find some rocks." She knew why. Along the trail she had seen buzzards and coyotes feeding on carrion. When she and Blue had heaped the grave with rocks, he threw on more earth and then covered the mound with grass and dried yucca stalks.

"We won't leave a marker?" Kirsten asked.

"So if Kelman's back this way he'll drag out his bones and hang them up for a warning?" Blue asked. "That sign on his chest, Miss Kirsty, the Committee took credit and said to leave the body on the tree. If you know a prayer, say it, and let's get out of here. We'll stop down the trail."

Kneeling, Kirsten tried to pray, but bewildered and outraged as she was at such cruelty and waste, the familiar words seemed blasphemous. She knelt to kiss the strewn grass. "Rest well, Bob Randall. I hope you're with your mother again, with all your family—"

At that moment, America, wonderful America, seemed very far away. She stumbled to her feet. "Come on, honey-girl," Blue said. He helped her into the wagon and hitched up, and they didn't speak again till they stopped a few hours later.

Kirsten mechanically set about fixing their meal, though she wasn't hungry, and felt as though she'd never be hungry again. That a young person could fall sick and die, she had seen with Lucia and other children in the village. But deliberate, violent severing of life—that was a crime against nature, against life itself, like trampling a flower before it has bloomed.

"There's no way for Kelman to be punished?" she asked after a long, heavy time.

"Not unless someone did it on their own hook. I 'member a few years back when the son of one No Man's Land rancher killed the son of a neighbor. The family of the dead kid brought it to court in Kansas, Texas, and Arkansas, but all the judges said there was nothin' they could do, their law didn't reach here."

"So we have ropes."

"Won't always be that way, Miss Kirsty. Soon as the government decides whether to tack the Strip onto Kansas or Texas or make it part of Indian Territory, there'll be law here. But let me tell you, a man looks the same strung up by vigilantes or all proper by a sheriff. That's why when I had to pick between hangin' and hamstringin', I figgered I'd rather have more days in the sun even if it meant I couldn't strut no more but would have to shuffle."

"And you don't hate the men who did that to you?"

"I stole their horses."

"But killing a man because he stole an animal!"

"That's how it is in cow country. It's not just a cow or two, Miss Kirsty, but what'd happen if folks could run off critters without havin' to pay the piper." Awkwardly, he patted her shoulder. "Want I should set up your sewing table? Depending on when we leave here, we'll get to Hardesty's tonight or tomorrow, and weren't you figgerin' on sending Annie's dress back on the stage?"

"I'm going to walk by the river. I—I can't sew right now."

At first she walked blindly, sometimes weeping, haunted by that terrible vision of Bob Randall's handsome face turned into a grotesque mockery, but a flock of prairie chickens whirred from in front of her, big black crows gossiped from the cottonwoods, and a bald eagle soared up from its perch to wheel toward the sun. How small, how earthbound, she and other humans must seem to him, yet he could spy an unwary prairie dog or rabbit and drop to one in a twinkling. A group of pronghorn antelope skimmed over the hills, white rump patches bobbing, fleet as the wind. There in a hackberry thicket a cardinal flashed scarlet and a woodpecker drummed on a dead tree.

Everywhere there was life, even with winter coming. Everywhere, creatures obeyed eternal cycles, mating, birthing, dying to yield place to others. This law endured; man's law came and went.

Kirsten still grieved for young Bob Randall as she walked back to the wagon; she still hated Kelman and his murderous pack, and she would never be able to see wavy black hair without a stab of pain, but she was able to eat now. After the dishes were done, she got into the wagon and worked on a green dress that would, she hoped, make a timid, overburdened young girl feel pretty.

They camped that night in sight of the Hardesty Half Circle S Ranch on Chiquita Creek. Probably trying to distract Kirsten from thinking about Bob Randall, Blue told her how Colonel Jack Hardesty lived in Dodge, but held fishing and hunting parties on his ranch that might last a week.

"Orders frozen oysters, olives and all kinds of fancy stuff. His hands think the world of him, even if he is tight in funny little ways—won't buy sugar for their coffee. Once a cowboy who was getting supplies bought a barrel of sugar and wrote 'sow belly' on it to fool Colonel Jack. Well, the colonel and a friend went fishing and needed to salt down their catch, so they opened up that barrel—sow belly is packed in salt—and put what they figgered was salt all over their fish. Another time—"

Kirsten put her hand on his arm. "Blue, please, will you play the violin?" *Play for young Bob Randall.*

Blue squeezed her hand. "Sure, I will, honey-girl. Long as you want, I'll fiddle."

He played wind songs and star songs, the Swedish hymns she'd taught him, the children's gay sing-songs, and then in a rusty but amazingly sweet voice, he sang:

> Go to sleep, my little baby,
> Go to sleep, my little baby.
> When you wake, you shall have
> All the pretty little horses:
> Blacks and bays, dapples and grays,
> Coach and six and all the horses . . .

Who knows? Maybe Bob's mother was singing to him now. Kirsten leaned over and kissed Blue on his weathered cheek. "Thank you, Blue. I can sleep now."

She did, heavily, but when she woke in the morning it was with an oppressed and weighted heart, though it took her a moment to remember why. "Could we camp here today?" she asked Blue. "I want to finish Annie's dress before we leave the stage route." True enough, but she could always dispatch a parcel from the ranch. The main reason she wanted to delay was that she was too deeply distressed to meet new people.

"Why not?" drawled Blue. "The grass is good and I'll just see if I can catch some fish."

Except for taking a few short walks to stretch her muscles, Kirsten sewed busily all day, and though she still saw flashes of a nightmare and felt waves of paralyzing grief and rage, and though she longed to pour out her heart to O'Brien, she was also able to picture Annie's delight in her surprise and imagine how the graceful, flounced sleeves would disguise the child's scrawniness, how the muted green would give Annie's carroty hair a mellow copper hue.

Next morning they put the dress in the box they'd brought along for that purpose and left it at the stage stop before leaving the Tascosa trail and following wagon ruts and horse tracks west along Hackberry Creek.

They pushed on early next morning. Soon Kirsten stiffened at a strange new sight: wire with sharp prongs! It stretched out of sight in both directions, though there was a gate across the road made of wire fastened to posts. This must be the boundary of Hi Allen's Hi-A Ranch. "Bob-wire!" Blue made it profane. "Be the ruination of the country! Wish the dang stuff had never been invented!"

Kirsten could move more easily than he could, even with her voluminous skirts. She climbed down, puzzled out which end of the gate opened, and pushed on the pole that formed one end of it while levering up the wire loop fastened to the main fence. The gate securely closed, they rumbled on while Blue called down maledictions on the wire that was changing the West.

"But Blue," said Kirsten, "what's so wrong with it? It's true that it's ugly, but—"

Blue whipped her a glance of surprise. He had to think a few minutes before he could put his feelings in words. "This country's always been wide open, Miss Kirsty. Buffalo drifted north to south and back again with the weather and grass; so did the Indians. And cattlemen couldn't afford to fence till this dang wire came along ten years ago. Whoever first moved their cattle onto a certain range was just naturally considered to have the use of it and control of the water. Of course, cattle drift, but they mostly get sorted out at branding time. Put up fences and you can't go where you want to anymore. Chops the country up in little chunks, 'stead of leavin' it high, wide and handsome."

"But farmers must have to fence to keep cattle out of their fields."

"Oh, there's reasons for the dadburned stuff, but I do purely hate it. Now what in the world is that rig up ahead? Kind of like an army ambulance, and would you look at them four matched mules?"

The vehicle, turning in from another set of ruts, pulled up as they approached. Both men on the driver's seat wore wide-brimmed hats and boots, and their browned faces showed exposure to all kinds of weather, but there all resemblance ended. The lanky driver had a bushy, sun-streaked yellow moustache and pale blue eyes and wore regular cowboy clothes. The man beside him wore a dark, well-tailored suit, white shirt and tie. He had a magnificent, tightly curling black beard frosted with white, and heavy black eyebrows above piercing gray eyes. The driver stopped the sleek gray mules, and both men doffed their hats as a smile changed the bearded one's face from stern to genial.

"You must be Miss Kirsten Mordal," he said, getting down and coming up to shake her hand. "My wife and sister will sure be tickled pink to see you. I'm Hi Allen and that's my foreman, Tom Reynolds."

"I am very pleased to meet you, sir," said Kirsten. "This is Blue Martin." She was glad the rancher shook Blue's hand, too, before saying expansively, "We were about to stop and eat. Unhitch and join us."

To Kirsten's surprise, Tom didn't build a fire beside the road but busied himself at the back of the wagon. "Want to look?" invited Allen. "Got a little kitchen built in at the back, and the benches make into good beds. The missus thought it up after I got rolled on by a horse a few years back and couldn't ride around my ranches the way I used to. At first I was kind of ashamed to have it so easy, but I've gotten to where I plumb enjoy it."

A table unfolded between the benches, and soon they were enjoying a feast, mostly from cans, served on delft plates. "Try the truffled woodcock," Allen said. "Salmon? Oysters? French sardines? The figs are good, and that Stilton cheese is excellent."

Kirsten nibbled at everything and found it all delicious. With their last cups of aromatic coffee, Tom put out a box of thin chocolate mints, the like of which Kirsten had never tasted.

"Have another," invited the rancher. "I'd better warn you, Miss Mordal, that you probably won't get a chance to rest from your journey before my womenfolk have you hard at work. The National Stockmen's first convention is going to be held in St. Louis this month, and that's a rare chance for the ladies to dress up. But once we're gone, you can recuperate." He grinned at his foreman, who had been stealing such admiring glances at Kirsten that she was embarrassed. "I'll bet Tom would like to take you riding. And of course you'll have to stay for our Christmas Ball. The cowboys would never forgive us if they missed a chance to dance with you."

"To dance is not fitting for me, sir. I'm in mourning for my sister."

His sharp eyes softened and he touched her hand. "I'm sorry for that, honey. O'Brien told us you'd lost your little sister, and that sure must have been hard, especially in a strange new place. Of course, no one'll push you. But lots of the men don't see a pretty single woman once in a coon's age. Do you think your sister would mind if you made a bunch of them happy?"

That put it in a different light. "Don't fret about it now," Allen said as Kirsten pondered. "It's seven weeks till Christmas." He proffered another mint. "These plains must be a sight different from Sweden. What do you think of America?"

Kirsten thought of O'Brien with a rush of longing, her first friend in this new country. She remembered Bridget and Minnie, her generous, good-natured patrons, and the parade organized to wish her well on her venture. There was Ash Bowden, who exemplified the pioneering entrepeneur; and there were the people touched by Blue's music. And there was August Kelman.

"America gives me opportunity I would never have in Sweden," she said carefully. "At first I missed the trees and lake and mountains very much, but now I think I would feel crowded by them. I have learned to love the way the plains sweep to the rim of the sky, so vast, so endless. But two days ago, sir, we saw a dreadful thing." Her voice broke and she had to swallow and wait a moment before she could go on. "This group of men called the Committee, they hanged a young man, Bob Randall, for butchering a cow he claimed was part of his wages."

Allen and his foreman exchanged glances. "I'm sorry to hear that," said Allen. "Randall was a likable young fellow, but he's been suspected of using a running iron now and then." At her frown, he explained. "That's a plain iron, ma'am, that can be used to make any brand on a cow critter. That's why we wouldn't hire him this spring."

"But killing a man for a cow!"

"Reckon it does seem hard," Allen said patiently. "But everybody knows thieving cows or horses may get them killed. It'll be different when we get law and prisons."

Anger swelled in Kirsten. "Would you have hanged Bob Randall?"

"Not the first time I caught him with one of my cows. I'd tell him to leave the country. But if he didn't——" Allen shrugged, unhappy but determined. "You're gentle-hearted, Miss Mordal. That's good in a woman. But if a man out here doesn't protect his property, he soon won't have any. That's the way it is."

Would O'Brien tell her the same thing? He'd defend what was his, but Kirsten couldn't imagine his ever being part of Kelman's Committee. "In America," she told Allen, "I think that is not how it should be."

He looked a whit abashed. "America's a long way from perfect, Miss Mordal, but we're not afraid to change."

"I will try to make that happen. So a man won't hang for a cow."

He slanted her a look of mingled respect and irritation. "You do that, ma'am. Good women, when you think about it, civilize a country a lot faster than all the laws in the world." He got to his feet, able to stand in the wagon, though Tom Reynolds had to duck his head of wild yellow hair. "We sure have enjoyed visiting with you, but I want to get to my Rock Spring line camp before dark. When you get to the ranch, would you tell the missus I'll be home in a couple of days?"

"I will, and thank you many times for the wonderful dinner."

"Our pleasure, wasn't it, Tom?" Allen smiled.

"You bet!" The rangy foreman had already jumped out of the wagon and helped Kirsten down, vigorously pumping her hand. "Good-bye for now, ma'am, but I sure am looking forward to showing you around." He paused, then burst out as if he couldn't help it, "I hope you'll dance at the ball. Why, if you don't, it'd be like a flower staying closed up tight instead of bloomin'." He blushed to the roots of his hair and looked so beseeching, hat in hand, that Kirsten had to smile on him.

"I'll think about it," she promised.

Much as Kirsten had enjoyed the self-sufficiency of having everything she needed in the wagon, even being able to sleep and sew there, it was good to be shown to a sunny room papered with a dainty flower pattern, with hooked rugs on the polished wood floor, a four-poster bed with an appliqué quilt in a rose design, a padded rocker by the fireplace, and a table and chair in good light by the glass-paned window.

"Oh, this is beautiful, Mrs. Allen," Kirsten breathed.

"If you need anything else for your work or your comfort, just tell us," Amanda Allen urged, beaming. She was small and huggable, with pale blond hair, wide-spaced violet eyes and a manner and accent reflecting her Virginia upbringing. She looked considerably younger than her husband, possibly in her middle thirties.

Her sister-in-law, Katharine, was probably near the same age, but she regarded Amanda with what struck Kirsten as envy and near scorn. It could scarcely be pleasant to be a dependent in another woman's home, but Kirsten wondered why, in this woman-hungry region, Katharine was unmarried. With black hair that waved around her face in spite of efforts to draw it back tight in a bun, splendid dark eyes and bold cheekbones, she must have been beautiful once and was still a striking woman, though lines of discontent had started to engrave themselves at the corners of her mouth. She was as tall as Kirsten, with a slender build verging on gauntness. Both women had greeted Kirsten pleasantly, with no hint of condescension, but where Amanda was warm, Katharine was guarded.

Two cowboys brought Kirsten's trunk, and Blue shuffled in with the Family Gem, which he set on the table. "So here you are," Amanda laughed. "And I'm glad you're not a day later, my dear, because if you can manage it at all, both sister and I need a new dress before we go to St. Louis. We're hoping you can refurbish some of our older things enough to get us by."

"If you're not careful, Amanda, you'll frighten Miss Mordal into leaving posthaste," cut in Katharine.

Amanda turned up her graceful hands. "Oh, don't let me do

that!" she implored. "Truly, I don't want you to work too hard. I'm sure you need a few days to rest—"

"I came to sew," Kirsten assured her with a smile. "I am tired now, but after supper we might look at the material you want made up and go through my pattern books. I'll start in the morning."

"My dear, that's not necessary!" protested Amanda.

"I'd rather get started, but feel free to stop, or to go for a walk when my neck and shoulders start hurting. And I've promised to make a dress for Mrs. Brown at the road ranch."

"I'm glad to hear she's getting a new dress," Amanda said. "Your hours are entirely up to you. Joey, the cook's helper, will bring you a tub and hot water. We'll dine at seven."

"And when my brother's here," put in Katharine, "we eat supper at six."

Amanda gave an airy shrug and slipped her arm through Kirsten's. "Come have some tea and cakes, dear, while Joey fixes your bath, and then you'll have time to lie down a while before we dine."

"Before we eat supper," Katharine amended.

10

After O'Brien had told the Allens about Kirsten, Hi Allen, on a business trip to Mobeetie, had bought material for his wife and sister, though they intended to shop for more while in St. Louis. For his wife he had selected crimson grosgrain silk and for his sister, midnight-blue satin.

"Isn't it sumptuous?" Amanda Allen said, holding up the heavy corded silk.

"It is," agreed Kirsten. She hesitated. The brilliant color overpowered Amanda's pale beauty, but how it would set off Katharine's stately darkness! And that smooth satin the hue of night would enhance Amanda's delicate blondness, but Amanda seemed to love the red and Hi had picked it for her . . .

Katharine held herself aloof, as if disdaining her sister-in-law's enthusiasm, but her eyes did linger on the rustling flame in Amanda's arms. Well, thought Kirsten, I'll do whatever they say, but at least I'll tell them they should trade.

Gathering up a fold of the deep-blue satin, she draped it under Amanda's chin. Facing the full-length wood-framed mirror, Amanda gasped. "Oh! That does become me!"

Kirsten took the heavy bolt of crimson and held it up to Katharine. "Good heavens!" cried Amanda. "Why, Kate, you're gorgeous!" She drew the taller woman over to see herself in the mirror. Her Kate's eyes widened and she looked almost frightened.

"It's too bright," she said. "Everyone would look at me."

"Why not?" inquired Amanda pertly. "Oh, Kate, you must have it!"

"My brother chose it for you."

"Fiddlesticks! I look worlds better in the blue. All Hi cares about is that we do him proud in St. Louis and are happy with our gowns. Now then, Kirsten, let's look at styles."

After much study and discussion, Amanda chose a princesse mode with a pointed, tight basque bodice, a draped overskirt trimmed with self-bows, and a scooped neck trimmed with small bows at one shoulder. The fitted sleeves ended at the wrist in tailored ruffles that would flatter Amanda's small, well-kept hands.

"This should do for me," said Katharine, pointing to a severe walking dress in the *Bazaar*.

"Oh, no, darling!" Amanda cried. "It hasn't a bit of dash. If you're going to wear red—"

"That wasn't my idea," retorted her sister-in-law. "As a married woman, you can be daring, but I don't care to be gawked at or gossiped about."

Kirsten had been going through her patterns, and now, pacifically, she held one up. "This would suit the grosgrain and become you, Miss Allen. See, the skirt has large, flat pleats opening over fan pleating that falls over a very narrow box-pleated frill at the bottom. The polonaise overskirt is caught up on one side with fabric roses for just a little fanciness. And see, the collar is pleated to stand up around the neck, but the throat opens in a narrow slit to the bosom, where there's an insert of more small pleats."

"It's perfect," declared Amanda. "Impeccable taste but with flair. You're lucky you can wear something like that, Kate. I'd look like a pickle barrel."

"You mean it would disguise where I'm bony?" Katharine's tone was acid, but she scanned the illustration. "Wouldn't those pleats be an awful amount of work?"

"I don't mind that," said Kirsten. "The important thing is that you have a dress you like, one that will make you feel good when you put it on."

"It is attractive," Katharine said grudgingly. "But I've always thought it was pathetic for old maids to go to a lot of fuss to deck themselves out."

"Don't talk that way, dear." Amanda's eyes darkened in distress. "Hi's told me you had simply scads of proposals back in East Texas, but you declined in order to take care of your invalid mother."

"I had proposals," Katharine said grimly. "From a pack of ninnies who wouldn't be able to stand up in the wind that blows out here. If I am ever in your way, Amanda, I'll remove to a place of my own, but I will never marry just to have a husband."

"We admire you for that, darling." Amanda embraced the other woman, who submitted but did not hug her back. "Gracious, this was your home before it was mine, and I hope you will never dream of leaving, unless you find a gentleman who deserves you." She surveyed Katharine somewhat in the manner of a pampered house cat accosting a battle-scarred alley tom. "There's bound to be lots of fascinating men in St. Louis. Tell me, sister, what type do you fancy?"

Katharine bridled for a moment. Then, with smile of defiance, she said, "If Patrick O'Brien had ever asked me to marry him, I'd have done it like a shot."

Amanda gaped. "Mr. O'Brien's charming," she said, recovering. "Handsome and extremely competent, from all I hear. But uneducated, dearest, born of Irish immigrants. Really not eligible."

"I am a Swedish immigrant," Kirsten said.

Amanda colored. "It's not the same at all, dear. You have very pretty manners, and it's clear you've been well taught. The Irish who came over here were starving and ground down to a stage approaching savagery. I rejoice that many have done well in America, and in a few generations—"

"What twaddle, Amanda!" broke in Katharine. "Everybody knows that plenty of the oldest Virginia families are descended from indentured servants. Our father poached a deer from the local lord, killed the bailiff who tried to arrest him, and escaped to America with a price on his head. That didn't stop you from marrying Hi. And I'll tell you straight, if O'Brien had ever asked me, you'd have had him for a brother-in-law."

It took Amanda a long moment and obvious effort to control herself, but when she spoke, it was gently. "I'm sorry, Kate. We never dreamed you loved him. Going to his wedding must have been painful for you."

"Wedding?" echoed Kirsten, going cold to the heart.

Suddenly faint, she sat down by the window and pretended to study the pattern. All the time, underneath what her conscious mind accepted, she had evidently persisted in hoping, dreaming, that something would intervene, that the marriage wouldn't take place. But it had. As for Katharine's startling declaration, Kirsten felt a secret glow of vindication that this independent and discern-

ing woman had preferred O'Brien to all her suitors. Face averted
to hide the tears springing to her eyes, Kirsten was even more
astonished at Katharine's next words.

"I don't love O'Brien. I was careful not to let myself do that,
because he never showed me any special favor, was never any
nicer to me than he was to Nora and Grace in the kitchen. It's the
way of him, you know, to flatter and tease. But if he'd given me
the chance, I would have loved him."

And in a way, you do, Kirsten thought in a flash of certainty.
Whatever you say, however careful you tried to be. It gave her a sense
of kinship with the formidable older woman.

"The Meadows girl is sweet and quite lovely," Amanda said.
"Not at all the sort for O'Brien, though, I would have thought."
She turned to Kirsten. "Her gown was absolutely ravishing. How
you made it fit her so well when you couldn't try it on her is a
mystery to me."

"It wasn't hard." The hard part had been making the dress for
the bride of the man she loved. Kirsten's mouth was so dry that
the words stuck. "O'Brien told me I'm much the same size as Miss
Meadows—Mrs. O'Brien—except for being several inches taller
and a bit slimmer. You went to the wedding, then?"

"Almost everyone did," laughed Amanda. "O'Brien's friends
came from all four winds and the celebration went on for three
days. Hi and other ranchers provided the barbecue, but O'Brien
paid for everything else."

"His way of showing he honors his wife," sniffed Katharine.
"Well, that's O'Brien for you. Generous, chivalrous—and crazy."

A wave of premonition swept Kirsten. "What do you mean?"

"Kate," began Amanda, but Katharine shrugged. "Kirsten's old
enough to know that babies are sometimes born six months after
a wedding."

Kirsten blinked. The full import struck her and she sprang up,
pacing the length of the room before, under the women's surprised gazes, she stopped and stared out the window at the mean-
der of trees along Hackberry Creek. She seemed to be expected to
say something.

"On Midsummer Night and at the harvest, our young people
often—frolic," she said. "No man wants a barren wife, so in spite
of what the minister preaches, little is said about a couple, provided that they marry."

"A sensible attitude," Katharine remarked drily. "But from

what I hear, if O'Brien hadn't taken over his dead friend's obligation and stood up for Lorena to her own parents, they'd have sent her packing."

Kirsten's head was still whirling. So this was why O'Brien, after acting so interested in her the night he took her to the Dodge House, speaking so confidently of their future, had then, on their next meeting, told her of his coming marriage! It was to his credit that, except in a general way, he hadn't explained why he was marrying his friend's sweetheart, and it was sad that in spite of his efforts to save her reputation, everyone between Dodge and Tascosa knew, or would know, of Lorena's plight.

"There'll be talk," Amanda concluded. "But no one'll care to tangle with O'Brien. He saw to it that she had a proud wedding, and though we've joked about O'Brien liking all the ladies too much to settle down with one, now that he's done it, I predict that he'll make an exemplary husband and father."

"He will," nodded Katharine, "because Lorena needs him and he's kind. But it's like seeing wild fire tame itself to a hearth."

"He makes a poet of you, Kate," rallied Amanda. "I think you loved him a little, no matter what you say."

"Didn't you, a little?" retorted Katharine.

Amanda started to remonstrate, then chuckled richly. "Who didn't?" Her eyes widened, coming to rest on Kirsten. "He was something of a rescuer to you, wasn't he, child?"

"He was. I can never repay him." In spite of a mighty effort at control, Kirsten's voice broke, and she busied herself with the many times overlapped pattern from the *Bazaar*, which she must trace on paper before she could cut out Amanda's dress.

"If we expect Kirsten to get our dresses made, we should leave her in peace," Katharine said. She gave Kirsten such a wryly sympathetic glance that Kirsten blushed, sure that the older woman had guessed her secret. "I'll fetch you a pot of tea, dear. From the looks of that dreadful pattern, you're going to need it."

"Nora rings the bell for meals," Amanda said, pausing in the door. "But if you get hungry, she always has tasty nibbles, so don't hesitate to visit the kitchen.

Kirsten thanked Amanda, grateful to be left alone to absorb the truth of O'Brien's marriage, which evoked in her so many conflicting emotions. She admired him for protecting a defenseless woman, keeping a pledge to his friend, honoring his bride before the whole country. At the same time, she burned with furious hurt that she had been shut out, that this man she loved and who, she was increasingly sure, loved her, had chosen duty without explaining it to her.

He couldn't have revealed Lorena's disgrace, though, and still been O'Brien. Kirsten knew that. She also knew, with a wrenching of her heart, that affectionate and protective as O'Brien was, he'd come to love his wife simply because she needed him. If Kirsten had needed him, too, he might have wavered, but oh, no, she had pulled herself together after Lucia's death, worked hard, and started a business. To his way of thinking, she didn't need him.

Well, she didn't, she told herself. Not to protect her, not to provide a living. But oh, dear heaven! how she needed him to love! And to love her.

Often during the next long days at the Family Gem, Kirsten blessed the window that let her watch a redtailed hawk survey his domain from an old cottonwood on the creek, see pronghorns skim like buff clouds over the slope, meadowlarks rise from the grass, and crows that had chosen to stay the winter chatter sociably at each other from bare branches. Such glimpses took Kirsten out of the room, back to the free openness she had traveled with Blue; refreshed, she would resume her work. The Allens remonstrated with her not to work so hard, but she had less than three weeks to complete the new dresses and refurbish old ones, so she dared not slacken. She did take a brisk walk daily, visited Honey and Stockings with tidbits in the field where they grazed near the corral, and every few days stopped by the cookhouse to see Blue. Though it wasn't expected, he had insisted on helping Pete Jones, ruddy-faced and white-thatched, cook for the eleven regular Hi-A ranch hands in return for his keep.

Her experience at Minnie's was useful now in dealing with the open admiration of the Hi-A men, from Tom Reynolds, who kept hopefully suggesting a buggy ride, to Joey, a red-haired, freckled fifteen-year-old who carried wood and water for both big house and cookhouse, and often brought Kirsten arrowheads or scrapers he'd found, a bird feather, or dried pods and stalks and grasses to make a winter bouquet. Kirsten was friendly with all the hands, but in such a frank, direct way that none of them could think himself signally favored. The Allens were renowned for feeding their hands well, so there was often a grubline-rider stopping off for as long as pride allowed. Since most ranchers let many of their hands go for the slack winter season, these out-of-work cowboys often spent those cold months traveling from one ranch to another for a few days' food.

In the big house, a white-painted two-storey building made of lumber shipped by rail to Dodge and freighted from there, Nora Farrell, her once black hair now streaked with gray, presided as cook and housekeeper with the help of her daughter, coltish fourteen-year-old Grace. Grace rapidly began to idolize Kirsten, imitating all she did to the point of trying to copy her accent. Kirsten had turned eighteen during the trip from Dodge, but she was close enough to Grace's age to remember how trying it was to feel oneself quite grown, to be expected to act and work like an adult, but still to be treated like a child.

Taught by her mother, Grace could sew neatly when she wished to and volunteered to help Kirsten with the basting when she wasn't doing other chores. Nora approved, so Kirsten gladly accepted, on condition that she could pay Grace. At first Grace demurred, but when Kirsten insisted, Grace's blue eyes glowed as she described the locket she was going to order from Montgomery Ward. She never tired of hearing about Kirsten's village and asked endless questions about Dodge.

"I've never been to a real town," she sighed. "I wish I could go to a lot of places, just the way you have."

Kirsten thought of Lucia, not much older than this girl, with a surge of grief and longing. "You're lucky, Grace, that you'll be able to travel a long way and see a lot of places and people without having to leave America."

"A worthy sentiment."

Kirsten whirled at the familiar lazily amused voice.

Ash Bowden stood in the door, silver hair making his browned face seem even darker. The black diamond winked from his tie. Gray, almost crystalline, eyes rested on her face, and as he crossed to her swiftly, his combative jaw relaxed in an exuberant smile.

"Miss Mordal!" The formal address was a mocking caress. "I've heard about you all along the trail, and couldn't resist stopping to see you and my friends, the Allens."

"That's kind of you, sir. I hope you left Minnie and Bridget well."

"They send their love, and I have a scrawl for you from Annie.

120

When the package came in on the stage, she thought it was a mistake till she found your note. She's a broomstick, that child, but somehow the way you designed the dress made her seem a budding nymph."

"I'm glad," said Kirsten. Opening the rumpled paper he offered, she felt a glow as she pictured Annie's delight and read, "Miss Kirsty—I love the dress and I love you! All the thanks in the world, Annie." When Kirsten looked up, Bowden was watching her with a bemused expression.

"Mrs. Allen tells me you've been working far too hard. She suggested that I borrow their surrey and take you for a drive."

"That's kind of you both, sir, but I really must keep at my sewing if I'm to finish before the Allens go to St. Louis."

His brow wrinkled before he made a glum face and said, "You take this very seriously, don't you?"

"Of course I do! It's my living."

"It doesn't have to be."

"Please, Mr. Bowden!"

"Very well, my dear." He shrugged philosophically. "I'd hoped that the rigors and dust of the trail would have dispelled your enthusiasm for this gypsy mode of mantua-making, but I see I underestimated your endurance. You still intend to travel the whole loop?"

"Yes, certainly."

He sighed. "Will you at least promise me one thing?"

"Mr. Bowden, I owe you for my wagon, but apart from that I cannot think of any reason why I should promise you anything."

"It's nothing you would do for me, but something for yourself."

"What?"

"If the time comes when you tire of the road, if your plan becomes only a dogged exercise in stubbornness, there'd be nothing wrong with setting up a business in town." As her mouth opened, he raised a silencing hand. "I won't speak of it again, since it vexes you, but do remember I stand ready to take the wagon back at any time and leave you unencumbered."

"I appreciate that, sir, but I think the wagon will be very useful on my farm."

He gave her a long stare. "Determination's useful, but don't use it to sentence yourself to a life you may not care for." She didn't answer but looked at him in a way that made his smile grow. "I must admit, Mrs. Allen predicted that you'd decline an outing, so she said you must come down for coffee and cake."

Intensely aware of the danger of being overwhelmed by his driving will, she wasn't sure that she was *pleased* to see him, but he made her feel vibrantly alive, speeded the blood in her veins, and there was no way to decline Amanda Allen's invitation without being rude.

"Thank you for helping, Grace." Kirsten smiled at the brown-haired girl. "If you'd like to use the machine to do your mending, go ahead." Grace was intrigued with the Family Gem, and Kirsten was teaching her to use it. Who knew? One day it might be the girl's way to independence and a choice of where and how to live.

"You have an adoring helper there," Bowden said as they walked down the hall to the staircase, which made a graceful spiral to the floor below. He turned to her suddenly. "Kirsten, Kirsten. O'Brien's married." Grasping her hands, he made her face him in the dimness that centered the light in his eyes. "You have good sense in other things. Why don't you show some in this?"

"You should not call me by my first name."

"Good God, what an answer! Well, my Kirsten, when we're alone, I will call you that, for it's how I've thought of you ever since I learned it. If there can't be love between us yet, at least let's have truth."

She didn't try to pull away. She knew she couldn't, and instinct warned her not to give him the arousal of physically mastering her. "Good," she said. "Let us have truth, Ash Bowden. Do you want me to try to love you because that would be the sensible thing?"

His hands tightened on hers to the verge of pain. She braced herself against the force that pulsed between them, barely controlled, ready to blaze, and forced herself to meet his searching gaze. *I don't love you,* she thought desperately. *Whatever this wildness is you make me feel, it's O'Brien I love.*

Out of this knowledge, she said gently, "You wouldn't want what I could give you. Not for long."

He smiled in that almost irresistible way. "Ah, but Kirsten, if I started with that, I'd win more." He released her, though, giving her his arm as they descended. "It's early days yet. But you're wasting time, our time, and when you're my age, Kirsten, maybe you'll understand why that drives me crazy."

She shook her head, able to smile now that the charged moment was past. "I don't think age has much to do with it, sir. I'm sure you've always wanted whatever challenged you just as soon as you could get it." She paused on the landing. "There's something I need to tell you. If you're going to build a town in No Man's Land, maybe you can do something about these men who call themselves the Committee."

"You encountered them?"

"That wasn't the worst part." She told him about Bob Randall, trembling and fighting back tears as she remembered how the rope had turned a handsome young man into an obscene scarecrow. "Can you do something to stop Kelman?" she pleaded. "You aren't a cattleman who's afraid he'd lose all his cows if men weren't hanged for stealing them."

"I'm buying up land for that Scottish syndicate," he said. "We'll run cattle. Harsh as their justice is, the Committee serves a purpose till real law comes to the Strip."

Was that what everyone thought? Even O'Brien? Defeat bitter in her mouth, Kirsten started down the stairs again, declining Bowden's arm. "One thing I will do," he vowed, "is see that Kelman knows he's never to trouble you again. For that I'd gladly shoot him if he didn't have his uses."

"What he did to me was nothing."

"Not to me it isn't."

His stern expression changed to a smile as he bowed to the ladies upon entering the spacious living room with its thick carpet, velvet draperies and imported walnut furniture. "Mrs. Allen, you said cake and coffee, not a feast!"

Amanda dimpled as her husband came in from the adjoining office and cordially shook Bowden's hand. "Since you won't stay with us even one night, sir, we must at least make sure you leave us well fortified. Really, though, you should reconsider. It's half past two now. How far can you possibly travel before dark?"

"Quite a distance, with my horse and myself both rested," he assured her. "I'm sorry, believe me, but some land I want near Tascosa is being dickered for by Kansas City financiers, and I need to be on the spot to counter their proposals."

"The Circle Cross, next to the land I sold you?" Hi asked.

Bowden nodded. "That'll be the south range of the ranch I'm putting together. I've already bought most of the north part in Kansas."

"So you need a chunk of No Man's Land to tie them together?" chuckled Allen.

Bowden grinned. "You know the old saying, 'All I want is the land next to mine.' I've made arrangements with folks in western No Man's Land to let me buy their places once they can get legal title."

Allen smoothed his curly beard. "I hope you don't grow old waiting for the government to make up its mind."

"I don't think it'll be long."

Nora, Grace's mother, a pleasant-faced tall woman, brought in coffee and added a plate of just-baked cinnamon rolls to the array of cakes, cold meats, cheeses and relishes that covered the serving table.

Kirsten had so often brought Bowden his food that it seemed strange to sit with him now as a fellow guest. Katharine, who was probably near his age, responded to his banter with an alacrity that made Kirsten suspect that here was a second man to whom Hi's sister might be drawn, and there was fiber in Katharine that should appeal to Bowden if he ever got to know her. But though he chatted with his hostesses and talked business and politics with his host, Bowden's gaze rested most frequently on Kirsten, and when he rose to make his farewells, she was the one over whose hand that shining head bent lowest.

"I'll see you again, Miss Mordal." Now that he had disavowed it so scornfully, that formal name was a private joke that almost made her smile. "Somewhere along your road. May you travel well."

His eyes held hers. Then, Allen beside him, he left the house and strode toward the corrals.

II

The gowns were ready, to Amanda and Katharine's delight, down to the last blue satin bow and crimson silk rose. When the women modeled for Hi, he looked slowly from one to the other several times, then let out a cowboy yell and hugged them both.

"You two will be the toasts of the convention, and I sure am proud of you both!" He beamed at Kirsten. "My wife and sister are fine-looking women, Miss Kirsten, so you had a head start in making them look beautiful, but I've never seen such pretty dresses or ones that just matched the ladies wearing them." He made a face of comic dismay. "And when I think I got the red for Amanda and the dark blue for Kate—" He stepped back and gave each a thorough scrutiny. "Kate, you look like a queen. Ought to wear red all the time. Makes your eyes flash and your hair black as a raven's wing. Amanda, you're a gold angel dressed in part of the night."

Amanda went pink. "Why, Hi, you're turning into a poet!"

"You're the poem," he retorted, unabashed, taking her hand. "And you'll always be my sweetheart."

Katharine's flush of pleasure faded. Splendid in crimson, she held her head regally high as she quietly left the room, where her brother and his wife seemed to have forgotten everyone else, but there was something disconsolate in her posture. It was a lover's or husband's praise she needed, not a brother's.

Quickly overtaking her, Kirsten said, "Miss Allen, if you'd try on your black silk, we can decide whether adding that ivory satin vest front will be enough or whether the lapels and collar need some kind of trim, perhaps some ivory appliques."

Pausing on the stair above, Katharine looked at Kirsten, and in the moment before the dark-haired woman spoke, Kirsten could almost read her thoughts. *Why should an old maid fuss about her appearance? Why make the effort if the only man to care is a brother?* Kirsten vastly admired the other woman when she smiled.

"I've been sick to death of that old dress, but your notion of a vest will change it completely. Yes, dear, if you're not too tired, by all means let's have a look."

In the remaining six days before the Allens' departure by privately hired stage for Dodge City, Kirsten, with Grace's eager help, transformed the black silk. Katharine's bottle-green cashmere took on new life with cuffs, collar, pockets and buttons cut from an old bronze velvet cloak. A new basque to replace a badly stained one restored Amanda's dark-gray taffeta to resplendence. Kirsten worked almost to the moment they departed, with all of them adjuring her from the buggy to take some of the rest she'd earned now, before starting the other garments.

"There's no hurry with them," Amanda called. "And remember, you have to stay through Christmas!"

Kirsten waved them out of sight, then hugged her shawl about her as she turned back to the house, her relief at actually finishing everything they needed ebbing into a sort of despondency. A natural result, she told herself, of sudden relaxation after weeks of hurry. While racing the Allens' calendar, she'd scarcely had time to think of anything but completing her work on time.

The house seemed huge and lonesome. Kirsten felt a wave of homesickness, of longing for her sister. But she no longer had a home in Sweden. Lucia was gone. In a few weeks now, on her birthday, Bridget would light candles on her grave, and again at Christmas. How strange to think that only a year ago, Grandfather Nils had been alive. . . . Yes, and hadn't he grieved because he couldn't put enough regular food on the table, let alone holiday fare? It was suddenly too much. Kirsten leaned against the bannister and sobbed, but, at a footfall, jerked up guiltily.

Nora stood watching her a moment before she crossed and took Kirsten in her arms. "Go ahead and cry, child. You've worked yourself to a frazzle, and it's times like that, when you've a minute to think, that the sad thoughts come."

What a relief to weep against that motherly shoulder! When the tears stopped, Kirsten drew back, feeling much better but sheepish as she used her handkerchief. "I'm sorry, Mrs. Farrell. I've got so much to be thankful for that I'm ashamed of being such a goose."

Nora's eyes, usually grave, danced as she took Kirsten's hand and led her toward the kitchen. "Now isn't that exactly what I tell myself when I go to howling?" she said. "I've got my health and a fine job with the Allens and Grace is a good girl in spite of her notions. But I miss my husband and my own little home and once in a while—not often, mind!—a good cry helps. Now you have some coffee with me, and another cinnamon roll, and then take yourself out for some fresh air before you go to work. Miss Amanda told me to make sure you didn't push yourself."

The Allens were gone almost two weeks. They returned laden with purchases and the news that a National Cattle Trail had been authorized. The purpose was to create a detour around cow country that had been claimed, when tick-infested south Texas cattle were being driven north. Kirsten had finished Mrs. Brown's brick-red dress of bombazine, a worsted wool and silk twilled fabric, and sent it to her, and made simple but pretty wrappers for Amanda and Katharine. She had also ridden several afternoons with Tom Reynolds, but though she liked the tall, yellow-haired foreman, being with him simply made her think longingly of O'Brien.

"My ladies were the queens of the convention," Hi told Kirsten, pride softening his craggy face. "They got asked over and over for the name of their—what do you call it, Amanda?"

"Modiste, dear," twinkled Amanda. "Anyway, Kirsten, I took the liberty of telling several of the nicest North Texas ladies that you'll stop off and see what they want designed."

"That's my business," Kirsten smiled. "Thank you very much. I'm glad the dresses were successful."

"You might say that," Hi said, with a mirthfully teasing glance at his sister. "Kate had three proposals that I know of, for the men approached me before asking her. Heaven knows how many tried their luck with her and got no further."

"The usual assortment," Katharine shrugged. "Old men looking for a nurse, widowers hunting for someone to mother their children, a few who think an alliance with Hi Allen would be advantageous."

"Tush!" chided Amanda. "If you loved a man, you wouldn't care how old he was or how many children he had."

"That's just it," said Katharine, pulling a comic face. "I don't love them. And they don't love me, either. How can you love someone you see a few times all gauded up at a convention?"

"You don't have to accept a gentleman at once—indeed, you shouldn't," Amanda pointed out. "But you could intimate that his company's not distasteful to you, and make a decision after you're acquainted."

"Do you think I'm a numbskull?" Katharine demanded. "If I were even feebly attracted to someone, I'd give him an opportunity." Gentling her tone, she kissed Amanda. "Don't worry about me, pet. I had a grand time at the convention, thanks to you and Hi, who didn't once make me feel I didn't belong with you."

"Of course you belong with us," said Amanda. "We're glad of your company, sister. It's just that—" She broke off at the look in Katharine's eye. "We can wear our gowns again for the Christmas ball," she went on vivaciously. "Goodness gracious, it's time we started getting ready for that! And Kirsten, just wait till you see the lovely wool ottoman we bought for riding habits. Mine is hussar blue and Kate's is purple."

"I can start on them tomorrow," said Kirsten.

Amanda shook head. "There's something I want you to make up in time for the ball, dear." Sorting through parcels, she undid the paper and unrolled yards of soft fine wool in a dark, gray-blue shade. "This is our Christmas gift to you, Kirsten. It would make us all happy if you'd wear it for the ball. It hurts me to see you always in black, and on the frontier no one expects observances to be as strict."

"You—you're very kind," said Kirsten, caressing the luxurious fabric with a lump in her throat. "I'll think about it."

"Do more than that," urged Amanda. "Please make the dress."

Kirsten thought of Lucia. Her sister would have wanted her to have a pretty dress and be as happy as she could, and no amount of grieving could bring Lucia back. In that sharp realization, a certain part of Kirsten's mourning ended.

"I'll make the dress," she said, a promise to Lucia. "I'll wear it to the ball." With a wrench of pain, she remembered how O'Brien had wanted to be the first man she danced with in America, but she smiled almost defiantly in spite of the ache. "And—and I'll dance!"

* * *

The dark gray-blue was just the color of Kirsten's eyes and brought out the richness of her gold-brown hair. Amanda told her to make her dress before starting on the riding habits, but Kirsten had two other gowns she wanted to help with before the ball. Every Christmas, the Allens gave Nora and Grace material for new dresses. Kirsten helped mother and daughter select patterns for Nora's rose wool grenadine and Grace's primrose sateen, and though the Farrells did all the handwork, Kirsten supervised Grace's use of the Family Gem for plain seaming and sewed the crucial parts herself.

And there were Christmas gifts to make: linen handkerchiefs for Hi Allen, smaller ones for Amanda and Katharine; lace cuffs and collar for Nora; a rustling black taffeta petticoat for Grace. Because Blue refused wages for accompanying her, she had ordered for him from Bob Wright's store in Dodge a pair of new Levi's, a red-checked flannel shirt, and a brown duck jacket lined with heavy red mackinaw. This took nearly all of Kirsten's ready cash, including the money Hoodoo had sent for his wife's dress, but there was a good sum due from the Allens.

Adding it all Kirsten gasped. Ninety-four dollars! And Amanda had told her to keep some leftover materials and trims. She had four more definite engagements, and surely there'd be ladies wanting dresses in Tascosa, Mobeetie, and the two forts. There shouldn't be any problem in paying Ash Bowden for the wagon, and as soon as the Allens settled with her, she'd send O'Brien what she owed for Stockings and Honey. After she and Blue picked a place to homestead, she was going to order a Singer sewing machine powered by a treadle worked by foot. That would be much less tiring on neck and shoulders, though she loved her Family Gem and intended to keep it always.

While Kirsten sewed upstairs, the big house hummed with preparations. Joey left his cookhouse chores to help with the floor-to-ceiling cleaning, which included laundering all the curtains, waxing floors, beating rugs and polishing the windows. Three days before Christmas, a two-foot-wide shelf was fixed to run the width of the kitchen, and Amanda and Katharine joined in the baking. Giving off tantalizing odors, the shelf steadily filled with burnt-sugar cakes; chocolate, spice and raisin pound cakes; brandied fruit loaves; and a dozen kinds of pie—mincemeat, cream, lemon, pecan and the inevitable dried fruits. Three ten-pound lard cans filled up with light bread. Kirsten left her sewing long enough to make *pepperkakor*, ginger cookies, and, since there were almonds, *mandelmusslor*, which had been special Christmas treats—when they could be afforded.

For her, there would be no *julotta*, the early-morning Christmas service, no lighting of candles on her loved ones' graves, but she hoped Sexton Carl would do that for her parents and Grandfather Nils, and she was sure that Bridget and Annie would for Lucia.

Of course, it didn't really feel like Christmas without tall, snow-weighted trees, white-crowned mountains, and children sliding on the frozen lake. Even finishing the gray-blue dress—with its Valenciennes lace-edged sleeves and collar and a polonaise that draped gracefully all the way around the skirt—couldn't relieve Kirsten's underlying sadness and a futile, yearning homesickness for those who were dead, for the home village she would never see again. How could it be otherwise, though? she asked herself, and kept her hands busy, though she sometimes was blinded by tears.

If O'Brien could have courted her—if she could have hoped to marry him someday, that would have filled the emptiness in her heart with joy she dared not imagine.

The day before Christmas, hams and turkeys were baked, and Pete, the cook, supervised the barbecuing of a whole side of beef. That afternoon, several ranching families who would be guests in the big house arrived, among them the next family Kirsten would sew for, Sheldon and Sally Rawlings with their twin sixteen-year-old daughters, Marilyn, who had her father's red locks, and Meg, dark-haired like her mother. Both girls had dark-lashed green eyes, but Marilyn had very fair skin while Meg's was creamy. They were dressed in identical mud-brown dresses that did nothing for either of them.

Kirsten saw that one of her first tasks at the Rawlings' would be to convince the mother that her daughters should dress to suit their coloring and personalities, though indeed Mrs. Rawlings seemed to prefer them to have no individuality, for she kept them near her and squelched any remarks they ventured. Kirsten had often longed for a mother, but she was glad she didn't have one like that and felt apprehensive about trying to please her.

An extra table was set up in the dining room that evening, and after an elegant repast, the cowboys were invited in for cake and coffee and to gather around the piano while Katharine and Amanda took turns playing Christmas carols. Kirsten listened carefully and joined in the chorus when she could. Next year, she wanted to know these songs. Next year, she hoped to feel like an American and not be yearning for the hymns and familiar tunes she'd grown up with.

Before noon on Christmas Day, buggies, wagons and riders streamed into the Hi-A, and Kirsten knew a few of them: Hoodoo Brown with Mrs. Brown, proud in her new bombazine; Captain and Mrs. Busing; and Bart, the freighter who'd wanted to enjoy his jug the night at the Cimarron crossing, when people on both sides of the river had listened to Blue's music.

It was a sunny day, so the meal would be served outside on plank tables set up near the barbecue. Kirsten was helping Grace and Nora carry out cakes and pies, when she noticed the driver of a wagon pulling up outside the corral.

O'Brien? He sprang lightly down, and she was sure of it; no one else moved exactly that way. The woman in the wagon wore a sunbonnet that slipped off and hung by its bow as he lifted her down, and even from this distance, Kirsten winced to see that he handled her with gentle protectiveness.

Oh, if he didn't already love the bride he'd felt honor-bound to take, he soon would! It was his nature to take care of the helpless, and Lorena seemed that. She waited as he unharnessed the team and turned the mules into a field, where he hobbled them. Kirsten wanted to run, to put off a meeting she dreaded, but O'Brien deserved better of her. He deserved that she befriend his wife. Setting down a pan of gingerbread, Kirsten hurried to greet the newcomers.

It wasn't cold, but Lorena clung to O'Brien and seemed to huddle within the cherry wool cloak that Kirsten would have sworn O'Brien had bought for her. Her dark-brown hair was fine and flyaway, escaping the combs that tried to hold it back from a high, broad forehead. Her melting brown eyes had a shy, questioning look. Her skin was ivory and she had a sensitive mouth. And yes, though the cloak hid Lorena's figure, Kirsten was sure they were nearly the same size, except that Kirsten was at least three inches taller.

It must have been hard for Lorena to come to this party. People would be watching her, guessing when her baby would come. No wonder she held on to O'Brien as if he were her only refuge. He smiled as he spoke to her, bending his head, and then he looked up and saw Kirsten.

"Miss Kirsty!" Those sea-colored eyes sparkled like sun on the waves. He took a stride forward, but Lorena impeded him. He slowed his pace to hers, but he held out his hand and laughed exultantly. "No need to ask how you've fared, colleen! You look bright as the day." He clasped her hand, and that warm, hard pressure radiated through her. How fortunate Lorena was, to have the right to touch him anytime, to have the physical comfort of his strength. Surrendering Kirsten's hands, he smiled down at Lorena. "Honey, this is Kirsten Mordal, who made you that beautiful dress."

Kirsten offered her hand and found it wasn't really difficult to smile at the other young woman. There was something childlike and appealing about Lorena, though she was the elder by a year. Her small hand crept out as if fearing rebuff, but once resting in Kirsten's, it seemed reluctant to withdraw.

"It's such a lovely gown, Miss Mordal, and fit just perfectly. I hope we'll have a daughter who can wear it for her wedding. Pat's told me how you're traveling the wagon routes with your sewing. That's clever of you, and awfully brave."

"It's a good way to see the country and become known to customers I'll hope to keep after I settle in one place," Kirsten said. "I appreciate your husband's getting me this work at the Allens'. It's led to other invitations, and I'm sure the journey will pay off the wagon with money to spare. That reminds me," she said to O'Brien. "As soon as the Allens pay me, I can send you the rest of what I owe on the team."

"There's no rush."

"There is for me. I don't like being in debt." *Though I will always be in yours, you, my first friend in America, who should have been my lover.*

Rebellion flamed in Kirsten. If only Lorena were strident or common, a woman she could detest! It was impossible to hate Lorena, who, in spite of O'Brien's championing, was bound to be the target of gossip. It was surely O'Brien who had insisted they attend the ball.

"It won't be long till dinner's ready," Kirsten said. "There's coffee in the cookhouse. Let me get you some."

As they entered the laughing, visiting throng, people called out jovial greetings to O'Brien, who stopped to talk and always brought Lorena into the conversation. As Kirsten went for their coffee, she saw more clearly than ever that O'Brien had not only given Lorena his name but a place in this far-flung community, insisting that she be treated with respect; ironically, though this was why Kirsten must not love him, it made her love him more.

Such quantities of food were devoured that it was a marvel anyone could dance, but after the dishes were bundled into the cookhouse, the company trooped into the big house, where living- and dining-room carpets had been rolled back and the floors gleamed with beeswax. Younger children were put to bed on pallets upstairs, while older ones perched on the stairs to watch their elders.

"Where will all these people sleep tonight?" Kirsten asked Nora as they placed more cakes and pies beside the eggnog and punch on the table in the hall.

"Bless you, they won't need beds!" Nora laughed, festive in her new rose dress. "Dance till dawn they will, have a big breakfast, and then they'll set out for home, except for the Allens' houseguests, who'll probably stay another day or two. Folks can't get together often in this big country, so when they do, they make the most of it." She smiled at Kirsten. "I declare, it's good to see you in something besides black! Aren't we all grand, though? This dress makes me forget I'm tired, and Grace looks like a prairie flower in her yellow. And how she does love that swishy petticoat you gave her!"

Indeed, Grace did look winsome, giving a glimpse of the woman to come. Joey, red hair slicked back, for once was not ignoring her. They sat on the landing, stealing glances at each other, too bashful to talk much but wearing beatific expressions.

There was a fiddler from over Wolf Creek way. He and Blue, shaved and natty in his new shirt and Levi's, tuned up and launched into "Turkey in the Straw." Hi Allen and Amanda opened the dance, and in seconds, both rooms and the hall teemed with whirling dancers. There were three times as many men as women. Tom Reynolds swept a protesting Nora onto the floor, and a young cowboy abducted Grace from under Joey's startled nose with a grinning "If you aren't goin' to dance, you cain't hog the lady!"

An earnest-looking rancher from Texas seemed already to be pleading his case to Katharine's ear as he joggled her about. When Kirsten realized that no one in skirts was to be spared, she fled to the kitchen, though she had, in fact, resolved to dance. And she would, but first she must have a few minutes to nerve herself up to it, to master the sudden, overwhelming surge of disappointment that her first dance in America would not be with O'Brien, as he had urged on that unforgettable night at the Dodge House, when she was sure he was beginning to love her.

She scrubbed back a tear. No use to think of that, mope over what might have been! She'd walk down the hall and dance with the first man who asked her; she, too, would dance till morning, and if her heart ached, no one would ever guess it! Lifting her head as if marching to battle, she moved out from behind the stove and almost collided with O'Brien.

"No fair hiding!" he teased, steadying her with a touch that left her most unsteady. "When I saw you run off, I hurried like the devil was on my heels. For sure, Miss Kirsty, I haven't forgot that it's with me you must have your first dance in America."

"But Lorena—"

"Has partners lined up ten deep." He tilted his head as the music changed. "Faith, now isn't that a fine waltz they're playing!" He smiled as one big hand almost covered the small of her back and the other caught her right hand, guiding her as they dipped and turned in a glide. "We've got more room here than anywhere else. I've got big feet, colleen, so feel free to step on my toes all you like."

"I'm afraid I can't help it," said Kirsten ruefully. "I don't know these dances."

"Just gives your partner an excuse to hug you tighter, but we'll dance a few tunes to give you the swing of it. I'd best enjoy your company while I can, because once we go back to the others, it's lucky I'll be to get another turn."

To be in his arms! The glow that sweetly, headily, warmed her was kindled from depths that knew nothing of marriages and rules, nothing of restraint. Yet nothing could happen, nothing ever would. Why not, for these few rapt moments, yield to the bliss of his touch, the joy of being with him? Smiling, face near his breast, she closed her eyes, shutting out everything but his nearness for this one, probably only, time, delighting in his embrace.

"Kirsty!" He spoke her name with such vehemence that she started and looked up. His eyes had darkened till she could not read them, but a muscle twitched in his jaw. As she gazed at him, alarmed, his long mouth compressed and he gave a strained smile.

"Guess I can't keep you to myself much longer, but first tell me how your journey's been."

"Well, you hear Blue playing my grandfather's violin," she said, trying to keep her voice even in spite of a shortness of breath that didn't come from exertion. "You should have heard his concert on the bank of the Cimarron." She told him about the band and firemen giving her a royal send-off from Dodge, how well Honey and Stockings pulled at the crossings, how Blue had told her about the Star Girls. Then she hesitated before she asked, "Did you know Bob Randall?"

"I did."

"Do you know the Committee hanged him?"

"That's the word they spread around. How did you know, Kirsty?"

"Blue and I—found him." She poured out the whole story, eyes filling with tears of grieved indignation. "You—you don't think it had to be that way, do you? Do you, O'Brien?"

They had stopped dancing, but he still held her hand. "No. I don't think, Kirsty, a man should die for a cow. That's as bad as the wicked laws England put over the Irish." He sighed. "It's not how it should be, but it is how it is."

What had she thought he could do? Change what had happened? Defy the Committee, when decent men like Hi Allen regretfully thought their tactics justified? "I'm sorry, Kirsty. Someday we'll have law here, proper law, and that kind of thing won't happen."

"But till then, the Committee is law?"

"They're protecting their property. Folks have to do that till we get law officers, or they'd be robbed blind."

"I don't want to live where such things happen."

He closed both his hands over hers, held her eyes with his. "Don't give up on us, Kirsty. The Strip's going to be what people make it, the people who settle and raise families. You have dreams about America. I can't think of a better place to help make them true."

After a startled instant, her heart opened and lifted. This was what she needed from him, the challenge to work in this raw new land for her dream of America rather than lament that the dream had not arrived before her. America wasn't completed yet, really never would *be* but would always be *becoming*, succeeding to the extent that people cherished and worked for the promise. Right then she determined that she would live in No Man's Land and she would be there long after the Committee was a not very proud memory.

"Thank you, O'Brien."

His brow furrowed. "For what?"

She couldn't put it all in words. After a moment, she smiled. "Thank you for America."

"You brought yourself here," he protested, puzzled.

"Yes, but you've shown me I can help make it come true."

He was silent before he touched her cheek. "I think you will, colleen." The warmth between them flamed. He drew back as if he had brushed fire, while need for him blazed up in her, not wistful, girlish yearning, but a woman's fierce hunger for the man who should be her rightful mate.

Lightning played in the depths of his green eyes. His face paled, and she knew with agonized triumph that what she felt, he felt, too. Roughly, he caught her arm. "The boys'll be coming after me with a rope if I don't get you back to the dancing."

They moved down the hall, and as Tom Reynolds rushed to claim her, O'Brien said, voice still husky, "Thank you, Kirsty. I'll always be proud it was with me you had your first dance in America."

"I'm proud, too, O'Brien." And glad for those moments of happiness, though they made a world without him seem bland. She fixed her concentration on Tom, following his steps, making conversation, but there was never a time the rest of the night that she didn't watch for O'Brien's bright head and wish she were in his arms.

12

The eastern sky glowed rosily before the music stopped. Some of the women had managed to slip away upstairs to snatch a bit of sleep before returning to eager partners, and Blue and the Wolf Creek fiddler spelled each other, but Kirsten was among those who got no rest all night, and when Nora and Pete hurried to the kitchen to start breakfast, Kirsten went with them. Joey had already built a fire in the cast-iron stove, and the air was redolent of the coffee beans Grace, apron over her yellow dress, was grinding for the two big coffee pots requisitioned from chuckwagons. When Nora looked at her child in amazement, Grace laughed and gave her a swift hug.

"This is my Christmas present to you, Mother! I'll try to help you without being asked—at least sometimes!"

"I couldn't have a better gift," Nora said. "Nor on a better morning. Will you fry the sausage and ham, Pete, while I do biscuits? Kirsten, would you open those cans of peaches and applesauce?"

Most of the year, Pete ruled the cookhouse, and Nora the big house kitchen, but they worked well together. In forty-five minutes, platters of meat and biscuits and pitchers of gravy covered the tables, surrounded by preserves, jellies, fruit and what was left of the pies and cakes. When people had filled their plates and found a place to sit or stand, Kirsten and Grace brought around coffee for the grownups and hot chocolate for the youngsters.

It was like serving *glögg* and cakes to holiday visitors in her village, but that had been impossible these last few years, and never, in any house, had there been such bountiful feasting. By now Kirsten knew all the guests at least by name, and as they began to take their leave, having eaten and drunk their fill, they warmly invited Kirsten to stop with them if she came near their homes. The Rawlings sisters, once more governed by their mother's wary surveillance after a gala night of dancing, murmured to Kirsten that they looked forward to her coming.

She wasn't sure that she did. That would be a very different household from the Allens', but it was her livelihood, so she smiled and assured them she'd be along as soon as she finished the riding habits for Amanda and Katharine.

"We'll be watching for you at Zulu Stockade, Miss Mordal," Jim Cator assured her. Shaking her hand, he held it longer than was necessary, though when they were dancing he'd confided to her that he was building a stone house beside the old picket dwelling because he was expecting a bride from England. He himself was English, son of a captain in Her Majesty's Royal Navy, who had shipped his two young sons off to make their fortunes in America. First freighters, then buffalo hunters, and finally ranchers, the brothers had ended their partnership the year before when Bob was lured to Oregon, but Jim still ran cattle on Palo Duro Creek and maintained a post office and road ranch. Kirsten enjoyed his British accent, so different from any American one, and his courtly manners.

"We'll stop," she promised, laughing. "Who could resist a place called Zulu Stockade?"

Jim's blue eyes twinkled in his sunburned face. "When we tried to explain to father what a ranch was, he called it a stockade, and seemed to think the Indians here were like the Zulus Great Britain was fighting in the Transvaal. We had to have a name for the post office and decided to have a little joke on father." He gave her hand a final squeeze, captured his hat and coat, and was on his way.

Lorena embraced Kirsten as they parted. "Come and see us when you can, Miss Mordal. You're very welcome." Kirsten murmured something. She could think of nothing more excruciating. O'Brien might have thought so, too, for he didn't press the invitation. "Travel well, Miss Kirsty," he said, reverting to the more formal address in public. "And watch out for blizzards. This is the time of year for them and they can come up in a hurry."

"We'll be careful," Kirsten promised. A trembling began within her. Suddenly weak, she couldn't meet the full force of his eyes. "Have a safe journey. May the New Year bless you." For a moment, her hand was lost in his, close and warm. It felt cold and lonely as her heart when he released it and took Lorena's arm.

After the mounds of dishes were done, it took the rest of the morning to set the house to rights. After a meal of leftovers, everyone, including the remaining houseguests, retired for a nap, but Kirsten, though light-headed with weariness, was far too strung up to rest. She had already cut out the jacket and skirt of Amanda's hussar-blue habit and started the basting, making swift, orderly stitches much at variance with the tumult of her feelings.

Reliving the waltz in O'Brien's arms, her eyes on the level of the artery in his throat that pulsed with the flowing of his blood, she thought that the workings of any body were a miracle: breathing, taken for granted till it ceased; the system that turned food into energy; the intricate meshing that gave the brain power to command this miracle of bone, muscle, flesh and blood. Any creature was a wonder, any human an awesome mystery, especially when you had seen that unity dissolve with age as it had with Grandfather Nils, with sickness in Lucia, or with the sudden violence that had in minutes changed young Bob Randall from a handsome, laughing man to carrion.

That being true, why couldn't she love another human miracle? Why was it that she longed to press her lips against only the pulsing of O'Brien's life force, why must her body, heart and spirit yearn for him and no one else?

Ash Bowden roused a frightening response from her own mystery of nerves, blood and flesh, and he commanded respect. She had sympathy for what he'd hinted of his struggles. But though this formidable, complex man could shake her with his presence, almost overwhelm her, when she was away from him, he didn't trouble her thoughts, nor haunt her in those unguarded moments between waking and sleeping.

O'Brien did. After he'd left her in Dodge City to sew his bride's wedding dress, Kirsten had battled her love for him, tried to banish him from her reveries; and on the trail, watching new country unfold, and during the busy weeks at the Allens', her aching sense of loss had gradually lessened.

Seeing him again had destroyed that easing, irrevocably fixed him as the center of her deepest secret life. First friend in America, first man she had danced with here, first man in her heart.

She worked with the fine woolen cloth, but touched O'Brien's flannel shirt with his muscular shoulder beneath it. She got up to make herself a cup of tea and remembered the champagne punch he'd given her in Dodge.

All she could think of was O'Brien, but she couldn't think of him now without seeing Lorena at his side, hand resting trustfully in his. What stabbed like a sword twisted through Kirsten was that Lorena trusted her, too. It was wicked, a betrayal of that faith, to dream of Lorena's husband. But, Kirsten vowed, she would never do more than that, and as much as possible, however hard it was, she would be Lorena's friend.

The riding habits were finished by the end of the first week of January 1885, but in St. Louis Amanda and Katharine each had bought material for a summer gown, which they wanted Kirsten to sew. It was nearing the middle of the month when Kirsten made the final adjustments, glowing in the Allens' delighted praise, and said that she'd leave the next day.

"Oh," cried Amanda. "I hate to think of you traveling so far in the winter, maybe getting caught in a storm. Why don't you stay till spring, dear?"

"I'm expected at the Rawlings'."

"We could write to them to send their measurements back by mail and you could do most of the sewing here, then stop at their place to do the finishing."

"That's very kind of you," demurred Kirsten. "But it'll be much easier, especially with three ladies, to be where I can do the fitting as I go along. Besides, from what I've heard, there's usually some problem any time of year: floods and bogs in the spring; heat, dust and scarce water in the summer. I'd as soon take my chances with the winter."

Amanda shivered. "When O'Brien told us what you were going to do, I thought it was exciting. Now that I know you, I think it's dangerous!"

"I don't intend to do it forever," Kirsten laughed. "I just want to make the loop once, to see what Ash Bowden calls the Triangle and to meet customers. After that, Blue and I will hunt for a place we can homestead."

"Oh, my dear!" Amanda took her hands, violet eyes distressed. "I know it's none of my affair, but you have no parents to advise you so I feel constrained to speak. It's clear that Mr. Bowden admires you. If you married him—" The look in Kirsten's eyes made her break off, then add lamely, "Homesteading's an awful life for women, Kirsten. If you don't want to marry yet, you'd be well advised to set up your business in town."

Katharine's color had risen during this exchange. "For heaven's sake, Amanda, don't try to discourage Kirsten from choosing the life she wants. Do you know what pressing to death was? It's how they killed some of the Salem witches, placing a board over the poor wretch and weighing it down, stone by stone, until the person died. What's safe and sensible can be like that—every day another stone, until there's no life left."

As his wife and sister stared at each other, Amanda hurt, Katharine indignant, Hi interposed. "You're a capable young lady, Miss Kirsten, and it's clear you've made your plans. We think the more of you for that. But remember, we're your friends. There'll always be a place for you here."

"Thank you." Kirsten looked at each one, strangers little more than two months ago, now indeed friends, ones she'd remember. And Grace and Nora, Tom Reynolds and Pete, the cook, red-headed young Joey, all the cowboys who'd snatched any excuse to talk with her awhile or to do her small favors. "I'll miss you, but we'll see each other again." She smiled, thinking of the difference between what the word *neighbors* meant here and in Sweden. "We'll be neighbors. Isn't that what you call anyone who lives within a hundred miles?"

"Anyone we like," Hi smiled. "All right, Miss Kirsten, if you're bound and determined to go, let's make sure you have everything you need. You're a day from Hardesty's, and then it's forty miles to Zulu Stockade."

They left before sun-up next morning, while the ground was white with frost, and the breath of people and horses rose in a vapor. Blue wore his new coat and Levi's and the gloves Pete had given him for being such good help. When Amanda learned that Kirsten had only a shawl, she insisted on giving her an old but warm and perfectly good cloak of dark-gray wool. With the hood snugged around the soft gray muffler Nora had knitted for her, and her hands in matching mittens fashioned by Grace, Kirsten felt warmed not only by the clothing but by her friends' thoughtfulness. The food box was filled with good things, and Hi, after testing the thickness of their bedding, had added two blankets apiece, refusing to take back some of the money he had just paid to Kirsten, ninety-six dollars in gold and silver, which made a lovely chinking sound when she put it in the bottom of the trunk.

"You've more than earned the blankets, Miss Kirsten, but if it bothers you, let's make them a credit on the next sewing you do for my ladies."

"I'll appreciate that," she said. She could finish paying for the team now, but would need to save up to pay off the wagon next October.

The women embraced her. Hi Allen and Pete shook her hand as they had Blue's, and Tom Reynolds helped her into the wagon, his yellow moustache seeming to have a more dejected droop than usual. Grace reached up and squeezed her hand. "Thanks for letting me use your Family Gem, Kirsten. Someday I'd like to travel around just the way you do and make my living sewing pretty clothes."

"By the time you grow up, there'll be a train thundering down the old wagon road, Gracie," predicted Hi. "But one thing won't change. Women will always want nice dresses. Watch the sky for northers, Blue, and take good care of Miss Kirsten."

Amid waving, farewells, and admonitions, Blue started Stockings and Honey, who seemed eager to be on the trail. Kirsten waved back at the Allens till they were out of sight over a slope; she had to blink back the moisture in her eyes.

"Nice folks," said Blue.

"Yes. They treated me like family. In Sweden, that could never happen."

Blue grinned. "Probably couldn't here in some big cities, where people have fancy ideas. But the West is full of folks who started from scratch, and most of 'em remember that after they get well-to-do."

The sun rose behind clouds streaked gold, peach and rose. The frost glowed softly with those colors before the sun burst through its veilings and turned the frost to diamond dust. Kirsten's heart swelled with the glory of the day and anticipation of what lay before them. It had been wonderfully pleasant, her stay with the Allens, but now she relished being in her own wagon—well, *almost* her own—with the wide plains before them, infinite-seeming as the sky, which increased in brilliance as the sun rose higher.

"Oh, Blue!" she said, bouncing a little as she turned to him. "Isn't it good to be traveling?"

"Sure is, Miss Kirsty." He pointed his chin at the horses. "They're glad, too. It's not healthy, I reckon, for man or beast to lazy around too long." He glanced at some prairie chickens that scrambled into the high grass, colors blending till they were invisible. "Won't be long now till the cocks start puffin' out those orange balls on their chests and struttin' around their booming grounds to impress the females. Sign that spring's comin', even if it's still winter."

"This winter hasn't been bad compared to those we get in Sweden."

"No. Just a few snows that didn't amount to much. Weather here's pretty mild except when a storm roars in from the north, and those blizzards are plumb terrible, Miss Kirsty. I hope you never see one, except from the inside of a nice warm house with plenty of grub and firewood. That's when cattle freeze, 'specially now they've strung up some damn drift fences."

"Drift fences?"

Blue aimed a spray of tobacco juice at a yucca. "It's a fence to keep cattle from drifting off their home range, but the devil gets in it when a norther whoops in. Cows just naturally turn tail to the blast and head south. They can usually outwalk a storm even if they wind up close to Mexico. A drift fence stops 'em. They freeze all along it and pile up till their weight breaks down the fence or they're stacked so high other cows can walk across 'em." He spat again. "I hate fences and I'm sure thankful I lived a long time without 'em."

As they rumbled along, it was like greeting old friends to see pronghorns race fleetly along the horizon, the yellow breast of a meadowlark rising to the sun, the circling of a prairie falcon hunting its breakfast, a bald eagle apparently sunk in meditation as he perched in a lofty cottonwood on the creek. A prairie dog sentry barked from his mound and crows gossiped raucously, gleaming black patches in the leafless branches.

At Hardesty Ranch Kirsten made a well-wrapped packet of the forty dollars she owed on the team, addressed it to O'Brien, and left it for the mail stage.

Back on the main road, they passed freighters on the way to and from Tascosa or points in between. Cattle drives stopped in the fall, but supplies had to be hauled year-round from Dodge to all parts of the Triangle. Nights were much colder than in early November, when Kirsten had last slept in the wagon. She was glad of the extra blankets Hi Allen had thrust upon them, and urged Blue to move his bedroll into the wagon, but he said he liked being close to the earth; it was sheltered enough beneath the wagon.

By pushing the horses, they could have reached Zulu Stockade in three long days from the Hi-A, but they decided instead to do it in four. Since leaving Hardesty's and passing into Texas they hadn't seen a dwelling, nor, except for freighters and the wide trail, any sign that humans had ever passed this way.

The third day dawned clear, and it was chill and bright when they began the midday rest. But when Kirsten brought the horses to be harnessed, she followed Blue's gaze north to a vast dark cloud. "Going to be a mean one," he said. "It'll hit us in a couple of hours. Let's get moving and see if we can find a bank to dig into or some kind of shelter."

Kirsten was used to storms in Sweden, but had never been far from the village when one struck. This was very different. They were far from any dwelling, out on the open plains, utterly exposed to the threatening sky. Fear hastened her movements as she stowed pans and food in the wagon, hampered by the rising wind that turned her skirts into sails and swept back her hood, stinging her face. She gathered the cow chips they hadn't used into a sack and wished they hadn't burned so many.

They were traveling southwest, thank goodness, so at least they and the horses didn't have to face the blast that grew stronger by the minute, swaying the wagon and flapping the canvas shades in spite of their being tightly drawn and secured.

"In Sweden we'd call this a troll-wind," Kirsten said in Blue's ear, trying to joke.

For once, he had no answering smile. "Here, we call it a blizzard. It's anyhow twenty miles to Zulu Stockade. So let's keep our eyes peeled for a place to hole up."

"The wagon—"

"Folks freeze to death in wagons. 'Less we can shelter it under the north rim of a bank or by some trees, it won't help much. If worst comes to worst, we'd better turn it on its side so the wagon bed'll make a pretty solid wall to the north, tether the horses and cover 'em well as we can with a couple of blankets. As the snow packs in, it'll keep the wind out and if we can keep a fire going, we've got a pretty fair chance."

Only a chance. Kirsten couldn't believe it. Her heart contracted with fear, fear that turned the food she'd just eaten into a heavy, nauseating lump. She tried to pray, but the old gentlemen-God of her village church with his long coattails and top hat had nothing to do with this prairie, and the power of Blue's spirits had vanished with the buffalo.

The horses moved fast without urging as the sky darkened and the wind howled. It was like being pursued by great troll-mountains that had somehow defied the edict that by day turned them into motionless hills. Kirsten scanned the flat grasslands for a line of cottonwoods that might signal a creek with a bank, or for a gully eroded deep enough to give them a wall, but she saw only pronghorns fleeing the storm and rabbits bounding for their safe burrows. It must have been less than an hour later when the first fine-powdered ice stung Kirsten's face, in spite of the shawl she had draped over her cloak and hood, after insisting that Blue tie his hat down with her scarf.

The cold sliced into her lungs, taking her breath away, squeezing her heart like an icy fist. This wasn't snow, melting on the face. The particles stung like pulverized glass and melted only enough to freeze on her face. With numbed fingers she muffled her head completely in the shawl except for an opening to peer through. The merciless wind, even though her back was turned to it, drove ice against her lashes and froze them shut.

"Blue!" She moved close as she could to him and shouted with breath that instantly congealed. "Shall we stop and turn the wagon over?"

He cupped his hand to her muffled ear. "We may have to, but we have a better chance if'n we can find some cover."

With each breath, it felt as if icicles stabbed down her nose and throat to her lungs. "How long do these storms last?"

"Some blow out in a day or night. Others last three or four days."

The team labored on, barely visible. The robe tucked over Blue and Kirsten's laps and legs was packed with the tiny crystals, which mounted in the wagon bed, pushed under the drawn front curtains. Ice caked on the horses' hooves, building to thick clumps that made the animals struggle for traction. The ice layers dropped off of their own weight but immediately started packing again.

The trail was obliterated. There was no horizon, no east or west or north or south, only the small space around them. It was like being the only living creatures left in a vast freezing whiteness. Would they die and be found after the blizzard passed? They went on and on, the wind shrieking like the lost souls of the Weird Hunt. Grandfather Nils had heard them once in the forest and hidden till they passed. But this frenzy surrounded its prey, rocking the wagon, whipping through their garments, starting already to bury them.

No shelter, no trees, no creek bank. They could never make Zulu Stockade. Wouldn't it better to stop before they froze and make the best refuge they could? Several times, Kirsten started to plead with Blue, but fought back the words. He knew the weather, the plains, and their best chance. She must trust him.

She could no longer feel her feet or fingers, in fact she couldn't feel much of anything. The ice razors didn't sting as much. Her body felt heavy, drowsy. She was almost indignant when Blue roused her.

"Guess we better stop, Miss Kirsty. If we start to freeze, we'll have to kill the horses, slit 'em open, and crawl inside."

"We can't do that!"

"Honey-girl, they've got a lot of heat in them big bodies. I'm alive 'cause I crawled into a buffalo's carcass in a storm like this."

Kill Honey and Stockings? Kirsten shuddered and kept on shuddering because she was so cold. "You're here on my account," she called at last, leaning against his ear. "You can kill one of the horses for yourself, but I—I can't do it."

"I wouldn't do it for me," Blue shrugged, dislodging a shower of ice. "If you feel that way, honey-girl, we'll just go on a while."

"Blue, it's my fault you're here!"

Incredibly, he chuckled. "Now don't you go takin' credit for the weather!"

"You'd be safe and warm at Minnie's."

"And feelin' about as useful as a chewed-up bacon rind! Miss Kirsty, being on the trail with you's been the best time of my whole life since I was a kid with the Kiowas."

"It's like Lucia," Kirsten said woefully. "If I hadn't brought her here, she'd probably still be alive. If—if I'm the cause of you freezing—"

"Don't talk crazy," Blue scolded. "I'm *somebody* again. I got a real job. You did that for me, honey-girl. It's worth whatever it costs."

"Kill one of the horses."

"No. We'll make it together or check out together."

They huddled together as the swirling ice searched through their garments, packed around their feet and legs, began to bury them. Ice must have melted, then frozen again, on the horses' moist muzzles, for their heads were white masses that dragged lower with each minute.

"Better stop while we can," Blue muttered. His voice sounded far away. Kirsten drifted in a warmth that embraced her like O'Brien's arms. "Whoa, girls!" Blue shouted, drawing in the reins.

That roused Kirsten enough to compel her to fight the comfortable drowsiness. She straightened under the thick shroud. Build a fire. They'd build a fire. But with the amount of fuel they had, it wouldn't burn for long. Would the upturned wagon and the heat or the horses' bodies be enough to save four creatures who seemed the only living beings in this strange world of white midnight and berserk wind?

The horses didn't stop. Blue yelled at them, then relaxed the reins and hope strengthened his voice. "Maybe they know something I don't. I'll give 'em their head for a little while anyways."

In spite of the ice burden weighing their heads, the horses moved faster. Then they all but stopped before they pushed forward against some kind of resistance. Ice showered from what loomed as a white hillock. Before ice covered it again, Kirsten saw the brownish-gold of dried grass.

"A haystack!" Blue dropped the reins and hugged her. "Outside of findin' a house, it's the best luck we could have." He worked his way off the seat. "Hop down, Miss Kirsty. We'll burrow out a nice comfy hole, get the wagon in as far as it'll go, and just wait this dadgummed blizzard out!"

Honey and Stockings pushed deeper into the sweet-smelling hay. The wagon stopped with the ambulance cover, but once the front seat was cleared, they could get to their supplies. Pressing through the hay had worked most of the ice off the horses' bodies, but their heads were encased in blocks of ice. Blue dug under the seat for a mallet. Carefully, while Kirsten soothed the animals, he knocked the heavy masks away and began to unharness.

"Purty smart of you gals to find feed along with shelter," he praised the horses. "Munch away. You've earned it."

How warm the grass cave was after the stinging blast! Holding her hands inside her cloak till they could obey her, Kirsten helped Blue clear the seat and entrance to the back of the wagon which was now protected by overhanging eaves of hay. They got out their bedding and food. A cup of hot coffee would have been wonderful but there was no way to safely build a fire here. They were close enough to the horses, though, that as the big animals warmed, they'd share their body heat.

Kirsten and Blue shook and scraped ice off their clothing and put on dry wool stockings. Filling a kettle with snow to melt for drinking, Kirsten put on the lid and set it near the horses.

Last night's beans were frozen, but there was bread, and Blue thawed the last of the fried chicken Nora had packed for them by wrapping it in a cloth and holding it against Honey's belly till it was chewable. The dried-apple pie had frosty shards in it, but Kirsten covered it with a cloth and put it on top of the water kettle.

They scooped out grass to scatter beneath the horses and to spread over the ice they'd brought in with them. Then they put down Blue's bedding, sat on it, and drapped Kirsten's blankets around them as they gnawed at their food.

"Takes some chewing," Blue said. "But say, honey-girl, ain't it good to be able to chew?"

13

As Kirsten slowly awakened, the smell of hay and horses made her think she'd somehow fallen asleep in Grandfather Nils's barn, but then she heard the wind wail and shriek and remembered. Sitting up, she rubbed her eyes and saw that it must be day again, for she could make out the pale bulks of the horses and the front of the wagon. Blue's bedroll was empty, but she heard movement on the other side of the horses and took the opportunity to press through the hay almost to the other side and there relieve herself. When she crept back to the main cave, Blue was cleaning out the horses' soiled hay, and Kirsten replaced it with clean.

Folding the bedrolls into seats completed their housekeeping. They breakfasted on snow-water, a can of peaches, and bread spread with jam. "How much longer can this last?" Kirsten asked.

"No telling. Blizzard usually wears itself out in two or three days, but they been shorter and they been longer. Why don't we give the horses a good currying? We'll never have as much time as we got right now."

Blue used the curry comb and Kirsten followed with the brush. Honey lipped softly at Kirsten, reveling in the attention, and Kirsten got each horse a handful of grain from the feedbox.

"When we find out whose haystack this is, we'll have to pay them," she said as they finished their task.

"More'n likely saved our lives," Blue nodded. "Sure would love some good hot coffee, but we can't risk a fire. Want I should fiddle, Miss Kirsty?"

"Yes, and I'll sing. We're lucky you can play, Blue. It's too dark to read or sew."

"Does pass the time." Blue taught her the words, the decent

ones at least, to "The Buffalo Skinners" and "Streets of Laredo." Then she tried to teach him some Swedish songs, but after several valiant efforts, he shook his head. "No way I can learn the words, Miss Kirsty, but I've got the tunes. Say, will you sing that real pretty one you turned into English?"

> *So night and day, and day and night,*
> *Are yours and only yours . . .*

O'Brien came so strongly into her thoughts that she could almost see him. Her voice trembled, and when she finished the last verse, Blue bowed into "Wonderful America." She clapped with her singing, causing the horses to look at her, and Blue was joining in the chorus, when a muffled sound came from outside.

Honey threw up her head suddenly and neighed. Blue stopped playing. Kirsten sprang up. "Kirsty . . ." came a faint voice.

Her heart turned over. She started to dash out, but Blue grabbed her as he shouted, "This way! Come on! This way!"

"O'Brien?" Kirsten tried to wrest herself loose, but Blue gritted his teeth, saying, "Stay here! He's almost with us. Let's clear him a way in by the wagon."

Calling steadily, they made an opening that sent powder-fine ice flurrying over them. They could see nothing else till a shape solidified from the particles, a shrouded rider on a horse whose head was a grotesque block dragging in the thigh-deep drift.

The man lurched from the saddle. Kirsten and Blue caught and almost dragged him in. The horse followed, sensing refuge, food, and his own kind; it stood heaving and spent, its ice-mask drooping to the hay.

"Take care of him," O'Brien gasped. "He's kept moving on heart."

Blue freed the gelding's head of ice, while Kirsten helped O'Brien shake off the ice and made him get between the bedrolls. Then she worked off his boots and frozen socks. His feet were bluish-white. Frozen? O'Brien a cripple? The only way to warm him was with her body. She put her skirts over his feet and pressed them between her thighs, too fearful for modesty. In spite of his protests, she fitted his hands beneath her arms. "Keep still!" she ordered. "We have to get you warm!"

He blinked as ice melted from his eyelashes, and even in the dimness, even in her dread, his eyes had the luminance of the ocean. She felt seized, swept high by a great wave. He grinned weakly. "So—you're real. When I heard you singing, I sure thought I'd died and some way sneaked into heaven."

"What are you doing out in this?" She was angry at him, angry because he had almost died.

"I tried to herd my cattle south toward the cedar breaks along the Canadian, where they'd have some protection. Hope some of them made it."

"You almost didn't."

"If you're close to the trail, we got mighty lost," he admitted. "I gave up on the cows last night and hoped Barney could find the way home. Kept thinking the storm had to pass." He sighed. "Hate for Lorena to be by herself in this, but the soddie's snug and tight, and it's just a step to the dugout that's full of corncobs and cow chips."

Kirsten felt for the young woman, even though she'd be able to have coffee and hot food. Blue brought water for O'Brien, held it to his lips, and then fed him a wedge of apple pie. In spite of Kirsten's warmth on his hands and feet, O'Brien was shivering.

"I'll get in next to you," Blue decided. "I'm too dang scrawny to throw out much heat, but I'm better'n nothing."

"Now stop the fuss," O'Brien grumbled, but his teeth were chattering and Blue paid him no attention but got into the bed-rolls and hugged O'Brien, who was curved in an arch, as close as their disparate sizes made possible.

"Sorry I'm not a plump, purty gal who'd thaw you out in a hurry," Blue chuckled.

Kirsten flushed, wishing she were in Blue's place. There was certainly no romance in the way she was trying to warm O'Brien's feet and hands, but they did seem to be less icy. "M-m-makes me feel like a durned fool," said O'Brien. "B-b-but it's a sight warmer."

He gradually stopped shivering. "Hope I get a chance to do the same to you," he mock-threatened Blue as he sat up, and Blue perforce released him. "Colleen, colleen, it's shamed I am that my hooves were against your fair, tender skin."

"It's no time to worry about things like that." She examined his fingers one by one. "Do they work? Can you move your toes?"

He flexed his fingers, but grimaced as he tried to do the same with his toes. "They're full of needles so they ought to be okay."

Fortunately, Blue had another pair of dry wool socks. He got these for O'Brien and Kirsten fetched him the last of the chicken. Barney, meanwhile, was munching hay as if he couldn't believe in such a feast. A third horse crowded the cave, so Blue and Kirsten carefully enlarged it, scattering dried grass over the melted ice shed by the new arrivals.

How lucky that they'd been making music! Had they been talking quietly or sleeping, O'Brien would have passed by and by now might have lapsed into that stupor from which he'd not have awakened. Kirsten's heart swelled with glad thankfulness, and again she resolved to try to be happy because he was alive, not be sour and angry that he couldn't be hers. The threat of death made her value the sweetness of life.

How good it was simply to breathe and eat and move! How blessedly wonderful to see the sun again! To be able to sing, work and have friends, that was to be rich and lucky. Still, when she looked at O'Brien, bright hair tousled, face stubbly with several days' growth of beard, resolutions and self-chiding could not check the melting tenderness that radiated through her.

He could not be hers, but she was his. That was a fact of her life. Maybe, as years passed, it wouldn't hurt so much. His eyebrow lifted. "Why are you frowning, Kirsty? Sorry you hauled me out of the storm?"

"I—I—" She cast about for an answer. "If we'd known we were going to see you, I could have paid you for the team now instead of sending the money by stage."

O'Brien stared before he burst out laughing. "Lord bless us, colleen, if we'd guessed we were going to wind up in a haystack, I expect we'd have all stayed under a roof!"

She had to laugh, too. "Now isn't it something," he went on, "that this team I sold you found the haystack so you were waiting when I came floundering along? I made myself a better deal than I'd reckoned. But I sure wish this blizzard would huff itself out. Lorena doesn't like to be alone, and I have to see if I've got any cows left."

"Listen to the man!" whistled Blue. "You won't do your wife or critters any good froze out on the prairie. Why don't we play some poker?"

"I don't know how," said Kirsten.

"That's what they always say before they clean everybody out," said O'Brien with a grin.

Kirsten did win, though the others had to help her pick her best hands till she learned that a flush beat a straight and three of a kind. As the day wore on, the wind's howling diminished, but there was no hint of clearing skies. They ate beans, cold biscuits and dried fruit. Then Blue played the violin and they sang.

O'Brien's roughly sweet tenor went to Kirsten's blood, resonating in every fiber of her being. Afraid to watch his face lest he read her feelings, she looked instead at his long hands, the brown fingers, graceful though work-scarred. That was worse. Before she could stifle the wish, she'd dreamed them on her.

Their eyes met. The song broke on his lips. The force that leaped between them, invisible lightning, stopped Kirsten's breath. He felt it, too. She didn't wrestle alone with her yearning. Made both exultant and more desperate by that realization, she stumbled up, retreating to her private passage, fighting scalding tears.

She was glad they were alive, she acknowledged Lorena's place as his wife, and she could make all sorts of sensible, honorable vows and resolutions, but this blaze between them heeded no rules. If ever they were alone together—That must never happen. For their peace and Lorena's, they must meet seldom.

Wiping away futile tears, she thought it seemed lighter outside, and when she made her way back to the hollow, there was no doubt. The wind had dropped. O'Brien had drawn away enough of the hay by the wagon to look outside. As they watched, a few last crystals drifted to the white expanse of earth that merged with a livid sky.

"From where Blue says you were when the blizzard hit, I figure this is one of Zeke Thomas's haystacks," O'Brien said. "Can't really see the sun, but it's bright enough over there to figure that's west, so Zeke's place on Sand Creek shouldn't be more than a couple hours' ride in that direction. He was at the Christmas ball, sawed-off little black-haired Welshman. We'd better head for his soddie. I'll go on home in the morning, but you two can ride the horses and leave the wagon here till it can travel."

"Miss Kirsty," said Blue, "if there's a place that close, let's make for it."

It would be foolhardy to do anything else. They bundled food and clothing into their bedrolls and packed their other things, except the violin, into the wagon, which they pulled deeper into the haystack. Blue strapped blankets as pads to Honey's and Stocking's backs and slipped on their halters. He mounted from the wagon, cradling the well-wrapped violin to his breast and ducking as Stockings reluctantly sidled into the crusted drift that had piled against the back of the wagon.

O'Brien gazed down at Kirsten. " 'Twas your singing brought me safe," he murmured. "I owe you for that, colleen." He hesitated, then blurted as if he couldn't help it, "Still, if I'd been fated to die, there's no way I'd have gone happier than with you beside me like an angel."

"I'm no angel, O'Brien," she snapped, and climbed from the wagon to Honey's back before he could help her.

It wasn't, she knew, so much the superior safety of Zeke Thomas's home that had spurred O'Brien to move them out that day. He had felt the fire, too, and was afraid to sleep by her that night, afraid of what might happen even with Blue close by.

Zeke had shoveled a path to his barn and was carrying a half pail of milk to the soddie, still buried to the windowsills in snowdrifts, when the three rode up in the dusk. Smoke curling from the chimney had been their beacon for several miles, but it was a vast relief actually to come in view of the buildings. More than once, as the horses gingerly picked their way on hooves that built up slippery ice cakes, Kirsten thought they might better have stayed where they were, for everything to help them orient themselves, except for the faint glow in the sky, was hidden under that unending white.

Zeke welcomed them in and helped O'Brien take care of the horses, who could shelter in the barn with the cow. "Isn't the fire beautiful?" Kirsten breathed, hurrying to stand by it.

"Yes, but the smell of that coffee's even beautifuller!" Blue drew in a rapturous whiff and poured each of them a cup, for Zeke had invited them to help themselves.

The soddie was a good-sized room with a bed built into one corner, a crude table, several crates for chairs, and a few shelves that held supplies, dishes, and pans. On the hard-packed earth in front of the fire, coals covered a Dutch oven, and a delicious odor of baking bread mingled with that of the beans simmering on an iron frame at one side of the fire.

Kirsten began to unwrap the food they'd brought: coffee, sugar, dried fruit, rice, ham, bacon, and most of a bourbon walnut cake, the last of Nora's delicacies.

"You folks didn't need to bring your own grub," said Zeke, coming in and peeling off his sheepskin coat. "But that cake and ham sure look scrumptious!"

They had a merry feast, the hot food and drink doubly invigorating after several days of ice water and barely thawed viands. Zeke scoffed away Kirsten's offer to pay for the hay they had used or damaged.

"Shuckins, it'd be worth the whole stack to have company, 'specially a pretty lady. I'm mightily glad you happened on to that hay." He frowned at O'Brien, leveling a fork at him. "Next time, lad, remember your hide's worth more than a cow's."

"Guess we'll soon find out," said O'Brien. "Reckon a lot of us'll be skinning cattle after this storm. Soon as I make sure Lorena's all right, I'm going to look for my cows."

"There'll be a lot drifted down from Kansas, even Nebraska," Zeke said. "And your cows may be way over on the Pecos."

"Rather have 'em there than frozen." O'Brien considered for a moment. "Ranchers aren't going to come a long way just to skin their dead cattle, Zeke, but if a couple of us teamed up to do the work, I bet they'd be tickled to give us a good share of what the hides bring, because otherwise they wouldn't get anything."

"Fine with me," said Zeke. "The ways a man figgers to make money here don't work out so often that I never pass up anything honest. Blue, I'd admire to hear some of your fancy fiddlin'." Zeke's bright blue eyes laughed at Kirsten. "If you're not too fagged out, ma'am, we can even have a dance."

As soon as the dishes were done, they moved the table back, and while Blue played beside the fire, Kirsten danced with Zeke and O'Brien, partnering one while the other clapped and kept time. It was high-spirited frolic, not a time for tender glances or languishing thoughts. When at last, gasping, Kirsten pleaded exhaustion, they had milk and cake before settling the sleeping arrangements.

"You have the bed, Miss Kirsty," Zeke urged.

She shook her head emphatically. "It's big enough for all three of you so it'd be silly for me to take it." When the men protested, she used another strategy. "If we put those crates end to end, I could sleep here close to the fire, and I'd much rather do that than be over in the cold corner."

"Makes sense," nodded Blue. "The three of us can pack in and keep each other warm."

The men moved the crates and turned their backs while Kirsten took off her shoes and dress and got into her bedroll. She was asleep almost before the sounds of the men settling themselves subsided into an occasional creak.

Several times during the night, she woke long enough to feed the fire more cow chips or corncobs. Once she roused to see O'Brien, clothed except for belt and boots, performing that chore. On his way back to bed, he paused beside her. Kirsten kept her eyes shut, scarcely daring to breathe.

If he kissed her, thinking she was asleep, that wouldn't be wrong, would it, for either one of them? She felt his breath on her cheek, grew tense with longing. Then, with a sort of muffled groan, he moved away, only permitting his hand to touch her hair.

Kirsten slept no more. She was up at faintest light to dress, build up the fire, grind coffee and keep her back decorously turned while the men yawningly arose and put on whatever gear they'd doffed for bed.

They were eating biscuits with real butter and coffee with real cream when the sun rose like a golden shout, turning the white waste into dazzling glory so brilliant that it hurt the eyes. O'Brien left right after breakfast, and though Kirsten felt some disappointment that they had no private farewell, she knew it was best.

"Don't be in a big rush to start out," he warned her and Blue. "Let the freighters and stages break the trail first."

"You can stay as long as you want to," Zeke said so eagerly that O'Brien scowled for a minute before he recalled his manners, thanked Zeke for his hospitality, and mounted. During the night, wind had scoured most of the ice-snow off the higher flats, drifting it deeper in lower spots. O'Brien made for the easier traveling, raising his hand as Barney gained a slope.

"He's got a long day's ride," said Zeke. "Thirty miles just to make sure his wife's feet are keeping warm."

"She must be worried sick over him," Kirsten pointed out. "You talk just like a bachelor, Mr. Thomas."

"Well, that's what I am," Zeke rejoined. He grinned behind his tangle of wiry black beard, but his eyes were wistful. "Sure could be talked out of it, though."

"I daresay you will be one day." Kirsten smiled at him, but in such an open, friendly fashion that he couldn't think she had designs on his bachelordom. "Gracious, it ought to warm up and start melting. Blue, do you think we ought to start today?"

"Rather not camp in this, Miss Kirsty, and it's a long day to Zulu Stockade. If the weather holds, let's get a real early start in the morning."

They breakfasted and set off before dawn, just as the sun edged over the horizon in a burst of gold and crimson that turned the white plains an incandescent rose.

"You be careful now," Zeke adjured, shaking hands and holding Kirsten's a good deal longer than he did Blue's. "You're welcome to my haystacks anytime, but I'd a sight rather have your company."

They thanked him and rode west, back to the haystack and their wagon. Staying as much as possible on the flats made the going easier than the coming, though frozen remnants of ice made footing treacherous. Where drifts couldn't be avoided, the horses plunged through the glazed crust and floundered laboriously to higher ground.

In one of these hollows, the horses snorted nervously, laying back their ears. Kirsten followed Blue's searching gaze, but she saw nothing till he pointed.

A hundred yards west, mounds rose above the drifts. "I'll look," said Blue. "Probably cattle."

Kirsten followed but Blue got there first; he scraped at one clump to expose dark hide and harness and followed it up to a horse's head, encased in the icy block congealed from its breath. Dismounting, Blue and Kirsten dug frantically at the largest mound to expose the front of a wagon, and clawed through the ice till they found blanketed forms huddled beneath them.

Blue hauled back the coverings. Ice had penetrated the blankets and partially covered the strangely peaceful faces of a man and woman who couldn't have been more than a few years older than Kirsten. Both were blond. In spite of their bluish pallor, she was pretty, and he would have made a handsome man when his features lost their boyish molding. One of his hands gripped the reins, but his other arm cradled his wife and her cheek rested on his shoulder.

Blue sighed. "Damn shame. But they went together and don't look like they suffered at the end."

Kirsten's eyes blurred. "Could—could we have passed them on the way to Zeke's?"

"Can't be sure, but I figger we came along that ridge on the other side of the hollow." Their tracks had drifted over so they were making their way by the sun and Zeke's directions.

"We can't just leave them here."

Blue considered. "We could hitch our horses to the wagon but I hate to wear the team out in these drifts. Guess the best thing's to pack the bodies out. Sure can't make a grave till the ground thaws."

"It can't be far to our wagon."

"Doubt if it's a mile. We'll tie these poor kids on Stockings and I'll hoof it."

"No, I will," said Kirsten firmly.

Blue opened his mouth to argue, then shrugged. "Guess you're right. My hobblin' would slow us down, and we sure want to hit Zulu Stockade before night."

Kirsten climbed into the wagon. It was dreadful to work the man's arm from around the woman, but it had to be done. Kirsten turned down the blanket and stared at the small bundle hugged between the woman's breast and her husband's side.

"Good Lord almighty!" whispered Blue. "Is that a baby?"

Lifting the little person from the mother's dead embrace, Kirsten raised the afghan and stared at the small face framed by golden curls. Long lashes lay against pallid cheeks and the lips were blue, but somehow the child didn't look dead, or perhaps Kirsten simply couldn't accept that the parents' efforts to shield her with their bodies had been in vain.

She remembered that in the Bible, Elisha had breathed into a dead boy's mouth and revived him, and once Grandfather Nils had done the same for a comrade overcome by cold and weariness in the mountains.

Holding the child on one arm, cupping its head with her other hand, Kirsten sealed her lips around the small mouth and nose and blew in. Did the chest swell? Taking a long, deep breath, Kirsten tried again. On the fourth breath, the child stirred and gasped, and the eyelids fluttered open.

Eyes blue as mountain veronica, the well-remembered blue of Lucia's eyes. These widened before they closed again. But color was returning to the lips and face and the child kept breathing. Wrapping her snugly in the afghan, Kirsten handed her down to Blue. "She must need food and water. Thank goodness Zeke gave us a bottle of milk."

"Poor little mite," Blue said, cuddling the baby, who looked to be about a year and a half old. "Or maybe we better say, lucky little gal! Few more hours and she'd of been dead as her folks, the poor young critters." He handed the child to Kirsten. "Keep her warm. I can bring Honey in close and get the bodies tied on her."

"Can you get the milk out and maybe a biscuit?"

While Blue went about his task, Kirsten labored out of the drifts with the little girl and carried her to a wind-bared stony outcropping on the flat above. Holding the body under her cloak, Kirsten unbuttoned her dress enough to tuck the icy feet against her flesh and sopped a bit of biscuit in milk.

"Here, darling." What was the child's name? Maybe there'd be something in the wagon to identify the family so the baby's relations could be found. Kirsten touched the morsel to lips that were already a healthier color. "Taste it, sweetheart." Then, without really thinking, she urged, "Eat the nice bread and milk, Lucy."

The child's eyes opened again. Golden eyebrows puckered, but she ate the bread and opened her mouth for more, just like a baby bird. Her clothes were wet and soiled, but changing her would have to wait till they reached the shelter of the haystack. The baby whimpered.

"It'll be all right, honey," Kirsten soothed. "We'll take care of you."

Blue was coming, mounted on Stockings, who broke the way for Honey, led by her reins and burdened with the blanket-wrapped corpses. How much would the baby understand? She was certainly old enough to know and miss her parents. Rising, Kirsten snuggled the child beneath her cloak so only the tiny nose peeked out, then started across the flats.

14

In a quick search of the dead couple's wagon, Blue had found nothing to identify them. The man's wallet contained a few dollars but no papers. The patterned wedding ring on the woman's finger was worn enough to convince Kirsten it was an heirloom. She thought of saving it for the little girl but couldn't bring herself to remove it. When they got to Zulu Stockade, she'd clip off locks of hair for a keepsake, and perhaps a close search of the wagon would turn up something to hint at where the family came from, or at least a few things to be saved for the child.

At the haystack, while Blue shoveled drifts away from the back wheels and the horses contentedly munched hay, Kirsten spread a bedroll in the cavern and, warming wet soft rags with her hands and talking gently all the while, cleaned the baby and dressed her in clothes Blue had found in a trunk in the wagon.

The child's mouth quivered several times but she didn't cry, only gazed at Kirsten with wondering eyes. She helped tug on her flannel petticoat and gown, though, and determinedly wriggled her toes to the end of diminutive wool stockings.

"That's a big girl," praised Kirsten. "What's your name, sweetheart?"

"Baby."

"Yes, but don't you have another name?"

Studying her intently, the girl shook her head. "Mama?" she asked. "Daddy?"

How much did that little mind comprehend of the ordeal? What could it understand? The bodies were frozen in a seated position, but the blankets concealed that rather grotesque posture. Would it be better to let their daughter see them and realize that they couldn't move or respond than perhaps to let her feel abandoned?

"Mama?" This time tears formed in the gold-lashed eyes.

"Blue," called Kirsten. "Do you think we ought to let Lucy see her parents?"

He glanced up from harnessing the team. After a moment, he said slowly, "Seems cruel, but I reckon that'd be better in the long run. Otherwise, she might keep expectin' them to come back."

"She may anyway."

"Sure, but kids and animals know things deep inside. She's going to miss her folks, nothing we can do about that, but if she sees for herself that they've changed, that they can't move or talk, I think she'll make peace with it better."

It was terrible, having to make such a decision, but Kirsten had to agree with Blue. It was out of the question to lie to the child, let her hope her parents would be with her again.

Agonizing over each word, Kirsten held the baby girl on her lap and said, "Darling, your mama and daddy got so cold they died. They'd like to hug and kiss you and play with you but they can't."

"Mama!" This time it was a wail.

Steeling herself, Kirsten picked Lucy up. "Come see her, darling."

Kneeling by the blanketed forms, Kirsten uncovered the faces. So young to be parents, so young to die. And of course they'd been seeking a better life, had dreams for their future.

"Mama," the child pleaded. She patted the face, tugged at her shoulder. "Mama up!" Thwarted, she turned to her father, calling him, trying to lift his head. She sat between them for awhile. Finally, she said, "Mama sleep. Daddy sleep. Kiss 'night."

She kissed each of them, stroking their hair and saying, "Night," clearly her shortening of "Good night." But somehow she must have known this was more than slumber, for she made no fuss when Kirsten drew the blanket over those quiet faces, and didn't resist sitting on Kirsten's lap, snugly bundled, as Blue started the team. She'd had a cup of milk and now she chewed on slices of dried apples. Gradually, her body went limp and she slept in Kirsten's arms.

"So she's Lucy," said Blue, glancing at a golden ringlet that curled from beneath the afghan. "She does have your sister's eyes and that real fair, see-through skin."

"Maybe her parents or their parents came from Sweden or

Norway," Kirsten speculated. "It's sad to think their families may never know what happened to them."

"Be sad if they knew," he reminded. "But the little gal pullin' through would be worth a lot. Hey, there's the trail! Glad we didn't stray too far off it."

Several vehicles had broken the way, and the horses drew the wagon more easily. By the nooning stop, the road was getting slushy and an occasional yucca stalk speared nakedly through the whiteness. In one draw they saw horns and hooves thrusting out of high drifts. "Cows piled on top of each other and the bottom ones suffocated or froze," Blue said. " 'Fraid there's goin' to be an awful lot of that." Indeed, as they traveled southwest buzzards circled over many spots and, satisfied that a meal waited, dropped down to what they had seen.

Lucy woke when Blue halted the team on a high stretch where wind had uncovered the tops of withered grass. He had stowed hay in the back of the wagon, too, to make sure the horses could eat. After rubbing her eyes and yawning, Lucy smiled, then focused on Kirsten with a startled look and sucked-in breath. Braced for screams or weeping, Kirsten was surprised when the child slipped from her lap and made her way to the bodies.

She tugged down the blanket, stared at her mother and father, knelt and patted them. "Mama? Daddy?" After a time, shaking her head in sad puzzlement, she told Kirsten, "Mama sleep. Daddy sleep." She pulled up the blanket and smoothed it down.

Scarcely able to speak, Kirsten said, "Come here, honey, and cuddle up in the seat. I'll get you something nice."

Rummaging in the food box, she located the dates and pushed out the pits before she gave two of them to Lucy, along with more milk. She helped Blue build a fire from twisted hay and the cow chips they hadn't been able to burn in the haystack.

When Lucy saw them drinking coffee, she stretched out her hand. " 'Fee?"

"Don't think it'd hurt to give her a snort," said Blue.

"Well, if I put just a few drops in her milk—" Kirsten decided.

The little girl laughed to have her desire fulfilled and sipped proudly, draining the cup and asking for more. "First, eat your biscuit," Kirsten said, glad Zeke had given them some of his butter.

Lucy polished off most of a biscuit sopped in gravy and then flourished her cup in reminder. "Sticks to her point," Blue grinned.

"Could you play the violin?" Kirsten asked, filling the cup half full of milk and tipping in a splash of coffee. "She'd like that and maybe it'll take her mind off coffee."

Had Lucy heard fiddling before? She bounced up and down to jig tunes, swayed to waltzes and began to drowse with the lullabies as Kirsten rocked her.

They needed to reach Zulu Stockade by nightfall. The horses had dined on Zeke's hay as well as whatever they could glean from the snow. Blue hitched up early and they started on, Lucy drowsing off against Kirsten's breast. What a mercy that they'd found her! Kirsten held the small body close. Feeling that in a mysterious way, her little sister had been given back to her, she hummed a lullaby.

The setting sun crimsoned the white vastness as they descended a long, sloping hill into a pretty valley watered by Palo Duro Creek. The big picket house, built of small, straight logs stood upright in trenches, was right by a roomy corral and stables. A stone house looked nearly finished; that was for Jim Cator's English bride. Though he'd just come in from an all-day hunt for his cattle, Jim made them welcome and exclaimed with quick sympathy when they told him about the dead parents of the sleepy child Kirsten held.

"I'll take care of your team," Jim said. He ruffled his light-brown hair. "Tomorrow I can knock some coffins together, but these poor young folks may have to wait to be buried till the ground thaws some. Let me take the child, Miss Mordal, and help you down."

Lucy's eyes flew open as the stranger took her. She reached for Kirsten and cried desperately, "Mama!"

"We'd better let her look again," Kirsten said, anguished. While in a way it was merciful that the baby didn't fully understand, it was also more difficult. She lifted Lucy into the back.

The little girl repeated her ritual of the nooning, lifting back the cover, touching her parents, calling them, but this time, when they didn't move, she began, sobbing, to try to shake them. "Up, Mama! Up! Daddy, up!"

"They can't get up, darling," Kirsten said through tears, unable to steady her voice. "They can't get up ever again." Climbing back into the wagon, she took Lucy in her arms. The child didn't resist, but clung weeping to Kirsten's neck.

Jim Cator helped them down. "Go on in," he said. "Tea's brewed. Make yourselves at home."

The Cator brothers had been the first permanent settlers in the Texas Panhandle. "Though I must concede that Bob wasn't too permanent," said Jim as they ate beef stew. "We lost so many cattle the winter of 'eighty-three that Oregon looked better to him, so he's up there. Another blizzard like this and I may join him." In spite of worry over his stock, Cator was a genial host. As well as a stage stop, this was a post office and store.

He located a stick of candy for Lucy, who held on to Kirsten as if fearful that she, too, might fall into the sleep that gripped her parents, and then he carved a piece of cottonwood root into a creditable buffalo, which he presented, kneeling to be on the child's level.

"Cow!" she laughed delightedly.

"Close enough," he grinned. "I suppose, little one, that you'll never see the originals." Entranced with the toy, Lucy got down on a wolfskin rug and began to gallop the beast through the wolf hair.

Watching her ruefully, the Englishman shook his head. "When my brother and I came to the plains, we didn't think any amount of hunting could much affect the herds. There were so many! But they didn't last long." He and Blue exchanged a deep look of remembering, and Kirsten felt a certain envy. New as this country was, she hadn't known it as they had, when it was still the domain of Indians and the great herds of humped, bearded beasts whose skins were everywhere in the house, spread on benches and beds.

Jim had to hear all the details of their surviving the blizzard and promised that when he could, he'd salvage the wagon of Lucy's family, search carefully for clues to their identity, save anything that might be of real or sentimental value to Lucy, and sell the wagon.

"When you know who's going to take care of the tyke, let me know," he said. "I'll get the money and other things to them." His eyes softened as he watched the child enjoy his candy and play with the "cow." "I'd fancy keeping the little blue-eyed angel myself, but she'd do better with a woman to mother her. Pity you're traveling around, Miss Mordal, or you could keep her yourself."

Kirsten had been so enraptured by the feeling that in a way

Lucia had returned to her that she hadn't considered the practical difficulties of keeping the baby. Now she had to, and an honest gauging of the situation forced her to see that she had no right to haul Lucy all over the plains, hazarding blizzards and other dangers, if a loving, settled home could be found for her. Of course, she could do what Ash and Amanda had suggested, rent a house in one of the towns and open a business there.

But she really didn't want to live in town. She wanted a place near trees and water, like this one, where she could look over a garden, orchard, and fields. And having started the circuit of Ash Bowden's Triangle, she was loath to abandon it. Still— Lucy brought the buffalo to her and walked it along her arm. "Moo-o-o!"

"Moo-o-o!" returned Kirsten and, her heart swelling with protective love, scooped Lucy up for a hug and kiss.

Unless she found someone who convinced her they could take better care of Lucy than she could, she'd give up her tour of the region and settle in Tascosa or Mobeetie. When Lucy was a few years older, they could think about homesteading. Blue, of course, would make his home with them. Realizing that she took that for granted, Kirsten glanced fondly at Blue. He had become like her family, and after the ordeal of the blizzard, she felt they were destined to be together the rest of their lives. He had even given her back Grandfather Nils's music, and she knew she had restored his pride.

He played that night and learned some English ballads from Jim. Kirsten moved with Lucy to a homemade rocker by the big fireplace and in lulling the child to sleep, almost lulled herself. She started at a light touch on her shoulder.

"Bless you, Miss Mordal, you'd best tuck in," smiled Jim Cator. "You have the bed here by the fire. Blue and I'll sleep in the next room."

"Why don't you sleep in here?" asked Kirsten. After the haystack and the crowding at Zeke's, she was more concerned about everyone being warm than conventional niceties.

"The fireplace is built to heat both rooms," Jim explained. "You can enjoy your privacy with a clear conscience." He touched Lucy's golden hair. "Sad about her parents. Not much more than a boy and girl themselves."

As she had when Lucia died, Kirsten felt the guilt of one who survives when others die. She assuaged it by swearing to the dead parents that she'd take care of Lucy. Placing the "cow" on the child's pillow, she began to get her ready for bed.

Next morning, Blue and Jim took the lumber, freighted from Dodge, that Jim had intended to use for doors and framing windows in his new house, and made it into a double coffin. "Saves wood," said Jim, "but I think they'd want to be together. And we can bury them after all."

"But the ground—" began Kirsten.

"Hole's already made. Hunters had a dugout down the creek a bit. We'll slip the coffin in and seal it with rocks and whatever earth we can chip off the top and sides."

Kirsten had loathed the thought of the young couple lying frozen in the stable till spring, but now she worried over what was best for Lucy. There wasn't any easy way to deal with the child's final good-bye to her parents' bodies.

"Let her go with us to bury the kids," said Blue. "If they just disappear, she'll keep hoping they'll come back."

That was what they did, after Kirsten clipped a lock of hair from each golden head and wrapped them in a scrap of velvet to save for Lucy. Jim hitched up one of his teams and they drove the coffin, lid unfastened, along the bank above the creek till they reached the old partially caved-in dugout. It was sealed by snowdrifts, so that the men had to use their shovels to clear a space.

Battling to keep her voice calm, Kirsten told Lucy, "We're going to let your mama and daddy stay here, sweetheart. They can't wake up again and they need a nice quiet place."

Lucy wailed and scrambled back to her parents. "Mama up!" she cried imperiously, tugging at her. "Daddy! Up!" When they didn't move, she sobbed against them but didn't resist when Kirsten, crying herself, lifted her so the men could bring the blanket over those handsome faces and fasten the coffin lid.

Using rubble left by the cave-in, the men soon covered the entrance to what was now a burial chamber. "I'll put up a marker," Jim said. "The little girl may want to visit the grave when she's older, or maybe some of their family will turn up."

Lucy cried on the way back to the house, but once inside Jim diverted her with another candy stick and carved her a fork-legged figure that could either stand or sit on the buffalo, and these she intently played with. Blue hadn't found a doll or any toys in the wagon, so Kirsten, out of one of his old socks, fashioned a rag doll with an embroidered face and a bandanna dress. After dinner, Lucy went to sleep cuddling her treasures. Fortunately, she understood the use of the chamber pot and said when she needed it.

A party of three mule-drawn freight wagons rumbled in that afternoon, and Kirsten helped Jim cook supper for the teamsters, who obviously tried to temper their language and tobacco spitting in deference to her. They were enchanted by Lucy, and when they heard her story, they took up a collection to be used for her clothing and care by whoever assumed responsibility for rearing her.

They reported hundreds of cattle dead along fences or piled up in draws, and when they heard that Kirsten and Blue were bound for the Rawlings' ranch and would have to camp out one night, they advised them to wait a day or two before journeying on.

"There'll be more grass in sight for your critters," a pock-marked bald man said. "And the road's still pretty slick."

Blue fiddled after supper. Several of the teamsters had good voices, which didn't inhibit those who lacked them from joining in so in spite of the shadow of death, it was a rather merry evening, though Kirsten declined to dance when asked by the lanky, fair-haired wagon master. She lacked the heart for it, though she understood that here, where death was a common risk and monotony commoner, people weren't callous to enjoy themselves when they could.

Next day, Kirsten performed what was becoming an habitual chore at bachelor outposts: sewing on buttons and mending. Blue made Lucy some soft leather boots, and Kirsten used a piece of hussar-blue wool left over from Amanda's riding habit to stitch a hooded cape that would give the child more freedom than the afghan. Lucy needed other clothes, too, since all Blue had found for her was an extra flannel petticoat and dress, besides those she'd been wearing. Kirsten had soaked and scrubbed these out and dried them by the fire, so Lucy had a change, but Kirsten, thinking of the leftover material in her chest, planned to make real little dresses and long-legged, lace-trimmed cambric drawers to keep Lucy warm; a bonnet and muff out of the midnight-blue satin; and dainty smocked nightgowns with embroidery. Lucy strutted so proudly in her boots and in the cape, which made her eyes even bluer, that Kirsten itched to begin her wardrobe.

The thought of Amanda's hussar-blue ottoman raised a possibility in Kirsten's mind. The Allens would certainly take Lucy in. They'd be kind to her—though Grace and Nora would take charge of her—and there was no doubt they'd love her. The Allens could give a child every advantage. Still, after reflection, Kirsten thought Lucy, who'd obviously adored her father and was amusingly coquettish with Jim Cator, would do better with a man younger than Hi to act as parent. That brought to mind a young man who soon would be a father, and Kirsten's heart leaped before it contracted.

O'Brien would make a marvelous father, and Lorena apparently had the nature of a good mother, but to give this child, already dear to Kirsten, to the woman who already had the man Kirsten loved? It was too much! The idea haunted Kirsten, though, in spite of her violent rejection of it.

O'Brien was the father she'd have chosen for her own children. Kirsten suspected he'd be firm if Lorena was too indulgent, and soon there'd be a baby of just the right age for Lucy to play with, as Kirsten had with Lucia.

If Kirsten had left an orphaned child, she could think of no one to whom she'd rather have entrusted it than the O'Briens, and a home with such a father was infinitely better than any that Kirsten, single, could offer. If Jim Cator found nothing in the death wagon that could be used to trace Lucy's relatives, Kirsten decided that she'd have to write to Lorena and O'Brien. But in her lonely depths she almost hoped they'd have some reason not to accept the responsibility. Knowing O'Brien's concern for the helpless, though, she didn't think it would happen. That night, cherishing Lucy's sweet warmth beside her, Kirsten rebelliously wondered if she was fated to have to give up to Lorena everyone she loved.

"Where the dadburned road's not ice, it's mush," groused Blue next day as they labored along the road that stretched like a ragged, rough-edged scar across flat prairie. "The turnoff to Rawlings' isn't quite halfway from Zulu Stockade to Little Blue Station, but we may have trouble spotting it unless someone's been down it."

Buzzards were still spying feasts from on high, and in several draws the wagon had passed coyotes feeding at mounds from which horns, hooves and other parts of cattle protruded. Beautiful prong-horns had perished with the larger beasts. Kirsten held the sleeping Lucy closer, shivering. If they hadn't found her, by now birds and beasts would be cleaning those fine, delicate bones. What a razor edge it was between life and death! Like O'Brien hearing their music and finding his way to refuge.

"This must be the turn to Rawlings'," Blue said. "See, there's ruts showing on that rise where the ice's melted off. According to what Mr. Rawlings said, it's ten miles to his house, so we'll go just a little farther before we camp, and then it'll be an easy haul to the ranch."

Within the hour, they found a good stand of buffalo grass and stopped there for the horses' sake. Jim Cator had given them a sack of corncobs and filled up a kettle with his good beef stew, so they built a fire and soon had a hot meal. It was no night for sitting around a fire, so as soon as the dishes were washed, they settled themselves to sleep in the wagon and didn't wake till the eastern sky began to lighten.

15

Being caught in the blizzard and having Lucy along made Kirsten eager to reach a dwelling, but as the wagon wheels churned through slush or groaned through mud, she became increasingly apprehensive about being part of the Rawlings' household for a month or more. It was a shame, for Marilyn and Meg, the twins, were so close to her own age that they could have had a lot of fun if Mrs. Rawlings weren't so overbearing.

Few of her patrons would be as warm and kindly as the Allens, though, and she was a businesswoman who could scarcely refuse customers because she didn't especially like them. What troubled her most was how Sally Rawlings would react to Lucy. She didn't behave like a woman who'd enjoyed her own children, let alone anyone else's. However, considering Lucy's plight, it was inconceivable that anyone would refuse to shelter her for a while, and on that point Kirsten didn't feel the slightest uncertainty: If Mrs. Rawlings didn't want Lucy in her home, Kirsten wouldn't stay, either.

Blue's sucking in his breath jarred her from such musings. "Lord help us, there's the damn drift fence!"

A dark line rimmed the horizon to the south, stretching out of sight on both sides. The road veered toward it. Gradually, they came close enough to see that the dark line was cattle heaped two- and three-deep for a long way, in places stretching perhaps as much as a half a mile from the fence.

Partially bared by wind and sun, the cattle were frozen in every posture, some trampled by others, many dead on their feet searching for a way through the fence, all huddling for warmth. And mingled with them were pronghorns who could have fleetly out-run the storm if they hadn't struck the barrier.

Kirsten had seen big herds of cattle driven into Dodge, but never in numbers to approach this enormity. Heads, horns, ribs and legs rose from the wind-drifted snow. Buzzards pecked at sightless eyes and scavenging coyotes scarcely gave the travelers a glance.

The ragged border of death was so immense that Kirsten felt less sickened than gripped with horrified awe and she held Lucy tighter. How lucky they had been to survive that storm!

"Bad," muttered Blue. "But there's bound to've been lots that walked right over these poor brutes and that danged fence and are down on the Rio Grande or over on the Pecos. Hey, there's a wagon up ahead! Skinners workin', looks like. Wonder if it's O'Brien."

It was. He was guiding the mule team that was pulling the hide off a frozen cow while Zeke Thomas and a younger man worked fast with their knives to free the hide from the icy carcass. Its head tied to a cedar post, its hide peeled back from neck and legs, the animal had been slit down the belly and a knot of hide from the neck had been secured to the mules' doubletree, the bar to which singletrees were attached. The mules' harness hitched to these bars and the purpose of the doubletree was to equalize the team's pulling power. The little mules didn't like their task. Their tails jerked, they kept their ears laid back, and it was all O'Brien could do to keep them from bolting.

The hide ripped loose as knives flashed swiftly. O'Brien handed the reins to the youngest man and, rubbing his gauntleted hands, came to meet Kirsten and Blue, Zeke behind him. O'Brien's eyes sought Kirsten's, though he spoke to them both.

"Reckoned you'd pass this way. Light down and have some coffee." A strong aroma drifted from a fire where other cedar posts crackled. O'Brien strode toward Kirsten, arms outstretched to help her down—so strong and smiling and alive, his eyes gold-green, the sun sparking glints from his hair, that her heart sang to look at him.

Lucy stirred and sat up, pushing back the afghan. O'Brien stopped, lean jaw dropping, and so did Zeke. "This is Lucy," Kirsten said, and told how they'd found her while the little girl looked at the men sleepily, and then with a sudden smile, held out her arms to O'Brien.

"Come along then, sweetheart." He swung her to his shoulder before he helped Kirsten down; then he brought them all to the fire.

The third man hitched the team and came over to warm his hands and drink the coffee Zeke handed around. O'Brien introduced the thin, dark young man as Bill Mabry, the son of a neighboring rancher.

"That steer we just skinned wore our brand," Mabry said gloomily. "What's worse, we've skinned out two of our best heifers this morning." Steers went for beef, but good heifers were kept for breeding.

"We tallied near a thousand head stacked up along two miles of fence," said O'Brien. "Brands from as far away as the Platte River country. Lots of Hi Allen's."

"How about yours?" Kirsten asked.

"We've skinned a roan steer I raised on a bottle when a cattle drive left him because he was too puny to keep up. I only had a couple hundred head." He shrugged. "Just have to hope most of them passed over this heap and got away from the storm. I reckon the outfits will send some crews down south to drive back whatever stock they can find. I'm sure going." He stared grimly at the endless wall of death. "Took me a long time to get that two hundred head."

"Anyhow," put in Zeke, "the hides'll bring three to five dollars apiece in Dodge. Better'n nothing."

Sitting on a post with Lucy on his knee, O'Brien poured a lot of canned milk into a little coffee and steadied the cup while Lucy drank it. Her blue hood had fallen back, and with her golden head near his, they could have been father and daughter. Had she gone to him so readily because his height and fairness reminded her of her father?

Kirsten watched them with bittersweet pain. She hadn't expected to have to part with Lucy this soon, though she'd made up her mind that she'd have to do it if the O'Briens were willing to take the child as theirs. Glancing at Kirsten, O'Brien asked the question that he, being O'Brien, would have to ask.

"Why don't you let us keep the darlin', Miss Kirsty? Lorena loves kids and she's hoping for a daughter. This way we'd have one for sure, and she'll soon get a baby brother or sister to play with."

Best for Lucy. Much the best. Kirsten held to that, though

beneath her cloak, she clenched her hands till they ached. "Are you sure, O'Brien?"

"Sure as I breathe," he said solemnly.

Averting her face to hide the trembling of her lips, Kirsten had to swallow before she could say, "I'd love to keep her myself, but I —I know she'll be better with a mother and father both. I suppose it's better to make the change before she gets too used to Blue and me."

"You'd make her a sweet mother," said O'Brien gently. "But it's hard while you're traveling around."

Kirsten nodded, unable to speak. "Aw, Miss Kirsty," said Blue, crossing to pat her shoulder.

Scrubbing back tears, she said, "I'll take her to Rawlings' for now. Will you come get her when you're through skinning?"

"That'd be the best way. We'll probably work another week. Stack and salt the hides we can't haul out and come back for 'em later. I'll ride over horseback for Lucy, but when we get back to the wagon I can hold her while Zeke drives. Don't worry, colleen. We'll take care of her."

"We'd better go on to the ranch," said Kirsten. "I wonder if the Rawlings lost many cows."

"His herds were mostly south of the fence," said O'Brien. "He ought to come off at least a sight better than Hi Allen."

He helped Kirsten into the wagon, kissed Lucy's rosy cheek and placed her in Kirsten's arms. "Good-bye, honey," he told the child. "I'll see you before long." To Kirsten, he said, "You'll be like her godmother, Kirsty. And someday you'll have a baby of your own."

"I don't know how you can be so sure of that," she retorted, and arranged the afghan to shield Lucy from the wind. She felt O'Brien watching her but couldn't bear to look at him as Blue started the team. She should be glad Lucy would have him for a father—and she was. But how it hurt to lose her!

While only one storey high and not as impressive as the Allen home, the Rawlings' house was also of milled lumber and was painted white. Two young trees, their branches naked, were planted precisely on either side of the front door, and the house sat aloof from the other buildings, a bunkhouse, cookhouse, stable and barn. Except for smoke curling from the cookhouse and smokehouse, the ranch looked deserted.

"Sheldon and the hands are prob'ly huntin' cows," Blue said. "Well, let's get you settled and then I'll unhitch."

"Let's go to the back door," Kirsten suggested. "It doesn't look like anyone goes to the front." Did the house really have an air of unwelcome about it or was she imagining things?

As they drove to the rear, a scrawny, middle-aged woman with sparse gray hair pulled back in a knot so tight that it seemed to sharpen her features appeared in the door, grasping a cloak around her.

"You're the sewing woman?" she asked suspiciously, small black eyes darting over Kirsten and fixing on the child. "You don't look old enough. And the missus never said anything about a baby."

"I'd like to get her in out of the cold," said Kirsten. "I'll explain to Mrs. Rawlings. If you'll be so kind as to tell Mr. Martin where to put my trunk—"

"Miss Mordal!" That was Meg, because her hair was browner than her twin's red curls. Both girls rushed past the disapproving sentry, laughing in excitement.

"Oh, we're so glad you're all right!" cried Marilyn. "Were you still at Allens' when the blizzard hit? Where'd you get the sweet little girl? Isn't that the darlingest hooded cape?"

"Come in and get warm," Meg invited. "You can tell us about everything while you're having a nice hot cup of coffee." She turned to Blue. "Won't you come in for a cup, too, mister?"

"Name's Blue. Thanks kindly, ma'am, but soon's I unload Miss Kirsty, I'd ought to take care of the horses."

"Hank's coming up from the cookhouse now," said Marilyn. "He'll help. Martha, will you show them Miss Mordal's room?"

"I don't know what the missus is goin' to say about a young'un," Martha grumbled.

Kirsten could have said that she'd only have Lucy a week or two before O'Brien fetched her, but she rebelled at the thought of working in a house that wouldn't cheerfully make place for an orphaned child.

"Blue," she said, descending, "since there seems to be some doubt about Lucy's welcome, maybe you'd better leave my trunk and things on the porch and go take care of the horses."

"Oh!" The twins' green eyes darkened with distress and they spoke in chorus. "You—you won't travel on right away?"

"That depends."

The sisters wore severe dresses of a dull, unfortunate brown without any of the resonant shadings that color can have, but away from their mother's reproving vigilance they bubbled with friendliness, and Kirsten longed to make them some pretty clothes. They hustled her into the big kitchen, and she was savoring a cup of steaming coffee while Lucy, in Meg's arms, sipped at her brew of mostly evaporated milk, when Sally Rawlings came in with a swish of skirts that reminded Kirsten of the tail lashings of a perturbed cat.

"Well, Miss Mordal, so you've finally arrived." Her eyes, which lacked the warmth of most brown ones, fixed on Lucy and gasped. "Good heavens! I didn't know you had a child. That was no part of our understanding."

"We were caught in the blizzard," Kirsten said, and explained the situation, except for revealing that Lucy had a new home, a father who'd claim her soon. "If Lucy is a problem, Mrs. Rawlings," she concluded, "we'll travel on in the morning."

Sally Rawlings stared before she went scarlet. "I can't believe what you're saying, Miss Mordal. You'd just ignore your agreement to sew for us? That's no way to get or keep customers!"

"I'll stay if Lucy's welcome."

"Oh, please, Mama!" Meg urged. "Marilyn and I will help look after the baby. She won't cry and make your head ache."

"It's aching now." Sally Rawlings gave Kirsten an accusing look. "I suppose I don't have much choice, since we all need new dresses, but please remember that I'm paying you to sew, not dawdle over a baby. The twins' old trundlebed's already in your room and Martha will get some padding to protect the child's mattress."

"She doesn't need it," said Kirsten defensively.

"All the same," shrugged her employer. "As soon as you've unpacked, let's look over what you're sewing for us. You should have time to lay out at least one pattern before supper."

After she left, the kitchen grew lively again. Marilyn got some dates for Lucy, and Meg, after asking if Kirsten was hungry, supplied her with a big bowl of rice pudding, which Lucy shared blissfully. By then, Blue had returned with Hank, a tow-headed boy of perhaps thirteen, who evidently served as general chore boy in the way Joey had at Allens'. They stowed Kirsten's belongings in a small room across from the kitchen.

Blue was feeling much more at home than Kirsten did. "Cook is Dan Ruggles," he told Kirsten with pleasure. "We cowboyed together in our young days. He used to break mean horses for fun, but one rolled on him and now he's purty nigh as crippled up as I be, but he sure makes good flapjacks." Blue rubbed his stomach. "He just built me up a big plate of 'em. Everything okay, Miss Kirsty?"

She nodded. As she had foreseen, it wasn't going to be like the Allens', but it was her business, after all, and she had forced Sally Rawlings to accept Lucy, so she had no real excuse for passing on to pleasanter engagements. Besides, it would be a challenge to see if she couldn't achieve individuality in Meg's and Marilyn's clothing. What a shame that their mother didn't seem to want them to be pretty! But even in her drab gown, Meg looked beautiful as she smiled and crooned to the little girl she held in her arms.

Ranged on a table in the stiff and obviously seldom-used living room, the materials weren't as hopeless as Kirsten had feared they might be, which made her suspect that Sheldon Rawlings had selected them on some visit to town. There was a russet silk foulard printed with tiny black and gold flowers; a gray-green wool grenadine; some black satin, presumably for Sally Rawlings; and for summer, gauze striped in various tones of green, and lavender muslin printed with violets.

"The twins turn seventeen in June," their mother said, as if this were somehow their fault. "Mr. Rawlings thinks they need more style to their clothes, though gawky as they are, I can't see the use." She fretfully indicated masses of braid, edgings, gimps, lace and ribbons. "I think he bought all the trimmings in Tascosa, but there's no call to use more than looks proper."

"Trims do have to be chosen with care." Kirsten was glad to be able to agree with Mrs. Rawlings on something, though she'd winced along with Meg and Marilyn at their mother's disparagement. "Style's very important for young ladies with such graceful, willowy figures. I have some patterns I think would suit."

Already she was seeing how cut and trim could vary dresses made of the same material. The foulard, for instance, could have, for Marilyn, a high collar edged with black braid, a fitted bodice with jet buttons, and braid banding the skirt, while gold velvet ribbon could accent Meg's dress, which should be made as a princess sheath to emphasize her slim, budding figure.

"I suppose we're paying you for your ideas as much as sewing,"

Mrs. Rawlings said without much grace. "Amanda and Katharine Allen praised you to the skies, so let's hope you can contrive some way to make the twins look less like beanpoles." She surveyed her own buxom curves complacently. "The black silk's for me, and you can make it from the same pattern used for my wedding dress. Let the girls help you with the basting and such, they've plenty of time."

She departed, leaving the younger women to go through patterns. "Which material do you want made up first?" Kirsten asked, and was pleased when they decided on the foulard. When she explained her thoughts, Meg clapped eagerly but Marilyn looked dubious.

"Mama may not like it. She says twins should dress exactly alike so there's no question of one being favored over the other."

It didn't seem to Kirsten that there was much danger of either of them being favored at all by their insensitive mother but she said reassuringly, "Your father seems to want you to blossom out, and your mother, I think, was leaving such things up to me."

"Don't be a goose, Marly," Meg adjured. "It's about time we looked different. What if we got married and our husbands couldn't tell us apart?"

"We may not get married."

"Oh, horsefeathers! We're a lot more likely to if men can see we're two separate people, not a team that has to be bought together like horses or mules."

"If Mama heard you!" cried the scandalized Marilyn. Meg made a face and went over to look at Kirsten's patterns.

Before supper, Kirsten cut out the first dress while Meg and Marilyn vied with each other to entertain Lucy—who had woken a bit crankily from her nap—beguiling her with toys they unearthed from their closet. By supper she was in a good mood and had graciously accepted her new vassals.

When they entered the large room that served as parlor and dining room, Kirsten said, "If you'd prefer, Mrs. Rawlings, I'll feed Lucy in the kitchen and put her to bed."

"You may as well try her here." Sally Rawlings shrugged. "Meg has dragged out her old high chair and Marilyn has located an oilcloth bib and her silver spoon. The tot *is* a pretty little thing, and thus far I'll admit I haven't heard her squawling."

Fortunately, Lucy liked the high chair and, when she wasn't eating, enjoyed playing with the wooden beads inserted in the tray. "Beautiful hair," remarked Mrs. Rawlings, as Kirsten bore Lucy off to bed. "It needs washing. I have some fine castile soap you may use."

"I'll do that tomorrow when she's rested," Kirsten said, letting Meg and Marilyn kiss the little girl goodnight. As she carried Lucy down the hall, she nuzzled her neck and laughed. "Goodness gracious, darling, I think Mrs. Rawlings is going to like you if she isn't mighty careful!"

That night, Kirsten cut out a simple gown for Lucy from the golden-brown bengaline she'd used for Bridget's dress, designed with smocking at front and back to allow for growth. Ruffles at wrist, throat and hem could be added to, and of course there'd be an ample hem and wide seams, so this should serve as a best dress for several years. When Meg and Marilyn saw the cut-out pieces for the little gown, they begged to help with it, and Kirsten was glad to let them baste while she proceeded with Meg's foulard.

The three of them, with Lucy playing on a rag rug a safe but warm distance from the small cast-iron heating stove, filled Kirsten's small room, but she enjoyed the company, and already it seemed that there'd never been a time without Lucy. The rag doll Kirsten had made her and Jim Cator's "cow" were still her favorite toys. She gathered up all her creatures and rocked them and at nap time carefully arranged those she didn't sleep with in the cradle, covering them with a seriousness that made Kirsten wonder whether she remembered drawing the blanket over her parents' faces.

Lucy didn't cry for her parents, but once or twice a day she would place a hand on either side of Kirsten's face, compelling full attention, and inquire, "Mama up? Daddy up?"

"No, darling," Kirsten would have to say. "They can't get up, not ever." Lucy's mouth trembled then, but she'd march away and start mothering her dolls as if that somehow comforted her.

Sally Rawlings looked in on them from time to time, apparently rather annoyed when she found nothing to fault. "I declare I don't know how you get anything done with all your giggling and chattering," she said. "But it seems you are, so I won't complain, even if the noise makes my head ache." Lucy was galloping her "cow" across the rug, and Mrs. Rawlings bent to watch the golden hair, turning with a sigh. "I always wanted a daughter with golden hair. When they were babies, the twins were fair, but the color changed before they were three."

"They have beautiful hair," Kirsten said, aghast, while Meg and Marilyn kept their eyes on their sewing. Why did Mrs. Rawlings make statements of fact into accusations?

"Oh, it's well enough." The woman shrugged and went her way out.

There was a moment's awkward silence before the sisters exchanged bitterly amused smiles. "Mama would have been happier with dolls than real children," Meg said. "Remember, Marly, she had fun dressing us up till we were nine or ten?"

Marilyn nodded. "I guess that's when she began to be disappointed in us."

Meg gave an indelicate snort. "No, Marly, that's when we got too big to be play toys. And I doubt Mama likes to be reminded that she's old enough to have grown children." Her green eyes rested on Lucy. "When I have a daughter, I'm going to tell her she's pretty, no matter what she looks like, and I'm going to tell her she's smart and can do anything she decides to, not make her feel awkward and stupid."

"So will I," said Marilyn. "And if someone nice doesn't ask me to marry him by the time we're eighteen, I'm going to leave home and teach school or something."

Meg nodded vigorously. "Kirsten's managed on her own, and in a strange country, too. It goes to show women don't have to just put up with whatever happens—they can make things happen!"

Startled and embarrassed, for it hadn't occurred to her that she might serve as an example to anyone, Kirsten glowed at the admiration in Meg's voice. "I don't deserve much credit," she said. "We left Sweden because we were tired of eating bark bread. I wanted something better for Lucia and for me. But Lucia—" She bowed her head. Even after all these months, grief could overwhelm her.

After a moment, Meg said gently, "We'd like to hear all about it if you want to tell us. We know you worked at a hotel in Dodge and that your sister died, but you've never said much else."

"Wasn't it scary to leave Sweden?" Marilyn asked.

Bending to her work, Kirsten began with Sexton Carl's stories of America, and she had reached the part about how O'Brien had rescued her at Selina's, when Martha Todd opened the door.

"Gentleman in the parlor to see you, Miss Mordal. Mrs. Rawlings is there, so it's proper. Miss Meg, Miss Marilyn, you're to serve coffee and cake."

Could O'Brien have come so soon? Surely not, unless his plans had misfired. Since no one would be left with Lucy, and Kirsten was nervous about the stove, she smoothed her hair, picked up the toddler and her doll, and went down the hall to the parlor.

16

Ash Bowden crossed to her in a long stride. She felt, as always, a shock at that thick silver hair, which made the pugnaciously attractive face all the more vital. *Of course,* she thought with a sense of inevitability, *it would be you.*

A lifetime seemed to have passed since she had seen him at Allens', and in a way it had, for near death in the blizzard and the tragedy of Lucy's parents had cut through her past like a dividing line as final as the voyage from Sweden. She knew he would have taken her hands if she hadn't been holding Lucy. As it was, he contented himself with an encompassing glance that she was sure noted everything about her before it fixed on her eyes.

"Well, Miss Mordal!" His smile mocked the formality. "So you are safe and sound, as Jim Cator, and just now, Mrs. Rawlings, assured me. I was in St. Louis when the blizzard hit but journeyed to the Allens' when I returned to Dodge. There's been a serious fire there that wiped out most of the buildings around the bridge."

"Minnie?" asked Kirsten, frightened.

He shrugged. "Her hotel escaped. Anyway, I was so concerned about you that I didn't linger. Some teamsters left word at the Hardesty Ranch that you were all right, or the Allens would have mounted a search." He included Sally Rawlings in his deprecating smile. "I still had to see for myself. In a way, Mrs. Rawlings, I feel responsible for Miss Mordal's enterprise, for I was impressed by her flair for designing and suggested she become a *modiste.*"

"Really, sir?" That clearly elevated Kirsten in Mrs. Rawlings's view more than even the recommendations of Amanda and Katharine Allen.

"You mustn't feel too responsible, Mr. Bowden," Kirsten said.

"I was already thinking of becoming a dressmaker. But it was your speaking of the Triangle that made me want to explore it."

"You've seen what happens to explorers," he said with a meaningful look at the child. "Jim Cator was just back from getting that young couple's wagon. He said to tell you there was no identification and nothing worth keeping except this."

From a table, he picked up a small wooden chest inlaid with mother-of-pearl. Opening it with a silent apology to the dead woman, Kirsten gazed through gathering tears at the small treasures of that life: a black velvet ribbon with a cameo, a brooch and earrings set with garnets that had the look of heirlooms, a tortoiseshell comb, and a little bottle encased in silver filigree that puzzled Kirsten till Bowden grinned sardonically. "To hold smelling salts," he explained. "Somewhere back in the poor girl's family, there must have been ladies with leisure to swoon when they laced themselves too tight."

Kirsten shut the box. It seemed they would never know where the young couple came from or who they were. "Thanks for bringing the box," Kirsten said. "It's good that Lucy will at least have a few keepsakes."

"Jim says when he sells the wagon, he'll send you the money."

"I have to get word to him to send it to the O'Briens," Kirsten said. "They're going to take Lucy."

Bowden's eyebrow raised, but Sally Rawlings made a sound of surprise. "You're not keeping the baby? When you made such a to-do about her being welcome here?"

"I'm to take care of her till O'Brien can fetch her," Kirsten said, feeling that was enough explanation for her employer. "Did you see O'Brien, Mr. Bowden?"

Ash nodded. "He's still skinning cows. But he stopped long enough to let me know you'd saved his life—'angel singing' I believe he called it."

Kirsten flushed at Bowden's tone but said, "It's lucky he heard us. And the luck for all of us was that haystack."

"Indeed." Eyes, cold gray as the cloud that had presaged the storm, probed hers and held them. "I trust that such a nearly fatal predicament and discovering the child's parents has led you to see you should give up your gypsying."

"No."

"No?"

"I intend to complete the loop, sir, just as I planned."

"That's crazy!"

"There may not be another bad storm for years. And we're usually only on the road a few days at a time between shelters."

Bowden gave an exasperated groan and might have argued further, had not Marilyn and Meg come in with trays of cake and coffee. Mrs. Rawlings was a bit cool to Kirsten, and her glance kept wandering back to Lucy, but Bowden exerted himself to be charming, and Meg and Marilyn met his banter first with shyness and then increasing confidence. He talked to them and their mother, but Kirsten had the uncomfortable certainty that he was studying her from the corner of his eye.

He was invited to spend the night as a matter of course, and at supper entertained them with how the "mugwumps," liberal Republicans, had helped the Democrats, called by some the party of "Rum, Romanism and Rebellion," to elect Grover Cleveland the past November, and what could now be expected from Washington.

"There's a lot of public pressure on Congress to make a law against fencing western public lands," Bowden said. "My friends in the Capitol think it'll pass this year."

"Laws are made a long way from where things happen." Sally Rawlings's lip curled. "Like the law the Texas legislature passed last year making fence cutting a felony." She studied Ash with less favor than previously. "I've heard that you're interested in promoting a town, sir, up in the Neutral Strip. That's not good in cattle country."

"The city I envision, ma'am, would, I am positive, meet with your approbation. A center of culture with an academy, a well-equipped hospital, and stores the equal of those in Kansas City. And of course the railroad that'll pass south through my town will relieve cattlemen of having to trail their herds to Dodge." When she looked unconvinced, he smiled. "Establishing a city that will be the heart of the Triangle isn't my only concern, ma'am. Among other undertakings, I'm acquiring land for a sizable ranch."

"Where?"

"I've already bought land in western Kansas and the Texas Panhandle, ma'am. As soon as the Neutral Strip's opened, I'll get the connecting territory."

"That sounds like quite an operation."

"It will be. The Scottish syndicate I represent will send over purebred Durham stock, and we'll experiment till we've produced a cross that's hardy but provides good beef."

"They'll gaunt up on the trail."

Bowden's smile flashed, and again Kirsten marveled at how relaxing his combative jaw turned him handsome. "Not when they only have a short amble to the railroad. Longhorns are going the way of the buffalo, and so will cattlemen who can't or won't adapt to new conditions. The plain fact is that the country's settling up." He looked straight at Kirsten with an intensity that jolted her. "The trail between Dugan's road ranch and Busing Crossing on the Cimarron has two new settlements just since you passed that way, Miss Mordal. Fowler started Christmas Day when Linn Frazier opened a general store in a half dugout, and they're building a hotel. Nine miles down the trail on Crooked Creek, some folks were platting a town when I rode through. Going to call it Wilburn. That stretch between Dodge and No Man's Land is filling up in a hurry." Platting, Kirsten knew, meant making a map or chart of a proposed town so that lots could be sold.

The rolling expanse of grass and sky broken by frequent towns of the raw sort spawned on the prairie? With a regretful pang, Kirsten mused, "I'm glad I traveled that way while Hoodoo Brown's was the only place between Dugan's and Odee."

Bowden's smile broadened. "Ah," he teased. "Spoken like a pioneer. 'Let me pass into the new land, Lord, but then slam down the bars and keep out the riffraff.'"

"Riffraff got here first," Sally Rawlings pointed out. "An ornerier, stinkier, meaner bunch never scratched lice out of their beards than buffalo hunters."

"Yes, but those who stayed are solid citizens now like Jim Cator." Bowden reflected dreamily a moment. "The men who come first to a region are like lovers. They relish the wildness and danger, sometimes wooing, sometimes ravishing, often passing on. The next men are like husbands. They have to study the moods of the land, know what they can change and what they can't, but they stay, and the country shapes them at least as much as they alter it."

"What about women?" Kirsten demanded.

"There, I defer to the wisdom of you ladies. But it seems to me that a woman's main energies are used within her home, and the constant in that, wherever she may be, is making a comfortable nest for her children."

"You sound as if a woman has to be married."

His mouth curved down. "Doesn't she? To be a woman?"

"No more than a man must be married to be a man."

To her surprise, he laughed. "It happens I agree with that. Now, if you ladies will excuse me, I'll step outside for a cigar."

"No need for that," said Mrs. Rawlings. "We're quite accustomed to my husband's enjoying his smoke of an evening. Come sit by the fireplace and the twins will serve coffee."

Kirsten helped clear the table but then escaped to her room with the excuse that she must put Lucy to bed. It was both flattering and disturbing that Ash Bowden, in spite of a press of important business, had made this journey to satisfy himself that she was safe. If she hadn't loved O'Brien, she might have been so drawn to Bowden's vibrant energy, so beguiled by his attentions, that she'd have mistaken the excitement he caused, the sensuous thrill, for true love.

That couldn't happen now, but she was wary of him, even while she was tempted to return to the parlor and enjoy his banter and news. She hesitated, then grimly took herself in hand, put fuel in the stove, and lit the lamp, setting it by the Family Gem.

Lucy's dress was basted. She could finish it in several hours. Kirsten smiled to think how delighted the child would be next morning to find the gown draped across the trundlebed. Sitting down at the machine, Kirsten was soon absorbed in guiding the magic stitches that were making something pretty for someone she loved.

She was sewing the last ruffle on the hem, when a sound made her turn. Ash Bowden stepped in, unbelievably silent, and closed the door. She rose, hand going to her throat where the pulse beat furiously. Had he moved toward her, she would have screamed; he sensed this, for he stood by the door, eyes brilliant, though his face was in shadow.

"My love," he said softly. "Oh, my dear, willful, foolish love."

His voice, though muted, deep and masculine in its caressing, stirred through her powerfully like a physical entity. "You should not be here." The words trembled as her body was beginning to; that angered her, and she stiffened her arms at her sides. "Kindly leave at once."

Far from going, he moved forward, though he paused beyond

arm's length. His tone grew richer, softer. "Will you shriek the alarm, my dear? Compromise yourself, so the only way to save your reputation would be to marry me? Go ahead, by all means. I'd rather you wed me from affection, but if necessary, I'll take you any way I can and win you after marriage."

"I wouldn't marry you if my reputation were ruined twice over!"

"Really?" He seemed to loom, though he was only a few inches taller than she and he had not moved again. "Strange, Kirsten, for my fairly well-trained instincts tell me that I'm not repugnant to you."

"That's not what we're talking about."

"But it's such an interesting subject."

She regarded him frostily. He gave her a rueful smile and surprised her by going to gaze down at Lucy, hair bright on the pillow, with her sock doll and Jim Cator's buffalo cuddled against her. "You love the child, Kirsten. You've named her for your sister. Why are you giving her up?"

Tears dimmed Kirsten's eyes, and she looked away, swallowing, forcing her words to sound matter-of-fact. "She'll be better off with a mother and father."

"I don't agree. Having you for a mother would outweigh the advantages of belonging to any number of normal families, even that of your idolized O'Brien. Lorena is a sweet child, but she can't begin to give a girl the example that you would."

"Lucy—she loved her father," Kirsten said. "She went to O'Brien right away. He's the best father I can imagine for any baby."

"That's obvious. But when I've considered the matter—which, I'll grant you, I hadn't till I met you—I think I have the stuff of a passable father myself."

"*You?*"

"Not a flattering reaction," he said wryly. "But think on it a moment, Kirsten, and be fair. Don't you believe I'd protect my children and imbue them with useful knowledge?"

In spite of the half-mocking tone, she felt constrained to ponder the question and answer honestly. "You'd protect your children as you would anything you claimed. There's no doubt you'd give them every advantage, and, if they had your interests, you could teach them a lot."

"And?" he prompted.

Feeling her way, Kirsten sighed. It was difficult, trying to assess this man who had so intrigued and puzzled her from the beginning. "I think, if you gave yourself time, you'd dote on young children, probably be overindulgent. But as they grew older, began to have ideas that might not please you—then, I don't know. You could be a tyrant."

To her surprise, he winced. "I suppose that could run in the blood," he said slowly. "A tyrant my grandfather certainly was, for all his being a Presbyterian minister. I don't blame my mother for running away with a handsome rascal and I cringe when I think how it must have been for her to crawl back to her father, swollen with me, abandoned by her lover." His mouth twisted and Kirsten looked away. So often she had wondered about his past. Now that he was telling her, it was painful to hear. "The poor girl died before I could remember," Ash went on. "I was left to my grandfather's mercies—grandmother was long dead and no wonder—and he did his best to thrash any hereditary vice out of me. I ran off when I was eleven, worked at whatever I could find, and it was in those years I determined, Kirsten, that though people might not love me, I was going to be strong and rich and powerful enough so that at least they couldn't hurt me." Shrugging, he switched back to his usual bantering tone. "So you think I'd be a tyrant?"

Taken aback by his baring what had to be his most painful secret, Kirsten flushed. "After that kind of childhood, perhaps you'd know you must let children learn their own lessons, find their own way."

"It's illuminating to hear your surmises." He looked away. For the first time it entered her mind that it might be as hard for him to meet her gaze as it was for her to encounter his. But that was ridiculous. The likes of Ash Bowden could never be abashed by a young foreigner of half his age and a tithe of his experience. If she hadn't known better, though, she would have thought he groped for words. "Has it occurred to you that how I behave to my extremely hypothetical children might depend on who the mother is and how I feel about her?"

"I—what's that got to do with the children?"

"Damned near everything, my exasperating innocent." He took her hands, and she didn't deny them to him, for the way they were talking, nakedly, was more intimate than touch. "I savor beauty in women, but it wasn't only that that I saw from the start

—maybe it was sadness for your sister or your homeland, but something about you well nigh broke my heart, and it is not, believe me, one easily marked. However, it was your integrity, your courage, and your sweet generosity of spirit that made me prize you. How could a child of yours lack those qualities? Or even one, like this mite, lucky enough to come in your path?"

What would he think of her integrity if he knew how she yearned for a married man? Shaking her head desperately, Kirsten freed herself. "I'm not those things," she almost sobbed. "I've been terribly afraid—not just in the blizzard, either—and I—" She gulped and snatched a word from the parson's homilies. "I've coveted what isn't mine."

"Oh, my Kirsten!" He laughed with tender delight. "That only makes you human—and lets me dare to love you."

He had bared himself to her. That gave her power she couldn't misuse. "Ash." She used the name timidly, though anything else at that moment would have been false. "I want to be your friend—"

"Stop right there," he commanded, covering his ears. "With artful variations, I've made that speech so many times that I've no curiosity as to your wording. God pity us all, my poor sweet. I know you're still mistaking gratitude to that big Irishman for undying passion. How could you know the difference?"

His eyes flared, and she took a quick step back. He fixed his hands behind him and paced to the sewing machine, studying the tiny dress. "For a moment, let's pass over how you regard me and consider your love for this little girl. I'm far from a mystic, but obviously you yourself find your sister in this child, who would be dead except for you. In a very real way, you gave her life. Since Providence brought you together, don't you believe you're intended to be her mother?"

She had to smile faintly at his ingenious argument. "It's odd to hear you invoke Providence."

"For your benefit," he shrugged. "Myself, I honor Fate, and she is seldom kind."

"Just so." Kirsten looked down at the baby with a surge of protectiveness and tried to express the deep convictions of her heart. "I suppose I do believe that in Lucy I can love Lucia again, make up in a way for taking my sister away from her home to die young in a strange country. That's why I can't be selfish and keep

Lucy, though it's what I'd like to do. Fate led me to her, and I *must* see that she has the best possible parents."

"Damn it, you're the best possible mother! And if you'll let me, Kirsten, I swear I'll cherish this child as if she were born of our flesh, for she is born of your heart."

"Ash—"

"Don't answer till you've thought on it. You're not deceiving me. I know the loyalty of your sweet, stubborn heart. But will you give up this little one, forego a home and the love of a man, all for the sake of a girlish infatuation?" He set his finger on her lips. "Think."

Unwillingly, but forced by his will to obey, she surveyed a future without Lucy or any child, without O'Brien or any husband. A dismal picture, however she tried to summon up visions of a snug house shared with Blue, a garden and orchard and ripening fields, and in that moment she found no thrill in imagining tremendous success with her sewing.

She treasured independence. It was gratifying to create becoming and useful garments, but wouldn't these satisfactions, strong as they were, dull with time if she never sewed a bride gown for herself, never stitched clothes for her own babies, never gave a bridegroom the shirt she had tucked and embroidered so painstakingly far away in Sweden? From childhood, she had always expected to marry. Must she deny that dream?

Her woman's nature reacted potently to Ash. She had shared with him her most secret thoughts, as he had with her. This brought them closer than she had ever been to anyone; and yet she did not love him.

He read her answer in her eyes. The look of ardent, eager youth left his face, though he still smiled. "In my way, Kirsten, I'm as faithful as you. Time changes many things, and I'm good at waiting." He glanced again at Lucy. "I hate to see you pain yourself so uselessly, but you'll do what you must." Taking her hand, he held the palm to his lips as he had done the day she left Dodge City. "Good night, my dear. Sit up late and finish the little frock. Isn't that what all good spinster aunties do?"

He left before she could speak, but she was glad of the caustic remark for it kept him from assuming noble proportions in her mind. Ash was a realist, and without being told, she sensed that he was not one to foreswear women. When he finally realized his suit was hopeless, he'd find another love.

Why couldn't she?

He left next morning without a private word to Kirsten, though he complimented Lucy on the gold-brown dress she'd hugged on waking and insisted on donning, holding out the skirt as she danced in circles and chanted, "Look at me! Look at me!"

When he was gone, Kirsten found an envelope pushed beneath her door. Inside was a hundred dollars in gold pieces and a note in a bold, slashing hand: *For Lucy—I was an orphan once.*

Shaken, Kirsten put it with Lucy's jewelry. What an unpredictable man Ash Bowden was! And why, after last night, did she feel a treacherous sympathy for him? Later, when Meg and Marilyn joined her, they talked on and on about him, plying Kirsten with dozens of questions.

"Oh," sighed Marilyn. "He's such a gentleman! Gallant and worldly. Isn't it astonishing he's never married?"

"I couldn't vouch for that," said Kirsten tartly, for Ash haunted her that morning, and she wished the sisters would find a less troubling subject. "For all I know, he's a bigamist."

"Kirsten!" cried Marilyn, eyes going wide.

Meg shot Kirsten a startled glance before she laughed. "Kirsten's right, Marly. Those charming manners could hide a Bluebeard, and that only makes him more fascinating. I've finished basting in the stays, Kirsten. What shall I do next?"

Sheldon Rawlings rode in two days later with his cowboys. They'd found thousands of cattle dead on the plains, some with the Lazy R brand, but Sheldon hoped most of his cows had drifted south. He'd called on a number of Panhandle ranchers, and they'd agreed each to send a wagon and ten or more men to scour the Pecos and drive surviving cattle back to their home ranges. As soon as they got organized, Rawlings's foreman and most of the men would join the expedition.

Worried as he was about his stock, Sheldon romped with Lucy, hoisted her on his shoulder where she gripped his sandy hair, and got down on all fours, dignity forgotten, to pretend to be a raging bull. "Fun to have a wee one around again," he said.

To Kirsten's surprise, his wife nodded. "Yes. Yes, it is."

Sheldon hugged the twins, one in each burly arm. "Well, girls, reckon it won't be too long till you give us some grandbabies to spoil."

Mrs. Rawlings said coldly, "A good many women of my age have children."

His jaw dropped. "Why sure, honey, but—I thought—You said—" He broke off in confusion. Clearly, they were getting into private matters, and he soon escaped to his office. Kirsten liked the bluff, ruddy-faced rancher and was sorry that he seemed to get scant pleasure from his home life, though he obviously adored his daughters and they him. Sally Rawlings controlled them all with an acerbic tongue against which her husband had no weapon, though her daughters would someday escape.

One afternoon, Mrs. Rawlings came to sit with the younger women in Kirsten's room, coaxed Lucy to her lap and began to brush her hair, a procedure the little girl enjoyed as long as the tangles were already out.

"The O'Briens are expecting, aren't they?" Mrs. Rawlings asked.

"I think so." Kirsten gave a brief answer because she didn't want to discuss the O'Briens' affairs. Surely Mrs. Rawlings wouldn't, in front of unmarried young women, speculate on who had fathered Lorena's baby and whether it would be born "early."

Sally Rawlings didn't say that, but her next words were almost as jarring. "Taking on another little one would be quite a burden and hard on Mrs. O'Brien. Her husband had no business assuming such a responsibility without consulting her. After all, she'll be the one who'll mostly have to take care of the children."

Taken aback and puzzled at her employer's concern for Lorena, Kirsten said, "O'Brien says Lorena loves children, and it's a long way to travel back and forth. But of course he knows I'd love to keep Lucy if for some reason they can't."

"We'll keep her," the woman said.

Meg and Marilyn quit basting, staring at their mother, and Kirsten ran the stitching off the seam. Her instinctive response was *No!* but before she could think of a polite rejoinder, Sally Rawlings added, "In our case, there's no need to wonder if the baby's really wanted. I talked it over with Mr. Rawlings last night and he thoroughly approves." She was forming curls around her finger, smiling fondly at the effect. "After all, Miss Mordal, you can't have the slightest misgiving about our keeping her. We can send one of the hands over to tell O'Brien he needn't bother to stop."

In Sally Rawlings's mind it was settled. Kirsten nerved herself with a deep breath. "I'm sorry, Mrs. Rawlings. It's kind of you to offer Lucy a home, but the O'Briens are much closer to the age of the parents she remembers and I'm sure she'll like having a brother or sister to play with."

Mrs. Rawlings's back stiffened and her dark eyes flashed. "Are you saying we're too old?"

"No, ma'am," said Kirsten miserably. "I just think she'd fit better with the O'Briens."

Mrs. Rawlings's cheeks flamed. "Don't you think it's presumptuous of you to make that judgment, especially when you're little more than a child yourself?"

"A child I am not." Kirsten reverted for the first time in weeks to her early use of English, caught herself and went on deliberately. "I found Lucy so I must decide what's best for her."

"And you've decided the O'Briens, living in a soddie and just starting out, will make better parents than we will?"

Meg sprang to her feet. "Mother," she cried, green eyes blazing. "What will you do with Lucy when she's too big to treat like a doll?"

The two stared at each for a taut moment. Then Meg, hiding her face, ran out of the room. Mrs. Rawlings, pale, looked at Marilyn, who bowed her head. Rising as if suddenly aged, Sally Rawlings put Lucy down and without a word or glance to Kirsten hurried from the room.

17

Kirsten half expected Sally Rawlings to pay her for the two dresses she had finished and send her on her way, but after shutting herself up for a day with a headache, the rancher's wife emerged and behaved as if choosing to ignore the whole incident, though she no longer paid any attention to Lucy. Surprisingly enough, she did carp less at her daughters, and occasionally Kirsten caught her scrutinizing them as if they were strangers. If Meg's outburst had jolted the woman into considering the way she treated her daughters, the skirmish might serve a useful purpose.

On the ninth morning of Kirsten's stay, O'Brien rode in. He had to get Lucy to his home as soon as possible and then join the Pecos cattle hunt while Zeke marketed the hides. He wouldn't stay for dinner, but put away half a peach pie and drank cup after cup of steaming coffee, keeping Lucy, who perched on his knee, supplied with her milk brew, while he and Sheldon rued the blizzard's toll and tried to estimate how many cattle might have taken refuge far to the south.

With Meg and Marilyn's help, Kirsten had finished a second dress for Lucy out of red bombazine left over from Mrs. Hoodoo Brown's gown. Lucy was already wearing it, with two new petticoats and a pair of the long flannel drawers Kirsten had fashioned to keep the little legs warm. As Kirsten packed Lucy's belongings, including the jewelry chest with Ash's hundred dollars, her eyes kept blurring and a big lump ached in her throat.

By actual count, it was only two weeks since they'd found Lucy, but in Kirsten's heart it seemed a lifetime. She was so used to rocking Lucy to sleep, rousing at night to soft baby sounds, watching her play. In these few weeks, she'd become the beloved center of Kirsten's life and now, suddenly, she'd be gone.

No one can love her more than I do, Kirsten thought, stifling a sob. But that's why I have to let her go with O'Brien. Look at the way she'd deserted everyone else that morning to run joyously to O'Brien, clamber up, and pat his face—his eyes and mouth, which could respond as her father's no longer could.

Holding to that image, Kirsten brought Lucy's hooded cape and explained to the little girl that O'Brien was going to be her daddy and take her home. Lucy took this news gravely.

"Kirsy come, too?"

"I can't, darling. But there's a new mama waiting for you and you can take your pretty new dress and your dolly and 'cow.' "

"She must have the elephant, too," said Meg. "And the doll," said Marilyn.

These were added to Lucy's plunder, but wrapped in her afghan, clutching her favored sock doll and buffalo, Lucy clung to Kirsten at the moment of parting.

"Kirsy and Blue come!"

"We can't now, honey, but we'll stop and see you someday. You be a big girl now for your daddy."

"Here, sweetheart." O'Brien reached down and took the child from Kirsten's arms, which felt unbearably empty. "There's a puppy at my house that sure will like to play with you. He's got one black ear, one white ear, and you can feed him."

"Puppy?" echoed Lucy.

"You bet. He can sleep by your bed at night." He let this beguiling promise sink in, settled her in front of him with a hug, and said, "Can you wave good-bye?"

Lured by the puppy and surely finding O'Brien's arms a comforting place to be, Lucy didn't cry, though she looked very solemn as she raised a small hand and named everyone in her farewells, ending with, " 'Bye, Kirsy! Come see Lucy!"

"I will, sweetheart." Reaching up, Kirsten grasped the plump little fingers and kissed them, stumbling blindly to the side.

"We'll take care of her, colleen." O'Brien's tone was soft with compassion. "And remember, you're her godmother."

Kirsten struggled to smile. "Yes. Maybe when she's older and Blue and I have a homestead, she can come and visit. And of course, if Lorena doesn't feel well enough to look after her, let me know and I'll come get her."

"Not much chance of that. Minute Lorena sets eyes on this baby, she'll be daft about her." He watched Kirsten with a concerned tenderness that strengthened her at the same time it made her knees feel as if they were melting. "Safe traveling, Miss Kirsty. You're mighty welcome at our place when you're heading back to Dodge."

He waved and reined Barney eastward. Lucy, peering past his shoulder, waved till they passed out of sight beyond a small slope. Blue said awkwardly, "We sure will miss that little gal, Miss Kirsty, but you done the best thing for her."

She nodded, unable to speak. The two she loved most in all the world had left her, traveling to another woman, and she was desolate. When Meg put her arms around her, Kirsten stopped trying to be brave. She lowered her head and wept.

Mrs. Rawlings was so pleased with the black silk gown that she asked Kirsten to restyle several old dresses, so it was the end of February by the time Hank helped Blue load the trunk and Family Gem into the wagon and Kirsten made her farewells. She embraced Meg and Marilyn and shook hands with Mr. and Mrs. Rawlings, Martha, Hank, and Dan Ruggles, Blue's friend of the cookhouse, who had baked ham and two apple pies to send with them.

With Martha's contribution, several loaves of her tasty sourdough bread and a spice cake, they wouldn't need to cook anything but a pot of beans the whole four-day journey to Tascosa. And in the trunk with the money left after sending O'Brien payment for the team was the hundred and eighteen dollars Sheldon Rawlings had paid her for nine new dresses and the two refurbished ones. Enough to pay for the wagon, with a fair amount in reserve!

That lifted Kirsten's spirits, and again she felt the excitement of taking to the road. She waved till the wagon dipped out of sight and faced the morning sun, humming as Blue whistled and the horses moved along springily, as if they, too, were glad to be traveling.

They were never out of sight of scavengers still feasting on cattle, pronghorns, deer, and even the occasional rabbit, prairie dog, or badger that had been too far from shelter when the blizzard caught them. But new life was beginning.

That evening, as they were looking for a good place to camp, they saw a few cottonwoods up ahead and found them growing in a wash that gave some protection from the wind. As they halted, a booming resonated across the plains, a curious sound, many times magnified, like that caused by blowing across the top of an open jar.

"Prairie chickens," Blue grinned. "Cocks'll be struttin' their stuff. Why don't you go watch the show while I make camp? It's worth seein'."

It was indeed, though Kirsten followed the sound for almost a mile before she sighted the huge bare space where dozens of males were in various stages of display. She took cover behind a small rise in the ground and saw one proud cock run to his selected spot, pat it with his feet, and swell orange sacs on his throat. Lifting orange eyebrows, stiffening a sort of crest on the back of his neck, he spread his tail as a lady snaps open a fan and began to boom.

The cock next to him deflated his orange sacs, drooped his wings and rushed at the newcomer. They hopped up and attacked each other with flailing wings, for all the world like rival roosters, but after a few flurries, each resumed his display. Females watched from the edges, and apparently one somehow notified a cock that he'd won her, for he left the shallow basin and disappeared with her into the buffalo grass. Kirsten watched a little longer, thinking the courtship in some ways very human, though women now, rather than men, used handsome garb to attract.

That night, Kirsten heard the eerie *hoo-hoo* of a horned owl, and next morning Blue pointed out the crows' nest appropriated by the bird that ruled the night as the eagle ruled the day.

"See those two tufts sticking up?" Blue asked. "That's the female on the eggs. And look to the side of the trunk, blending in with that knob. Daddy's having a snooze."

The owl's brown, black, and white plumage made it seem part of the trunk. The bird's body looked as long as Kirsten's arm. "Bet when he stretches out his wings they're five feet tip to tip," said Blue. "And the feathers are so downy on the edges that they don't make a sound."

Had he swept up one of those posturing cocks? The owl opened yellow eyes and regarded them drowsily, without alarm, confident in his sovereignty. "He looks like a cat with those ear tufts," Kirsten said.

"I've heard 'em screech like cats, too, and they can make a mewy sound. Hiss, they do, and click their beaks. Well, we'd better mosey along if we're goin' to make Little Blue tonight."

The mail stage stopped at Little Blue, of course, and as the sod way station came in view where it nestled in a stand of trees along a draw that Blue said ran into Little Blue Creek, Kirsten was much tempted to dispatch Ash Bowden's money to him, the whole eighty dollars with interest, and rejoice in owing not a dime to anyone.

An exhilarating prospect, but her next definite appointment was at a ranch north of Mobeetie. She intended to look for business in Tascosa but would have to pay for lodgings, meals, and the horses' keep at a livery stable, the same situation she'd find in Mobeetie. Till she saw if her skills were in demand, she'd best save her money.

The way station was so crowded with tobacco-spitting, whiskey-guzzling freighters that Kirsten and Blue slept in the wagon, but the food was decent so they had supper and breakfast inside. Leaving early, they angled around the head of Big Blue Creek and turned south to Tascosa Creek.

"Now," said Blue, "we just keep to the east side of the creek till it brings us right spang to Tascosa's main street."

That sounded easier than it was; the country grew hillier and rockier, and numerous sandy draws made the horses labor. They camped near a small butte that night, out of the wind enough so that Blue got out the violin. It was good to have music again and they sat up later than usual.

"Star Girls goin' to bed with us," Blue said, pointing toward the sinking Pleiades. " 'Member, Miss Kirsty, when we started out, they were rising just about this time? And come April they'll plumb hide away till October."

"By then we'll have done the whole Triangle."

Blue nodded. "Maybe we'll even be settled on our land. You still want to homestead, don't you, Miss Kirsty? Not goin' to marry some rich feller like that Ash Bowden?"

"Has that been worrying you?" Kirsten laughed and squeezed her companion's hand. "No, I'm not marrying Ash, and yes, I want to have our farm, and whatever I do, Blue, you'll have a place and part as long as you want."

"Then you sure are stuck with me for life. Lord, Miss Kirsty, I was hangin' around Minnie's just waitin' to die and now I'm startin' over, got another chance."

"I don't know what I'd do without you," she said truthfully.

Tascosa's main street was even sandier than the washes and only two blocks long, with several other equally sandy streets cutting through, though several adobes east of town, from which came sounds of revelry, made up what Blue called Hogtown.

First a settlement of sheepmen from New Mexico, then a hangout for Comancheros and buffalo hunters, now a supply point for cattle ranches, this bustling town built on the north bank of the Canadian was the county seat, and a stone courthouse loomed among tall cottonwoods that also shaded the streets and boardwalks.

"We could stay at the hotel," said Kirsten. "But I'd rather take rooms in someone's house."

"That'd be more respectable for you," Blue agreed. "Why don't we ask at the livery stable?"

Mickey McCormick, the genial, ruddy-faced, leonine owner of the stable, knew of her from O'Brien and had heard through freighters of their ordeal in the blizzard. At Blue's query, he rubbed his chin in thought.

"You'd be purely welcome at our house, Miss Mordal, but that might keep some of the high-nosed old biddies from patronizing you." He grinned. "I'm a gambler and my wife's the best monte dealer in the country. She's sure to want some new dresses, but I guess to keep the prissy females happy you'd better lodge with Betty Trube. Before you unhitch your wagon, let's go have a word with her."

Mrs. Trube was as big as he was, and it didn't seem she'd often need the six-shooter she wore at her broad waist to control the men devouring platters of food in her small adobe. Her yellow hair was fading, but she had merry blue eyes.

"So you're the lass O'Brien's mentioned!" she said after a searching look. "The one who lived through that storm in a haystack and rescued that poor little orphaned mite. Well, I've a room that's better than a haystack, and we'll move a table in for your sewing machine. Have your meals here or cook for yourself if you'd rather. You can pay in sewing for me, if you want." Her laughter boomed infectiously. "I'm outsize enough that you'd ought to charge as much for one of my dresses as you do for two ordinary ones."

"A fine figure of a woman you be, Mrs. Trube," said McCormick. "And a fine woman with it. We'll unload Miss Mordal's things, then." He said to Blue as they walked to the wagon, "I could use some help at the livery, and I'd reckon your reputation can stand boarding with us."

"I'd reckon," chuckled Blue.

Within the hour Kirsten was settled in a small, square room in Betty Trube's dwelling that adjoined the "eating house." A table got the light from the one window. A washstand, narrow bed and chair were the sparse furnishings, but there was a cheery blaze in the fireplace, a rag rug on the floor, and a bright quilt on the bed; with her chest and Family Gem, Kirsten felt immediately at home.

"You'll get a lot of customers here," said Mrs. Trube. "And I won't be a plumb hog of your time. If you make me two dresses, let's call that six weeks' board and room. After that, seventy-five cents a day should square things."

"That's more than fair," Kirsten nodded, relieved. She wouldn't have to dip deeply into her savings. "I'd like to make one of your dresses first thing. Do you have some material?"

"Would you go to the mercantile with me and help me choose?" Betty Trube glanced at her loud calico. "I'm big as a barn, I know that, but maybe—well, maybe you could figure out what'd look nicest."

Betty was entranced with an orange foulard splattered with enormous purple flowers that had just come in from Dodge, but Kirsten held up a length of nun's veiling, a fine worsted fabric, striped in harmonious blues. "This darkest blue is just the color of your eyes," she said. "Set off with this deep blue edging, it'd be most becoming."

"M-m-m." Betty considered and yielded up the orange abomination without too heavy a sigh. "I suppose the other dress better be black for Sunday best and funerals, which we have often enough for such a little wrinkle in the road."

"Black's always in good taste." She herself was heartily sick of it; when her year of wearing mourning was over, she didn't think she'd ever have another black dress.

"May be in good taste," Betty grimaced. "But it casts down my spirits."

"Then you shouldn't wear it."

"Maybe brown?"

"Gracious, no!" Kirsten explored along the counter, located a taffeta so blue that in the shadows it looked black. Bringing it into the light, she said, "I can make this with a detachable bertha and set of cuffs in this tawny cotton lace." She had seen a dress with a particularly fetching bertha, a wide, round collar covering the shoulders, in her *Delineator*. "For a change I can do a scarf of black chiffon to wear draped around your shoulders and fastened with a taffeta rose."

As Betty exclaimed in rapture, Kirsten thought aloud. "I could also make an overskirt of chiffon to attach on either side with more roses. That would really give you three dresses in one, and if you'd like, I think I can make you a fetching hat from scraps."

Betty's eyes widened and she laughed, giving Kirsten a hug that squeezed the air from her lungs. "I thought O'Brien bragged overmuch on that dress you made his wife, but now I don't reckon he gave you credit enough! You make me that kind of a rig, the striped outfit, and a hat, Kirsty, and your board's paid for two months!"

Betty's large frame called for great adjustment of patterns, but Kirsten got the striped gown cut out that day and was sewing, when Betty pounded on the door. "Come out of there, dear, and eat your supper! Mrs. McCormick's come to meet you."

"I'd rather you called me Frenchy," said the petite dark woman seated at a table in the corner. She wrinkled her nose and her dark eyes laughed. "That's not my real name. I was born Elizabeth McGraw, but that'd sound funny in a dance hall. Of course I quit that life when I married Mickey, but I feel a lot more like Frenchy than Elizabeth." Her beringed hand gave Kirsten's a friendly pressure. "Betty says she's already got you at work, but I'd love for you to make some things for me."

"That's why I'm here," Kirsten smiled, and sat down. Frenchy dimpled, and a winning smile took years off her age, which Kirsten guessed to be early thirties.

"I thought I'd better get in line before you got more customers than you can handle." She glanced at her scarlet gown, which was trimmed with gilt braid and buttons. "Mickey likes for me to wear bright colors and I like them, too, but maybe I could look more—well, sort of genteel. Not dowdy, mind you!"

"I think we can manage that," Kirsten assured her. "Why don't you take my style magazines home and look for ideas?"

Frenchy's laughter bubbled like the champagne punch O'Brien had ordered for Kirsten at the Dodge House that one wonderful evening—before he'd discovered that he had to marry Lorena. "Kirsten—may I call you that? I wore spangles and bangles so long that I'm scared of *my* ideas. I'd rather leave it to you to pick out some possibilities and I'll choose from them." She got to her feet, smoothing her dress in a way that called attention to her slender waist and swelling bosom. "I've got to get home and fix Mickey's dinner before he starts dealing faro. Why don't you come have a bite with me at noon tomorrow? Mickey'll be off in the hills hunting with his dogs. If we decided on some patterns, I could start shopping for the material."

Kirsten agreed to come and watched Frenchy depart with a swaying gait that drew the gaze of every man in the room. Over the years, Frenchy had acquired certain habits that nothing would disguise, and it wouldn't work to try to dress her sedately. She needed dash.

As Kirsten ate the heaping plate of beans, cornbread, and beef that Betty served her, she knew that if she could design clothes that made Betty stand out more and Frenchy blend in, her reputation in Tascosa should be assured.

Kirsten missed Lucy with a sort of dull ache that a reminder could change into throbbing pain. In spite of knowing it was best, it gnawed at Kirsten that Lorena now had not only O'Brien, but the child. Still, being in a place that held no memories of the little girl at least made those stabbing reminders less frequent, and as always, Kirsten found her work and its results the best panacea.

When Betty Strube donned the completed blue striped dress and looked in the mirror, her eyes glowed an even more vivid blue and color brightened her cheeks. "I'm not going to wear my six-shooter with this," she declared. "But I look so nice I reckon that'll keep the men in line. My hair's not right, though. Could you help me figger out a way to fix it?"

"You've got some natural curl," said Kirsten. "Let's try catching it up almost on the crown of your head and letting it wave a bit around your face."

"I wouldn't know me!" cried Betty, beaming at her image after

Kirsten had brushed and arranged her hair. "Who'd have thought loosening up that bun and lifting it could make such a difference?"

"A lot of it is that you're smiling and look happy," Kirsten demurred.

Betty laughed. "Well, that's because I know I look pretty. I'd meant to keep this dress for special, but doggone if I'm not going to wear it for work, and have you make me one more. If dressing up makes me feel and look this much better, it's money well spent. But I won't hog your time. Go ahead and sew for Frenchy and some of the other ladies."

"I'll finish your taffeta first," said Kirsten. "I'm dying to see how that lace bertha and chiffon overskirt and scarf look."

The effect was all she'd hoped, and more. The chiffon, secured with taffeta roses, created glamour, and the lace, while feminine, had what Betty rapturously termed a "high-falutin'" air. When she saw the rose and chiffon hat, she gasped, gasped again when she tried it on, and caressed it with her big, rough hands.

"This is what I'll be buried in, Kirsty. This hat and the plain dress. Shucks, you could make a pile of money just doing hats. Could you make me a bonnet out of the blue stripe?"

"Of course. But if there's a little material left over, could I pay you for it and use it in a dress for Lucy?"

"Use it and welcome and any scraps from the taffeta, too. It's mighty nice of you to sew for the poor little tyke."

"I like to," Kirsten said and turned away before Betty could see her tears.

18

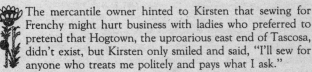The mercantile owner hinted to Kirsten that sewing for Frenchy might hurt business with ladies who preferred to pretend that Hogtown, the uproarious east end of Tascosa, didn't exist, but Kirsten only smiled and said, "I'll sew for anyone who treats me politely and pays what I ask."

"That's your lookout, miss," the sharp-featured balding man shrugged. "Just thought you bein' a foreigner and all you might not understand."

"Oh, I think I do, but I've enjoyed sewing for Mrs. McCormick. She has a lovely figure and an elegant carriage that sets off her garments."

"Well, I've got to admit she looks like a queen in that red velvet coat thing—"

"It's a *casaque*. Yes, that did turn out nicely, didn't it?" The sleeved cloak was gathered in front to form a vest defined with bars of heavy braid, which also banded the cuffs of scarlet angora wool lace. Two rows of the same braid trimmed the back with its broad pleats. All in all, Kirsten thought it her most successful creation to date, and she had deliberately made it first to sate Frenchy's love for red.

The merchant actually twinkled. "Doubt if you'll lose much trade, Miss Mordal. My wife, for one, is going through the pattern books and'll be over to see you soon."

Kirsten paid for the blue edging she needed to finish Lucy's new dress and, stepping out on the boardwalk, hesitated. Her shoulders and neck ached from sewing, and it was a sparkling though chill afternoon. A brisk walk would loosen her tight muscles and clear her head. She followed the boardwalk to its end and then, delighting in signs of spring, proceeded along the trail that she and Blue had followed into town three weeks ago.

The grass was still brown, but the first tiny plants were greening, stalks of prickly poppies thrust upward, and masses of short-stemmed white and pale pink daisies nestled among narrow leaves. From above came a distant calling and she glanced up to see a wedge of geese winging north. The same ones that had flown above her in the autumn, bound for a kinder wintering? She watched till they were tiny specks, then bent to examine a blue-purple flower that somewhat resembled the mountain veronica of Lucy's eyes.

"Pretty, isn't it? But that's locoweed, Kirsty, and you'll want to keep horses and cows away from it."

"O'Brien!" she cried, whirling.

"Betty Strube saw you headin' this way."

Kirsten felt herself sinking, sinking, into those eyes, the ocean closing over her, and had no desire for anything but to be lost there—no, not lost, but *found*, as this man alone could discover and know her. Touching her only with those dark-green eyes, he looked weary till he smiled, and then it was like the sun bursting through thick clouds. "Come eat with me, Kirsty. Can't stop long, but I guess what's left of my cows will push along with the rest for a couple of hours."

"You lost a lot of cattle?"

His grin was so crooked it hurt her. "Didn't have a lot to lose by most reckonings, but out of my two hundred, we found a hundred and twenty head. Hi's foreman, Tom Reynolds, tallied about ten thousand head and says they lost just about that many. Sheldon Rawlings came out a little better, but none of the outfits that worked the Pecos brought out more'n two thirds of their stock, and for most, it was half. Still better than losin' the whole caboodle."

Dazed at such numbers, such losses, Kirsten shook her head. "In Sweden, we must keep cows in the byre all the winter, so no one has hundreds. I'm glad you found more than half your cattle."

He nodded. "Some lost tails or ears, but they'll be all right. What made me sick was the ones whose feet had frozen and dropped off. We had to kill them." At Kirsten's cry of pity, he said roughly, "I didn't come to bellyache. Let's go see what Betty's got for dinner. I sure am tired of chuck wagon grub."

"Did you get Lucy home all right? Was Lorena glad to have her?"

"Tickled pink. Of course the little colleen missed you something fierce, and Blue, too, but she fell in love with that black and white pup and that helped a lot. Kirsty, that hundred dollars in gold—"

"It came from Ash Bowden and he can certainly afford it."

He looked ready to argue, then shrugged. "Fine. We'll put it with the forty dollars Jim Cator got for the wagon and a few other things, and save it for her."

"You're feeding and clothing her. You should use the money if you need it, O'Brien."

"Might if we get to starving. Otherwise it's hers." His tone softened. "Did you come out to see the springtime?"

"I didn't know it was here—but I'm glad it is." A rush of homesickness came over her as she remembered how joyous she and Lucia had been to find the first tiny blue anemones and sudden bursts of golden coltsfoot, the first spring flowers.

These were among the seeds she'd planted on Lucia's grave. Would they bloom in this strange country? O'Brien had enough trouble of his own, so she tried to think of something amusing. "When the first cuckoo called, we'd know it was spring. Some people even ask the bird questions and take the number of his calls as an answer."

"Cuckoo, eh? Well, you needn't get too homesick, Kirsty. See that bird raising and lowering his tail and huffing up his feathers? I've been told he's a sort of cuckoo. We call him a roadrunner. Look at him go after that lizard!"

The large crested bird with blue and red markings around the eye seized its victim and dashed off, long tail dragging. "He's not much like our cuckoo," Kirsten said. "But he is very handsome." Walking along with O'Brien, her heart seemed to dance and she felt as if the sunlight coursed through her blood. "Oh, O'Brien, I'm so glad you stopped!"

"Now would I ride through without seeing you, colleen?"

Their eyes met, to her a sweet wounding. Oh, if one time, only once, she could love him with hands and arms and lips! For that grace she would gladly renounce a lifetime with any other man. *So night and day, and day and night, are yours and only yours . . .*

That was true, would always be true, though his nights were Lorena's. In him, that yearning must be a desperate urge, for his nostrils showed white at their curving and the muscles in his jaw corded before he said, "I told the boys I'd be back in time to help chase those cows across the Canadian. This is just the northern bunch. Around thirty-five thousand head, including ten thousand of Colonel Slaughter's, have already veered east toward Big Spring. The Texas and Pacific Railroad will let 'em water at its tanks till the owners get them. There'll be some big outfits go bust over this."

Everyone in the eating house knew O'Brien and shouted questions about the cattle drive or came by the table to visit, so Kirsten was grateful they'd had a few private moments on the road. How could anything that pained her so much be her greatest joy? Tracing every angle of the beloved face, she ached to see that though he smiled and laughed, it was without his old rollicking gaiety, and the lines edging his mouth and eyes had grooved deeply just since the Christmas ball.

"Is Lorena feeling well?" she asked.

"She doesn't complain, but she's mighty uncomfortable. Feet swell real bad. Just seems too much weight for anyone so little to pack. I'll be glad when that baby's born."

His friend's baby. "I'm sure Lorena will be, too." Kirsten tried to make it a small joke, though she realized immediately that Lorena's relief at the birth would be mixed with shame. Was it the same everywhere, that ugly back-count of nine months?

"Is Lucy excited about the baby?"

"Reckon she doesn't quite understand." He chuckled. "Right now, she's a lot more interested in Patchy. That's what she calls the pup. He'll be a good protector, won't let her out of his sight. When you swing up our direction, you've got to come see us."

"We will, then or after we've been to Dodge and start back south looking for a place to settle."

"Know yet where that'll be?"

"Someplace in No Man's Land." She smiled. "I know it's not officially open for homesteading, but if we wait till it is, Blue says all the good locations will be taken."

"He's right about that." O'Brien rubbed the cleft in his chin. "There's some nice land along Kiowa Creek, adjoining us—"

See him often? Entwine her life with his family's? Part of her desired it passionately, promised abnegation, but the deepest center of her knew better. If they were frequently together, soon or late that magic between them would change to a curse, a dream would become a nightmare.

"That wouldn't be a good idea," she said woodenly.

Flame smoldered far back in his eyes; answering fire shimmered through her. No, no, they must never be alone. A heavy sigh broke from him and he stared at the table. "Guess you're right about that, Kirsty. But I wish you'd live close enough that I could help you build your house, lend a hand when you need it. There's a pretty place on a little creek that drains into the North Canadian—big trees with a good spring, grass waist-high in the bottomland. If I'd seen it before I built on Kiowa Creek, I'd have settled there."

"How far is it from you?"

"Something over thirty miles." The side of his mouth quirked. He knew so well what she was thinking, in his man's way must be thinking the same thing. "That's a long day's ride, Kirsty. Too far for me to be a nuisance but close enough to help out if you need it. And you could keep track of Lucy."

"O'Brien!"

He shrugged. Some of the old devilment danced in his eyes. "Sure, that's underhanded, but I'll say and do whatever I have to, Kirsty, to have you where I can sort of make sure you're all right."

"I'm not your problem."

"Reckon you are." He smiled and his voice reverberated through her. "I'm your first friend in America, remember? And till you marry, Kirsty, I guess I'll feel it's kind of up to me to look after you."

"That's your trouble," she blurted before she could stop. "You think you have to look after everybody! Well, I'm not helpless, O'Brien! You don't need to worry your head about me for one single minute!"

The instant it was out, she could have bitten off her tongue. His face closed, the sparkle in his eyes died, and he got to his feet. "I still hope you'll let me show you the place. So long, Kirsty. I've got to be riding."

She had hurt him and that shamed her, but it was better to have restraint between them than that treacherous, overwhelming current that even now had her inwardly trembling.

"Let me get Lucy's dress," she muttered and fled blindly from the room.

* * *

Sew, she told herself in the next weeks. *Don't moon around over him.* Use of the American expression came naturally. She no longer thought much in Swedish, but she still dreamed mostly in her mother tongue. When that ceased, she'd feel that her spirit, too, had finished its journey and was at home here.

About this time last year, Grandfather Nils dead and only bark bread in the house, she had decided that she and Lucia must leave for America. Only a year, yet it seemed a lifetime—and it had been Lucia's. Oh, let the anemones and coltsfoot bloom on her grave, let her have home flowers in this strange land.

Swept by sudden grief, Kirsten worked doggedly till noon on Betty's third dress, a beige calico strewn with small blue flowers, but was very glad Frenchy had invited her for dinner, more for the older woman's lively company than for the imported delicacies she always served.

"Pretty girl, pretty girl!" squawked Frenchy's parrot as Kirsten entered. He'd cost Mickey a hundred fifty dollars, but the gambling livery-stable owner never counted money when he thought Frenchy might enjoy something.

Frenchy gave the brilliant-feathered bird pâté on a cracker before she set a tureen of gumbo on the table. It was flanked by olives and imported cheeses.

"This gumbo's even better than what you had last time I was here," Kirsten praised, savoring the blend of flavors and spices.

Frenchy laughed. "I like to cook now for Mickey, but it would've bored me stiff when I was young. By the time I turned fourteen, I was working in a St. Louis dance hall, by the time I was twenty, I was in Dodge City, and a few years later I went to Mobeetie. Booming it was in 'seventy-five with the buffalo trade, but when that started going flat, I came on to Tascosa. Met my Mickey, and thank God, he loved me in spite of all those miles and men. No matter what happens to the cattle business, we aim to stay right here."

As they ate she reminisced, about Billy the Kid, killed by Pat Garrett in New Mexico four years earlier, Temple Houston, old Sam's son, and many others. "Oh, they've all had their fun in Tascosa, Kirsty. Bat Masterson, Charlie Siringo, Frank James, John Poe, some outlaws, some the law, and you couldn't always tell which one was which." She switched subjects abruptly. "Do you think you can have that shamrock dress ready by Sunday? That's Mickey's birthday and I want to surprise him."

Kirsten nodded, though it would mean working after supper for a few nights. "Come over in the morning and I'll fit the pattern to you," she said, rising.

As a break from working at the machine, Kirsten had already made the hat, shamrocks of deep-green velvet outlined with white chiffon, which clustered around a big velvet bow and wisp of veiling. It exactly suited Frenchy; it was dramatic and feminine but in impeccable taste, like the dress with its basque slightly rounded in front and graceful half-length sleeves trimmed with pleated batiste, which also made up the collar.

Just thinking about it made Kirsten eager to begin. She finished Betty's calico that evening, and the shamrock gown was ready for Mickey's birthday celebration at the Exchange Hotel. Kirsten was invited, the only guest, and drank her first undiluted champagne. The McCormicks were still so much in love that she felt like an intruder, and as soon as was courteous, she escaped to her room. There was no escaping, though, the longing for O'Brien that the champagne released.

Could she risk living thirty miles from him? In sober daylight, she thought she could. It would be wonderful to see Lucy now and then, perhaps as she grew older have her for several weeks at a time; and how comforting to know O'Brien was only a day's ride away! Yes, in the day, that seemed quite feasible. But tonight— Kirsten felt his eyes on her and fever raged, till at last she had to get up, dress and walk through the deserted proper part of Tascosa while distant whoops and loud music floated from Hogtown.

The thought of Ash Bowden rose unbidden: that oddly attractive smile, that coolly penetrating glance. Inexperienced as she was, the female in her knew he could quench the fever that consumed her, seemed to devour her bones.

Why not have that, at least? And children? Why not?

Then she saw O'Brien's face, weary, with deepened lines. He couldn't be hers, mustn't be hers. Why then did even thinking of another man as lover or husband feel like gross unfaithfulness, as if she were abandoning him?

Kirsten departed Tascosa the third of May with the great satisfaction of having sent Ash Bowden his eighty dollars plus interest.

Now, she owned her wagon and team outright and had one hundred and seventy-eight dollars in cash at the bottom of the trunk. Besides her sewing for Frenchy and Betty, she'd made six more dresses and two cloaks for other women, and it seemed assured that so long as she was in town, there'd be customers. However, if she and Blue hoped to be building a house before next winter, they needed to move on. Kirsten was not enthusiastic about living in a dugout.

"Let us know when you're settled," Betty called from outside the livery where she stood with the McCormicks, waving the travelers off. "I'll be wanting another dress next fall!"

"And so will I," Frenchy added. "And hats and a cloak."

"I've got your measurements," Kirsten assured them.

There'd been no rain, but melt from the blizzard had soaked the earth. The prairie was green, including the buffalo grass, which Kirsten had seen only in varying tones of brown, and the rolling country was brilliant with pink gayfeathers, bronze and scarlet Indian blanket, yellow paintbrush, daisies, primroses, winecups and cone flowers. Butterflies of equally dazzling hues hovered over the blossoms. Morning glories trailed like bits of sky wherever they found support, and large white prickly poppies looked as ethereal as the long snow-pure trumpet blooms of jimsonweed, another poisonous beauty.

After that winter of death, Kirsten rejoiced at the meadowlark's melodious whistle and the flight of swallows, those Swedish harbingers of spring. Bob-o-links and bluebirds were flying north, and longspurs, pipits and lark buntings rose from their grassy nests. In spite of the numbers of pronghorns that had perished, small bands grazed here and there with gray-brown fawns tagging their mothers or frisking with each other.

Tiny prairie chicks, balls of fluff, followed their diligent mothers, pecking for seeds, snipping off tender leaves, and relishing any insect they could catch. "So that's what came of all that strutting and booming," Kirsten laughed to Blue.

He nodded. "Young things everywhere." With a stab, Kirsten thought of the new life that must by now have come into being at the O'Briens' and was glad that Blue felt inclined to discourse. He raised his elbow toward some small prairie dogs frisking upon their mounds. "They won't have been out of the burrow long. After six weeks below, they must think the big world is really something."

"There's a snake after that one!" Kirsten cried.

An adult barked a warning. The babies dived into a hole as the snake's head lashed forward. He just missed the last flirting tail. After a moment, he slithered off in disgust. "Bet he's cussin' in rattlesnake," Blue chuckled.

They camped that night on Lahey Creek and had a fire of fragrant mesquite wood, for many of the trees grew along the water, their frondy new leaves with fragrant catkins the fresh, soft green of the taller cottonwoods. Being out of doors was so delightful that they took a week to cover the hundred miles to Mobeetie, making the noon stops extra long to avoid the heat and let Honey and Stockings revel in lush grazing.

There were several way stations for the mail, but after weeks in town, it was refreshing to sit by the embers while Blue fiddled, or simply to watch the stars till it was time to sleep. The Star Girls were gone till autumn, and so was Orion the hunter, who had frightened them, though his following dog could still be seen on the rim of the horizon at nightfall.

The violent winds of April had calmed so that only a playful breeze fingered Kirsten's hair as she slept in the wagon with the curtains rolled up, and it was blissful, when half-roused by the shrill gossip of coyotes, the howl of a wolf or the eerie call of an owl, to watch the stars a moment before snuggling deeper into her pillow. But sometimes instead of sleep, thoughts of O'Brien filled her, stripping away her drowsy contentment.

Did he hold Lorena in his arms, face buried in her hair? When such thoughts tormented her unendurably, Kirsten put on her shoes and robe and walked, though Blue had warned her that rattlesnakes often hunted in the night coolness, until she was exhausted.

19

Having begun as Hidetown, a rip-roaring buffalo hunters'
gathering place that had sprung up near the protection of
Fort Elliott, Mobeetie was also a county seat boasting a gray
stone courthouse where school was held in an upper room.
Overlooking Sweetwater Creek, the town with its adobe
and frame buildings spread out along the hills made an attractive
sight.

"The Comanches told the settlers Mobeetie means 'sweet water,'" Blue laughed. "But it's really the word for prairie coal—
buffalo chips."

Kirsten took a room in the Grand Central Hotel on a block
shared by a saloon, the Cattle Exchange, and a wagon yard and
livery stable, where Blue got work. Beyond, a whole block was
fenced in with pickets to form a corral for the freighters' teams.
All the town's and fort's supplies had to be hauled in from Dodge
City, two hundred and eighty miles away, the apex of Ash
Bowden's Triangle.

A camp house and saloon were inside the corral, but of course
the freighters visited the other saloons and frequented the women
of Feather Hill on the town's north edge. So did the soldiers after
their payday every third month. Black soldiers were stationed
here, and many lived with their families in small cabins on the
post. The center of business for miles around, Mobeetie had two
banks, barber shops, a drugstore, a hardware store, several general
stores, a dry goods shop, and even a ready-to-wear establishment.
Temple Houston had his law office here; with his brown hair
curling about his shoulders, the towering, slender man was a romantic vision in cowboy boots, Prince Albert coat and white Stet-
son, though he occasionally wore fringed buckskins.

Houston's beautiful southern wife was Kirsten's first patron, and she was rapidly followed by Judge Woodman's pretty, auburn-haired wife, whose slim figure made her a pleasure to dress. Mrs. Boles of the dry goods store traded material for Kirsten's making her a cool muslin summer dress, and officers' wives from the fort hastened to bespeak ball gowns and riding habits. She even made one black satin gown for Ella, the "Diamond Girl" from Feather Hill, so named because she glittered with the jewels.

As in Tascosa, Kirsten could have set up a profitable permanent business, but she was eager now to finish the circuit and have a home. She left Mobeetie at the end of May with another hundred and twenty dollars in the trunk.

That night, pointing out their first nighthawk since last autumn, Blue said, "Summer's here. And a parcher it'll be if it don't rain soon. Course I'd just as soon it held off till we're on the other side of the Canadian. That can be one mean river in flood. Lots of quicksand."

Plain sand was bad enough, but the Canadian was four hundred yards wide, every inch of it fine sand with no rocks for solid footing. A stone abutment placed in the middle of the bed to anchor one of the telegraph poles stretching from Fort Elliott to Camp Supply had sunk into the sand till only a few inches showed of the platform; a freighter told them that the year before it had reared seven feet into the air from its base six feet below the surface.

To lighten the load, Kirsten and Blue got out and waded through the shallow water, urging the horses along, pushing on the rear of the wagon when it threatened to mire down.

They were watching for a good nooning spot next day, when they came over a rise and saw in the broad, shallow valley, as far as the eye could reach, a vast gathering of cattle and men riding in from several directions with more.

"General roundup," Blue explained. "All the cattlemen in an area send men and a wagon. A captain's elected to boss the show, and he splits up the country betwixt the different outfits. They comb all the ravines and draws and drive their bunch down to the main camp, where they sort 'em out and split them into bunches according to brands. When an outfit's got most of its cattle, they're herded to their home range for branding and marking the calves. That's when they get looked over for screwworms, blackleg and that pleuropneumonia that's been so bad. As the roundup moves on, outfits drop out or join up. There'll be reps here—that's men representing their ranches to claim any of their cows—from as far away as Nebraska."

"Would O'Brien be helping?"

"More'n likely. For sure Hi Allen and Sheldon Rawlings will each have sent men and a wagon. Truman Hollister or his foreman may be captain for this particular gather, since we're prob'ly on the Hollister range."

As their wagon rattled down the slope, a man who with several other hands had just driven some cattle into the valley swung his horse toward them. Could it be O'Brien? No, Kirsten thought in disappointment. This rider wasn't tall enough, and long white hair blew from beneath his black hat, which he swept off as he came within hailing range.

"Howdy!" he called as he rode alongside on his big sorrel gelding. "Reckon you're the sewing lady, ma'am. I'm Truman Hollister. My wife, she sure has been looking for you ever since we heard you were in Mobeetie."

She introduced herself and Blue, at once liking this wiry man with keen gray eyes and a weathered face that looked even browner because of his white mane, bristling eyebrows, and moustache. "Come down to the chuck wagon and have dinner before you go on," he urged. "You're only about four hours from the ranch."

"Oh, let's do," said Kirsten, turning to Blue. She hoped to see O'Brien, and besides, she'd never seen a roundup.

"Fine by me," said Blue.

Truman Hollister kept his horse beside them as they angled toward the wagon, which was drawn up under some big hackberry trees overlooking the creek. They unhitched a good way from the commotion of the camp, Blue taking the horses down to water before he hobbled them as Kirsten went on with Hollister.

"Glad you got here," he said. "It'll cheer up Persia—that's my wife—to get some new riggin's and you ought to have time to make 'em before we start packin' up."

Kirsten's look asked a question. Hollister's bushy white eyebrows knitted and pain flashed across his face before he shrugged, jerking his head toward the cattle grazing in the fine grass along the valley.

"Looks like a bunch of cows, and it is, but I reckon I lost more'n half of mine in the blizzard. We got a good offer for the ranch, and Persia, she's always honin' to get closer to town, so we're dickerin' for a smaller place a tad south of Abilene."

Regret sounded in his tone. Kirsten knew that, losses or no, had it been solely his choice he'd have stayed where he was. He grinned hardily. "We got no children to take over, and Persia didn't complain when I wanted to move up here ten years ago. Reckon it's time to do what she wants. We're not either of us spring chickens." Dismounting rather stiffly, he turned his horse over to a dark-haired youngster who came to meet him. "Ever see a chuck wagon before, ma'am?"

She shook her head, momentarily distracted from searching for O'Brien among the men who were riding up and unsaddling, leaving their horses to water and graze under the surveillance of the dark-haired boy, who was evidently in charge of the extra mounts. She had thought her wagon a model of efficiency, but this one was a marvel.

A sort of box cupboard was built into the back of the wagon, and its hinged lid let down to form a work table supported by a single leg. The shelves held cooking supplies along with tin cups, plates, and cutlery. A coffee grinder was clamped to one side of the food box. Beneath the wagon bed was a box that held the few pans that weren't in use and a dried cowhide filled with wood and cowchips. Fastened on the outside of the wagon was a water keg, and the wagon bed behind the cupboard was heaped high with bedrolls. What amazed Kirsten most, though, was a sleek Jersey cow feeding placidly near the wagon, content to remain aloof from what must have seemed to her a wild rabble of fellow bovines, and two red hens that scratched and pecked as blithely as if they were in their own barnyard.

One flapped up on the wagon seat and then scuttled into some straw spread in one corner. "Penny lays us another egg and we'll have Indian puddin' for supper, boss," said the perspiring, bald-pated man in a floursack apron as he stirred one of the kettles suspended over the fire from a pothook attached to an iron rod supported by two iron stakes. Another big cast-iron kettle steamed from the pot rack, a two-gallon coffeepot exuded a fragrant aroma from its position on a rock edged over the fire trench, and three Dutch ovens gave off delicious smells of sourdough biscuits and—was it apple pie?

The red-faced cook smoothed his black moustache and his brown eyes rested approvingly on Kirsten. "Good day to you, ma'am. You sure are welcome to camp."

"This is Miss Mordal, the sewing lady," Hollister said. "Miss Mordal, Shang Phelps makes the best coffee and sourdough biscuits you'll ever taste. That's why we put up with his mean temper and chickens and cow."

"Ain't noticed I ever throw out any milk, Tru," returned the cook. "And my sourdough ought to be good. Isn't it from the starter my great-granny gave granny when she was leavin' England? As for the coffee, secret is to grind it the night before and let it soak in water till mornin' when you sets it on the fire to simmer. Just simmer, ma'am, never boil."

Hollister wrinkled his nose. "That son-of-a—pardon me, ma'am! Is that son-of-a-gun stew I'm gettin' wind of?"

"Reckon it is. Calf broke a leg this mornin'. You take the marrow-gut, ma'am, some liver and sweetbreads and—"

"Shang," cut in Hollister, "most ladies'd rather not hear about what all you put in that stew."

The cook's thick chest swelled even more. "Never met a one yet too finicky to relish it, Tru."

"Yeah, but—"

Brushing away the ashes and coals on top of the Dutch oven nearest him, Shang raised the lid with a pothook to reveal golden-brown biscuits. Grunting, he returned the lid and straightened. "Ma'am, you git your plate and cup and go through first."

"Come on, Miss Mordal." Hollister motioned her in front of him and called Blue to join them as Shang cupped his hands and bellowed, "Come an' git it!"

Eagerly, but not jostling, cowboys of assorted sizes and shapes made for the wagon to claim their eating paraphernalia, while Kirsten, Blue, and Hollister took their heaped plates and occupied convenient stumps.

Most of the hands were young and lanky and watched Kirsten with such intentness that it was embarrassing. One was very dark, and when he turned toward her, for a flash he looked like young Bob Randall, handsome Bob Randall, who, when she'd help bury him, had been no longer handsome.

This man smiled shyly and she saw that beyond coloring and build, there wasn't much resemblance, but the shock brought back her angry sorrow that a boy should be killed for a cow. She was sure that, like Hi Allen, Truman Hollister might not have hung Bob but would agree he'd earned his fate. Of all the people she'd spoken to about the killing, only O'Brien felt it shouldn't have happened. Even Frenchy had raised an elegant shoulder and said, "It's a pity, child, but he knew what he was risking."

Again, Kirsten cried inwardly, *Such things shouldn't happen—not in America!*

"Miss Kirsty!" As if her thoughts had drawn him, O'Brien dropped on one knee before her, taking off the old gray hat. He must have washed his face in the creek, for it was clean though his clothes were dusty. His man scent was strong, salty, mingled with odors of horse and cattle. "Tru said you were coming but I reckoned it'd be after the roundup moved on. How in the world are you?"

"Well, thank you." He was even leaner than when she'd seen him in Tascosa, and she noticed the elbows were out of his shirt and some buttons missing. "How is Lucy? And Lorena? The baby has come?"

"Has he! As fine a lad as ever hollered the roof down. Almost a month old he is and already a curly head of black hair on him. Lucy brings his diapers and helps us rock him. She says she loves him almost as much as Patchy. We've named him John Matthew after—well, after my good friend who was engaged to Lorena, and my father."

No need to ask how O'Brien felt about this child, not his own, who had forced him to marry a woman he didn't love; tender pride lighted his eyes, and Kirsten, between exasperated despair and admiration, thought, *You want to protect everyone who needs you, O'Brien, and you, being you, can't help loving them. But that doesn't leave anything for me.*

The sudden twist of his mouth told her that wasn't true. Love wasn't like water in a vessel, only so much and that hoarded. It was an ever-filling, ever-sustaining spring, and though she could not bathe in it or drink her fill, she could wet her lips. She tried to be grateful for that, but then a smoldering fire in his eyes torched flame in her that coursed through her body, dissolved her loins.

Holding her breath, she wrenched her gaze away, watched his scratched, muddy boots retreat toward the chuck wagon. By the time he returned, hunkering down on his heels to eat, she could ask him in a normal voice whether the cows he'd driven up from the Pecos had dropped many calves.

"More than I expected after what they'd been through." He grinned.

"What we all need, Tru, is cows that have twins, and heifers at that."

"Might be kind of dangerous for anyone to have many cows like that," said Tru. "The Committee's run out three or four men they suspected of cattle theft, and a cowboy from the Indian Nations was found last week hangin' from a tree up Kiowa Creek."

"Plain murder," said O'Brien hotly. "The Cattle Growers' Association could stop Gus Kelman if they wanted to."

"Son, a lot of Association members don't like Kelman's methods. Told him to go to hell—pardon me, ma'am—when he tried to get them to check the identity of any stranger crossing their ranches. Since there's no law in the Strip, that bunch has taken it on themselves to ramrod things. But the Association's all for hanging cow thieves, and they don't want a lot of farmers movin' onto what they figger's their land." He went over for a second plate of stew, beans, beef, rice and biscuits. Returning, he said, "Want to take your pay in a good Hereford-cross heifer, O'Brien?"

"Better'n money," O'Brien explained to Kirsten. "I'm gathering my own cattle at the roundup, but I'm also working for Tru." Turning to the cattleman he asked, "You didn't sell your stock with the ranch?"

"No." Hollister grinned sheepishly. "I think I've bred up some pretty good cattle, but Ash Bowden don't. His partners are sendin' over some purebred critters that they don't want associatin' with plain old range cows."

"Ash Bowden?" Kirsten gasped.

Hollister nodded. "Know him?"

"From Dodge City. I knew he was buying ranch land but—well, it's still a surprise."

"Several big spreads are goin' belly-up, but he liked our place because it's well-watered and the grass is good," Hollister said with mournful pride. "That's because I never did like some who stocked according to years when we get lucky with twenty-eight inches rain. I know the average is goin' to work out under twenty, and that's what I figgered on." He sighed, wiped his brow, and grinned philosophically. "One thing about that blizzard, it culled out the weak stock. I'll be driving a good bunch south and just about enough of 'em for the size operation I'm wantin'. Say ma'am, if you'd like some apple cobbler, you better dig in."

Getting stiffly to his feet, Hollister winced. "Durned if I'm not gettin' just like my horse. He tries to roll over but he can't cut the mustard. Time we both took things easier."

He hobbled to the Dutch oven and insisted on dishing a big spoonful of juicy crust and apples onto Kirsten's plate before he helped himself. "Tell Persia I'll be home in a couple of days," he requested. "After we clean up here, I'm leavin' the rest of the roundup to my wagon boss. See you soon, Miss Mordal."

Moving more easily now, he ambled over to talk to one of his men. Kirsten gave Blue most of her cobbler, saving just a bite so she could truthfully praise Shang for it.

"How long will you be at Hollisters'?" O'Brien asked, returning with a cup of coffee.

"I don't know." She hoped he wouldn't importune her to visit Lorena. Much as she longed to see Lucy, Kirsten didn't think she could endure, just yet, to see Lorena the center of O'Brien's cherishing and Lucy's love, the center of their world.

"Well, if you're at the ranch a month, colleen, be sure and come to the Fourth of July celebration." His smile was teasing yet it embraced her. "That's America's birthday, you know, and the biggest blowout we have in these parts."

"Oh yes, the Declaration of Independence!" Sexton Carl had made it one of their English lessons to translate the document, and she had thrilled to the simple but stirring words: . . . *that all men are created equal, that they are endowed by their Creator with certain unalienable Rights.* . . . "How do you celebrate, O'Brien? Do you read the Declaration and Constitution and—"

He rubbed his chin. "Guess we don't," he admitted. "Mostly it's a big two-or three-day picnic. But there's speechifyin' and fireworks and dancin' and games. Try not to miss it. It'll be held on Wolf Creek, not far from Buzzard Roost, and won't be out of your way at all."

"You'll bring Lorena and the babies?"

"Sure am counting on it." He reddened, and Kirsten was positive Lorena shrank from venturing out with the baby born less than seven months after her wedding. "Lorena'd love to see you, and, well, it'll be easier for her if she's got a woman friend. Anyway, don't you want to see Lucy? She still asks when you and Blue are coming."

Want to see Lucy? Even after all these weeks, Kirsten missed those little arms around her neck, the trusting smile on her lips when waking, that busy little body absorbed in play. Meeting at a big celebration where it would be possible to visit Lucy without being in Lorena's home would be a tolerable way to get used to seeing herself replaced as Lucy's mother.

"We'll be there if we can." Kirsten dared not look into his eyes as a storm of rebellion wracked her.

O'Brien at least had a home and family. She never would, for to her a house without a family wasn't really a home. Of course, she might take in another child, gladly would if one needed a place, but there'd never be one like Lucy, Lucy who was the image of baby Lucia and whose care had filled that starved, half-guilty void in Kirsten's heart.

Frowning, O'Brien probed. "Is something wrong, Kirsty?"

What if I said my heart is breaking, that I can't go on without you? Hearts, Kirsten was learning, became bruised and ached and grew oppressively heavy, but they didn't break, at least hers didn't. And she could go on without him, where Lorena couldn't.

Straightening, almost defiantly meeting his troubled gaze, Kirsten took a long, deep breath against the pain. "What could be wrong? I own my team and wagon, I know for sure now that I can make a living anywhere I care to go, and I've saved some money to start farming with. Everything's fine!"

He winced at her tone. "I'm glad to hear that, colleen," he said after an awkward moment. "That's how it should be for you." Turning away, he called over his shoulder, "We'll see you then, at the Fourth of July."

Kirsten thanked Shang Phelps and Truman Hollister for the good meal. Since the team would have a long spell of restful grazing, it wouldn't hurt to cut short this nooning and get on to the ranch. She caught the horses for Blue, and before the cowboys had gone back to their labors the travel-proven but still brightly painted wagon splashed across the creek and followed the ruts that climbed to the flats.

Three hours later, they stopped in front of a long stone house shaded by large black locust trees and trellised with roses and honeysuckle.

A porch ran the length of the house; a woman spilled a green-eyed black cat out of her lap into the rocker as she rose and hurried to meet Kirsten.

"Land's sakes, I know who you must be! Judge Woodman was this way last week and he told us the dress you made his wife is just as pretty as you are! Get down, child. I'm Persia Hollister." Her broad smile included Blue. "Come on in, mister, after you've taken care of your horses, and have a bite and some coffee. The cook's out with the roundup, but there's plenty of victuals in the cookhouse and you can have the room behind the kitchen. Shang's married and has a cabin."

Slipping an arm around Kirsten, the small, bouncy, white-haired woman drew her up the steps and across the porch. "I was so afraid you wouldn't get here before we moved down toward Abilene," she confided. "Come in, do, and as soon as you've freshened up, we'll have a nice cup of tea—"

Seizing a slight pause, Kirsten started to explain that they'd eaten at the camp and that Hollister had said he'd be home in a few days. The words died on her lips as she entered the big main room. Ash Bowden crossed from a window and smiled at her.

"So here you are," he said, taking her hands. He even kissed her cheek, laughter in his silvery eyes. "I hoped you'd come before I had to start back to Dodge."

"You know each other?" Persia Hollister seemed more intrigued than scandalized by the bold intimacy of his greeting.

"Indeed we do," said Bowden, releasing Kirsten with a look that said he was, in his mind, still holding her. "In fact, you might say I'm a partner in her traveling *modiste* business."

"No, you aren't! I sent you the money with interest, in care of Minnie. Didn't you get it?"

"Have you done that well, my dear?" He beamed at her. "There was no hurry to repay the loan. I've enjoyed the association. No doubt your payment is waiting for me in a stack of letters."

"No doubt," echoed Kirsten. He treated so airily what was to her tremendously important. "When you have a chance to read your mail, I'd appreciate your signing a bill of sale that says I've paid in full."

Not the least daunted by her chilly tone, he said with a crinkling at the corner of his eyes, "Your word is sufficient. Remember, Miss Kirsten, I found out early on that you're impeccably honest. I'll give you your bill of sale here and now."

He took a fountain pen and notepad from inside his gray linen coat and, standing by the handsome mahogany sideboard, wrote for a moment, signed with a looping slash, and handed the paper to Kirsten. "There you are. All legal and proper."

"But if the money's been lost—"

"That's not your worry, Miss Kirsten. I'll take it up with the stage line if necessary." He rocked back on his heels, arms behind his back, and as always she was struck by how a smile altered the combative underthrust of his jaw. "No need to ask if your enterprise has flourished. Were you impressed enough by either Tascosa or Mobeetie to decide to set up shop there?"

"I liked both towns. People were very pleasant. But I still want a farm."

With an exaggerated sigh, he turned to Mrs. Hollister. "Please, ma'am, won't you tell her that a dressmaker should locate in a town?"

Persia's hazel eyes twinkled. "From what I hear, sir, this one will do well wherever she is. Isn't it right, dear, that the patrons you've made along the trail can just write you their needs along with the cloth, and you'll make the garment from their measurements?"

Kirsten nodded. "Once I've sewn for someone and been able to fit a pattern and dress to them, I find I scarcely need to fit them again. It's better if I can, of course, but—"

"Bound to be a better fit than mail-order clothes," said Mrs. Hollister. "Not that I haven't blessed Montgomery Ward and Sears Roebuck many a time. But let me show you your room—may I call you Kirsten? It's a pretty name and I hate Miss-ing and Mrs.-ing. Please call me Persia. Right down the hall here. Shall I have Mindy and Jess, that's our cook and her son, fill you a tub of hot water, or would you rather bathe later?"

"It would be wonderful right now, if it's not too much trouble." Kirsten was in no hurry to be exposed again to Ash Bowden's unsettling presence, and if she must be, she preferred to be as clean and tidy as possible. "Could someone help Blue with my trunk and sewing machine?"

"I saw Jess making for the wagon. Hark! They're coming in now from the back door. Here you are, then, dear. Let me know if you need anything."

They held the door open for Blue and a chubby dark-skinned youngster who carried in the trunk. When it and the Family Gem were in place, Kirsten looked around the white plastered room with its blue curtains, coverlet and rug, and thought this would be a happy place to work.

If only Ash Bowden didn't stay too long or come back often to this ranch that he had bought! It struck her that she was under his roof, in his house, and that gave her a panicked feeling till she reminded herself that she'd also lived in what was actually his wagon, and besides, the Hollisters would be here as long as she was. All the same, a sense of being in his domain lingered, and even the luxury of a hot bath with scented oil couldn't quite wash away her uneasiness.

20

As if divining Kirsten's wariness, Bowden exerted himself to charm Persia, first over tea and then at supper. He didn't look directly at Kirsten except when addressing her in a half-teasing way.

"So when, Miss Kirsten, do you expect to make your triumphal entry into Dodge?"

It was irrational, but she felt that any knowledge he had of her gave him power. "I don't know," she said almost curtly.

Persia looked surprised, and Bowden's left eyebrow rose toward thick waving hair that still shocked Kirsten with its silvery color. "Will the Camp Supply ladies get the benefit of your talents?"

"If they want them. But I have to stop at a ranch just over the Kansas line, where a friend of Mrs. Allen's needs me."

Now why had she told him that? It was none of his business.

"Ah, so you'll return by way of Deep Hole and Soldiers' Graves, rather than Odee and Busing Crossing." He did silent calculations as Mindy, a tall, moccasin-shod woman with handsome features, brought in a tray of cake and coffee. "Well, my dear, it'll be September before you raise the dust of Front Street. Surely, after your experience with the blizzard, you'll winter in Dodge."

"I'll winter at my farm." He had a way, devil take him, of goading her into saying things.

"Oh? You've decided where to live?"

"No."

"Then let me beseech you not to get in such a hurry that you choose an unsuitable place."

"It's kind of you to concern yourself, but Blue knows the region. I'm sure he'll help me pick a good location."

Bowden dropped his jocular tone. "I hope you don't settle too far from my town, Miss Kirsten. If you find you can't get enough sewing, my offer of a choice lot is still open."

"That sounds like a grand opportunity!" Persia exclaimed.

"Mr. Bowden's generous," said Kirsten drily. "But there isn't any town, and I daresay I'll have my house built before there is."

He chuckled. "I'm not as secretive as you, Miss Kirsten. I'll be glad to show you exactly where I'm going to platt the town as soon as the Interior Department rules that the Neutral Strip is public land. I'm sure that'll happen before the year's out."

"If that happens, there'll be squatters rushing in before the land's even surveyed for homesteads," sighed Persia. "Be the end of it as cattle country."

"Let's say the end of cowmen grazing on free range," said Ash. "But they can get their cowboys to homestead land around the best water, buy cheap from the railroad when it comes through, and buy out homesteaders who decide to quit, as a good many will. Stock growing won't end in the Strip; it'll just change."

"A mighty big change, what with the government ordering cattle off the leases on the Cheyenne-Arapaho reservation," Persia said. "Tru's going to drive ours straight down to Abilene. You'd better take your time stocking this place, Mr. Bowden, be sure you've got enough grass."

"I intend to do just that, ma'am," he said easily, not revealing the extent of his land purchases for his Scottish syndicate. He glanced at Kirsten. "Since you don't have that lovely little girl with you, I assume she's with the O'Briens." He spoke their name so contemptuously that Kirsten flared up.

"She is and she's happy! She's got a dog and a little brother and—and it's the right thing for her!"

"Of course," agreed Bowden. "Everyone knows children thrive in soddies with dirt floors, dirt and bugs falling from the roof into the food and rain dripping in to soak the bedding and everything else."

"I'm sure the O'Briens' house isn't like that!"

"If that big Irishman knows how to make a sod roof clean and tight, he could certainly improve his fortunes by sharing the news."

Kirsten choked with wrath. "Lucy's a lot better off with people who love her than she'd be in a mansion with cold hearts."

"My dear, there can be cold hearts as well as cold feet in soddies and warm ones in mansions. I'll warrant no one's been kinder to you than the Allens."

Ignoring the jibe, she asked eagerly, "Have you seen them lately?"

"Just before I cut across country to travel here. Hi's naturally glum about losing so many cattle in the storm. They send their love and say to come visit them when you can, even if you haven't time to sew."

"They're all well?"

"They looked to be so, especially Miss Katharine. She wore that red gown you'd designed and the effect was enchanting."

Kirsten, in amazement, felt a swift pang. How could she be jealous over a man she didn't want? It forced her to admit that though he made her nervous, the attention paid her by such a handsome, important and, above all, virile man was certainly flattering, balm to the woman part of her that felt rejected by O'Brien—no matter how often she told herself that it was because he did care about her and was honorable that he hadn't made love to her. Her body and instincts cared nothing for morality and reason. Love for O'Brien had roused them, and been frustrated by him; they quested for fulfillment. Ash Bowden, therefore, was dangerous.

Steeling herself against him, quelling that spurt of jealousy, Kirsten said, "Katharine is a remarkable woman, too strong and intelligent for most men."

"Is it that you have an exalted opinion of Miss Katharine?" His eyes danced and an improbable dimple showed in one cheek. "Or a low opinion of men?"

"I think men like to be told they're wonderful."

His eyes laughed even more. "Don't women?"

"Well, of course, but—men—men seem to need it more," she finished lamely.

"You make us sound like not only the weaker vessels, but empty ones, unless a kind lady's handy to pump us full of pride and vainglory." Through his chuckle, he gave her a straight look like the flash of a blade drawn from velvet. "Unless memory fails me, Miss Kirsten, you've never paid me a compliment or been more than passably civil. How do you explain, then, my pleasure in your company?"

"You don't need my compliments."

"Ah, but wouldn't I revel in them!"

Persia, who'd been listening to this exchange with unconcealed fascination, rose in a rustle of skirts. "I'd better talk to Mindy about tomorrow's meals," she said, and disappeared before Kirsten could escape.

"Considerate of her," murmured Ash. "While we're making sweeping remarks about the sexes, I must say that I've never seen it fail."

"What?"

"If a woman doesn't want a man herself, she can't resist matchmaking. I suppose Darwin would call it an adaptation to ensure the survival of the species."

Kirsten got to her feet. "If you'll excuse me—"

"No, Kirsten." He rose, too, and was between her and the hall. "I have a few things to say to you, and unless you'll consent to go riding with me in the morning, I'd better say them now."

She was stonily silent, though her heart faltered before it began to pound, and to avoid his eyes, she fixed hers on a framed hair wreath hanging by the door. Embroidered in the center was a date and Persia's name entwined with Truman Hollister's. Those locks of hair, gold and dark brown, must have been cut from their heads thirty years ago. How much must have happened to them since then! Their love must have changed, just as they had, but it was warmly evident in the way they spoke of each other.

Tracking her gaze, and her thoughts also, Bowden said softly, "Yes, that's the way it can be. Truman Hollister can weather losing this ranch because he has Persia, just as she was willing to come out on the prairie because that was what he wanted. Passion may start love, Kirsten mine, but it's caring that sustains it. I care for you."

"I wish you didn't."

"Nevertheless." His glance touched her black gown. "Will you wear mourning all your life?"

She touched the ruffle at her throat defensively. "In August I will leave off black."

"That's not what I mean." He didn't move toward her, but it seemed he had and she stepped back, putting a chair between them. There was no defense, though, against his words. "Will you mourn all your life for a man you can't have?"

"I'm not mourning!"

"Yes, you are. You're shrouding your womanhood, denying

what's right and natural in favor of being Auntie Kirsten to O'Brien's brats!"

The savagery hurt. She bit down on her lip to keep it from trembling. "What I do is none of your business."

"It is, because it drives me wild!" He ran his hand through his hair. "Do you know how wild, Kirsten? I've actually considered, in this day and age, of carrying you off like some ravishing robber baron from the medieval Rhineland."

She laughed out loud at that, though a thrill of danger ran along her spine. "That's not just wild, it's ridiculous."

"Perhaps, but that's not what stops me." He moved his head wearily. "I've also thought of offering O'Brien a big chunk of money for his squatter's claim and a partnership in some far-off enterprise of mine, say in Alaska, which has interesting prospects. Do you know why I don't?"

"I long ago gave up, Ash Bowden, on trying to guess why you do or don't do anything."

"Then I'll tell you. I have my own kind of pride. I don't want you through force or hopelessness or trickery, for though I don't scruple over ways to my means, such methods would bar me from what makes you a cool spring in the wasteland." Now he compelled her eyes as he chose each word. "There are other women as lovely as you, some few as resourceful. I lust for the first and admire the other, but what makes me love you is your honesty, grit, and most of all, your loving-kindness."

Stirred and regretful, she whispered, "I'm sorry. But it's no use. Can't you—won't you understand that?"

He turned from her, crossing his hands behind his back and she saw the nails go white. "Only two things would make me give up."

"If I married?"

"Only if you married O'Brien," he said with a grim laugh, swinging around to confront her. "If somehow that happens, I'll fold my campaign tent, because I know that'd bar me from you just as finally as the other reason: if you should die."

"Neither is likely to happen."

He nodded, and his insouciant grin widened, giving her a glimpse of the tough young orphan who'd fought his way up, scorning the love denied him when he needed it most. "Don't waste your pity, my sweet. Power and wealth are fairly satisfactory substitutes for love. And I'll tell you frankly that if it were a choice between them or having you and being forever poor and negligible like your own true love, I'd stay as I am."

Affronted at his slurring O'Brien, Kirsten shot back, "I'm glad you said that! Because now I don't feel sorry for you—or even like you much."

"Good. I've no use at all for your liking or your pity. Save them for O'Brien."

A hot retort sprang to her lips, but she stifled it as Persia returned with a tray of small glasses, brandy, and liqueur. "Shall we go out on the porch?" she asked, scanning each guest. "The breeze is cool but not chilling."

Kirsten pleaded tiredness and escaped, but long after she lay between Persia's lavender-scented sheets, Bowden's words taunted her. *Auntie Kirsten!* Aunt, never mother; friend, never wife.

Since the ranch was his, Bowden could have stayed as long as he pleased, but to Kirsten's relief, he left the next morning. He'd already made his farewells, but as he mounted the splendid black horse that gleamed like the dark diamond pinning his master's tie, Ash said to Kirsten, "No doubt we'll meet in Dodge City, if not before. I hope to be on hand to celebrate when you come out of mourning."

Speechless, she flushed at his double meaning. Persia would have waved him out of sight, but after he had turned once in the saddle, saluting them with his hat, Kirsten said, "I have all my patterns and fashion magazines out, if you're ready to look at them, ma'am." In spite of Persia's request, Kirsten didn't feel comfortable first-naming the older woman, at least not so soon.

"I suppose we had best get started," Persia said, entering the house. "I got the material out this morning, if you'd like to see it first." She smiled at Kirsten, inviting a confidence. "It's plain Mr. Bowden's daft about you. Did you have a spat last night?"

"We always quarrel." They were in the Hollisters' bedroom now, and Kirsten exclaimed at the purple cisele velvet with its floral pattern formed by cut loops contrasting with uncut ones. "What a marvelous color for you!"

"Tru picked it out in St. Louis last fall. You don't think it's too gaudy?"

"It's—" Kirsten groped for the English word. "It's for a queen! I have just the right pattern." She touched the sheer mesh fabric. "And this pale-green marquisette will be wonderfully cool."

"I'd like the marquisette for the Fourth of July." Persia smiled and stroked the velvet. "This is the one I can't wait to see, though. I've got slippers to match, but I'll need a hat. Maybe one with egret plumes—"

"Oh, please, no!" Feathers and even whole birds were very stylish now on hats, but Kirsten winced when she saw a creation that had surely cost a free, winged creature's life. "The egrets are so beautiful, and they're killed for their plumage. Please, I'll make a hat that will match your dress exactly."

"Have a go at it, child," shrugged Persia. "Now, shall we look at patterns?"

It was the second of July when Kirsten finished the last chemise and added sixty-five dollars to her trove.

"I'll give a big party at Christmas in our new home," said Persia, "and wear my purple dress—if I can stand to wait that long!" She gave Kirsten a hug and kiss. "You were right, dear. The hat looks better on me than anything from Paris, and you'll have to make my hats from now on, since you've put me completely off feathers. We will see you at the celebration on Wolf Creek?"

"Course we will," said Truman, shaking Kirsten's hand. "Matter of fact, lass, why don't you camp by us? We'll start in the morning with the buckboard and take a shortcut your wagon can't. Should be there by the time you are."

"I'd like to do that, thank you," said Kirsten. Hollister helped her onto the seat and in a moment the wagon was rumbling away.

They crossed the boundary between Texas and Indian Territory and camped that night near the Polly Hotel, a stage station of several cedar picket buildings situated under a cliff that rose above the Commission Creek Crossing. Oliver Nelson, the wiry, gray-eyed, rugged young man who ran the station, had cornbread and an appetizing stew ready, so Kirsten and Blue took supper with the Mobeetie stage driver, his two passengers, and the driver from Fort Elliott on his homeward swing from Camp Supply. Several Cheyenne, long hair braided but in white men's clothes except for moccasins, lounged around the buildings. These were the first recognizable Indians that Kirsten had seen, and she tried not to stare, though they certainly looked at her and one made a remark that amused his companions.

"Do you know what he said, Blue?" Kirsten asked in an undertone as they sat down at the table.

"He said your hair would make a first-rate scalp."

"Ten years ago it might have," said Oliver Nelson, bringing their heaped plates. "This hotel's where the cavalry left little Adelaide and Julia German after getting them back from the Cheyenne in 1874. The family was traveling along the Smoky Hill River when the Cheyenne attacked. Killed the parents and three other children. Poor kids were sent up to Fort Leavenworth, where General Miles's wife took them in." He gave Kirsten a keen glance. "Reckon they'd be close to your age now, ma'am."

As she and Blue walked to their camp, Kirsten shook her head. "I can't believe these things happened only ten or eleven years ago."

"Guess nobody can. But Apaches are still raidin' out in Arizona and the Army can't stop them, 'specially when they duck over into the Mexican-Sierra Madre. When folks holler about Indian devils, though, just keep in mind that time and again, whites who claimed to be good Christians have murdered Indian women and kids."

He didn't fiddle that night but went straight to bed and Kirsten soon followed. Killing off the buffalo, forcing Indians to settle on reservations instead of ranging free—these, like Bob Randall's killing, tarnished her dream of America, but they were indisputably part of the reality. Maybe from reality you worked toward the dream.

By the time they reached Buzzard Roost station, with its picket house, dugouts, log mess house and blacksmith shop, on the evening of July 3, hundreds of the big black birds with crimson heads were settling in trees along Buzzard Creek, in the valley where that stream ran into Wolf Creek.

All that day horsemen and lighter vehicles had been passing them, and at the crossing, travelers could be seen turning off from the other direction and heading west. "Goin' to be big doin's," grinned Blue. "Bet you'll have a lot of friends here."

Soon they could see wagons, tents, buggies, horses, and some oxen spread out along the valley. Blue gave a long whistle. "Whooee! It seems like people are far and few between in this country, but when you get 'em all together, they're quite a bunch! Look, there's that fancy wagon of the Allens', and the Hollisters are next to 'em. Looks like they saved us a place in the shade."

Amanda and young Gracie rushed to meet the wagon, followed more sedately by Nora and Katharine, scarcely waiting for Kirsten to descend before they embraced her. "Oh, my dear!" Amanda cried. "We were so afraid you'd been lost in the blizzard! It was a glad day when we heard you were safe!" She and Katharine both wore dresses Kirsten had made for them, and Persia had on her green marquisette. There was a joyous shout, and Meg and Marilyn Rawlings ran up to hug her.

"Mama said the drive would give her a headache," Meg said, "but Papa let us take the stage to Hardesty and Mr. and Mrs. Allen brought us with them. Oh, you do look well, Kirsten!"

"So do you," she said, laughing, glad to see that Meg wore the airy gauze with varying green stripes while Marilyn floated in the lavender muslin with printed violets. In the five months since she'd seen the sisters, they'd acquired much more assurance and looked like young women instead of girls. They were plying her with questions about the rest of her journey, when a shadow slanted across them and a small hand seized her shoulder.

"Kirs'n!"

"Oh, Lucy!" Whirling, Kirsten caught the child in her arms and held her tight, kissing the golden curls while Lucy patted her face, smearing the tears that coursed down Kirsten's cheeks, dimming her eyes so that she couldn't make out the expression on O'Brien's face.

After a moment, Lucy wriggled, reached out and touched the wagon. "Where Blue?"

"Taking care of Honey and Stockings." Kirsten set the little girl down and knelt so their eyes were more on a level. The child looked adorable in a blue dress Kirsten had sent from Mobeetie. "You're a big girl, Lucy. You must help a lot with your baby brother."

Lucy considered that. "Rather play with Patchy." She tugged at Kirsten's hand. "Come see Patchy!"

O'Brien chuckled. "Little Jack's in the wagon, too." Greeting the other women, he said, "You ladies want to come over and meet our son?"

Our son! The words plunged deep, even though Kirsten knew them for a gallant lie.

"We won't all descend on Mrs. O'Brien at once," ruled Katharine, checking Persia and her sister-in-law. "Meg and Marilyn, why don't you go with Kirsten and we'll come later."

Blue returned, and after a violent hug and exuberant kisses, Lucy appropriated his hand, too, and trotted between him and Kirsten as O'Brien led the way to their wagon a little way along the creek.

Kirsten's mouth was dry. It had been torment to see Lorena at the Christmas ball; how much worse now that she had a baby O'Brien acknowledged and was mother to Lucy! If there'd been a way to escape, Kirsten would have, but Lucy, chattering, tugged her along.

Canvas was secured over the wagon for privacy. "Mama!" Lucy called, and the word twisted like a blade through Kirsten. "Mama! Kirs'n's here! And Blue!"

The flap lifted. Lorena came out, cradling a dark-haired baby, and stood graceful and shy as a startled doe. Then she handed the infant to O'Brien and sprang down, catching Kirsten's hands.

"Thank you," she said in a soft tone and, bowing her head, brought Kirsten's hand to her lips. "Thank you for my husband."

21

Kirsten's heart stopped. Could Lorena know how she felt, sense that O'Brien had given her, Lorena, his name and protection though he loved another woman? While the black-haired baby got a grip on O'Brien's red-gold hair, and made soft little cooings and gurgles, Lorena smiled shakily at Kirsten.

"If Pat hadn't heard you singing in that blizzard—if you and Blue hadn't been in that haystack—oh, I can't bear to think of it!"

Almost sighing with relief, Kirsten smiled back, for what else could one do with Lorena? "It's because O'Brien sold me Honey and Stockings. They found the haystack." *Besides, what your husband did for me and my sister when we were strangers, that I can never repay.*

But Lorena persisted. "And then you let us have Lucy!"

"Not everyone would call that a favor," Kirsten protested. "I'm sorry there was no way to make sure you wouldn't mind—"

"Mind! I don't know how we got along without her. Pat knew how much I wanted a little girl. Now we have her, I'm glad Jackie turned out to be a boy." Who must surely resemble her dead lover. But that wouldn't disturb O'Brien. He'd be glad his friend wasn't wholly gone, and this generosity shamed Kirsten into asking to hold the baby.

Even through the silky curls she could see the pulsing in the top of the skull where the bones hadn't grown together. That and his translucent skin, soft as a rose petal, compelled wonder. His tiny fingers made Lucy's seem big. Peering into some secret world adults had long forgotten, his eyes were an indeterminate deep color that looked as if it might turn either blue or brown. He had a sweet, milky odor and wore one of the flannel gowns Kirsten had sent.

Laughing, he reached for her face. Kirsten nuzzled his neck and gave him back to Lorena. "He's beautiful," she said. Was she fated never to have such a miracle of her own?

Lucy had clambered into the covered part of the wagon. Now she emerged, clutching a wriggling puppy almost as big as she was. "Patchy boo'ful, too!" she insisted earnestly, hauling him over for Kirsten's inspection. "Kirs'n hold Patchy, too!"

The black and white dog with his floppy ears and piratical spot over one eye was a good deal harder to hold than Jackie. Ducking to avoid his pink tongue, Kirsten got well-slathered before she put him back in the wagon, assuring Lucy that he was indeed beautiful.

"Gracious," said Lorena with an apologetic laugh. "It must make you glad you don't live in such a zoo. I hope Patches didn't get you dirty."

"I wish I had a zoo just like it."

"Oh, someday you will." With a proud smile, Lorena let Meg take the baby while Marilyn admired the dolls and Jim Cator's buffalo that Lucy brought out for presentation. "Pat says you and Blue are going to homestead this fall. I wish you'd settle close to us, but he explained that with your business, you need to be closer to the stage route. Do, please, let him show you that pretty place with the trees and spring. He could help you when you needed it and we'd be able to visit sometimes."

How could any woman be so blind and unsuspecting? But that was just it; in some ways, Lorena was as guileless as Lucy. "It does sound like a good location," Kirsten said, feeling irrationally guilty at Lorena's pleased look.

Persia and the Allen women joined them then, and after making over Lucy and the baby, Amanda suggested that they all eat together. Several beeves, donated by ranchers, were already roasting in earth-covered barbecue pits, but they'd be eaten tomorrow and polished off the next day.

They had a merry supper; Lucy divided her favors among Kirsten and Blue, Marilyn and Meg, but always ran back to O'Brien, confident of her place in his arms. Perhaps, in her memory, her real father, whom she hadn't been able to coax awake, had merged with him. Several times, like a butterfly in transit, Lucy cuddled by Lorena for a moment and talked to the baby, but it was clear that O'Brien was the center of her world, and though Kirsten ached not to be part of it, she rejoiced at seeing the child she loved so happy and thriving.

After supper, Blue got out the violin. Soon he was joined by the fiddler who'd played with him at the Christmas ball, several cowboys with harmonicas and Zeke Thomas with a new accordion— bought, he told Kirsten, with part of the proceeds from the cattle hides he and O'Brien had garnered along the drift fence.

In no time, a dance was underway. Grass had already been cleared from a large square and though it was far from a smooth surface and didn't lend itself to graceful waltzing, the space was quickly filled. Seeing lanky Tom Reynolds, the yellow-haired, bushy-moustached Hi-A foreman, moving toward her, Kirsten hastily took little Jackie from Lorena and urged, "Go ahead and dance. I'll watch the children."

Lorena hung back, but O'Brien swept her along with him after beaming on Kirsten with a "Thank you, colleen."

Tom slowed his purposeful gait till his eyes lit on the Rawlings sisters. After a second he made for Meg, just as young Bill Mabry, O'Brien's other helper in the hide venture, hurried up to Marilyn.

"You should be dancing, too, child," said Amanda. "I can hold the baby."

"There's no more room," said Kirsten. "Anyway, I'd rather watch."

"You won't get away with that for long," Persia predicted. "Look at all these cowboys moving in close so they can grab you fast for the next dance."

A dozen or so men did seem to have positioned themselves as close as they could get. Since men outnumbered women ten to one, Kirsten knew she should take part, and she would, but Tom's approach had panicked her.

There were five sets of four couples each, and as the Wolf Creek fiddler called the steps, the dancers obeyed, men bowing, ladies curtsying. "Salute your partners! Join hands and circle to the left!" And so it went to his droning singsong and tapping foot. "Lady in the center and three hands round, mind your feet, fellas, don't stomp on her gown . . ."

At his concluding "Ringtailed coons in the trees at play; grab your pardners and all run away," Bart Reed, the black-whiskered, barrel-chested freighter Kirsten had met the night Blue played at Busing Crossing, grinned at her as she knelt and took the baby.

"You're purtier than ever, Miss Mordal. Not fair for you to hide behind this little guy." He nodded at a tall, thin, red-haired cowboy who had his elbows out to repel intruders. "Have a trot with Jake here, and then he'll hold the young'un while you'n me sashay."

"Please, ma'am," stammered Jake.

Kirsten didn't get to sit down again that night, and from what she could see, neither did Marilyn, Meg, or Lorena. Because only forty could dance at a time, Persia and Amanda were allowed some respite, but once Bart dared ask Katharine to dance, she, too, was kept in the clearing for one set after another.

O'Brien, Kirsten noted, took over the care of the children, obviously delighted that Lorena was having a good time. Men would have been attracted to her in any case, but that most of the women had come over to speak to her and praise the baby whenever the musicians paused to rest was largely due, Kirsten suspected, to the young woman's sitting with the Allens and Hollisters.

Only when the caller hoarsely shouted this was "plumb, absolutely, entirely the last dance" did O'Brien appear beside Kirsten and draw her into one of the sets. This swift, partner-changing, rollicking dance was nothing like the waltz, her first dance in America, that they'd had in the Allens' kitchen, but even the fleeting touch of his hands sent sweet wild quivering through her.

Would that never change? Would it always be this way, even in front of his wife and children and most of the people of this prairie world? Under the gay music sounded the other refrain, yearning, tender, that echoed through her when she saw O'Brien, or even thought of him. *Oh, will the time yet come, love, when day and night are ours?*

There was no honest, decent way. But if there had been, if she could have traded one night with O'Brien for a lifetime with any other man, she would have taken that single measure of joy and with it comforted her allotted round of night and day and day and night that belonged to him anyway, although he was Lorena's.

At sunup, Captain Busing, resplendent in his Union officer's garb, ran up the flag of the United States and led the pledge of allegiance. Kirsten had seen the flag at Ellis Island and again in the Dodge firemen's parade that had escorted her out of town, but never had those stripes of red and white, those stars on a blue ground, looked so beautiful, so full of hope and promise as on this grassy plain against a brilliant azure sky drenched with sun.

Though she had seen Bob Randall hanging, though she knew some thought the guarantees of the Constitution didn't reach to Indians or Mexicans or Blacks, the ideals *were* there, law of the land. Wasn't she saying now "with liberty and justice for all," along with most of those around her, though a few former Confederates like Hi Allen kept silent. She had to live in this country five years to become a citizen, but that morning, eyes misting, she committed herself with all her heart. America wasn't all that she had dreamed, but she would work to make it so.

As the pledge ended, she turned to find O'Brien standing behind her. "Sure, 'tis a glorious flag, colleen. When my parents came from starving Ireland, they knelt and kissed the earth."

He went then to help erect the fifty-foot-long plank table under the shade of some great cottonwood trees, and Lucy tugged Kirsten over to the swings put up for the children beside a few teeter-totters. Marilyn and Meg came to help Kirsten swing the little girl, but before long Bill Mabry wandered over and eventually worked up the courage to invite Marilyn to walk down the creek with him to see a hawk's nest. Then Tom Reynolds, wild moustache somewhat subdued with rose-scented pomade, importuned Meg to come see his saddle horse. Zeke Thomas strolled up, helped swing squealing youngsters, and confided in Kirsten that he'd never have gotten the accordion if he'd realized he'd have to play it instead of dance.

He looked so mournful that she laughed and said, "Well, just don't play it all the time, Zeke. Why don't you ask me for the first dance?"

She blushed then, hoping he wouldn't think her shameless, but he let out a whoop and exulted, "If I have that dance with you, Miss Kirsty, I don't mind workin' that accordion the rest of the time!"

Oh dear! she thought, hoping she hadn't falsely encouraged him. It was pretty clear that cowboys wearing jingling spurs cut dashing figures with the daughters of ranchers and farmers alike, and this condemned farmers like Zeke to hermitdom or seeking a bride elsewhere.

Suddenly, Kirsten thought of Bridget. Why not? Her brood wouldn't be a burden to Zeke, but would provide company in his long solitary hours and help with the work. "Zeke," began Kirsten, "have you ever stayed at Minnie Tolliver's hotel in Dodge?"

All that morning people kept arriving in wagons and buggies, on horseback and even on foot. To Kirsten's relief, August Kelman wasn't there, nor any of his Committee. As noon approached, women spread tablecloths end to end on the table and covered it with dozens of kinds of pickles and preserves, corn pone and light bread, fancy rolls, slaw, potato and cucumber salads, hominy, sauerkraut with sausage, crocks of butter and cottage cheese, and every sort of cake and pie that could be produced by resourcefulness and available ingredients. Big kettles of beans and barbecue sauce and two-gallon coffeepots simmered on cookfires. Kirsten's contribution was Swedish fruit soup, much like a pudding, concocted of stewed dried apricots and sandhill plums, thickened with cornstarch and a little precious sugar.

When the men tending the roasting beeves proclaimed them ready and carved off big pans of meat, everyone took plates and, after getting ample servings of beef, spicy barbecue sauce and beans, proceeded to the table.

The first couple wasn't through the line when a wagon wheeled up, stopping beneath the trees far enough away so as not to raise dust, and Ash Bowden sprang down.

He spoke to a couple of boys coming up from the creek, and coins flashed as he handed them some silver. With alacrity they began to unhitch his matched bays. He got a sizable box from under the seat and brought it to the table, sweeping off his flat-crowned black hat to the ladies.

"Do you suppose there's room for these things?" he asked Persia with his charming smile. "The back of the wagon's full of fireworks, but I wanted to make some contribution to the feast."

"French chocolates!" exclaimed Persia, lifting a gilt box out of the large one. "Bonbons! English toffee, nougat, nut creams! Figs, dates, salted nuts—goodness gracious, Mr. Bowden, you never found all this in Dodge!"

"I'll confess I raided St. Louis," he smiled, eyes questing till they fixed on Kirsten. "I thought this would be a special Fourth of July and wanted to help make it an occasion."

"Well, you have. Here's an extra plate, so join in," Persia invited. She stared at the wagon. "That load's all fireworks?"

"The fanciest I could get. Ought to light up the sky awhile."

"Should," agreed Hi Allen. "Mighty generous of you, Ash."

Bowden shrugged. "I live here—or soon will. It's my party, too." He stopped beside Kirsten. "Will you be surrounded on all sides by your beaux, Miss Kirsten, or is there a spot for me?"

"Why, of course you'll sit with us," declared Amanda. "We're glad you came to help us celebrate."

"Thank you, ma'am." He bowed, including Katharine, whose color heightened. "I'll most gratefully join you." He sauntered off to the barbecue servers and stopped to speak with Judge Woodman, up from Mobeetie to make the principal speech. Meg and Marilyn were among the women whose admiring eyes followed him, and Marilyn sighed.

"How can you resist him, Kirsten? He's such a gentleman and so—so worldly!"

Behind her, Bill Mabry scowled. "He's a speculator, Dad says, and prob'ly crooked as a dog's hind leg."

"I don't think you'd better let him hear you say that," sniffed Marilyn.

Persia also frowned. "We sold our place to Mr. Bowden, Bill, and I assure you, he insisted on paying more than we asked and has given us every consideration. I'm disappointed to hear you talk like that about a public-spirited man who wants to help the region go forward."

Besieged, Bill ducked his head so his cowlick stood up boyishly. "I still say he's too smooth," he persisted. "Aims to build a town in the Neutral Strip and get rich selling lots—"

"He's already rich," said Amanda, giving the young man a motherly pat on his muscular brown hand. "Don't be a grouch, Billy. You can eat with us, too."

"Maybe I'm not wanted," he said stiffly.

Marilyn raised a dainty shoulder and her coppery hair glinted. "You're welcome if you can be polite, Mr. Mabry."

There was no way to keep Ash out of their group, but Kirsten took her plate to one of the blankets spread by the wagons and sat down between Amanda and Lorena. As if to cooperate, Lucy settled against her knee. The Rawlings sisters with Tom Reynolds and a rather glum Bill Mabry shared another blanket. O'Brien leaned against the wagon with Hi, Blue, and Truman Hollister, but when Ash came up, he nonchalantly sat beside Persia and

Katharine in a way that put him squarely in Kirsten's line of vision.

"I've always wondered what ladies say when men aren't listening," he said, glancing merrily around. "I seem to have interrupted some interesting observations. Are they a secret?"

Persia bridled but Amanda giggled. "Oh, do tell him, Persia! It'll teach him not to pry into female conversations."

"If you must know," Persia said a bit crossly, "I was saying that some Mobeetie friends told me Mrs. Judge Woodman's hair's not naturally auburn. She colors it by using soda shampoos and drying it out in the sun."

"Scandalous!" said Bowden enthusiastically. He looked around till he spied the lady in question and sadly shook his head. "I'd gladly render an expert opinion, but I can't see her hair for her hat. Fetching gown, though. Did you make it, Miss Kirsten?"

Kirsten nodded, and all the women in the group laughed. "She made all our dresses," Persia said. "Walking advertisements, that's what we are—"

An explosion cut off her words, followed by rapid popping and more eruptions. Even in the sunlight, dazzling patterns formed in the sky and starlike bursts of various colors rose high before showering down.

"The fireworks!" Ash jumped up and so did the rest of them, peering toward the wagon from which explosions large and small continued to come as more rockets hissed into the blue or sputtered as they caught in tree branches. The boys Ash had hired to tend his horses were doing their best to slink out of sight. Ash took a step and then shrugged.

"Guess the lads tried to filch a few firecrackers and set off the whole shebang. Can't stop it now, so we might as well enjoy it."

It was several more minutes before the wild display ended. If Ash was chagrined, he didn't show it and brushed aside the embarrassed apologies of the boys' fathers. "Just makes more time for dancing tonight," he laughed and went to choose dessert.

At such times, it was impossible not to like him. As people returned to their spectacularly disrupted meal, Kirsten's smile faded. Those horsemen riding in . . .

Their leader, bulky in the saddle and sitting it awkwardly as few men from these parts did, looked familiar. She shaded her eyes to see better. Flat nose, eyes sunk deep in a heavy face, reddish fringe of beard and side-whiskers. August Kelman!

She made a choking sound, started to spring up, but swirling blackness dizzied her, and in it she saw Bob Randall on the rope, the Committee's sign on his chest. Shaking her head to clear it, she tried to rise again but strong fingers caught her wrist.

"Colleen," said O'Brien softly. "Don't give that hooligan a chance to demean you or I'll have to fight, maybe kill him, and though he'd be no loss to the Triangle, it would sort of spoil the party."

"But he—" O'Brien's eyes checked her protest even before he spoke with quiet sympathy.

"I know, Kirsty. His kind make mock of what we celebrate today. But when law comes to the Strip, he and his Committee will be out of business. I know it goes against the grain, but try to ignore him."

"That's good advice," said Bowden, on Kirsten's other side. "I hope Judge Woodman's speech is short, because I want to make one myself before I start back to Dodge."

"You can't leave so soon," objected Amanda. "The fun's just starting! There'll be races this afternoon, and I'll wager the dancing won't stop till the sun comes up."

Bowden slanted a glance at Kirsten. "I wish I could stay, dear lady, especially with such delightful company, but some of my Chicago partners are arriving tomorrow, so I'll keep them waiting for a few days as it is."

"But to come all this way for just a few hours!" exclaimed Persia.

Ash smiled at Kirsten, thrusting jaw relaxed. "Ah, but I knew it would be a very special Fourth. Besides, even if my fireworks went off prematurely, I do have something to say."

Kelman and his companions filled their plates, though they'd brought no contribution, and located some shade at the far end of the wagons. Kirsten was glad they were out of sight. Someone banged on a kettle, and Judge Woodman, a tall, courtly man, ascended the improvised platform of a wagon with wheels blocked to keep it stable.

"My friends," he began in a sonorous voice. "Let us consider today our sacred Bill of Rights, the first ten Amendments of our Constitution, which guarantee our freedoms."

Kirsten had studied them in Sexton Carl's book. They were part of her dream of America, and now she listened intently:

freedom of religion, of speech, of the press, of peaceable assembly; freedom to bear arms in order to act as militia; no quartering of soldiers in homes without owner's consent; no search without a warrant issued upon probable cause . . .

As the judge read on, Kirsten realized that five of the Amendments dealt with the rights of a person suspected or accused of a crime, and this increased her outrage at Kelman. He had not only robbed a young man of life but acted in scorn of the supreme law of the land. *He* should be accused; *he* should go on trial. She joined fiercely in the clapping and cheering at the end of the judge's speech and didn't notice that Ash Bowden had left their group till she saw him striding lithely to the wagon.

The judge, still standing on the wagon bed, lifted his arms for silence. "Ladies and gentlemen, though we're gathered in Indian Territory, and come from Texas, Kansas, and the Neutral Strip, we all live in a region bound together not only by stage and freight wagons, but by common interests and needs. We're fortunate to have among us today a man some might call a dreamer, and some a hard-headed entrepreneur who knows a winning thing when he sees it." Pausing, Judge Woodman grinned. "I think he's both and I know he's worth hearing. It's rare to find a man of energy who knows how to get things done and also has the vision to know what these things should be. The fireworks he brought in the wagon went off a little early, but I'll wager he has more up his sleeve. Friends, I'm honored to present another friend, Mr. Ash Bowden."

Climbing down, the judge led the clapping, which exceeded even that the judge had received. Clearly, the early blast of rockets inclined the crowd to give him credit for his generosity at the same time that it created sympathy for him—and a certain satisfaction in seeing that even such a successful man's intentions were sometimes amusingly thwarted.

Ash ascended, bowed, and took off his hat. "Thank you, ladies and gentlemen, for letting a stranger speak at your celebration, though truth to tell, I don't feel strange, for I've done business with a number of you and count many as friends." For a while, he spoke of the Triangle and its prospects, before, more somberly, he detailed its problems. "With more people coming into this country, Dodge City can no longer be the main city, but should, like Mobeetie and Tascosa, stake down one corner. What the Triangle needs is a centrally located hub that is served by a railroad. It will have stores rivaling those of Kansas City, a hospital, opera house, churches, and excellent schools, including an academy or even university so our sons and, yes, daughters—" did he look toward Kirsten as he said that?—"will not have to go far away for higher education.

"The natural location for such a city is the Neutral Strip." He raised a hand at the murmuring. "Yes, I know the Strip isn't open to settlement, but take my word, the Interior Department, before this year of 1885 is out, will rule it public land. Settlers will rush in and legalize their claims later. Towns will sprout like mushrooms, most of them no more substantial than mushrooms. Central City, my town, won't be like that. Till the Strip's formally opened, I won't sell lots." His smile flashed. "That would be illegal. But I'll provide titles that will be regularized as soon as a land office is set up, and meanwhile I'll lobby for the railroad that will carry your stock and produce quickly and cheaply to market. What I'm here for today is to tell you the future I see for the Triangle and to ask your support for its future heart—Central City!"

Bowing to thunderous applause, he stepped down and was immediately surrounded by congratulators and questioners. Extricating himself as soon as he civilly could, he made his farewells to Kirsten and his other dinner partners. Katharine furrowed her brow at him.

"I think the crowd applauded you with extra warmth because your fireworks did go off ahead of time," she remarked. "It proved you human. May I ask, sir, if it was really an accident?"

"Kate!" gasped Amanda.

Ash Bowden smiled. "Astute of you, Miss Katharine, but you can't expect me to plead guilty to such a trick." He regarded her quizzically. "Would there were some way to let you evaluate my business partners!" His gaze swept round to Kirsten. "Again, thank you all for your company. Miss Kirsten, I hope that I'll see you in Dodge."

The same boys brought his team and hitched them to his wagon. Paying them, he lifted his hat toward Kirsten's group, and stepped lightly to the seat. Katharine watched him with a grudging smile. "One has to admire his nerve."

"Kate," Amanda chided. "How you could make such an accusation!"

"He didn't deny it," said Katharine.

Kirsten scarcely heard them. To her wrath and dismay, August Kelman was moving to the speaker's wagon. And it wasn't only the men who'd come with him who were cheering and applauding.

22

Even so, the clapping was thin and scattered. It couldn't have escaped Kelman's notice that none came from cattle-men or cowboys. He reared back, thumbs hooked in his belt, and his attempt at a smile only bared his teeth.

"Neighbors," he began ponderously, "the judge made a dandy speech about the law and Mr. Bowden told you about what the Triangle can be. But you folks livin' in the Strip know well that right now we don't have law and till we do, we won't have any towns that're more than hangouts for drunks and thieves. Some of you already know about the Committee. We've brought back your stolen stock. We've smashed distilleries that encourage men to get hog-drunk. We've cleared off outsiders who've come in and tried to take over your claim. There's not enough law and order in the Strip, God knows, but we're all there is."

At this, his companions whooped and cheered, shouting, "Pour it on, Gus!" "Tell 'em straight!" and similar exhortations.

A farmer woman rose, one baby in her arms, a toddler hanging to her skirt, and called shrilly, "Gus Kelman brought back my milk cow some no-goods ran off. 'Thout him, my children wouldn't have milk to drink. I say God bless Gus and his Com-mittee!"

That evoked more spirited applause, and Kelman's smile be-came less of a snarl. "It was your cow, ma'am," he called. "Me'n the boys only done what was right. And that's why I'm here, neighbors, to ask you to help. First, if you live in the Strip, I'm invitin' you to join the Committee. Second, I'm askin' you ranch-ers, wherever your range is, to stop feedin' and shelterin' every deadbeat that comes your way."

A roar of derision came from bunches of cowboys, but Kelman

went on doggedly. "You ranchers have a responsibility to keep out riffraff. 'Less'n a stranger has a good, honest reason for being in the Triangle, you'd ought to run him off."

Hi Allen stepped forward, face stony. "Kelman, like I told you before when you came around with this nonsense, no man's ever stopped at my ranch without getting meals and a bunk, and never will. I'm not checkin' into their pedigrees. None of my business and sure none of yours."

Kelman reddened, head coming forward on his thick shoulders. "That's fine for you ranchers who've got men to chase after your stock and protect you. But what about the rest of us? You've had it your way so long, you big bugs, that you reckon you're kings and farmers don't count."

A rumble of agreement came from his supporters. Hi said, "I don't have to make excuses to you or anyone, Kelman. But I do know I've sent many a quarter of beef over to settlers who were havin' it rough. And I'll tell you this. Don't come on my land huntin' for men to hang!"

He moved back to lean against the wagon. Kelman glared, small eyes protruding from puffy fat. "It's not your land," he blasted. "You don't have legal title to a single acre!"

"No more do you," returned Hi, unruffled. "But you know my range. As of today, I'm warnin' you and your gang to keep off it."

Kelman spread his hands as if appealing to heaven and shouted, "Hear that, neighbors? Maybe we'd ought to decide right now if'n these ranchers can harbor claim jumpers and thieves!"

Amidst roaring applause and cries of approval for Kelman, Kirsten sprang up and almost ran to the wagon. Clambering into it, she cupped her hands and called loudly as she could, "Americans!"

Hulking above her, Kelman glowered. "What're you doing, you crazy female?" His eyes widened slowly in recognition. "Why, you're that foreign gal with the wagon we met whilst we were—"

He broke off, but Kirsten picked up his words. "We met while you were hunting Bob Randall, Mr. Kelman." Raising her voice, she looked out at the faces, all startled, some hostile, others concerned. "I did some counting while Judge Woodman read the Bill of Rights today. Five of those Amendments protect the rights of a person suspected of a crime. Half of the ten!"

"What about it?" growled Kelman.

"You searched my wagon," said Kirsten. "That's against the

Fourth Amendment. You hanged Bob Randall without a trial or due process of law and that broke the Fifth, Sixth, and Seventh Amendments and I believe you broke the Eighth, too, because if taking a man's life for stealing a cow isn't an excessive fine or cruel and unusual punishment, I don't know what you'd call it. Bob Randall said he didn't steal the cow, that it was due to him in wages."

Kelman advanced on her, working his big hairy hands. "So you did hide him!"

"Yes, and I wish I'd hid him long enough that you'd never have caught him!" Too furious to fear him, Kirsten turned and, though she was trembling violently, was herself amazed at the strength of her voice as she appealed to the crowd, friends and foes alike. "In Sweden, there is a song about 'Wonderful America.' But it's not wonderful when a man is killed for a cow!"

There was stunned silence. *I've only made them angry,* she thought. *Even my friends.* But O'Brien was striding toward her. "Good for you, colleen!" he shouted.

The wildest applause of the day burst out, joined by all but the rest of the Committee. Dazed and spent, Kirsten felt as if her knees were buckling. Kelman's face worked. "You're going to wish you'd kept out of this," he grated beneath the shouts and clapping. "You little foreign slut!"

O'Brien jumped into the wagon, ducked a wild swing from Kelman, and hit him so hard in the fleshy middle that Kelman was knocked out of the wagon. O'Brien sprang after him. Gasping, Kelman got halfway to his knees; with amazing rapidity for such a heavy man, he lunged at O'Brien and bore him to the earth.

They toppled back and forth, Kelman so much the heavier that it seemed he would crush O'Brien if he got on top of him or could grasp him in those bearlike arms. Kelman, gripping O'Brien, rolled over, pinning him, and groped for his throat. His fingers closed, dug in, but O'Brien wrenched free, got a knee up, and sent Kelman over backward.

Panting, O'Brien rose to a half crouch as Kelman caught his breath and lunged again. O'Brien leaped to one side and kicked Kelman in the rump, sprawling him face down. From the corner of her eye, Kirsten saw one of Kelman's men feel under his vest as if for a hidden gun. Truman Hollister saw it, too, and reaching into his wagon produced a double-barreled shotgun.

"There'll be no shootin'!" he commanded. "Anyone draws a gun is goin' to get full of shot."

Pushing himself slowly to his feet, spitting dust, Kelman didn't face around but stood heaving. "This ain't no way to do, O'Brien."

"Then tell Miss Mordal you're sorry."

Kelman spun, sledging his huge fist out. O'Brien almost went down at the force of the blow. His nose gushed blood. But as Kelman whooped and dived for him, O'Brien, still bleeding from his nose, sidestepped and thrust out a foot that tripped the bigger man. He was on him as Kelman hit the earth; he dragged back both Kelman's arms, forcing them upward till he screamed.

"Stop it, O'Brien!" Kirsten begged. "What good's an apology he doesn't mean?"

O'Brien continued the pressure. "All right!" Kelman choked. "I—I'll apologize!"

"Do it."

"Didn't mean no harm," Kelman muttered. O'Brien drew the arms higher. Kelman yelped. "I'm sorry, ma'am!"

O'Brien let him up. Kelman, still bent, grabbed O'Brien and threw him over his shoulder. O'Brien lay stunned. Kelman drew back his booted foot in line with O'Brien's head. Kirsten grabbed one of the chunks of wood blocking the wagon wheels and swung it against the back of Kelman's head. He went down on top of O'Brien, who was reviving now.

People came running. Kirsten's fear that she might have killed the Committee leader subsided as he moved dazedly. His friends helped him up, supporting him between them. Hi Allen said to them, "Let me just tell you boys now that if you give O'Brien any trouble over this, let alone Miss Mordal, I'll make it my business. Now why don't you just pile on your horses and get out of here?"

Kelman sagged half-conscious. One of his friends said, "Fine way of thankin' Gus for all he's done!"

"I don't thank him for anything," Hi said. "And keep off my range or you may find out you're not the only ones who know how to toss a rope over a cottonwood limb."

Sullenly angry, Kelman's men got him in his saddle, one walking along beside him as they started off. Lorena ran up, dropping on her knees beside her husband, and Persia followed with water and a cloth.

Expertly washing away the blood, she peered critically at his nose. "Guess it's not busted," she said. "But it's a good thing he never sat down on you good and proper. You'd be a pancake!"

Aghast at what she'd caused, Kirsten whispered, "I—I'm sorry. Oh, O'Brien, are you really all right?"

"No need to be sorry, colleen." He got slowly to his feet, wincing but able to move everything. "You made us remember what today's all about. I'm doggoned proud of you."

"So are we," said Katharine, and Persia and Amanda nodded. Judge Woodman bowed to Kirsten and, though his eyes twinkled, they were respectful. "You win the honors today, Miss Mordal. That's a most interesting point you made, that half the Bill of Rights protect a suspect's freedoms. An excellent point."

"Well," said Truman Hollister, still holding his shotgun, "if a sheriff won't run in anybody who steals my cattle, I reckon I'd do my best to hang the fella high. But, Miss Kirsten, I'll make durn sure he's guilty."

"Heavenly days, Tru!" sniffed Persia. "Only thief you ever caught, you wound up givin' him a quarter of beef on account of his family was hungry."

"Time for the races!" someone shouted.

"I was goin' to race," said O'Brien, and grinned. "But you know, I've plumb lost my ambition."

"Come with me, Pat," urged Lorena. Lucy, who looked as if she'd been crying but was now prattling relieved endearments, caught his other hand, and the crowd moved over to watch the races. Kirsten, drained from the encounter with Kelman and the fight, would have liked to go off by herself but thought that might look as if she regretted what she'd done. She was abashed, but not sorry, so she stood with her friends to watch the contests.

Tom Reynolds on his claybank won the mile. Bill Mabry triumphed in bareback racing, and a Lazy R hand won at leaning from the saddle of his galloping horse to pick up sticks. Meg won the ladies' race, causing Tom Reynolds to beam as proudly as when he'd collected his winner's purse. There was a race for children under twelve, and the events finished with three-legged races for the children, who tried to hop fast with their right legs in the same sack.

By then it was time to eat again, and after the food was cleared away, the dancing started. Zeke Thomas eagerly came to claim the first dance with Kirsten, and afterward picked up his accordion with good grace. Every partner Kirsten had praised her for speaking out, but her head throbbed. She worried that in spite of Hi's warning, Kelman might try to get back at O'Brien, and finally, pleading a headache to Tom Reynolds, she started to her wagon.

O'Brien, who'd held Jackie and Lucy while Lorena danced, got up with a child asleep against each shoulder, and said quietly, "Rest you well, colleen. I was feelin' kind of sorry your first Fourth went the way it did, but when I chewed it over, I'm glad. You saw the law may be there but people have to keep it true. And you made everybody think." His lips brushed her hair. "Bless you, Kirsty."

He couldn't touch her. The babies were between them, neither his by blood yet his all the more since he claimed them. "I'm sorry you were hurt," she said softly. "But thank you, O'Brien. Thanks for taking my part."

He gave a wry chuckle. "I better thank you for taking mine. From what they say, if you hadn't knocked Kelman flat, he'd have caved in my skull." His tone changed and that almost painful sweetness flowed between them, that invisible but imperious current that threatened to sweep them off their feet. "Anyhow, Kirsty, I'll always take your part."

To hide her feelings, she kissed the children and, unable to resist, let her mouth touch O'Brien's hand. "Kirsty!" he breathed. She turned at once and fled to the wagon.

Yours and only yours . . . She was sure he loved her, too, but it never must be spoken.

The music and dancing went on till nearly dawn. Kirsten drowsed fitfully, Kelman stalking her fleeting dreams so that she was relieved to awaken. She was up and had biscuits in the Dutch oven when Blue, exhausted, but grinning happily, got into his bedroll for a quick nap.

The giant coffeepots had never stopped simmering, and as the eastern sky flamed gold and rose, leftovers were spread on the table along with pies and cakes and newly made biscuits and gravy. Many of these people wouldn't see each other till the next Fourth and made haste now to finish their visiting.

"I wrote Mrs. Harding, the Camp Supply chaplain's wife, dear," said Persia. "She says you're welcome to stay with them. Their only daughter married a surgeon recently posted to Alaska and they'd be glad for company."

"Oh, I shouldn't trouble her," Kirsten demurred. "Surely I can find something in the town."

"Lord love you, there isn't a town! Just the stockade out in the middle of the Cheyenne-Arapaho lands." At the face Kirsten made, Persia said bracingly, "Of course you should stop there! I'm sure the ladies have already heard about you from friends at Fort Elliott. They'd be mightily disappointed if you skipped them—and they'll make good customers later, for they're always getting sent off to some camp in the wilderness, but they have to dress nicely and keep up appearances."

She and Truman made their farewells, promising to send their new address when they were settled, and drove off as five women approached Kirsten about sewing for them. Seeking cover between her wagon and the trees, she took their measurements, made notes on what each wanted and her own private observations about what colors and styles would suit, and asked if they'd like her to buy material in Dodge, make up the dresses, and send them by stage with a bill.

"Oh, would you do that?" asked Daisy Ballou, a young yellow-haired farmer's daughter of about Kirsten's age who planned to marry that autumn. "Ever since I saw that beautiful red dress of Mrs. Hoodoo Brown's, I've had my heart set on having you do my wedding dress, and mama's let me save butter and egg money. I can't afford a white dress, for just this one time, but if you could make it blue or pink or pale gray—"

Another wedding dress! Kirsten wondered if she were fated to sew dozens of them but never her own. Controlling the rush of envy, she compelled herself to study Daisy's milky skin and dark-lashed hazel eyes. "Why not a soft dusty green? I can use lots of ecru lace to trim the wedding gown but make a different collar and cuffs for when you don't want to be so dressy."

Daisy glowed. "That sounds lovely! I'm really thrilled about it, Miss Mordal. It'll be the first dress I've ever had that we didn't make out of hand-me-downs from my aunt back in Iowa."

It might well be the last such gown, since she was marrying a farmer. Kirsten resolved that the material she found would be priced as low as credibility allowed and she'd do a wedding cap and fancy sunbonnet.

A rancher's wife who was a friend of Mrs. Judge Woodman's had brought her material, gauzy black silk crepe, but the others were glad to trust Kirsten's selection.

"Don't forget us," said Amanda, giving Kirsten an affectionate hug. "If you don't have your house built before winter, you're welcome to stay with us." She glanced significantly at Tom Reynolds and Meg. "It may not be too long till there's another wedding dress to sew. And from the way Bill Mabry's stayed close to Marilyn, there could be a double wedding. All the twins needed was a chance to get away from mama, where they could laugh and act natural."

Kirsten felt another pang, though she was glad for her friends. When she'd met the sisters at the ball, she'd thought them too meek and spiritless to ever escape their mother's domination, but that had certainly changed. Perhaps Sally had realized that she'd better treat her daughters with more consideration if she hoped to see much of them after they left home.

Almost floating in their pretty summer dresses, they came over to embrace Kirsten warmly. "Remember, once you're settled, we'll come see you if you don't visit us," Meg threatened gaily. Tom and Bill helped them into Hi's elegant wagon.

Brushing a kiss on Kirsten's cheek, Katharine spoke so softly no one else could hear. "Two men love you, dear, but only one's free. You'd better take him."

Softly also, Kirsten said, "Why don't you?"

Katharine stiffened. Then her thin, handsome face broke into a smile. "Maybe I will!"

Their wagon rolled away in the stream of other vehicles and horsemen. The O'Briens came over to say goodbye, and Lucy clung to Kirsten, giving her resounding kisses. "Bye-bye, Kirs'n. Come home with Lucy and Patchy?"

"Not now, honey."

"I wish you would," said Lorena. "Pat could make you a house close to ours. Do think about it, Kirsten."

Trying not to betray guilty shock, Kirsten said, "You're very kind, but we'd better settle on our own land."

"Try to let me know about when you'll be getting to Jim Lane's road ranch," said O'Brien. "I'll meet you there and show you that good location I told you about."

Dare she live within a day's ride of them? Bowden's taunting words came back: *Auntie Kirsten.* But what was wrong with that? If she couldn't be Lucy's mother, that was the next-best thing.

"Whatever I decide, I'll let you know," she said, and got into

the wagon, quickly, before he could touch her and and rouse that
futile hunger that understood no laws but its own.

The horses were well rested, so Kirsten drove part time while Blue
slept, and they made the twenty miles to Camp Supply in time to
hear silvery bugle notes as the flag was lowered from its pole on
the parade ground. Indians—according to Blue they were Cheyenne, Arapaho, and some Kiowa off the Fort Sill reservation—
were camped outside the stockade but showed no interest in the
travelers. Freight trains with supplies, mail and passenger coaches
from Dodge and the daily stage from and to Mobeetie were more
exciting than a single wagon.

A young sentry called an officer, who paid a lot more attention
to Kirsten than the Indians had and escorted the wagon to the
Hardings' quarters. Pink-cheeked, gray-haired Mrs. Harding made
Kirsten feel immediately at home, and showed her to their daugh-
ter's room. There was a small room at the back, and Blue, Mrs.
Harding said, could stay there.

"Thank you, ma'am," he said, then surprised both women by
adding, "but if it's all the same to you, Miss Kirsty, I'd like to visit
with the Kiowas while you're busy here. Maybe some of my old
friends are out there."

"Well, of course, Blue, if that's what you want. Why don't we
plan to leave in about a month?"

He nodded. "I may see you before that, but for sure I'll be back
then. Is it all right if I take the team so I can look after 'em good?"

"Take the wagon," Kirsten urged.

He shook his head. "Better not, Miss Kirsty. Indians believe in
sharing everything, and they'd think I was stingy if I didn't hand
out our supplies."

"Well, you should take some presents. Get whatever you think
they'd like."

He thanked her and left as soon as her things were unloaded.
Alone, glancing around the rose organdy and satin room, Kirsten
let her hand rest on the wheel of the Family Gem. "We've traveled
a long road, my good helper," she said as if it could hear. "This
last stop, and then we'll be in Dodge close to one year from when
Lucia and I got off the train."

Lucia. Kirsten's eyes filled.

Would the Swedish wildflowers be blooming on her little sister's grave? Kirsten touched the black ruffle at her wrist. She thought her heart would always constrict with pain when she thought of Lucia, but she was forced to admit that days could pass now when she remembered Lucia only at night when she said her prayers. Often, and for this Kirsten was grateful, she thought of Lucia in some happy or funny moment, and would smile fondly before grief stabbed her. As time passed, the good memories lasted longer and the pangs hurt less. It was as if Lucia were still alive but living at a distance.

"Supper, dear," called Mrs. Harding at the door. Kirsten straightened her hair, gave the Family Gem a final pat, and went out to get better acquainted.

23

As the wagon crossed the bridge over the Arkansas, which was running low because of the continued drought, and rolled up Bridge Street to Front Street, Kirsten gasped and caught Blue's arm. She remembered Ash's saying, after the blizzard, that there'd been a fire in Dodge that January, but she hadn't realized its destructiveness. A grocery store and the Union Restaurant on the north side of Front Street were still in charred ruins; and the flames had jumped the railroad track to devour several warehouses and stores and damage the east side of the Iowa Hotel.

"It hit that brick store on the corner, and that's where folks must have finally got it stopped," said Blue.

Thank goodness the rest of the town had escaped, including Minnie's hotel. And there was the depot, where one year and ten days ago, Kirsten and Lucia had been approached by Selina. Kirsten glanced at Selina's place, and though saddened to remember her little sister's illness, a smile touched her lips, for it was in Selina's that O'Brien had come to their aid.

That seemed long ago, but after all, it was a year in which more had happened than in all the rest of her life. She had come to America, lost her sister, earned her living while acquiring the language she now dreamed in most of the time, started her own business, which she now owned completely, and journeyed the roads that were the Triangle's lifelines, meeting the ugliness of the Committee and the shock of Bob Randall's lynching. In the blizzard, she'd learned the fragility and sweetness of life and found Lucy, whom she'd had to let go. She'd danced her first dance in America with O'Brien and all the time loved him more, in spite of his belonging to Lorena—and Ash Bowden's attractiveness.

"Shall I let you off at Minnie's before I go on to the livery?" Blue asked.

Kirsten shook her head. "Let me off at Lucia's grave, Blue. Will you please see if Minnie has room for us? If she does, you might unload our things. I'll walk back."

Bless Bridget! She and Annie had faithfully tended the only land Lucia would claim in America, the small plot beneath the locust tree, enclosed by the wrought-iron fence. Wild roses scented the air, and sure enough, bright among them were golden coltsfoot and anemones, blue as Lucia's eyes. They had dared to bloom in this dry, hot country.

Sinking on her knees, Kirsten talked to her sister, blinded by tears, hoping she somehow might hear, and told her about her namesake, Lucy. Then she was silent, waiting for some answer, some sense of response, but there was only the sweetness of the Kansas flowers and the beauty of those sprung from Dalarna seed, flourishing here.

Perhaps that was an answer. And suddenly, the blue of the anemones became Lucia's eyes. *Take off that black, Kirsten, for goodness' sake! I'm happy where I am, with mother and father and Grandfather Nils. Remember us, never forget, but live in your new world and be happy.*

The words, of course, sounded only in Kirsten's mind, but she felt they came from her sister. Bending to kiss the flowers, Kirsten said a prayer for all her beloved dead, and then, facing the wind, walked back to town.

She was scarcely inside the hotel when Minnie and Bridget embraced her, laughing and full of questions. "What'll you have first?" asked Minnie, taffy curls dressed as preposterously high as ever. "A bath or dinner?"

"A bath would be wonderful! You have room for us, Minnie? I want to make up some dresses before we look for our homestead." Besides the five dresses she'd promised to do at the Fourth of July celebration, Kirsten had six orders from ladies of Camp Supply, and thought it best to get them done as soon as possible.

"Your old room's ready," said Minnie. "If Blue'll help out a little, I'll board you both for fifty cents a day, which I'm hoping you'll pay off by making me a cloak out of some lovely superfine wool from Tibet I bought in Kansas City."

"I'd love to make it," Kirsten said. She caught sight of Annie carrying buckets of hot water from the kitchen to the hall. "Annie! You've shot up like a lily!"

The thin, pale young girl set down the buckets and ran to give Kirsten a hug. "I'm glad you didn't say I've grown like a weed the way everybody else does! Oh, Miss Kirsty, thanks for my pretty dress! We've run out of hem to let down, though."

"A flounce should fix it," Kirsten said with a smile. Annie's carroty hair had darkened, and her figure revealed a hint of budding. "I think we'll need to let out the bodice, too."

"Oh, do you?" Blushing with pleasure, Annie hugged Kirsten again and ran off to her task.

There was something different about Bridget. Her face looked softer, younger. "Why, Bridget," Kirsten said. "I didn't know you had wavy hair. It looks pretty, fluffed around your face like that."

"You're not the only one that thinks so." Minnie sighed between annoyance and resignation. "Bridget turned down three proposals last winter because she didn't think the men would make good fathers to her kids, but last month here comes this black-haired Welshman out of No Man's Land and may I be switched if he didn't court Bridget like they were both sixteen!"

"He's grand with the children," Bridget glowed. "They're that wild to move to his farm where they can have a dog and ride horses and—"

"Muck out stables," supplied Minnie. "Hoe corn and milk cows and fight the grasshoppers for crops."

"Sure, and the young ones know they'll work," said Bridget.

"So will you, and harder than you do here."

"That may be," returned Bridget patiently. "But 'twill be in my own house for my own family. I call that happy work, Minnie."

Kirsten intervened. "When's the wedding?"

"As soon as Zeke harvests his corn and builds on two rooms for the children." Bridget's golden-brown eyes shone. "I'd thought all I could do was get my children raised, but now there's a father to them and a man who makes me remember I'm a woman. I just hope I'm not dreaming."

"I wish I were," snorted Minnie. "Drat it all, I bet I have to go through a dozen cooks before I find one who doesn't booze on the job, isn't dirty, and who makes good pies. If I find a halfway decent he-cook, I think I'll marry him just to make sure he stays.

Run along and get your bath, Kirsty, so we can hear your adventures before time to start supper."

Before Kirsten stepped into the round zinc tub, she opened her trunk and shook out the dress she'd made at Camp Supply, a cool gray-blue lawn trimmed with pleated ruffles, very simply cut. She had packed it in tissue so that it wouldn't need pressing. All this past year, except at the Christmas ball, she had worn one or the other of her two black gowns, faded now from sun and wear. In time, she'd take out the seams, brighten the cloth with vinegar, and renovate them, but for now, she was heartily sick of their somberness and was hungry for colors.

Beside the filled tub, Annie had left buckets of warm water. Kirsten used them to wash and rinse her hair and give herself an initial scrubbing before she got into the tub and soaked. The Family Gem sat on the table by the window as if it had never been away. The bed still had those familiar hollows, worn somewhat deeper. Lucia had lain there. Until she died.

Kirsten didn't fend off the rush of grief, felt it till it eased to sadness. She would always miss Lucia; always wonder if she might have lived had they stayed in Sweden. But at the grave, Kirsten had known a flash of communion with her sister's gentle spirit. That was infinitely comforting. And the flowers had bloomed, the flowers of Dalarna.

With a sense of having come full circle, Kirsten dried with Minnie's big soft towels, and when her hair was dry enough to braid, she slipped on her new dress. She had done what she set out to do: found a way to make her living, traveled the boundaries of the Triangle, where she would make her home. In the bottom of her trunk was five hundred dollars and she didn't owe a dime. As soon as she caught up on her sewing, she and Blue would lay in supplies and start for No Man's Land—a piece of which was going to belong to a woman!

When she stepped out into the hall, Ash Bowden was waiting.

What was it this man aroused in her? Some of the lightning shock she felt with O'Brien, but none of the protectiveness, none of the loving, which, ironically, she sensed was what Bowden desired far more than the passion he could doubtless evoke, given the opportunity.

He raised her hands to his lips, slowly kissed each palm. Beneath his warm mouth, her naked flesh felt dangerously vulnerable, as if his breath reached to her blood and entered it, ran through her veins. Before she could break away, he released her.

"So here you are, Kirsten, back where you started from, but now a successful businesswoman with a burgeoning clientele—and something of a heroine for bearding Gus Kelman. I'm sorry I missed your lecture on the Bill of Rights." His mouth quirked down. "It might have roused a glimmer of patriotism in even my cynical heart."

"I don't care if it roused patriotism," Kirsten retorted. "I wanted people to see that letting the Committee hang men isn't— well, it's not what ought to happen in America."

"My dear," he said with mocking tenderness, "it's fine to cherish dreams. But you'll break your heart if you can't remember that's exactly what they are—even in America."

"Is that how you got to be what you are?"

"Ah, but my dream was easy! I wanted money and power." His eyes held hers. "Now I'm daring to dream of love, Kirsten. That's not so simple." At her dismayed look, he laughed and slipped his arm under hers. "Don't be apprehensive. I know this isn't the time to blandish you. Maybe in a year or so, when the delights of homesteading have paled and you've had your fill of being Auntie Kirsten and yearning over another woman's husband—"

"You—you—don't talk to me like that!"

She tried to free herself, but he held her inexorably, and at her resistance, something flashed in his eyes that told her once again that struggling might bring a disastrous consequence. She let him move her up the hall.

"All I meant," he resumed amiably, "was that I'm not foolish enough to weary you with courting till there's a chance you'll be receptive. Till then, my Kirsten, you're tolerably safe, so do take that prim look off your face and behave like a gracious guest of honor."

"Guest?"

"Indeed. When I explained to Minnie that I have to leave tomorrow, she was kind enough to let me host a party for you here tonight."

Kirsten tried to draw back, but it was too late. The dining room was crowded with everyone she'd known in Dodge, and Bowden brought her in to resounding cheers and greetings. Jim Carson from the livery told her he was repainting the wagon wheels and varnishing the wagon. The Wrights from the mercantile wanted news of their friends in Tascosa and Mobeetie, and those of her former steady patrons who were in town, cattlemen, businessmen, and officers from Fort Dodge, seemed genuinely proud of her, though some of them tried to persuade her to stay in Dodge. Several ladies asked for dresses, and Mr. Wright offered to be her partner in a dress shop. Blue basked in approving interest, which must have been doubly sweet after years of being considered a derelict. Bridget and Minnie had conjured up a lavish buffet, and customers who came in for supper were invited to help themselves.

Kirsten had enjoyed quiet triumph in returning to town with her aims accomplished, and her embarrassment at this public celebration eased as she realized that these people were glad for her, and moreover, just as she had her dream of America, so did they. Her success fitted that vision, was an echo of what their foreign-born parents or grandparents had done.

When the last guests departed, Bowden walked her to the door of her room. "I probably won't be back till after you've set forth to homestead," he said, "but I'll find you this autumn and see how you're faring."

No use protesting. He'd do as he pleased. "Why," she demanded, "did you give this party?"

"Didn't you enjoy it?" The corners of his eyes crinkled. "Come now, Kirsten! Wasn't it fun to be congratulated and made over?"

She blushed, for it had been sweet, even though she knew one should be modest. She *had* worked hard and with imagination; in her own way, she had conquered a new country, and certainly she was proud.

"Yes," she said honestly. "It was fun."

"Good. It was my celebration, too, love. For the first time, I've seen you out of mourning." He let his hand rest on her cheek, for just a moment. "Now when you leave off your guise as Auntie Kirsten—" Laughing at her outraged gasp, he kissed her mouth swiftly, before she could move, and went down the hall without a backward glance.

* * *

Kirsten trusted Blue to buy the kind of plow that could break the prairie sod and choose the other necessary tools and implements. Building a frame house right off would devour their savings, and though Minnie offered to sign a note for a bank loan, Kirsten hated to go in debt.

"If we start with a soddie, Blue, we can pay cash for lumber in a year or two and then use the soddie for a barn or storage. But let's do have a good shingled roof. I don't want mud leaking on whatever I'm sewing—or in our food and bedding, either."

"Sod walls keep in the heat or cool," said Blue. "Don't look bad at all lined with muslin. But you'd ought to have real glass windows, Miss Kirsty."

Kirsten agreed fervently with that. As she studied their growing list, she said between a sigh and a laugh, "I'm glad we have the money to buy all this, but I'd planned to order one of those treadle machines from Montgomery Ward. I love my Family Gem, I'll never part with it, but my arm and shoulder wouldn't ache with the treadle, and I could sew a lot faster and easier. It has attachments for hemming, ruffling, quilting, gathering and adding braid, and Blue, it has three drawers on each side and a big center one lined with velvet! But it costs twenty dollars plus freight—"

Blue gave a snort. "Miss Kirsty, you order it or I'll use a hoe instead of a plow! Working hard as you do, you need the best machine you can get. Cheaper in the long run than abusin' your arm and shoulder."

She knew he was right. Besides, she should clear something over a hundred dollars for the sewing she wanted to finish in Dodge, though she'd take some of the less urgent orders with her. Before she could worry herself out of it, she borrowed Minnie's catalog and ordered the machine.

Bridget departed before Kirsten did, for, wearing her gold-brown dress, she married Zeke Thomas early in September. After a festive dinner, which Kirsten helped Minnie hostess, the couple set off for his claim with the wagon full of possessions and children.

"I'm glad for her," Minnie said, turning back to the hotel after she and Kirsten and Blue had waved the Thomases out of sight. "And Chet Brophy knows how to make pretty fair pies. But the Lord knows these old chuck wagon cooks are cantankerous, and I hate to think what'll happen first time someone complains about his cooking."

"Maybe they won't."

"Someone always complains," grumbled Minnie. "But he says he's tired of ignorant cowhands who don't know slop from stew, so if I brag enough on him, maybe he'll stay."

He was still there, and had promised to look after Lucia's grave, when Kirsten and Blue rolled out of town in the middle of September, the new machine, still in its wooden packing case, carefully surrounded with bedding and a hooked rug Minnie had given Kirsten for her new home. They'd save freight on everything they could carry themselves, so the wagon was loaded with as much as Honey and Stockings could pull without straining. There was a sturdy, straight-backed chair to go with the sewing machine, but Blue had urged Kirsten not to buy furniture till they saw what he could contrive out of boxes and framing and other odds and ends of wood that would be left over from building.

A house, a *home*, in America! Where the centuries-old chest would again have an honored place, where the Bible, with its generations of Mordal weddings, births and deaths, would bless the household. Kirsten had recorded Lucia's death last year. She herself was the last of the family. The Dalarna folk had been rooted from pagan times beside their lake and mountains, had thrown off Danish tyranny under the lead of Gustav Vasa, only to lose their ancient freedoms when Vasa sacrificed liberty—and men —to unify the country. He had beheaded two of Kirsten's ancestors in their own valley, yet the family survived.

Would it end here when someone wrote a date of death after Kirsten's birthday? Would there be no more weddings, no children's names? Kirsten brooded as Bowden's taunt sounded in her mind. *Auntie Kirsten.* Then she thought of Lucy. She hadn't borne her, but she had saved her life, and that was surely a kind of birthing. It wouldn't be cheating too much to put Lucy's name in the Bible with the account of how it came to be there. Kirsten had already decided that if she died single, Lucy would be her heir. Much as she treasured her heritage, Kirsten wasn't going to marry without love in order to have children—or company in her bed.

Blue jarred her from this reverie. "Did you write O'Brien about when to meet us?"

"Last week. I told him we'd get to Jim Lane's about Saturday and would wait for him there."

"Hope we don't run into Gus Kelman and his Committee. One thing for sure, Miss Kirsty, I'm goin' to keep the rust cleaned out of that old shotgun."

"After what Hi Allen said, I doubt Kelman will bother either O'Brien or us."

"Yeah, but there can be accidents." At Kirsten's startled look, Blue shrugged. "Don't fret about it, Miss Kirsty. Kelman's prob'ly so busy tryin' to be the law in the Strip that he can't worry about old grudges."

"A man like that, he is not the law!"

"Maybe not, honey-girl, but he's the one with the rope."

Kirsten shivered, though the day was hot, but the menace of Kelman faded as she watched a flock of prairie chickens swarm through the sagebrush that was in silver bloom. In spite of the drought, white prickly poppies looked incredibly delicate on their spiny stalks, and sunflowers and purple asters brightened the sides of the road. It was a little less than eleven months ago that she and Blue had rumbled along this way, beginning their journey of well over six hundred miles.

This time it was different. They were traveling to their home.

The trail was different, too. Last year, from Dugan's road ranch on Mulberry Creek, where Ash had taken her on that fateful picnic, there'd been nothing the whole thirty miles to Hoodoo Brown's. This time, at nooning of their second day out of Dodge, Kirsten and Blue ate a good dinner at the Wilburn Hotel while Stockings and Honey were treated to grain at the livery and got a loose shoe secured at the blacksmith's, and they marveled at how quickly a bustling small city had risen from nothing since its platting that February. Houses, frame and sod, were rising on lots around the main street, which had a hardware and a grocery store, a lumberyard and several other businesses, including a real estate firm.

"Country's getting plumb cluttered," mourned Blue as they started off. He was still bemoaning the change next day when they came in sight of more buildings rising from the plain. This had to be Fowler, started last Christmas with the opening of a half dugout as a store.

They paused only long enough to water the horses from a well in the town square. They camped that night near Hoodoo

Brown's, and during supper at the road ranch Hoodoo said that the town of Meade Center, two miles west, was putting him out of business.

"They've already got over two hundred houses and eight hundred people," Hoodoo said. "It was voted the county seat before it even got its charter back in July. I may move over there and start a hotel—if'n I can stand that kind of crowds."

After Meade Center no new settlements aroused Blue's ire, and when they pulled off the road to let a trail herd pass, he gave a soft whistle as he grinned at the lead steer of the strung-out hundreds. He had impressive curved horns and a bell around his neck that clanged as he marched, like an officer ahead of his troops.

"Danged if it's not Old Blue, Colonel Goodnight's pet steer," said Blue. "Only steer I ever heard of who'd let them hang a bell around his brisket. They stuff it full of grass or rags at night 'cause if the cows hear it, they're on their feet pronto, ready to hoof it. There's many a thousand head he's brought up the trail to Dodge, but he'll come back eatin' corn, whilst the herd's shipped to slaughter."

"Do you think he wonders what happens to the cattle?"

"He's good at leadin'. Maybe, like some of them fancy generals, that's all he cares about."

On their sixth day out, Friday, they reached Jim Lane's road ranch on the north fork of the Canadian, the Beaver River. Kirsten had a hard time going to sleep. Tomorrow she'd see O'Brien. Tomorrow she'd see the homesite where, if things had been different, they might have lived together. Shutting out such thoughts, she took bittersweet comfort in thinking that in showing her the location, he'd have a share in her home. Owls hooted along the river and a convocation of coyotes sang in the distance; finally, she slept.

She went from dreaming into waking so swiftly that when she opened her eyes and saw O'Brien, she thought for a heartbeat that she was still asleep and smiled drowsily. His eyes changed, the pupils widening, and the curve of his nostrils paled. He stepped back, and for a moment, all they desired, all that could not be, was between them like the body of a stillborn child. He managed a smile.

"Get up, sleepyhead! We've got to rustle if we're going to get to your place tonight. Eighteen miles it is, and not much of a road."

Hugging the quilt to her chin, Kirsten said in puzzlement, "I wouldn't have thought there was a road at all. Didn't you say it's ten miles or so off the Tascosa Trail?"

"Just a manner of speaking," he said hurriedly. "I'm making flapjacks, colleen, so you'd best get 'em down while they can be chewed. I'm told when they cool off they're tough as an old saddle."

Actually, served with canned peaches and a taste of molasses, the pancakes were so good that none were left to dry out. The sun was barely tipping over the eastern horizon when the wagon rolled off with O'Brien alongside on Barney. They had spent the night a few hours down the trail and started for Jim Lane's while it was still dark.

They nooned about eight miles west, where wagon and horse tracks turned abruptly south off the main trail. "Are you sure no one's taken the site?" Kirsten worried.

"Well," grinned O'Brien, "they hadn't as of yesterday morning."

What had gotten into him? All morning, he'd brimmed with excitement. He couldn't be that happy, could he, about her settling thirty miles from him, when he must know as well as she how hard that very closeness would be to endure till time and habit tamed the urgency—if they could—that ran through her now each time she looked at him. As they grew old, that might gentle into a pleasant warmth; now it was wildfire.

Watching his long, shapely hands, Kirsten felt a rush of panic. Were they both fools? Mad, to tantalize themselves? How could they possibly live in reach of each other and in some hour of extremity, keep from reaching?

Well, whispered a voice in Kirsten, *would that be so awful?* He'd married Lorena from pity and obligation to his dead friend. She had O'Brien's name and protection. What if, leaving her those, Kirsten took some small part? Kissed him, shared love words, slept now and then in his arms?

For that, she might have gone against what she felt was right, defied her upbringing, risked her reputation. What she couldn't risk was Lorena's happiness, the home she and O'Brien had made for Lucy and small Jackie. Kirsten started to tell Blue to turn the wagon around right now, make some kind of excuse, but as she called his name in a strangling voice, O'Brien turned to her with a smile so radiant and eyes so joyful, that "I can't" died on her lips.

He wanted her there, it was important to him. Besides being the lover she couldn't have, wasn't he her dear friend, her first friend in America? Taking a deep breath, Kirsten smiled through her pain and made up some question before O'Brien could wonder why she had called him.

24

The wagon topped a rise above a valley that followed the curve of a creek with a good source of water, for it was flowing in this time of long drought. At the bend of the creek, on the south side, silt deposited by many floods formed rich bottomland, acres of it. Above the bend, a stand of big trees flamed gold and orange—not just cottonwoods but what looked like hackberries, box elders, and ash. All along the valley grass grew high and thick, and this north rim would offer winter shelter for animals.

It was by far the most inviting spot Kirsten had seen in her travels, so she was not surprised to see several wagons drawn up near the trees, loaded with what looked like blocks of white stone. Hobbled horses and mules feasted in the meadow, and a campfire blazed on the knoll by the trees.

"Someone's got a wonderful place," she said wistfully.

She had come to love the far expanses, the ever-changing cloudscapes. Here, one looked to the skies for beauty: the majestic rearing of thunderheads; clouds, from thick, plump, cottony forms to mare's tails and ribbed waves like a shallow sea; each dawn and sunset prodigal glory; and grandeur even in the dark threat of blizzard or tornado. Yes, she looked to the sky, but she hungered for trees. Not forests, but some trees to commune with and thank for their green and gracious shade. Well, it couldn't be much farther to the place O'Brien liked, and though it couldn't be this lovely, he'd said there were trees.

O'Brien's startled look changed to a slow smile. "Like it, Kirsty?"

"Who wouldn't?"

"What do you think, Blue?" O'Brien persisted.

"Mighty close to paradise. Must be a good fifty acres of bottom that can be irrigated from the creek. Bet a spring in amongst them trees helps feed the creek—an unfailing spring, to still be runnin'."

"Think it's worth claiming?"

Blue stared, comprehended before Kirsten did, and let out a whoop. "Hot diggity durn! But if this is the place you had in mind, what're we goin' to do about them folks?"

"Let's go see 'em."

"We don't want trouble," Kirsten said nervously. "Please, O'Brien—"

But he was riding ahead while the team came cautiously down a dip less steep than the rest of the cliff. Where were the people? The aroma of coffee and baking bread, the tang of spicy beans, made Kirsten's mouth water, but no one was in sight. As the team drew up by the other wagons, she wondered where the blocks of white stone came from. Mortared, they'd make a house as well insulated as a soddie, but perfectly clean, and free of the spiders and insects that thrived in earthen walls.

Admiring the stone, wondering if she might possibly be able to afford some like it, she didn't see or hear anyone approaching till a familiar voice called, "Welcome to your place, macushla!"

"Bridget!" Kirsten almost fell off the seat. Zeke stood grinning behind his wife. And coming out of the trees, laughing like boys at her bewilderment, were Tom Reynolds, tow-headed Hank, the Hi-A chore boy, and young Bill Mabry.

"Lorena wanted to come," said O'Brien. "She sends you her love and so does Lucy. But she's feeling kind of poorly." Before she could ask what was wrong, Tom Reynolds thrust out his hand.

"Howdy, neighbor! The boss and Miss Kate and Miss Amanda, and maybe the Rawlings twins'll be coming for the housewarmin'."

"But—" It was all happening too fast, too unexpectedly. Kirsten shook her head to clear it. "I don't understand—"

"Simple, colleen," said O'Brien. "Cabin raising's a good old American custom. We don't have logs, but I reckon limestone will do just as well."

"The rock, it's for our house?"

"Well, we sure aren't makin' a barn out of it, though that's not a bad idea for later. There's tons of it a few miles west, just for the taking."

"And much, much work! These blocks look like they've been cut with a saw."

O'Brien looked sheepish. "Well, sure, but—"

"You could sell them," said Kirsten, aghast at the labor. "So you must sell them to me, O'Brien, at a fair price, or I won't let you use them here."

"Colleen, it's—" His eyes pleaded. "It's something we wanted to do for you. Lorena'd scalp me if I took a dime off you."

"I'll scalp you if you don't." As always, she longed to bury her hands in the thick springiness of his hair. "You found the land for us—wonderful land—and I know neighbors help each other, so I am very grateful for your helping with the house. But it will be of sod, not stone, unless you let me pay."

His mouth set stubbornly and she said, "Please, O'Brien. I would love the clean walls. I never dreamed there could be such a house, here on the prairie. Do let me buy the rock." With sudden inspiration, she beamed at him. "You can give me a very good bargain!"

Everyone else laughed at that, and reluctantly, after a moment, so did he. "All right, you stubborn Swede! With men working for a dollar a day, let's say you owe me twenty bucks."

"And your board and use of your team."

"Make Lorena a dress and we'll call it even."

"Whisht!" scolded Bridget. "You wanted a good bargain, macushla! Take it."

"That's my last word." O'Brien spoke so ominously that Kirsten had to smile. They shook hands on the deal and he swung her down from the wagon. "All right, Kirsty. You and Blue just stroll around till suppertime figurin' where you want the house, and first thing in the morning, we'll get started."

Kirsten and Blue agreed there was really only one place for their home, on the rise above the creek bend, out of reach of floods, with sweeping views in all directions but still somewhat protected by the opposite cliff from storms howling out of the north. Thinking of summer heat made it tempting to build among the trees, but that would have meant clearing some of them out, and Kirsten was resolved never to cut a single one, except from direst necessity. In this treeless land, they were blessed coolness, a feast to the eyes and senses. But the house could be raised near enough for the small grove to serve as a windbreak. There was a tall ash, somewhat sequestered from its kin, that stood where it could shade a dwelling in summer but in winter would let sunlight stream through its leafless boughs.

The spring flowed out of a limestone fissure, collected in small rock hollows, and ran as a miniature waterfall into the creek. "We'll dig a well later," planned Blue. "Close to the house. But it won't be bad carrying from this. Bet I could mortar the sides up on one of these little pools and make us a place to keep milk cool, if we get that cow you've talked about."

"I can't believe it." Kirsten sighed happily. "It's a miracle someone hasn't already settled here."

"Too far off the trail. But when the Strip's declared public land and folks start crowding in, this'd get taken mighty fast."

Kirsten frowned. "Can someone take the land away from us later?"

"Not if we've stayed on it, built a house, dug a well, and got ten acres under cultivation," he assured her. "The government allows what's called 'squatter's rights,' so when the Strip's surveyed and there's a land office, we can file a claim and get credit for the time we've already been here."

"*I* can't file, Blue."

"You can when you're twenty-one, long as you declare you aim to become a citizen. You can file then on another hundred and sixty acres, which is a quarter of a section. And we can stake us out a tree claim while we're marking this one."

"A tree claim?"

"Long as we're willin' to plant forty acres of it in trees and keep 'em alive for eight years, we can file on another hundred and sixty acres."

Another quarter section! Gazing across the plains where the only trees grew by the creek, Kirsten said, "I want an orchard. But forty acres! We'd have to carry water till the trees had a good start. Anyway, where would we get so many trees?"

"Cottonwoods'll grow from cuttings. And we could prob'ly move a dozen saplings out of the hardwoods." Blue pondered, obviously unwilling to abandon this entitlement. "Know what, Miss Kirsty? Nothin' to keep us from making the house site on the far edge of one claim and plant your orchard and whatever other trees we can rustle up on the near side of our tree claim. And then there's preemption."

"You tried to explain that to me once, Blue, but I didn't understand too well."

"Preemption's where you file a claim and pay the government a dollar twenty-five an acre. You're only supposed to preempt once, and of course it can't be done till there's a land office. That's a wad of money, anyhow."

Kirsten shook her head in amazement. "It seems to me that everyone in America would homestead, preempt, and file for tree claims!"

"Plenty have. But a good many came from the East or from cities and don't have a notion of what it's like to farm out here. They say Uncle Sam bets you a hundred and sixty acres against your fourteen-dollar filing fee that you can't stick it out for five years. For those who do, that land costs a power of work and grief. 'Tain't free.''

It was still a marvel to Kirsten. As they walked back to camp, she did swift calculations. A preempted quarter section would cost two hundred dollars. Money, yes, but coming from a country where only the rich owned more than a field or two, Kirsten prized land as the only lasting wealth, the only source of food. She and Blue would preempt as soon as there was a land office, and she'd preempt under her own name when she was twenty-one, if there was still adjacent unclaimed land. She wouldn't file for a homestead because the law required her to live on it, and she never wanted to leave this lovely place. Even so, she and Blue could claim a whole section, six hundred and forty acres, one square mile.

It seemed a kingdom. And most of it would stay wild, a refuge for pronghorns, prairie dogs, and other creatures, for she and Blue had agreed to concentrate on an orchard and raising hay. There would be chickens and a cow or two, but neither of them wanted to raise animals for slaughter, though Blue had laughed and said, "Unless'n we get heifer calves every time, Miss Kirsty, we're goin' to need a lot of pasture for the bull calves!"

"But we'll know them so well, Blue, that it would be like killing friends." She still remembered an orphaned calf she'd raised on a bottle—how she'd cried when Grandfather Nils sledged him between his big, fawnlike ears where he'd loved to be rubbed. Half starving though she'd been, she couldn't eat the meat. "Blue, on our farm, let's have milk and eggs and butter and cheese, all those good things that do not cost a life. But when our hens are too old to lay, we'll still feed them, and our cows can have shelter and grass as long as they live."

Blue gaped a moment before he scratched his head. "All right, Miss Kirsty, if that's how you feel. But I hope you'll let me bag a prairie hen now and then, long as we're not acquainted with her!"

When they got back to camp, O'Brien asked them to drive a stake at one corner of where they wanted the house. After supper, he tied a cord to the stake and with great care lined it up with the North Star and pegged it down.

"There's your north-south wall," he said. It pleased Kirsten mightily that the star that had guided her Viking forebears on their long voyagings now, in this distant new world, decreed the line of her home. And though he could not live under its roof with her, she felt deep joy that O'Brien had quarried the rock and would raise up the walls. Always, she would feel surrounded by his caring, sheltered by his skill and strength.

After breakfast next morning, O'Brien suggested that Blue and Kirsten stake the claim. "The southern boundary of the Strip was surveyed back in 1860," he said. "But the survey team that came through in 1881 couldn't find the first markers, so they laid out the boundary again and then surveyed the Strip into six-mile-square townships and marked the corners with zinc stakes. There's one stake just on top of that little slope yonder. Starting there with a marker of your own, you can pretty well guess what's a quarter mile north—I'd reckon it to be close to the cliff across the creek. Stake that, and then the other two corners. Be a good idea to put your name on the stakes, and the date."

The west border of the homestead included the spring and house site, then stretched across the bend of the creek, taking in more good meadow and bottomland to the east. Kirsten and Blue used the west corner stakes as the eastern ones of the tree claim, and hoped to preempt the next hundred and sixty acres as soon as homesteading was official. They walked the claims on foot, and by the time they had finished, the wall of the house was rising, O'Brien and Zeke fitting and dressing the blocks, while Bill and Tom took O'Brien's heavy wagon after more stone and Hank hauled mud from the creek to be used as mortar.

In contrast to the dense grass in the bottoms, there was only short buffalo grass on the knoll, and O'Brien had used a sort of sled with a horizontal steel blade fastened between the runners to clear the building site. The sled sliced off one-and-a-half-foot-long sod bricks, and with these Kirsten, Blue and Bridget began a stable for the horses. Held together by interlocked grass roots, the sod had a warm, living smell, and O'Brien cut more bricks from the place Kirsten chose for a garden. Taking off a layer of sod would make breaking the ground much easier.

By afternoon, Tom and Bill had hauled enough stone to complete the house and joined in the building, while Zeke, the best carpenter, made the door, the door and window frames, and sawed the rafters. There was plenty for the finishing and a good roof, for in addition to the shingles and wood Kirsten and Blue had brought from Dodge, Hi Allen had sent over some cured hardwood lumber. For the floor, O'Brien had shaped flagstones to be fitted in creek sand.

When Bridget and Kirsten weren't cooking, they worked on the stable, lifting the heavy sod blocks together. Once the walls were waist-high, Blue, because of his maiming, couldn't heft the bricks in place, so he made the door frame and contrived, from scraps, a strong big door. Then he took the wagon down the creek a way and felled enough of the plentiful young cottonwoods for poles to support the sod roof. Sawed cottonwood warped badly, but left as poles it was reasonably serviceable.

Many hands made quick work, and O'Brien had already shaped and dressed the stone blocks so well that they needed little additional smoothing. At noon of the sixth day, Zeke finished hanging the door, which faced south. Glass sparkled in the four windows of the fourteen-by-twenty-four-foot house, two looking south, one east and one west. Though the north view of the creek was beautiful, it was folly to have either doors or windows leaking the wintry blasts that would come from that direction. O'Brien had tested the rock fireplace, built into the middle of the long north wall, to make sure the chimney drew properly. A six-foot-high wood partition on the west end gave Kirsten a bedroom but allowed heat to flow over the boards and through the wide passageway. She suspected that in winter she'd move her bed, removed from the wagon, in by the fireplace opposite where Blue planned to build his bunk, which would serve as a bench by day.

The splendid new sewing machine with its burnished walnut cabinet was positioned for best light at a slant from the east window, where Kirsten, as she worked, could see the changing trees and the bend of the creek. The big ash, its leaves now blazing gold, would in summer shade much of that side of the house and give some protection from scorching southern winds.

The sewing machine's packing box served as a table, and there were crates to sit on as well as Kirsten's sewing chair. The rug Minnie had given her brightened the flagstones, and the old, old chest stood against the partition with Grandfather's Nils's violin resting on top.

O'Brien oiled the hinges of the door, straightened and said, "That's it, Kirsty! How do you like it?"

"I—I—" Heart filled to bursting, she broke off, swallowed, and smiled through tears as she looked from O'Brien to the other friends who had joined in this. "Oh, wonderful it is!" For the first time in months, she reverted to the way she'd spoken when she came to America. "My dear friends, all of you, I cannot thank you enough!"

"Oh, there'll be ways," Tom Reynolds laughed. "For starters, I bet it's not long till the Rawlings girls write you they need some bride clothes."

"Both of them?" Kirsten glanced at Bill Mabry, who colored to the edge of his brown hair.

"Well, yeah," he said with shy pride. "Marilyn might have fought me off a little longer, but Meg's talkin' her into a double weddin'. Prob'ly be the first one in the Strip."

"That's lovely! Tell them to send their material and some ideas about what they want."

"You can tell 'em yourself," grinned Tom, shading his eyes toward the west. " 'Cause here comes Hi's fancy wagon and I'll bet the twins are in it."

They were, along with Amanda and Katharine. After a flurry of laughingly excited embraces, the newcomers came inside. Standing by the fireplace, Meg cried rapturously, "Oh, Tom! Let's have a house just like this!"

"Whatever you want," said Tom fondly before he chuckled. "Reckon it won't be long, though, till we'd need an extra room or two."

"Tom!" blushed Meg. "If Mama heard you!"

"Do her good," said Tom, and Kirsten suspected that Sally Rawlings's tyranny by headache wouldn't get far with either of her sons-in-law. And the long-outnumbered Sheldon should feel bolstered by the addition of more men to the family.

Hi brought in a double armload of bundles and Amanda and Katharine began unloading them. "There's four laying hens and a rooster in the stable," he said.

"We brought a few things for the house," said Amanda, shaking out a blue and white quilt with a star pattern. "This rug sort of matches." The rug was braided of various shades of blue, and there was a larger oval rag rug in bright colors, which helped dispel the bare look. Frenchy McCormick and Betty Strube had sent an ornate bronze clock for the mantel along with orders for new dresses, and Jim Cator's gift was a Rochester brass bowl lamp with the bright-burning round wick and a green shade, the kind Kirsten had wanted to buy but had decided was too expensive. From the Rawlings came a Carlsbad china tea set patterned with delicate forget-me-nots, a fine plate-glass mirror in a carved oak frame, and tea towels and pillowcases embroidered by the sisters.

"It's too much," Kirsten protested, stunned and gasping as Tom and Bill carried in a rocker. "That's from Persia and Tru Hollister," said Hi. "Had it special made in Mobeetie from seasoned mesquite and sent to us by freighter. They've bought a smaller ranch south of Abilene. They like it, and say for you to visit any time you can."

The rich, eccentric grain of the wood was polished to shining and the ample back and seat were padded with red velveteen cushions. It was a beautiful chair, but what made it perfectly Kirsten's was the drawer beneath the seat, which Amanda pulled out to show chintz-lined compartments holding a pincushion with needles and pins, assorted thread, hooks and eyes, and other sewing needs.

"Try it out," urged Katharine.

Kirsten sat down in the most comfortable chair she'd ever used. Remembering how she'd rocked Lucy at the Rawlings', she thought how perfect this would be for holding a child and glanced involuntarily at O'Brien. He watched her with a darkening of his green eyes that made her look away, grateful when Hi put his arm around Amanda and turned her toward the door, calling over his shoulder, "Am I the only one that's starving?"

The women got pies and cakes and light bread out of the wagon, pickles and relishes, olives and ham. With the beans, rice, and sourdough biscuits ready at the campfire, they had a festive meal underneath the trees.

That afternoon, Blue used wire Hi had brought to fence a yard for the Rhode Island Red chickens, who'd live in the stable till he could make them a coop. The other men finished the stable roof by laying grass and sod over the poles and propping these up from the inside with more poles—for many a rain-soaked dirt roof had grown so heavy that it had come crashing down. After admiring the strutting rooster and his hens, the women went inside where Kirsten fitted Marilyn and Meg to the pattern they'd chosen for their wedding dresses. They'd brought satin and lace and seed pearls in a big box, so Kirsten could go to work as soon as she was settled.

"I think it's good luck that the first dresses I make in this new home on my new machine will be for a wedding," she said.

"Mama won't let us get married till next summer," Marilyn said ruefully. "So you certainly needn't rush. But it'll be encouraging to have the gowns to look at this winter, especially when the weather's too bad for Tom or Bill to ride over to see us." She smoothed the satin dreamily. "This is one time we don't mind dressing alike. But I wonder. If we hadn't worn different dresses to the Fourth, Meg, do you think our men would ever have got us sorted out?"

"Fiddle!" scoffed Katharine. "You looked so pretty that you knew you were, and acted like it. That draws men like hornets to molasses."

"Katie!" Amanda's smooth brow wrinkled. "That sounds so ungenteel! Can't you say bees to honey?"

"Hornets or bees," laughed Meg. "We're glad they took notice! I've adored Tom for years, but till the Fourth, he treated me like a little sister."

"And Bill's so bashful," said Marilyn fondly. "If Tom hadn't set an example, Bill would've torn his hat in half just working up nerve to ask for a dance."

Kirsten was glad for her friends, radiant with loving and being loved, but couldn't smother her envy. Would she be Auntie Kirsten to their children, too, and to all the children of marriages for which she'd made the bride's dress, till she at last withered into the venerability that would make her, in this informal country, everybody's aunt? She looked past the sisters to Katharine and they exchanged wry glances.

It was warm enough to have supper outside that evening, but Kirsten wanted the first meal in the house to be special, blessed by the presence of the friends who'd helped build it, particularly

O'Brien. She roasted and ground the coffee, set on the pot, made biscuits in the Dutch oven, put on the beans to heat, suspended by a pothook from the built-in rod, and put on water to heat for doing the dishes.

Meg came in with a jar filled with purple Michaelmas daisies, cone flowers and sunflowers and set them in the middle of the packing crate, over which Kirsten had spread a new blue-and-white-checked oilcloth. The table was set with the pair of white ironstone plates she'd bought in Dodge, and the guests' dishes and cutlery. There wasn't room for eleven people to sit *at* the table, of course, but the men rigged up benches on either side out of planks supported by stone blocks.

When everyone had filled their plates at the fireplace, Kirsten, feeling the occasion should be solemnized, asked, "Please, will we say the Lord's Prayer?"

As her friends' voices mingled in the beautiful, ancient words, Kirsten, in her mind, repeated them in Swedish, feeling that somehow the spirits of her family were there, wishing this new home well. Her eyes were misty when the prayer ended. As she glanced up, she met O'Brien's eyes.

What she saw there made her catch her breath and hold it against the trembling that threatened to overcome her. Wrenching her gaze from him, she translated the Swedish phrase. "If you will be so good . . ."

They had a merry feast then, those on the ends holding their plates in their laps and reaching for their cups on the table. After the dishes were done, Blue, at Meg and Marilyn's urging, tuned the violin. Furnishings and rugs were moved against the walls, and everyone danced, the four older women taking turns sitting out so the sisters could make the most of this time with their sweethearts.

When even they admitted to weariness, there was a midnight treat of coffee and cake before everyone retired to their various beds. Blue slept in the wagon and Kirsten yielded her bed, spread with the new quilt, to Bridget, unrolling a pallet beside Meg and Marilyn. She thought she was too happily excited to sleep, but after she closed her eyes, she drifted quickly into sleep beneath the roof her love—oh, yes, he was her love—had made for her.

25

After a big breakfast next morning, the house raisers and warmers departed, Zeke and Bridget calling back, "Remember, we're neighbors!" and Amanda saying, "You'll have to come to Hardesty for mail, so you can travel another fourteen miles sometimes and visit. Be sure to come to the Christmas ball."

As the Allens' elaborate wagon rolled off, Meg and Marilyn waved till they were out of sight. Bill and Tom rode alongside, so they, at least, wouldn't find the thirty-five miles and overnight trip to the Hi-A a wearisome one.

Turning to O'Brien, who was hitching up his team, Kirsten said, "I must get the twenty dollars for the rock hauling, and you must look at the material I brought from Dodge, O'Brien, and tell me what you think Lorena would like best for her dress."

"I hate to take your money, colleen."

"You promised you would—and I've got witnesses," she said gaily, as she ran inside to fetch the money from the trunk.

"No arguin' with you, is there?" he said when she returned. He took the money reluctantly. "I'd better leave decidin' on the material to you, Kirsty. Just remember Lorena hates pink. That was the color of the hand-me-downs she always got from a cousin back East."

"I've got a beautiful myrtle-green challis in a Persian design. Are her measurements about the same?"

He went scarlet. His eyes fell before he looked straight at Kirsten. "Lorena's going to have a baby. That's why she doesn't feel so good."

A baby? This time, it *was* his. A desolated sense of betrayal overwhelmed Kirsten, till it was stemmed by a blaze of jealous

279

anger. He could look at her with longing, but he didn't sleep alone. There was a young, lovely woman in his bed.

What did you expect? Kirsten demanded of herself. *That they live like brother and sister? You know better than that, you always have; you just don't want to think about it. Of course, you fool, they're going to have a baby, and it may not be their last one.*

Still flushed, but meeting Kirsten's stricken gaze, O'Brien said, "Lorena's sort of low in her mind. A pretty dress should perk her up."

"It'll be pretty." Each word hurt as if it cost blood.

He took her hand, this man she loved, who loved her back but must also in a fashion, love the woman he'd married, whom he lived with. "Thank you, Kirsty. Let me know if you need anything."

She looked from the trees and stable to the solid, clean, rock house. He had found this place, made her a home. Though he was Lorena's husband, he was Kirsten's friend, dear friend, first friend in America. He could be that without shame or wronging anyone, and that was very precious. Why did she have to need more?

"Thank you, O'Brien." She pressed his hand firmly. "Hug Lucy and little Jack for me and tell Lorena I hope she feels better soon." There! Spoken without a bobble.

The men shook hands, and climbing into the wagon, O'Brien started the team. "If you follow this creek," he said, "it runs into Kiowa Creek and we live where they join. Come see us when you can, but not after the snows start. I'll get over now and then to see how you're doing."

He waved before passing from sight around the bend of the creek. Kirsten turned to Blue, suddenly almost frightened. They had neighbors, yes, fine ones, but all were a day's ride away. At twenty miles, Jim Lane's was the nearest habitation, about the same distance as Hardesty, where they'd get mail. Weeks would pass, even months, when they'd see nobody.

Fighting a wave of fear, Kirsten caught Blue's arm. "Oh Blue, I'm so glad you came with me!"

"So'm I," he grinned, and as if he read her anxieties, added briskly, "Lots of things we need to do before cold weather. I'm startin' with a chicken coop. I'll build it right on to the side of the stable and save makin' one wall."

"I'll help you," Kirsten said, and went to change into the old green dress she'd brought from Sweden. She paused long enough to get the Bible from the chest. It was wrapped in the ruffled, embroidered bridegroom's shirt, and as Kirsten shook out the garment, she thought before she could check herself that it should just fit O'Brien.

Hastily refolding it, she closed the chest and opened the Bible. She had no pen or ink, but taking a pencil, she wrote carefully beneath the last entry in the family record, which gave the time and place of Lucia's death, *Lucy, found in blizzard January 20, 1885, perhaps eighteen months old. Given to Patrick and Lorena O'Brien to raise, but Kirsten Mordal's heir.*

Feeling better, as if she had just claimed part of the future, Kirsten placed the Bible on the mantel and went to help Blue.

It was nonsense, but Kirsten didn't want the first thing made in her new home with her new machine to be a dress Lorena would wear while carrying O'Brien's child. She got around this by cutting out Meg's and Marilyn's wedding gowns before devising for Lorena a dress with a softly smocked bodice and concealed drawstring waist. After the baby came, the challis could easily be restyled.

Kirsten worked on it several hours a day, her wonder at the ease and speed of the treadle machine and interest in learning how to use the attachments alleviating some of the bitterness of her task. Cruelly hard as it had been to sew Lorena's bridal gown, this pained Kirsten more. Perhaps till now, in some secret part of her mind and heart, she hadn't really considered O'Brien married; maybe she had harbored some vague hope that after her child had a name, Lorena might leave him. Kirsten had never allowed herself to think about whether they made love. Now she knew, and it did not the slightest good to tell herself what she'd always heard, that men were different about such things than women, that their urges, powerful as they were, could be gratified with women they didn't love. That was the reason for Selina's Palace.

Maybe, since Lorena owed so much to O'Brien, she'd insisted that he take his husband's rights. That explanation eased Kirsten a little, though the practical part of her mocked the notion that anyone as masculine and vital as O'Brien needed much seduction.

When Kirsten could endure such thoughts no longer, she left her sewing and helped Blue, for there was much to be done while the weather was fine: scything hay, the high wild grass, stacking it into piles, filling half the long stable with it, and piling more around the walls—both to have it close and to insulate the inside; building a shed of cottonwood poles and sod adjoining the south side of the house for storing winter fuel, which would mostly be hay twisted tight to make it burn longer; breaking crop and garden land so the grass roots would rot through the winter, making the earth easier to plow next spring; planting an acre of wheat, with arms and shoulders still aching from the jerk of the plow.

Each day, while cranes and geese winged over with their distant calling, the leaves flamed more brilliantly till they began to fade. By the time they began to fall, the nighthawks living among them disappeared, gone south, and some crows departed. But meadowlarks still rose with a golden flash of breast and cheery whistle, promising that they, too, would stay the winter.

Blue, Kirsten thought, was working too hard, so when she'd finished Lorena's dress, and made a matching one for Lucy, she asked if he'd deliver it. "Don't you want to go?" he frowned.

"I don't like to leave the chickens cooped up for several days, and if they're left overnight in the pen—well, you know it won't take that horned owl long to have a banquet. Besides, I really need to catch up on some of these orders."

"You don't mind staying alone?"

She did, but thought she might as well get used to it. With chickens, and after they got a cow, she or Blue would have to stay at the place to look after the animals. "If I get lonely," she said, "I can go visit the chickens and Stockings or Honey, whichever one you don't ride."

He was off next day at dawning, mounted on Stockings, using an old saddle and bridle Hi Allen had left them. Kirsten scythed hay till noon, just as she had in Sweden, taking pride in the rhythm of the swinging blade. This was one labor that would be easier next fall, if she could save enough to buy a mower. Sweating and dusty, she was washing in one of the rock hollows below the spring, when she saw riders.

The four of them sent their horses scrambling down the cliff across the creek. They didn't sit their mounts with the easiness of cowboys and there was something alarmingly familiar about the thick-bodied man in the lead.

Kelman! Freezing, Kirsten thought of trying to hide, but they had surely already seen her. Blue's old shotgun was in the house, but she didn't know how to use it. She buttoned her dress to the chin, rolled down her sleeves and, carrying the scythe, walked toward the house, forcing herself not to hurry.

Not hurrying, either, Kelman and his men watered their horses in the creek and rode up at a trot. "Well!" Kelman's small black eyes beamed from the sunburned flesh around them. "If it ain't the loudmouthed foreign gal!" He glanced around at his friends and laughed. "Guess she ain't learned American hospitality—don't know it's plumb bad manners not to ask us in to eat."

"If you're hungry, I'll feed you," said Kirsten. "But you will please stay outside." She felt a deep revulsion at the thought of their entering her house, being under the roof O'Brien had helped make for her.

Kelman's grin tightened till his eyeteeth showed. None of the men had removed their hats, and that, in this part of the country, was an insult. Kirsten was barefoot, liking to feel the grass beneath her. A man with greasy yellow hair and pink skin, one who'd been with Kelman on the Fourth, stared at her feet, which suddenly seemed to her a great nakedness. Fear rose in her, but she kept her pace deliberate as she started for the house. It was almost unheard-of for men, even outlaws, to molest a woman, but instinct warned her that Kelman hated women. At least she had the scythe, and she wouldn't put it down till she had a knife in her hands. If these men meant her harm, she'd aim for the soft parts below the ribs and carve across.

Kelman walked his gaunt sorrel in front of her. "Got grain for our horses?"

"There's plenty of grass."

He glanced toward the stable. "Nice place you got here." He leered. "Guess you got a lot of help."

"We did."

When he didn't move, she started around, but he kicked the horse forward. "See you got some nice, plump hens. Me'n the boys would sure relish fried chicken."

Anger swelled through Kirsten's fear. Stepping back toward the stable and chicken pen, she gripped the scythe. "Go home, then, and fry up your own."

Kelman glared, but the yellow-headed man, whose gaze kept drifting to Kirsten's feet as if he knew how uncomfortable it made her, chuckled and said, "Aw, Gus, let's just take whatever the little lady's willin' to give us."

They got down from their horses and began to unsaddle. Going inside, Kirsten leaned the scythe against the table so she could grasp it if anyone tried to follow, set the biggest knife within easy reach, and built a fire to heat the beans and coffee. She put tin plates, cups, and cutlery into a basket, cut cold cornbread into chunks, filled a jar with molasses, and placed these beneath the ash tree. That the men had unsaddled and hobbled their horses was an ominous sign that they meant to stay awhile. She only prayed they'd leave before dark. Meanwhile, however her insides twisted, she must keep a cool demeanor and act as if the intruders were ordinary wayfarers. She took the smaller knife, though, wrapped the blade with a rag, and thrust it in her apron pocket. She also put on her shoes.

When the beans were hot, she dished them over a piece of cornbread she had saved, poured her own coffee, and carried the steaming kettle and coffeepot outside, ready to dash the scalding contents at anyone who made a suspicious move.

Only the pink-faced man thanked her, grinning at her shoes as he did so in a way that made her sure he knew why she'd put them on. "Hold on," said Kelman, as she turned away. "This is a mighty fine place and you're goin' to need help to keep it, now the government's finally got around to declarin' the Strip is public land."

"That's happened?"

"They got the word in Kansas October the thirteenth, just a few days ago. Settlers already swarmin' in. You bein' a foreigner and not twenty-one yet anyhow, you're goin' to need all the help you can get to hang onto this."

"Blue's a citizen. It's his claim."

The fat around Kelman's eyes creased as laughter rumbled up from his belly. "That broken-down old Injun-nigger? There's some white folks would run him off just on general principles. To prove I don't hold grudges, I'm offerin' to let you join our claim club."

"We have staked the land. There's nothing more to be done till a land office opens."

Kelman chortled and his men laughed, too. "It'll take some doing to keep this place till then. That's what the claim club's for. Members promise to uphold each other's property rights and run off any claim jumpers. I'd reckon you'll need that help a sight more than most. Twenty-five dollars and we'll protect your claim."

"We'll protect it ourselves."

Kelman's black eyes glinted and he spoke through a mouthful of cornbread. "If you're countin' on Hi Allen and O'Brien to look out for you, you might think about gettin' them hurt or killed. And they can't help you and that redbone much if you're dead."

"We won't join your club, Mr. Kelman."

"Then I reckon we'll pull up your stakes. The club decides who has a right to claim, and anyone who won't join us ain't got that right."

"You can pull up the stakes but we'll put them back."

"Will you? It's funny how a prairie fire can jump inside a rock house and burn everything and everybody in it."

"If you're saying—"

There was a whistling sound as Kelman's hat ripped off his head. The yellow-haired man's went next. By then, all four men were on the ground, reaching for their revolvers.

"No need for that, boys," came a pleasant voice. "Just wanted to remind you to take off your hats when you're lucky enough to meet a lady."

Ash Bowden moved from behind the stable. He must have seen the group and advanced from beyond the creek bend and the trees. Grabbing his hat, Kelman looked aggrievedly at the hole. "You didn't have no call to do that, Mr. Bowden. We stopped by, neighborly like, to tell the young lady about how she needs to join the claim club—"

"She doesn't." Ash's tone was soft but his eyes were not. "Miss Mordal's none of your concern, Gus." The Colt's barrel drooped negligently, but the men all watched it. "Can you remember that?"

"We was only tryin' to help," Kelman growled.

"Yes, I heard you offer to pull up her stakes. Pull your own, Gus. If you ever set foot on this claim again, I won't just tip your hats for you."

They were armed and four against one, but like spanked school-boys, they caught their horses, saddled them, and rode off the way they'd come. Bowden gave Kirsten an ironic smile. "For once, my dear, I'll wager you're glad to see me."

"Yes," she said, too relieved to dissemble. "Blue's away. But maybe that's lucky. He'd have tried to make them leave, and they'd probably have shot him."

"Don't sell Blue short. He was mighty good with a gun once, and I expect he can still shoot rings around any of that bunch."

"He's only got an old shotgun, and against four of them—"

"I'll leave him my rifle. Claim jumpers may try moving in on such a choice place. But Kelman won't bother you again. I sent him word after the Fourth, but it must not have been plain enough."

"If you can make him leave us alone, can't you stop his hanging men?"

"Yes, if I wanted to shoot him." Bowden shrugged. "He has his uses, Kirsten. But if he troubles you again—" The bulldog jaw clamped before relaxing in that singularly winning smile. "Let me take care of my horse, and then if that gang left anything to eat, I'd certainly appreciate some dinner!"

He'd brought a saddlebag of imported delicacies, but what delighted Kirsten was the small, soft ball of gray fur he placed in her hands. "A kitty!" It mewed plaintively, squirming, and she held it against her heart, murmuring endearments. "Oh, doesn't she have beautiful green eyes? And the sweetest little face!"

"Whether a he or she, I can't say," smiled Bowden. "But any proper household needs a cat."

"She's a darling, and she will be wonderful company! Thank you, Ash. Will you hold her while I get your dinner?"

Settling into the rocker with the kitten in his lap, Bowden looked from the wildflowers on the table to the violin on the chest, Blue's bunk covered with a bright Navajo blanket, the cupboards made from boxes and scraps, the sewing machine with Meg's bride gown over the arm.

"No need to ask if you like it," he said wryly. "Already, you've made it a home." He heaved a mock sigh. "I'd expected to find you bravely enduring a dark sod hovel. This is small, and you need a good cookstove, but I must admit, by the standards of the region, it's quite a respectable house."

"It's a beautiful house," she said fiercely. "My friends built it."

"I regret I wasn't here to join in, but I just got back from Washington. I want to get my town platted before the Strip fills up with settlers."

"Where will you start it?"

"Where Coldwater Creek runs into the north fork of the Canadian, about eighteen miles northwest of here. It's as close to the center of the Strip as you can get and still be where the railroad can reasonably come through." He took the plate Kirsten handed him, and she cuddled the tiny smoke-colored kitten. "I can see I'll never get you off this place, but I hope you'll accept a town lot. Someday you could open a shop there—hire someone to run it while you sewed at home."

"I don't see how you can give—or sell—lots when there's no way to take title."

"I won't take money till I can actually give buyers official title to their lots. Till then, I've had my lawyers make up agreements protecting and binding both buyers and my company."

"But why would people want town lots when they can homestead?"

His deep laughter boomed. "Bless you, Kirsten, you may not believe it, but not everyone wants to battle dust, drought, grasshoppers and blizzards. Plenty prefer to live in town and run stores, hotels, liveries and such. But they can file claims, too, as long as they 'prove up' on them—that is, build a residence, cultivate some land, and live there five years."

After he had finished a piece of plum cobbler that she hadn't offered Kelman's gang, he folded his hands behind his head and smiled in vast contentment. "It's good to see you in your home, Kirsten. You're the kind of woman who lights and warms a house. Is there something I can help you do?"

"Don't you need to get your town platted?" she asked half mockingly.

"Yes, but unless you expect Blue back tonight, I'm staying here." His smile broadened at her startled look, and he glanced toward the scythe, which still leaned against the table. "You won't need a weapon. I'll sleep in the stable, or in the yard if you prefer, but there's no way I'll leave you by yourself overnight."

"You got rid of Kelman, I'll be fine." Kirsten brushed her cheek against the kitten's pricked-up ears. "Especially now I have Dimma. I'll make a nest for her right by my pillow."

"Lucky little beast. Is that a Swedish name?"

"It means fog. She's that color and her feet are that soft. Truly, I won't be afraid." He stared at her and she added, "Not very."

"I'll stay," he said with finality. "It looks like you've been haying. I haven't swung a scythe in quite a while, but when I was a boy my grandfather had me flogged into a pretty fair hand."

"Your clothes," she objected, for as usual, he wore an expensive suit cut to make the most of his broad shoulders and flatter his powerful, compact body.

"I've got some rougher clothes in my saddlebag. Figured I might need them while laying out Central City." He rose and picked up the scythe, holding her gaze. "You know, Kirsten, if I could share this house with you, I'd gladly work in the fields and make my world this small homestead. That's something I would never have believed."

She laughed to ease the tension building between them. "I don't believe it now, Ash. You'd be tired of it in a week."

His silvery eyebrows arched. "Will you place a wager on that?"

"Ash!"

"If I swing your scythe for a week or do whatever work you set for me, would you let me court you?" His gaze rested on her mouth like a physical touch. She moved back, lifting her hands as if to ward him off, but he pursued her only with his voice. "Would you, even, Kirsten, give me one kiss?"

"Don't be ridiculous! You're all full of your new town. If I said you could stay, I'll bet you wouldn't!"

"Try me."

"You know I won't," she said crossly.

"You won't because you know I would." He shouldered the scythe and paused in the doorway. "But you can't keep me, when I'm coming up from work this evening, muscles creaking and dewed with righteous sweat, from imagining that I belong here, too, and that you are my woman."

"Don't—"

"But I do. And I do it all the time, so you might as well get some work out of me."

He went out whistling. Restraining the urge to hurl something after him, Kirsten, feeling as usual with Ash that she had been bested, revenged herself by opening a tin of his fancy sardines and mincing one up for Dimma.

Kirsten was ruffling a flounce in the last good daylight hour, Dimma asleep beside her in a padded basket, when the door darkened, and only by the shining of his hair could she tell it was Bowden. He stood as if savoring the moment: That he could see her face while his was blurred by the light behind him gave her an uncomfortably exposed sensation and brought her quickly to her feet.

"Do you need a wash basin?"

"I took advantage of the spring." He stepped inside, and she saw that he was sunburned and flushed—and, yes, for once he exuded a male smell instead of the scent of bay rum. He sniffed as if trying to distinguish odors, named them as if reading off the most extensive menu of the finest imaginable restaurant. "Sourdough biscuits! Beans! Rice! Dried-apple pie! I hope there's plenty because I'm hungry as a wolf!"

"I remember when you turned up your nose at dried fruit," she teased.

"Ah, but you hadn't baked the pie." He crossed to grin at the kitten, who stretched and yawned, showing sharp little milk teeth and a pointed red tongue before jumping from the basket and devouring the last bit of sardine. "I *thought* I smelled something else," he said.

"There's no milk, and I was afraid to feed her eggs in case that might start her raiding the nests."

Ash didn't seem perturbed by this use of his imported gift. "Let's hope the sardines hold out till the wee one can control your mouse population." Pulling the sewing chair over to the table, he seated Kirsten in spite of her protests. "I'll dish up our plates," he said. "You're just as tired as I am."

Never in all her life had a man served Kirsten with food. It was strange to the point of discomfort, which made her wonder why, for indeed, when both had worked equally hard, why should the woman always wait on the man? She was glad that she and Blue never thought about such things but did whatever was needed without worrying over whose job it was.

"A boy should know how to cook," she observed. "And a girl should learn to drive a wagon."

"I do agree," he said lightly, pulling up a cushioned box and twinkling at her. "I solemnly promise that if we have children, the little rascals will have to pass exams on boy-girl chores. This may scare off prospective wives and husbands, but at least we'll have equipped them to be self-sufficient old maids and bachelors."

Better not to respond to his mention of "our" children. "You make a joke of everything," she accused.

In the darkening room, his eyes reflected the flickering light from the fireplace and his face was suddenly a hard-planed mask. "Shall I be serious then?"

Shock ran through her, left her weak. She lowered her eyes,

searching for words to armor herself against the force radiating between them. "Tell me about Washington," she said in desperation. "Do they have castles there?"

He laughed at that, described the White House and the Capitol and went into detail about how the city had been planned so that every neighborhood would have its park for strolling and pleasure. "I'd like to show it to you," he said. "It lacks the age-mellowed elegance of European capitals, but is really quite beautiful."

"Have you ever seen the President?"

"I dined with him last week." At Kirsten's look of wonder, Bowden grinned. "A stodgy affair it was, too, but useful. Cleveland needs to hear support from Westerners for legislation forbidding the fencing of public lands by ranchers."

"You own a share in a ranch."

"Yes, but the main reason I came to the Strip was to develop settlement." She had put the china teacups on the table and he raised his in a toast. "Of course, I've found a better reason."

To her relief, he made no more personal remarks, but talked entertainingly as he dried the dishes she washed, and afterwards when she lit the lamp and worked by its light, basting Marilyn's dress. What made her uneasy was the way he positioned himself in the shadows, able to watch when to her he was only a dark presence.

"That looks like a bridal gown," he commented.

She told him about the Rawlings sisters. "Good for them!" he chuckled. "I thought mama might make spinsters out of them, which would have been a pity, don't you think?"

"Not as much as marrying men they didn't love."

"Most women wouldn't agree with you."

"That's because they can't support themselves. *I* can."

"Yes," he said ruefully. "You've proved that to the whole Triangle. What if a generation of maidens adopt your views and look for employment instead of husbands? You'd undermine society."

"That part should be undermined. Women may work hard at home but never see a penny of their own or have much say in things. If both a woman and her husband knew she could earn her living, that would be different. And I'd think a man would like knowing his wife married him for love instead of necessity."

His question was like the swoop of an eagle, though it came in an amused drawl. "Have you ever discussed these views with O'Brien?"

She blushed and jabbed her finger. "Why would I do that?"

"Can you imagine sweet, timid Lorena making a living in any way except providing a home for her man?"

"It's the way she was raised," Kirsten retorted.

"Yes, but be honest. It's how O'Brien was raised, too, and it suits him right down to the ground. He may hanker after you—who wouldn't?—but that big Irishman wouldn't have the dimmest notion of how to deal with you."

He wouldn't have to, Kirsten thought. You deal with opponents, not those you love. To Bowden, she said coldly, "O'Brien's married, and that's the end of it."

Bowden rose like an uncoiled spring. "I wish it were! But we both know why."

Unable to contain her bitterness and hoping to silence her tormentor, she said, "That's not all, not anymore. They're going to have a baby. One of their own."

"Oh, Lord!" Bowden crossed to her, stood staring down at her lowered face. A tear dropped on the satin. He swore beneath his breath, pulling out a snowy linen handkerchief, dropping to one knee and wiping her eyes. "My God, Kirsten," he said helplessly. "How can I feel sorry for you when I want to shake some sense into that ordinarily all-too-level head of yours? Here, blow your nose, and I'll give you the latest news from Dodge. From the way she flutters around him, I really think that Minnie's going to marry her chuck wagon cook."

That jarred Kirsten out of her upset, and they chatted amiably for the rest of the evening, though as the clock ticked off the minutes and bedtime approached, Kirsten grew nervous and her stomach twisted into a knot.

At last, rising, she said, "You may use Blue's bunk if you like."

He rose, too, frost-gray irises only a thin rim around dilated pupils, the curve of his nostrils pale. "Thank you, Kirsten, but we'll both rest better if I'm outside."

He kissed her forehead. "I hope you know what that cost me." Before she could speak, he was closing the door.

26

That night Kirsten learned what it was to be divided in two: one woman who loved O'Brien and another primeval one who burned to go to Ash Bowden. *Do that and he'll make you his woman, sear away these useless dreams. Why shouldn't you both have what you can? Why should you sleep alone when O'Brien doesn't?*

Once she threw off the coverlet, but her feet touching the cold stone O'Brien had laid roused her like a slap. Clenching her hands against a wave of shame, she moved to the window and leaned her forehead against the cool glass till the fever in her quieted.

It made no sense, but she felt unfaithful. And, she realized, she had too much respect for Bowden, too much sympathy for his neglected boyhood, to cheat him. She knew him well enough to marvel at the restraint he showed her, at his obvious decision not to try to take her by storm. More than her body, he wanted her love, and that she could not give him.

A light touch on her cheek woke Kirsten from fitful sleep. Her eyes flew open to gray fur and a tiny paw just descending. "Dimma!" Sitting up, Kirsten nestled the kitten to her breast, humming along with the purr that seemed too loud for such a diminutive creature.

"Did you sleep well? Do you miss your family? Come on, you little gray fog, let's get you a nice sardine."

The smell of coffee came from the main room. Ash! Hot shame for what she had almost done last night flooded Kirsten. Thank heaven she hadn't done it. And thank heaven he couldn't guess. Dressing quickly while Dimma explored beneath the bed, Kirsten went into the main room.

The coffeepot sat on the grill: Ash had been up early. It was only now getting light. It might not have been a restful night for him, either. Could he be gone? Going to the window, she caught sight of motion along the creek. There he was, swinging the scythe. She'd make him a good breakfast and insist that he get on with his town platting.

He ate a stack of pancakes with stewed dry peaches. When he finished his second cup of coffee, he caught her glance for the first time that morning and smiled in triumph.

"So you do look at me sometimes."

"How can I help it?"

"I've wondered that."

"I appreciate what you've done," she said. "But you'd better go plat your city. Blue should be home this afternoon."

"When he is, I'll leave."

Useless to argue. When he went out, she sat down to her sewing. Dimma played with a sunbeam, sat in all the windows, and batted a curl of thread. Her frolics diverted Kirsten, both from remembering the bad dream of Kelman's bullying and from the unreasoning wildness that had, last night, almost brought disaster.

By the time an exhausted kitten jumped into the basket, moulding herself into a smooth gray ball, Kirsten was absorbed in her work, soothed by the whir of the machine. Still, she was glad that Blue rode in just before dinner so that she could avoid the unsettling intimacy of another meal alone with Ash.

Blue didn't come alone. He led a fawn-colored cow with black markings on her face, and at a distance behind them limped a shaggy, hump-shouldered beast with narrow flanks and a massive head.

Seeing Blue from the window, Kirsten ran out to meet him. "Blue! Where did you get the cow? And that other animal, is it a buffalo?"

"Nothin' else. We found the poor old fella in a coulee. Reckon he figgers Dolly here is some kind of buffalo. He just started in a-followin', and I hadn't the heart to run him off. He's got an arrow broke off in his hump, all festering."

Shuddering at a glimpse of the crusted, oozing wound, Kirsten asked, "Can't we get it out?"

"No way he'd let us, unless he was roped and held down. Don't get close to him, Miss Kirsty. Poor old brute's staved up, but he can still do plenty of damage. Got to admire him. I bet that's an arrow from last fall and somehow he made it through that blizzard and is still hangin' on."

Bowden had washed after his morning's labor, for drops of water gleamed on his silver hair and sun-reddened face and throat. Nodding to Blue, he studied the buffalo and sighed. "I can see it now, Kirsten. The hay I've been making at the cost of muscles I didn't know I had will go to feed that ugly varmint and God knows what other unprofitable creatures. So be it, but don't you go near that beast. I'll send a couple of men over from Hardesty to help rope him."

Kirsten hated to accept more help from him, but the poor animal couldn't thrive till the arrow was out, and that was a task beyond her and Blue. "Thank you," she said. "But I'll pay the men."

"No need. I'm sending a wagon over anyway with a load of wood."

"We don't need it. We have plenty of hay and we've been gathering fallen limbs along the creek. There's even one big dead tree we can saw up."

"Fine. But what if another blizzard hits? Or two or three in a row? It can happen. Would you like to burn that old chest to keep from freezing, or your new sewing machine?" His vexed tone changed to one of cajolery. "It's your housewarming present, Kirsten, and can you deny that's what it'll do?"

She had to laugh at that, and yield. While Blue unsaddled and rubbed down Stockings, Kirsten tethered the cow in choice grass while the buffalo watched from a distance and began himself to graze when he decided that his companion was going no farther.

At dinner, Blue explained about the cow. "Thought it'd be a nice surprise for you, Miss Kirsty, and you know I did earn some money here and there on our loop, so I took some cash along. Good many settlers comin' in since the Strip was called public land for sure, and a family from Arkansas who've taken up land a couple of miles from the O'Briens were sellin' this cow." Everyone was well at the O'Briens', Blue went on to report, except that Lorena looked peaked, though delight over her pretty dress had brought color to her cheeks. Jackie was starting to crawl, so it was a big help that Lucy guarded him from harm, rocked the cradle O'Brien had made, and ran many small errands that saved Lorena steps.

"Lucy was sure excited over her new dress," Blue said. "Good thing you put in a big hem. She 'pears to have grown a couple of inches just since the Fourth." A remembering look passed over his face and he reached in his pocket. "She sent you this." He produced an old envelope scribbled with pencil. "That's a picture of Patchy," Blue grinned. "Maybe our little gal's goin' to be an artist."

As Kirsten smoothed out the paper, joy at being remembered mixed with a pang over all that she was missing, these precious days of Lucy's discovering the world. She must be nearing two and a half, though her birthday could only be guessed at. The O'Briens had decided to make Midsummer Day, June 24, her birthday.

"Nice that the little tot remembers Auntie Kirsten," Ash said blandly.

Kirsten scowled at him. After a puzzled glance, Blue went on with his news. "The Taylors, the folks I bought Dolly from, have joined Kelman's claim club, and so have most of the other grangers who've been takin' up land."

Kirsten told him then what had happened the day before. He let out a long, angry whistle. "Why, them polecats! Want I should load up the shotgun, Miss Kirsty, and dust Kelman's britches?"

"I had a word with him," said Ash. "But I'm leaving you a Winchester, Blue. There'll be lots of squatters swarming into the Strip. Some may need a little convincing that you were here first." He slanted a lazy smile at Kirsten. "That's my other housewarming gift."

"I don't like to be beholden—"

"To me?" The corner of his mouth tucked down. "I'm building a house, Kirsten, at Central City, and I certainly do expect a housewarming gift from you."

"I'd be glad to make your curtains."

"That would be a waste of your skills, but what I'd most value would be your advice on decorating."

"I'm sure Amanda and Katharine Allen would be delighted to help you, and they know how fine houses should look."

"They're very gracious ladies, but I doubt they'd approve of the kind of furnishings I want. Solid, simple wood, no gewgaws. All you'd need to do is give me your views on the finishing touches."

It wasn't much to ask and he had done a lot for her. Besides, it would be fun to let her fancy, uninhibited by costs, run wild in the sort of mansion Ash would build.

"I'll do it." She spoke so suddenly that Bowden's jaw dropped before he recovered and smiled.

"Good. When the house is ready, you'll be the first guest."

"Only if you have a mightily respectable housekeeper."

"I'll hire a veritable dragon. She can even sleep outside your door if you like." He rose, chuckling. "The sooner I'm on my way, the sooner my city begins and my house with it." His gaze brought blood to her face. "I intend to hold you to your word, Kirsten." He put on his fine gabardine coat, gave the kitten a caress, and strode into the sunlight.

Luxuriating in the plentiful grass, Dolly showed no hint of straying and after a few days was allowed to graze untethered. Chief, as they called the buffalo because of his majestic head and shoulders, never got really close to her but was never out of sight. Kirsten milked Dolly morning and night, luring her into the stable with some of the horses' grain. Kirsten didn't skim cream off all the milk but kept some for drinking, which Dimma shared, little tongue splattering white on her whiskers. Dimma also loved the cottage cheese Kirsten made by heating sour milk till it formed curds and draining these to form a white, delicious ball.

With her forehead pressed to Dolly's flank, Kirsten experienced a contentment in the familiar chore akin to that of scything, a linking of her old life with the new. Though she'd never return, she missed her homeland, and it was good to know that some things were the same.

Five days after Ash's visit, she was churning the first butter from Dolly's rich cream when she heard the creaking groan of wagon wheels. Hurrying to the door, she saw that Bowden's gift had arrived, a heaping load of split wood. Bart Reed, the black-bearded, barrel-chested freighter she'd first met at Busing Crossing, swept off his tattered hat and grinned at her.

"Nice place you got, Miss Mordal. Here's some good cedar from down on the Palo Duro. Where shall we put it?"

It filled one end of the fuel shed to the top, a trove to be saved for emergencies; its scent had such a fresh pungency that Kirsten put several chunks inside the house. As a matter of course she invited the men for dinner.

"Thanks kindly, ma'am. We'll sure take you up on that. Give our horses a chance to rest before they have to help rassle that buffalo Mr. Bowden asked us to lend a hand with. I'm not much shakes with a rope, but Monty is."

"Never roped a buffler, though," said Monty Hall, a sandy-haired, skinny young man. "Ought to be interestin'."

It was—after their meal enhanced by fresh butter on golden cornbread. Keeping where the wind wouldn't carry their scent to the massive animal, they were close before he detected them and charged, head lowered. Swerving out of his path, Blue got a loop on a forefoot after several casts, while Monty snared a rear one and sprang down to tie the hind feet. Bart, taking over from Blue, who couldn't move fast, secured the front legs, and then, with all his great strength, hung on to the horns, arching the head back. Blue tossed his old coat over the shaggy head. This seemed to befuddle the buffalo, and Blue straddled him and produced his knife.

Blue had commanded Kirsten to stay at a safe distance, but he seemed to be having trouble. She hurried down and went sick at the bloody yellow ooze welling from around Blue's knife. Faintly, she said as she knelt, "If I pull back on each side of the wound, you can see better."

"Doggone it, Miss Kirsty! Oh, go ahead then, guess we've got the critter down." He grunted as more corruption spewed up. "There, I'm hittin' the arrowhead, unless'n it's bone."

Sweating, Kirsten closed her eyes, but she couldn't escape the smell. After what seemed forever, the buffalo roared and wrenched his great body so that he sent Kirsten tumbling. "I've got it!" Blue exulted, holding up the stained, splintered shaft with a triangular head. "Hey, this is iron, not flint."

"Never mind what it is, perfesser," panted Bart. "Can you get the front rope loose and then get out of here? You git along, too, Miss Mordal! When Monty and me let go of this ole boy, we ain't waitin' for no one or nobody!"

"You can leave that coat over his head," said Blue. "Should give you a couple of extra seconds after you let go."

Monty and Bart were mounted and off before the buffalo lurched dazedly to his feet. He pawed the grass, snorted and bellowed, but with his dim vision he probably couldn't see the riders.

By the time they reached the house, he had moved nearer to Dolly and resumed his grazing.

"I wish we'd had some ointment," Kirsten said.

"Not the time of year for blowflies, and he's tough," said Blue.

Bart and Monty had more cornbread and butter, which they claimed was better than dessert, tossed their saddles in the empty wagon, and started back to Hardesty. Both had signed up for lots in Central City, planning to be partners in a livery stable. "Wagon freighting'll die soon as there's a railroad," Bart said. "But we reckon folks'll always need buggies and horses."

"Then the town's really starting?"

"You bet! We've got our soddie started and there must be ten more a-buildin', with the town just platted. Inside of a year, I'll bet it's bigger than either Mobeetie or Tascosa and may be givin' Dodge a run for its money."

They waved and rumbled westward. Kirsten and Blue looked at each other. He said wryly, "Well, looks like we've got Bowden for a neighbor, but it could be worse. Guess I'll go see if there's anything left of my coat."

Chief put on flesh, and though he was free to range as he willed, he could always be seen in sight of Dolly. They never rested their heads on each other's backs as Honey and Stockings did. Blue kept the broken arrow on a shelf that held his things, and Kirsten knew he felt a kinship with the animal who had survived, though maimed, after his kind had been slaughtered to near extinction.

Bob-o-links, black-faced with pert yellow hoods, paused on their way south, but the robber-masked shrikes who had raised a brood in the honey locust by the tree claim seemed prepared to winter over, and so did some of the crows along the creek. A pair of bald eagles flew in to take up residence in a huge cottonwood. On the night that Blue, who always went out for a while before bedtime, called, "Come see the Star Girls!" Kirsten felt both a sense of completion and of starting anew. She had come a long way, both in miles and experience, since the Pleiades had risen last October. With a successful business and a start on a homestead, she had everything she could wish for—except O'Brien and Lucy.

At least they had each other, she had given them that, and that sustained her through sloughs of self-pity and the corrosive bitterness that gnawed at her when she thought of the baby O'Brien had made with Lorena, the baby who'd be born in the spring with all the other new creatures.

A man sleeps with his wife, she told herself. *What would you expect?* But still it burned, like a molten substance that couldn't be scraped off but seared ever more deeply. The best escape was work, and there was plenty of that.

Since she could sew during the winter, she worked now with Blue to scythe all the hay they could and mound it by the stable and the north side of the house after the inner storage was full. They gathered dead wood from along the creek and sawed several fallen logs into lengths for the fireplace. These were cottonwood and would burn quickly, though nowhere as fast as the twisted hay. Cattle had ranged here, and their dried chips, too, went into the fuel shed.

Kirsten also did most of the digging of a well near the fuel shed, for Blue's maimed legs lacked the thrust to send down the shovel, though he could scoop at the sides. As the hole deepened, they laid a log across it; Kirsten filled buckets with earth, which Blue hauled up and dumped before lowering them for a refill. He wouldn't let her work alone.

"There's a kind of heavy gas may settle at the bottom," he warned. "It's killed many a well digger." He lowered and raised Kirsten by the same rope, looped beneath her arms, that was used for the buckets. Fortunately, water began to seep into the well at about twenty feet. They paved the bottom with stone left from the house and lined the sides with hollowed sections of cottonwood trunks. Blue made a stone curbing around the top, mortaring it with mud from the creek, and made pole uprights with a connecting one from which a rope and water bucket hung.

"There we are," he said, beaming. "Water right outside the door. In summer, you might best do the washing over in the shade of the trees where things are now, but for winter, I can move the boiling kettle over here and rig some benches to hold the tubs."

"That would be handy," Kirsten admitted, for she had actually enjoyed washing over near the grove and hanging the laundry over limbs and bushes. "But could you put the kettle and benches on the other side of the fuel shed? They'd still be close to water but pretty much out of sight."

"Sure," said Blue. "And I'll string a clothesline there, too." He glanced around their domain and smiled at the silhouette Chief made on the slope above the creek where Dolly and the horses grazed. "Next year we'll put up a hay barn and dig a cellar, but I'll tell you, honey-girl, we ain't done bad at all."

As could be expected with the Strip declared public land, a number of wagons and horsemen came their way. Kirsten fed them all, sympathizing with the women, who exclaimed wistfully over the clean stone house and its location. For the few men who might have thought of trying to force a woman and partially crippled man off their claim, the Winchester hung above the mantel and the shotgun fitted between Blue's bunk and the fireplace. As the Strip settled up, such men might try to steal a claim, but while there was plenty of open land, they evidently preferred not to risk getting shot.

A chunky, balding freighter, Seth Collings, did stake out a claim three miles to the west, make a dugout, and returned to freighting. He made no bones of the fact that he was merely speculating, intending to sell the land as soon as he proved up on it. Because few settlers could hope to live off their farms for a number of years, the Homestead Act was fairly liberal in allowing people to be away from their claims part of the time if they were working.

Yellow-haired Daisy Ballou, glowing and just married to tall, dark Win Kelly in the bride dress Kirsten had made, stayed with Kirsten a few days, till Win found them a good location five miles east. Blue went to help them build their soddie while Kirsten stayed home to do the chores. She was glad to have a woman neighbor, though with all their work and the distance between, there wouldn't be much visiting. The comfort was in knowing that someone was there, and could be called on in time of need. It would also save trips, for the neighbors could collect each other's mail and take care of store needs when one or the other had to journey to Hardesty, as Blue did in mid-November to mail the Rawlings sisters' gowns.

"Ash is in Kansas City," he said, as Kirsten helped unload their purchases off the wagon before he drove on with the Kellys'. "His house is goin' up, though, wagons rattlin' in most every day with lumber and fancy fixin's. It sets on a rise above the town, I reckon like one of them king's castles."

"What about the town?"

"Must be close to fifty houses, some of them frame. Hear tell Bowden's lumberyard and hardware stores will give credit for building because he'd a sight rather have good solid houses in his city. There's a big general store, two hotels, a couple of restaurants, and Bart Reed and Monty Hall have their livery goin' and a blacksmith shop. Bowden's puttin' up a school that can be a church on Sunday." Blue took off his hat and scratched his grizzled hair. "But can you believe, there's nary a dance hall? And not a single saloon or gamblin' house? One of the hotels has a bar, but the drinkin's quiet and gentlemanly like."

All that in little more than a month! Central City was a long way from Bowden's dream, but he'd made an amazing beginning and was evidently enforcing, right from the start, rules that would send on their way anyone looking for a congenial binging place. Such an atmosphere, as Ash had predicted, was bound to appeal to women and sober, substantial businessmen and home seekers. Getting a crock of butter for Blue to take along to the Kellys, Kirsten had to confess that she was curious about Ash's town and, even more, his house. It would be a challenge to suit him.

One thing she needn't have worried about. She wasn't going to see much of O'Brien, and though she knew this was better for everyone, her heart still ached with yearning, especially when Dimma waked her with a soft touch, and Kirsten, in a dreaming flash, thought it was her love.

Winds shrieked out of the north, bringing lung-piercing cold but no moisture. When Kirsten milked Dolly, their breath clouded like smoke in the stable, and Dolly and the horses were let into their stalls each night in case of a sudden storm. Chief escorted Dolly from several hundred yards away and spent nights fairly near the stable, but remained wary.

Twisting hay for the fire was an unending chore when a fire was needed all day instead of only for cooking. Hay gave off copious smoke, and wisps littered the floor, but the precious wood must be hoarded for when the dry hay might give out, or the weather was too fierce to allow frequent trips to the fuel shed. As it was, hay and cow chips were stored in the front of the house—a practical necessity, for every time the door opened, cold rushed in. The chips burned longer than hay and smoked and smelled less.

"Next winter," Kirsten said to Blue, blinking her smarting eyes as she glanced up from her sewing to the naked trees outside, "we won't burn hay if there's any way to manage without it."

"We'd ought to have some corncobs and cornstalks," said Blue.

"And I can take the wagon next fall and fetch a load or two of cedar from the river breaks."

Only Dimma approved of the hay. She pounced in and out of it, pursuing real or imaginary mice, and scattering showers of hay on the floor. Her antics more than compensated for the mess, though, in giving them something to laugh about. She loved to hear Blue play, and if he was slow in picking up the violin after supper, she jumped onto the chest and touched the strings, not with her claws, but just enough to make them reverberate. She had a wonderful time playing with the shavings that uncurled from Blue's knife as he whittled the inhabitants of the Noah's ark he was making for Lucy and Jackie. Kirsten had made them both red flannel nightgowns for Christmas and cuddly stuffed donkeys with floppy ears. She had also knitted mittens for the whole family, a hood for Lorena, and a warm cap for O'Brien.

Not all days were blustery, of course, and it was then that they fenced the garden and wheat field with posts and barbed wire Blue had bought at Ash's lumberyard and hardware. If wheat sprouted next spring, they didn't want their animals to eat it.

The time for the Christmas ball drew near. By now, fond as she was of Blue, Kirsten longed to see her other friends; much as she loved her house, she wanted a change. After almost a year of traveling, she hadn't been off the claim in nearly three months except for taking one pleasant afternoon to ride over to visit with Daisy Kelly. With Lorena's baby coming in the spring, Kirsten doubted if the O'Briens would make the tiring drive, and that would make it easier, much as Kirsten missed O'Brien, for her to attend the ball.

The trouble was that both she and Blue couldn't go. One had to stay to milk Dolly, shut her in the stable at night, and feed and water the chickens. The matter was settled when Win Kelly brought the news that the Wolf Creek fiddler had gone back East. Kirsten was sure that Blue's playing was needed more than her presence and insisted that he go, taking the O'Briens' presents to mail if they weren't at the ball.

With him gone, the house was lonely. Kirsten was grateful for Dimma and talked more than usual to Dolly while milking her that evening. After supper, indulging herself with a log for the fire, Kirsten tried to knit, but was stricken with homesickness as she remembered her village. Had Sexton Carl got the money she'd sent for candles to burn on her family's graves? Would Chet

Brophy remember that Lucia, half a world away, should have her candle, too?

At last, to comfort herself, Kirsten got down the old family Bible, and with Dimma nestled in her lap, read the story of the shepherds, the star, and the baby. The Swedish words seemed strange to her now, and lost in a sort of musing sadness, she watched the flames curve and flicker.

She was drowsing, when there was the crunch of steps outside and a knock came on the door.

27

If it hadn't been for Kelman and the chance of claim jumpers, Kirsten would have hurried to open the door and invite the wayfarer in to warm by the fire, have a meal, and take shelter for the night. As it was, her heart pounded and she started to lift down the Winchester, though she couldn't use it, when a familiar voice called, "Blue! Kirsty! It's O'Brien."

Then she did run to open to him, drawing him quickly in from the cold wind and looking at him as if he were an apparition materialized from her longing before she urged him to the fire. He dropped his saddlebag and stood in his sheepskin coat, rubbing his hands, while she put coffee on, trying to control with that ordinary task the trembling that spread from within her to her fingers.

He had come. Almost like a spirit. "Are you hungry?" she asked and stepped back, less from the kindling in his eyes than the answering blaze that devoured her bones like quicklime, leaving her powerless.

"I ate on the trail. Came to bring your Christmas, though I figured you'd be at the ball."

"They needed Blue's fiddling more than me."

"I'll bet none of the men would agree to that. Lorena wasn't up to travelin', but she just finished her present for you yesterday and was set on your havin' it."

"I sent your gifts with Blue," Kirsten said ruefully. "He'll mail them, but they'll be late."

"Christmas is anytime you get a present," he laughed, taking off his coat. "I hope you'll like yours."

Opening the saddlebag, he took a folded piece of paper from

the bottom. "Lucy sent you a picture of herself in the dress you made. Lorena spent hours embroiderin' these pillowcases. And she liked the bread bowl I made her out of black walnut so much that I thought you might like one, too."

The big, slightly oval bowl had a hand-rubbed mellow grain and could be used for many things other than making bread. "It's beautiful," Kirsten said, caressing it with pleasure in the smooth rounding. "We used many wooden things in our kitchen in Sweden, but there was no room to bring them. It's the nicest gift you could give, O'Brien. And the pillowcases are lovely."

In truth, the stitching of the seams was crooked and the embroidery awkward, but knowing the time Lorena must have employed on a labor so difficult for her, Kirsten valued them and felt a sting of self-reproach for feeling as she did about O'Brien. Smiling fondly at Lucy's smudged, jagged drawing, Kirsten pinned it to the curtain by her sewing machine beside the first picture of Patchy.

"You made it a lovely Christmas, O'Brien. Now sit down and have your coffee and plum cake. I made two for the holiday, and lots of ginger cakes. You must take some home."

Prodigally, she put another log on the fire, cedar this time, for its bracing odor. She brought a plate of ginger cookies and plum cake and a pitcher of cream and poured coffee in the china cups. Not by a glance or tone would she betray more than friendship, taint the joy of his being in her house this special night.

Night? Her heart stopped before it began to pound, driving blood into her ears. He had come expecting to find an empty house, or Blue there alone while she went to the ball with the Kellys. In either case, he'd have spent the night. But did they dare, whatever their resolves, sleep in this house he'd made for her where they might do what they must not, in irrepressible desire or that half-dreaming state that freed the body to wholly seize its dreams?

When she had started, that other night, to go to Bowden, it was love for O'Brien that had stopped her. Tonight, that same force could sweep her away. And while she swore it must not, part of her cried, *This one time, this one night to last my whole life—what can it matter when she has him always?*

They spoke of the surge of people into the Strip, of Ash's town and mushroom settlements like Beer City, which was little more than a place for men to carouse and drink the whiskey they couldn't legally buy in Kansas.

"Most of the folks comin' in are decent," O'Brien said. "But there's some rough ones, too. There've already been some fights in our part of the Strip, where settling's thickest. Couple of men who wouldn't join Kelman's claim club found nooses in front of their dugouts and decided it wasn't healthy to stay. I hear the Committee's tossin' tobacco sacks full of bullets in front of places where someone's staked land any of them want. A squatter was found hangin' over by a distillery he had in a canyon off Coldwater Creek. The sign on him said he was sentenced for making rotgut, but the word is he ran Kelman off and wouldn't join the club."

The nape of Kirsten's neck chilled as she remembered the day Kelman and his gang had ridden in. They might well have killed Blue if he'd been there. She didn't think that even they would kill a woman, but remembering the pink-faced man's opaque blue eyes on her naked feet, she knew there were things as bad. O'Brien didn't know about that day, and she wasn't about to tell him, though she wondered with a rush of fear whether Ash Bowden's warning would serve to keep Kelman away from her if the vigilantes' power grew.

"It's not right," she cried. "Kelman's worse than the men he kills!"

"You and I think that, and he hasn't even asked me to join him —knows I won't and wants to save his face. But to most of these new settlers, he offers protection for their claims and some sort of order."

"We don't need his kind of order. We need law."

"Yes, but we won't get it till Congress decides to tack us on to Kansas or Texas or maybe Indian Territory. And let me tell you, in spite of Judge Parker and his lawmen out of Fort Smith, the Territory's probably got more outlaws per square mile than the Strip. Sure, and they've always ranged over here when a marshal got too hot on their heels. But till we're part of a state or territory, Kirsty, the only way to stop Kelman would be to form another bunch of vigilantes, and now that he's got so many new folks behind him, that sure would be a mess, damned near a war." Brooding as he watched the flames, O'Brien finished his coffee and rose to his feet, summoning a smile. "Hang on, colleen. There will be law here some day. Our kids won't believe us when we tell 'em about these times."

Our kids? He'd have a child of his body now, but she would not. That bitter inner cry must have flashed from her eyes for he drew in a sharply sighing breath and said in a whispering murmur, "Oh, Kirsty! Oh, colleen—"

Turning blindly, he started for the door. "Wait," she called, moving after him. "You can't ride home tonight."

"I've got to." Not looking at her, he shrugged into his coat and had his hand on the latch when a voice came from the other side.

"Pardon me for eavesdropping, but I had to know if virtue and duty would triumph yet again." Ash Bowden stepped in, a caped black cloak over his fine black suit. He gave O'Brien a cool smile in which there was more than a hint of envious disbelief before he swept off his broad-brimmed hat and bowed to Kirsten. "Don't ruffle up, my dear. Accept, both of you, the homage of my cynic's soul. Surely, between the three of us, we can be honest."

Kirsten stared at him, transfixed, while O'Brien went scarlet and then pale. Uninvited, Bowden moved to the fire and turned his back to it, warming his hands behind him.

"What are you doing here?" demanded O'Brien.

Bowden grinned hardily. "Like you, I wanted to see Kirsten."

"I didn't think she'd be here," O'Brien blurted, and then swallowed hard. "You came from the ball, didn't you? You knew she was here alone."

"Of course, and on Christmas Eve, I found that to be a good deal too much like Cinderella and hastened to bring her holiday cheer and company, not realizing she had the last." Reaching inside his cloak, Bowden produced a handsome bottle, a book, and a gilt box with a red satin bow. "The etiquette guides say a young lady may accept chocolates from a gentleman, even if they're from New York," he said, handing the box to her. "I think you'll like the book, it's a history of the United States. As for the champagne, let's all have a glass."

Frowning, O'Brien said, "We'd both ought to leave, Bowden. Or go sleep in the barn."

"Do as you like," smiled Bowden. "But unlike you, unfortunately there's no reason why I can't spend a blameless night under Miss Mordal's roof."

"You slept outside last time!" Kirsten blurted, and then, while

Bowden's smile broadened, blushed hotly at O'Brien's startled and indignant glance.

"That was warmer weather," Bowden said. "Unless you're unkind enough to deny what you offered last time, I'll take Blue's bunk."

"If you think I'd leave you here—" O'Brien began.

"Stop it! You're both staying in the house!" Kirsten glared at them. "It's the dead of winter and anything else would be ridiculous."

"You're absolutely right." Putting on his hat, Bowden started to the door. "I'll take care of my horse and bring in my bedroll. Since you were here first, O'Brien, I'll yield the bunk to you."

He went out, leaving them staring at each other. Kirsten started to explain, but O'Brien raised a silencing hand. "It's none of my business, Kirsty, long as you're satisfied, but if he ever does you a meanness, I'll break his damned neck. I'm not leavin' till he does or till Blue's back, and right now I'd better fetch my bedroll, too."

"You won't get in a fight?"

"Not unless he starts it."

In turmoil, Kirsten ground coffee and put on a fresh pot. O'Brien was shocked and hurt to learn that Bowden had stayed overnight at her place, but after all, it *was* none of his business! She was glad that at least Bowden now knew that O'Brien had behaved honorably toward her, though again, *damn* him, that was none of *his* business.

"Men!" she said to Dimma, who purred agreement.

Ash brought disturbing news. Late in November, another conflagration devoured most of downtown Dodge and a mid-December blaze swept away what was left, including Minnie's hotel. "Minnie's all right," he assured Kirsten. "She had a nice amount of money saved and is putting up a new brick building for a restaurant. Says she's tired of running a hotel. Bob Wright's rebuilding, and so will others, but I've offered the reputable merchants free lots and loans to build in Central City."

"Sure and the fires came at a lucky time for you," remarked O'Brien.

Bowden shrugged. "If Dodge can't change from a cow town, it's finished anyway." He poured Kirsten more champagne, and she was soon so drowsy that she went to bed, though the conversation had taken a turn that ended the men's sparring.

"I've put all the pressure I can on friends in Congress," she heard Bowden say as she lay down, Dimma curled under the covers at her feet. "With settlers coming in the way they are, we can't wait years for the government to do something about the Strip. We may have to organize our own territory and ask Congress to recognize it."

Grudgingly, O'Brien said, "Sounds like a good idea, except I sort of had the notion that only Congress can make states and territories."

"That's true, but when so many people move into a region that they need law and government for protection, they have a natural right to form their own if Washington won't."

O'Brien rubbed his jaw. "Fair enough on the face of it, but who's goin' to do the organizing? Someone like Kelman, who's already got lots of the new folks in his pocket?"

"There'd be a meeting. Everyone could come, have a say, and set an election for officials."

"Officials!" growled O'Brien. "What good are officials that don't have any legal authority?"

"They'll have the authority of the people who vote for them," said Ash. "It's the kind of law that's been set up in mining camps and other places with no sheriff and judges handy. Works a sight better than vigilantes who just elect themselves."

At that point, Kirsten roused herself and tried to listen, but the champagne fuzzed her mind, and though she grasped at their voices, meaning dulled and soon she was asleep.

Next morning, she gave them breakfast and sent them both on their way. "Bad enough that you weren't with your family Christmas Eve," she told O'Brien. "You've got to at least get home today."

"I don't have a family," Bowden said plaintively, though laughter sparkled in his eyes.

"That's your fault," retorted Kirsten.

He gave a resigned sigh and offered O'Brien an expensive cigar. "All right, O'Brien. I guess we'll ride off at the same time, though not in the same direction."

And that was what they did, Kirsten looking after, not knowing whether to laugh or be angry.

Blue brought many greetings, parcels of cake and ham, and a number of dress orders, the material folded up in his bedroll. He also had much news. Meg and Marilyn loved their bride gowns and had persuaded their parents to let them have a June wedding. "Tom and Bill strutted around like peacocks," Blue chuckled. "But not the match of Zeke Thomas! Bridget was there but she wasn't dancin'. Be a baby in their house this summer, I reckon."

"A baby?" echoed Kirsten, aghast.

"Well, Zeke ain't got none," Blue pointed out. "And Bridget sure looks happy, so where's the harm? Anyhow, her young'uns are startin' to spill out of the nest. Annie was dancin' a lot with Monty Hall and lookin' mighty purty."

"She's only fourteen!"

"Plenty of gals marry then."

"Well, I hope she won't!"

"Oh, Bridget will prob'ly rein 'em in for a year or two," Blue said, soothing her. "Jim Cator was there with his English bride, she's sure a nice lady, and the Hoodoo Browns—the missus ordered another dress—and Colonel Jack Hardesty down from Dodge. Lots of new settlers."

As he talked on, Kirsten wondered at her vehemence over Annie and Monty Hall. Wasn't jealousy mixed with her honest concern that the girl for whom she'd made a child's curveless dress fifteen months ago and who'd been burdened with the care of her younger brothers not marry while she was still a child? It seemed that everyone else was either getting married or having a baby. This gave Kirsten a curious feeling of being left apart, stranded, while the mighty, changing flow of life swept past. And just then it did no good to look from stable to house to field and meadow or hold in her hand the packet of orders that proved her success.

New Year's Day, 1886, dawned bright, but when Kirsten went to milk Dolly, she froze at the sight of a huge blue-black cloud obscuring the sky to the north. Blue had already seen it and was stringing joined ropes from the stable to the house.

"We're in for a storm, honey-girl. I'll draw plenty of water and stow wood and hay in the house."

"Should we bring the horses and Dolly inside?" Kirsten asked. She didn't welcome stained floors, but that was better than letting the animals die.

"The stable's good and tight and their body heat ought to be enough," Blue said. "We can hang on to this rope to go out to the stable if the storm lasts into tomorrow."

Kirsten glanced at Chief, a hump-shouldered dark figure on the slope. "I wish we could get him into the stable."

"No way to do that, but maybe he'll come down to the hay stacked around it. He made it through last year's blizzard, Miss Kirsty, and others before that."

She hurried to give the chickens fresh water and grain and shut them in their coop before filling the mangers with hay and starting to milk. Thank goodness there was more than plenty of hay to last a whole winter of storms. But what of O'Brien with his hundred head or more of cattle on the range? Would he risk his life as he had last year trying to keep them from drifting south?

Fear for him almost blotted out her own anxieties, and she realized that hard as it was to miss him, it was infinitely worse not to be able to help him at a time like this, not even to know where he was. She murmured a prayer for him and his family and their painfully acquired small herd as she gave her animals farewell pats.

"Keep each other warm," she told them, picked up the bucket, and met a blast that sent her reeling backwards as she opened the door. Gasping, she got outside, fastened the door securely, and fought her billowing skirts as she bowed her head against the howling wind, which was beginning to spit ice that stung her face and hands like finely splintered glass.

The blizzard keened all night long. Well fitted as the door was, snow almost as high as the latch sifted in at the cracks while the windows were banked with it so that daylight, when the storm abated, was only a lessening of darkness. Both Kirsten and Blue shoveled hard for two hours to clear a path to the stable, which was completely drifted over. The animals would have to stay in till the snow melted, so while Kirsten milked, Blue cleaned the floor and put down clean hay.

It was a trackless world so white that it hurt the eyes and bewildered the mind; there was no seam between sky and horizon. The house was a mound, except for the clearing at the door Snow weighted the ash tree's branches and those of the trees above the spring. Staring, she saw no sign of Chief, till suddenly the mass at the rear of the stable moved and a dark form emerged, scattering hay.

"He did the same as us last winter," Blue said with a grin of relief. "Snugged into his feed. Guess we won't have to worry about him after this."

"I wonder if O'Brien's got enough hay," said Kirsten.

"Oh, he's got enough to feed through this snow if it don't stay on too long. But if it's a bad winter—" Blue shook his head.

"We've got a lot more hay than we need," said Kirsten. "When the wagon can get through, I'd like to take over a load and tell him to come for more."

"I'll take the wagon," said Blue. "You drive fine on a road, but there's tricks to goin' cross-country."

Five days later he delivered the hay, getting back just as a second storm swooped over the plains. Kirsten helped unhitch the team and gave them grain while Blue rubbed them down. Blue opened the stable door to a stifling flurry of wet snow, coming so thick and fast that he shouted, "Hang on to the rope, honey-girl, and stay right behind me!"

Buffeted by the gale, blinded by the swirling flakes, they struggled their way to the house, which they couldn't see till they reached the door. Inside, stamping and shaking off the snow while Dimma mewed her displeasure at their messiness, Kirsten said remorsefully, "Blue, you were almost caught in that storm!"

"I've almost been a sight of things," he teased. "O'Brien was much obliged. Said if we've got extra hay, he'd like to buy more. He sure doesn't want to lose his good heifers and is tryin' to keep all his stock pretty close."

"He won't be out in this?"

"No. Lorena and the kids have grippe or somethin', but he'll come when they're better." Blue gazed out at the whiteness packing the windows. "And when this is over."

The storm raged most of the next day, and they were grateful for the wood, which made frequent trips to the fuel shed unnecessary. Following the rope to the stable, they cared for the animals and milked, but apart from that, they stayed inside while snow buried the walls and roof.

O'Brien came for hay the next week. Not wanting to leave Lorena longer than necessary, he didn't spend the night but left as soon as he'd rested and grained his team. He looked so gaunt, the hollows beneath his cheekbones like gashes, that Kirsten asked, "Have you been sick, too?"

"Too mean for that," he said with a fleeting grin. "But Lorena's poorly. She—" He broke off and swallowed, meeting Kirsten's eyes, though he went crimson. "She'd like for you to help birth the baby. Her mother did last time, but they've moved back to Arkansas."

Kirsten went cold, then hot, then cold again. Help bring the baby that her heart cried out should have been hers? How could she? "I've never helped with a baby," Kirsten said. "Don't you have neighbors? The Steiners who sold Blue our cow?"

"Yes, and I'm sure Mrs. Steiner will come over, but Lorena wants you. It'd make her easier in her mind if I could tell her you'll be there."

Kirsten stopped trying to evade the pain, the jealous anguish. She let it fill her, and said from its depths, "Then I will. Just to be sure, I'd better come a week or so ahead of when she's expecting."

"There's no way I can thank you."

"You did, before I'd been in Dodge half an hour." She forced a smile. "It'll be fun to have some time with Lucy."

"Sure, and she's always prattlin' about Aunt Kirs'n," he said. "Reckon the baby should come about the middle of March." He brought out a shabby wallet and tried to hand her a bill. "For the hay."

She recoiled. "Not unless you let me pay you for all the work you put into my house. We're neighbors, aren't we?"

His eyes embraced her. That wild, sweet yearning stopped her heart. "Yes, colleen. We're neighbors." He touched her face quickly and sprang into the wagon.

He'd been gone two days before the next storm darkened the sky, so as she and Blue assured each other, he was bound to have been safe at home. It was well he'd come when he had. During the next ten days, storm followed storm. Blue and Kirsten quit trying to clear snow from the windows. It was all they could do to keep a path shoveled to the stable and chicken coop. During lulls, Chief left his hay shelter to labor through drifts as tall as he was to the slope, which the wind scoured off quickly. But when sleet or snow started falling, he made for his refuge. The creek froze solid, so Dolly and the horses had to be watered in wash tubs filled from the well.

Still, Kirsten knew they were lucky. With a soddie, in this kind of weather at best, snow would sift in, at worst, the heavily weighted roof could collapse. She and Blue were in a good house with fuel, food and kerosene for the lamp, and she could sew while Blue played the violin. It oppressed her, though, to think of wild creatures and tame caught far from shelter, and remembering Lucy's young parents, she prayed no one else would die like that.

When the storms finally passed, the snow melted to reveal small deaths all over the plains, sodden heaps of feathers that had been cheery, winter-braving meadowlarks, and prairie chickens that wouldn't gather soon on the booming grounds. A pronghorn had died against the garden fence, and without walking far, she found a coyote, a quail, and several rabbits.

Blue rode to Hardesty to mail four dresses Kirsten had finished and returned with news that Dodge City had been snowbound, trains unable to get through, and ice a foot thick on the Arkansas River. Two men had frozen to death trying to reach their homes, so had a stage driver bound for Camp Supply, and several people had lost limbs to frostbite.

"Critters dead everywhere," Blue said. "Wild things or cattle or horses, if they couldn't find shelter, they died. It's lots worse than last year, Miss Kirsty. Hi Allen lost at least half his stock and at that came off better'n most."

There was a letter from Minnie, inviting Kirsten to dine free anytime at her new restaurant, and one from Ash, sent from Washington. "I'll be back soon," announced the bold, slanting scrawl. "Remember, Kirsten, you've promised to turn my house into a home."

Her cheeks burned as she put the letters in the Bible, where she saved precious bits of paper for using again. She hadn't promised that at all, yet guiltily and in spite of herself, in this winter of disaster, she looked forward to his return, his confidence and energy; and it preyed on her that in little over a month, she must keep her promise and be with Lorena when she bore O'Brien's child.

28

The snows brought death, but they soaked the earth, parched from a year of no moisture, and the first greening of brave little plants began under a mantle of withered grass. On a visit to the Kellys, Kirsten heard an unmistakable booming and followed it to watch cocks strut in a wide, bare shallow basin while hens pretended indifference. Their numbers were few but this courting would help replenish the flock. There still were meadowlarks, and the horned owls were making a nest in a high leafless fork of the biggest cottonwood.

Kirsten plowed the garden. It was exhausting work to hold the share in the furrow; had O'Brien not used the sod cutting sled on the place last fall and had she not plowed afterwards, it would have been impossible.

"This kind of work needs oxen and a man with good strong legs," growled Blue. "Seein' you behind that plow makes me hate bein' hamstrung more'n anything else ever did, Miss Kirsty."

"You have plenty of other work," Kirsten said, rubbing unsalted butter into her blistered palms. "Anyhow, each time the soil's worked, it'll be easier." She made a joke of what she suspected might be the truth. "Why, I'll bet in ten years, there's not a buffalo grass or bluegrass root left in the garden!"

She was also able to plow out grass and weeds between the rows of sprouting wheat. But when it came to land for corn, oats, maize, and more wheat, which they would need to feed themselves and the animals, Kirsten paid Win Kelly two dollars a day, his board, and feed for his oxen to bring them and his sod plow and break fourteen acres of virgin soil, and another dollar a day and board to help Blue fence the new fields. She blessed the fact that she earned enough from sewing to afford it.

By the end of February, Kirsten and Blue had sowed four acres of oats, and they hurried to plant potatoes before Kirsten needed to leave at the end of the first week in March to stay with Lorena through the baby's birth. With a bucket of potatoes cut in pieces so that each had an eye from which a plant would grow, Kirsten was kneeling to cover one and mound a hill around it, when a shadow fell across that of the garden fence and she glanced up to see Ash Bowden sitting on his black horse.

His expression made her feel as though she'd been caught in doing something wrong. She was barefoot, since her shoes got small clods inside them from walking in the plowed ground, and her skirt was kilted up to keep it clear of the dirt. Hastily releasing it, she said, "Welcome. Take care of your horse and I'll get dinner as soon as I finish this row."

"Go ahead now, Miss Kirsty," said Blue. "Reckon I can finish by the time you have our grub ready."

Ash came up as she was washing her hands at the high bench that held the wash basin, the pail, and the milk buckets and vessels after they'd been scalded. Taking the towel hung on a nail, he dried her hands gently and thoroughly, in spite of her protests, and in a tone that allowed no argument, said, "Sit down, there, on the curb of the well."

Before she knew what he was about, her feet were in the basin. "Ash!" she cried, but he prevented her from rising by clasping a foot in his hand and kneading the sole and ankle and each toe with a strong yet calculated touch, before he took the other and gave it the same careful attention.

It felt wonderful, but Kirsten knew she shouldn't allow it. "Don't!" she said. Looking up at her, Bowden dried her feet and for just a moment held them against his chest, hands firm on their high-arched slenderness.

"These have no business getting bruised and sore and calloused," he said. "For heaven's sake, Kirsten, if you must homestead, let me pay a man to do what Blue can't."

"I have money." She drew her feet away from him and stood up. "It's my affair, not yours, to decide when to hire help."

His jaw made a rock-hard square of his face. She stalked past him to the house. When, after a few minutes, he came to watch her mixing cornbread, his face was smooth again and his tone amiable.

"I've come to ask you to keep your promise. My house is built and mostly furnished, with even the most straight-laced house-keeper you can imagine. It's time for you to see it and use your special magic."

"I did promise, and I will come, but not just now."

"Why not? Blue said he'd finish the potatoes today, and I'm farmer enough to know you can't plant row crops or much else till April."

Avoiding his gaze, she set the Dutch oven on the coals. "I'm going to the O'Briens' this week."

Bowden started, recovered, and said, "The baby? You're actually going to be there when it's born?"

"Lorena wants me."

"Why, then, by all means, she must have you." Bowden's voice glinted with irony. "I knew you were hellbound to play Auntie Kirsten, but I didn't dream even you had such a taste for punishment."

Furious tears spilled from Kirsten's eyes as she spun around to confront him. "How can you be so hateful?"

"Will you let me be loving?"

Their eyes dueled. Hers dropped first, and she swallowed wrath that could only, with him, put her at a disadvantage. "After the baby's born, if you can wait that long, I'll do my best with your house."

"I can wait as long as it takes." He sat down, took Dimma in his lap, and stroked her to purring while he talked of the new town of Beaver, just being platted by promoters from Wichita, Kansas, at Jim Lane's road ranch on the Beaver River.

"Won't that hurt Central City?" Kirsten asked, hoping to keep the conversation off all too personal things.

Bowden laughed. "I never intended for my town to be the only one in the Strip," he said. "Only the best."

When it was time to go to the O'Briens', Kirsten took the Family Gem with her, wrapped in dress materials and blankets, and secured in a slicker behind Honey's saddle. On the long day's journey to where her creek flowed into Kiowa Creek, she counted half a dozen claims besides the Kellys', all with dugouts, except for one soddie. The same thing must be happening throughout the Strip wherever there was water. Hurrying to reach the O'Briens' before dark, but not wishing to seem rude if invited to stop, Kirsten kept a distance from the dwellings but thought a woman must live in one soddie, for curtains showed at the windows.

Living in a dugout or soddie was the mark of the true pioneer, Kirsten supposed, but one she was happy to forego, and she was glad that, as Blue had reported, the rock and wood cabin overlooking the meeting of the creeks was well made and shaded by ashes and cottonwoods. Kirsten would have thought considerably the less of O'Brien had he left his wife in a soddie while he raised a stone house for another woman.

The barn and stable were sod but, like the house, were roofed with cedar shakes. A windmill reared like a sentinel above the corrals, and from the number of longhorn crossed with Hereford cattle that had come to water at the big tank, Kirsten dared hope O'Brien had saved most of his herd.

He came out of the barn as she approached, carrying a bucket on which Lucy also had a grip. The last sunlight torched the man's hair and the child's into living flame, and Kirsten's vitals twisted with yearning for these two, best loved of all on earth.

As if to rebuke her sense of desolation, Lucy saw her, let go of the bucket, and ran forward. "Aunt Kirs'n! Aunt Kirs'n!" Setting the bucket on a stump, O'Brien hoisted the little girl, laughing as he put her in Kirsten's arms for a rapturous embrace and a short ride to the stable.

"So you've come, colleen." Joy lit his eyes as he lifted her down, with Lucy still clinging to her neck, but there was underlying sadness in that deep green look, and the angular face was much too thin. "You're mightily welcome. Go on to the house while I look after Honey. Lorena will be that tickled to see you!"

She clearly was, throwing her arms around Kirsten and kissing her as if they were sisters. "Sit there in the rocker and I'll fetch you some coffee," she urged. "Supper won't be long. Oh Kirsten, I'm so glad you've come! The baby dropped two weeks ago, and it feels like it's pressing against—well, the bones down there. Margrit Steiner says that happens a lot with second babies, but it's terribly uncomfortable and I feel big as the barn and not a whit prettier!"

Quelling the thought that there could be no sweeter burden than O'Brien's child, Kirsten said cheeringly, and with truth, "Your face looks beautiful, and you haven't long to wait now for a little son or daughter. I came to help, not sit, Lorena, so tell me what to do."

* * *

After supper, Kirsten washed dishes while O'Brien dried and
Lorena sat rocking Lucy and small Jack, whose cheeks pulsed with
the rhythm of strong tugs at his bottle. He'd been weaned from
Lorena's breast early because of the expected child, but at eleven
months he already looked heartily vigorous beside Lucy's petite
delicacy. With Patchy lying by the chair, one paw crossed daintily
over the other, Lorena and the children made a beguiling picture.
No wonder O'Brien smiled on them with tenderness before his
gaze struck Kirsten's like a clash of swords.

Feeling as if a blade had plunged into her to cause concealed
bleeding, slow and secret, Kirsten averted her face and in so doing, glimpsed the brass bed in the corner. There was nothing for
it; this stay would be an ordeal, and the hardest part would be not
to betray that her friend in America was also her first and only
lover.

Three nights later, as she bathed Lorena's sweating face, whispering encouragement as the gasping woman gripped her hands, Kirsten berated herself for what now seemed a childishly selfish,
wicked thought. When Lorena's pains had started three hours
ago, early in the afternoon, O'Brien had brought in fuel and water
before leaving to bring Mrs. Steiner.

Surely, they must come soon, *must*, before the baby began to
emerge. Lucy, detailed to rock Jackie to sleep in his cradle and
amuse him when he woke, was in the small bedroom Kirsten
shared with her, where the cradle had been moved, and was
spared at least the contortions of Lorena's face, though she must
have heard her moans. O'Brien had considered taking Lucy to the
Steiners' for a few days, but in the end agreed with the women
that Lucy knew a baby was to be born and that being home would
upset her less than being abruptly left with strangers.

Squeezing Kirsten's hands till they ached, Lorena arched with a
contraction and then lay panting, very pale except for her bitten
lips. "I—I'm sorry to be such a baby, Kirsten."

Kirsten wiped her face, smoothed the moist dark hair away
from that wide-eyed, childish face. "Do whatever helps, Lorrie.
You're not trying to win a soldier's medal, but get your baby
born."

"Yes." Lorena grasped Kirsten's hand. "I've got to tell you something, Kirsty. Little Jack isn't Pat's, but Pat married me to take care of both of us. He's—he's been so good to me, I won't feel right till I can give Pat a child of his own."

"You shouldn't feel that way, Lorrie. O'Brien loves Jackie and Lucy as much as if they were his."

The dark head moved stubbornly. "I can't give Pat much compared to all he's done for me, but I will do that. I will if it kills me."

"Don't talk that way." Kirsten was genuinely shocked. "The children and O'Brien need you a lot more than they do another baby."

Lorena's teeth clamped her lip, but a groan broke through them as pain wracked her again, and she gripped Kirsten's fingers till the bones ground together. When the tide of that agony subsided, Lorena whispered, "It feels like the baby's head's trying to come out. Can you see if it is?"

The last thing in the world Kirsten wanted to do was lift up the sheet and peer at the distended opening between Lorena's bent legs, wet with blood and secretions. How could a baby possibly come from there? But in the strained orifice, she saw what looked like golden hair plastered to what must be a skull.

"The head's showing a little." She fought nauseated horror to make her voice calm and steadying. "But I think it will still be a while."

Was this how it was supposed to happen? Was there anything she should be doing? "I'll bring you some tea," Kirsten said, cursing her ignorance.

To her vast relief, she only had to attend Lorena through a few more violent contractions before Margrit Steiner came in, a tall, raw-boned woman with blue eyes and graying blond hair. She surveyed her patient, scrubbed strong, blunt hands and took charge, telling a white-faced O'Brien to take the children outside and relegating Kirsten to wiping Lorena's face and bracing against her gripping fingers.

"Won't be long, dear," Margrit encouraged. "That little head's just about ready to move. Pain comin'? Good, that's what'll bring your baby. Bear down and yell if you want."

A scream tore from Lorena's throat. Her frail body arched, the belly monstrous, and Kirsten thought, *She's been through it before, she knew what it was, but she was willing to do this for O'Brien.*

Humbled at the other woman's courage, appalled by her suffering, Kirsten prayed with all her heart and will that Lorena wouldn't die. In that moment, if foregoing even O'Brien's smile for all time would have ended Lorena's travail, Kirsten would have gladly struck the bargain.

There were more screams. Kirsten's hands were crushed almost beyond sensation. She kept talking, hoping that perhaps a voice gave Lorena something to hold to in the intense loneliness of her struggle. "Jackie's such a beautiful little boy. This baby will be even prettier. And it won't be long till we know whether you have another son or a sweet little daughter."

"I want a boy," choked Lorena. "A son for Pat—" She screamed again and Mrs. Steiner grunted.

"Push, honey. That's the way. Good girl! Just breathe down like you could send the babe out with it. I've got my hand on top of a head of red hair so it won't come out too fast."

Lorena cried out as if riven in two. "The head's come," called Mrs. Steiner. "That's the worst part, honey. Take a deep breath and let it go, baby ought to just slip on out now."

But it didn't. Unable to see what was happening, Kirsten read the alarm on Mrs. Steiner's broad face. "Got big shoulders," she said with a matter-of-factness that the fear in her eyes belied. "Let's see if I can move them just a little."

This scream reverberated, ending in a snarling wail. Mrs. Steiner's face dripped sweat. She concentrated on her task. There was a crunching sound, like a thick eggshell breaking. All the time cries were ripping from Lorena as if they were all that could come from that tormented body.

Straightening, hands globbed with blood and mucus, Mrs. Steiner implored, "Try again, Lorrie. Push hard as you can."

After a mighty, convulsing effort, Lorena went limp, but after a moment her eyes fluttered open and fixed on Mrs. Steiner, who held a slippery little form head downward over her arm, cleaning out the nose and mouth before she gave a slap between the shoulders. When nothing happened, the woman hurriedly set her mouth over the tiny nose and mouth, puffing in a breath. The tiny chest rose, but apart from that the infant was still.

"My baby!" Lorena tried to sit up but fell back, possessed by a contraction that sent out a slippery reddish mass.

When no effort could evoke a sign of life in the small body, Mrs. Steiner gave it to Kirsten to hold while she tied the bluish cord and cut it. Tears mingled with sweat on the weathered face as she examined what must be the afterbirth and gently rubbed Lorena's abdomen.

"The baby," Lorena gasped.

Taking the child from Kirsten, Mrs. Steiner cleaned him before resting him in his mother's arms. Kirsten had never seen a new baby before, but she thought he would have been the image of O'Brien with that red-gold hair.

"I'm sorry, dear." Mrs. Steiner stroked Lorena's forehead. "His shoulders were too big. I—I had to break one to get him out and I think his little ribs cracked, too. I'm sorry. There wasn't any other way."

"He has to be alive!" Lorena stared down at the baby, pulled open the front of her gown and tried to suckle him at a swollen, blue-veined breast, which now must ache—oh, how it would ache —for the want of a hungry little mouth to draw milk from it. When the fair head rolled limply, the eyes shut without ever having seen this world, Lorena clutched him wildly, sitting up, to rock him. Mrs. Steiner shook her head.

"I had to do it before, but that time the baby lived." She looked helplessly at Kirsten, who wondered whether they had the same thought, that broken ribs might have punctured the baby's lungs or heart. What a waste, a terrible, senseless waste, of a perfectly formed small new person. And how bitter for Lorena, to endure the weary months of carrying, the cruel pangs of labor, and then hold a dead child to her breast.

Kirsten had thought it would be hard to tell O'Brien that he had a baby by Lorena. How gladly she would have done that now, if only it were true. Telling him his son was dead was the hardest thing she'd ever done.

Kirsten had knitted the baby a soft white blanket. They wrapped him in it, once Lorena was persuaded to give him up with the promise that he'd be buried on the slope above the house, where he wouldn't be lonely. O'Brien thought of that, and when she couldn't bear for the child to be buried without a coffin, he made one with boards from the wagon.

There was no minister closer than Dodge, but grizzled, burly Joseph Steiner, an elder in his Iowa church, spoke of how Jesus had taken children in his arms and said, "Suffer the little children to come unto me and forbid them not, for of such is the kingdom of heaven."

Lorena wept almost continually, till she kissed the baby and brought the blanket over his tiny face. Then, as O'Brien and Steiner fastened the lid and lowered the little box into the grave dug out of the thick sod with picks, Lorena knelt with Jackie and Lucy in her arms, and a strange, still look masked her, a look that frightened Kirsten, for it was as if Lorena's rounded, almost infantile face had in these few days aged into that of an old woman.

Kirsten stayed another week, till Lorena was strong enough to take care of herself and, with Lucy's help, see to Jackie. Fortunately, her breasts, though enflamed and tender at first, began to dry up without caking. She would sit for hours by the window facing the white headstone on the slope, rousing only when Jackie pulled up on her skirts or Lucy ran to her with some question or discovery.

Lucy had wanted to see the baby, and after considerable discussion, O'Brien had prevailed in his view that she would be less troubled if she was allowed to touch and kiss him before he was buried. Probably there was no good way to handle her worries, but Kirsten thought the dead child might have harrowed up in Lucy some vague memory of the mother and father who had lain quiet, too, and could not answer.

However that was, the little girl, usually romping with Patchy when she wasn't tending Jackie with earnest exhortations to "grow up and be a big boy," now held the black-haired child in her lap till he squirmed and howled and had to be rescued. She also woke him from his naps, and was herself fearful of going to sleep.

"Jackie not go dead?" she queried. "Jackie not go to sleep in box?"

Gathering Lucy up, Kirsten soothed, "Jackie's fine, sweetheart. He needs to sleep, everyone does, but that's not like being dead the way the new baby boy was." Who never breathed the air of this world but slipped into the eternity from which he'd come still linked with his mother's body.

Lucy's fair eyebrows puckered. "Baby not wake up? Never, never, never?"

"Not with us, honey, but he's in a good place."

Later, Kirsten heard Lucy solemnly repeating this to Jackie, and by the time Kirsten had to leave, Lucy was again starting to race with Patchy and lead Jackie around by his hands, chiding him when his chubby legs buckled and he sat down kerplunk. He never cried at such times but pulled himself up on something and progressed from one support to the next, till he tired of that mode of locomotion and reverted to his knees.

Before she left, Kirsten caught up the washing, including the blood-stained bedding, which she'd soaked in cold water, and baked a dozen loaves of bread, several pies, and a lard tin full of ginger cookies. When she told Lorena good-bye, the other young woman, jarred from some secret world, embraced Kirsten and thanked her.

"I don't know what we'd have done without you," she said, brown eyes filling. "I hope I can pay you back sometime, Kirsten."

"You already did, by letting O'Brien get my house built. Besides—" Kirsten's heart swelled and she spoke through an aching tightness in her throat. "I didn't do anything, there was nothing I *could* do, Lorrie."

"You were with me," said Lorena, pressing Kirsten's hand to her lips. When she looked up, her face settled again into the bleak cast it had had at her infant's burying. "I'm going to have another baby. I'm not much use to Pat with the outside work and really not very good at keeping house, but I am going to give him a child."

"Of course you will," said Kirsten, and hoped it was true, for these days of grief and loss had deepened her love for O'Brien, till her earlier longing for his mouth, for his arms, for the joining of their bodies, had been tempered in the crucible of birthing and death. Beside those, desire seemed brief. So long as O'Brien lived and was well, she vowed that she wouldn't let herself want anything more, and now she firmly grasped Lorena's hands. "Don't hurry, though. Wait till you're strong."

Lucy ran out with Kirsten to where O'Brien waited with Honey. Kissing Lucy, Kirsten hugged her, savoring the child's sweet warmth before giving her to O'Brien. Their eyes met over the curly golden head. Jolted as if by lightning, Kirsten felt the ashes of her renunciation burst into flame. Very well. Her feelings hadn't changed, but she had new feelings, too. These gave her the strength to mount without O'Brien's aid and say, meaning it, "Take care of Lorena, O'Brien. Tell her you need her and love her."

"Oh, aye. But Kirsty—" He carried her hand to his face, head bowed, and she saw the sun-browned back of his neck joined to flesh as white and smooth as Jackie's. Yielding to irresistible tenderness, an overwhelming need to comfort, she cradled his head just for a moment against her breast, smoothing the waving mass of red-gold hair.

There were no other words and that was their farewell.

29

The white of bones, skeletons of creatures small as prairie dogs or large as Hereford bulls, showed through the green of the freshening prairie, and this spring, because many coyotes had also perished and it had been the work of insects and returning buzzards to dispose of rotting flesh, the bones were less scattered than they had been last year. Kirsten scarcely heeded them, or even the windflowers, Easter daisies, and white and purple mats of vetch.

She saw instead that little face with its flattened nostrils that had never breathed, eyes that had never opened, mouth that had never tasted, and again she rebelled, not only at the grief, but at the waste of anything so wonderfully and intricately made. Honey shied at the dainty hoof of a skeleton pronghorn hidden in a clump of sage, and as always when she saw any death without being steeled for it, Kirsten felt a wave of pity and anger.

The pronghorn, too, was awesomely made, beautiful, and joyed in its speed, the company of its herd. There was no answer to why lives brought into the world at the pain of mothers, human or animal, and lovingly nurtured by them, were cut off at random, as Lucia's had been.

No answer. Yet in those prairie dog mounds on the flats above, young were snug in their burrows; in that cottonwood beside the creek, crows were nesting. The killing blizzard also brought life, moisture to quicken the dead brown prairie into verdant freshness. The sandhill cranes and geese flying north had surely lost some of their numbers, but these would breed and the young would wing south again next autumn. Birth, breeding, and dying flowed inexorably but naturally into each other. Kirsten could accept that as abstract law but not when it happened; not when

Lucia died or Lorena's baby never lived, and especially not when people killed someone as they had Bob Randall.

She was musing on these memories, when she saw a cluster of men where a tree forked over a gully. For a moment she thought her mind was throwing out an image of young Bob's lynching. She blinked. The men were still there, and now she saw that the slightest one had his arms tied, saw the others shoving him roughly to the edge of the bank. Her spine chilled as she recognized August Kelman and several of his cronies, including the pink-faced, yellow-haired man who had enjoyed her discomfiture when he stared at her naked feet.

They mean to hang that little man!

She shouted and sent Honey loping forward. A bright red wagon stood on the bank, the horses tied to a tree. MAURY'S TRAVELING EMPORIUM was gilded in ornate letters on the side.

Why on earth were they hanging a pedlar? The wispy little man wore a brocade vest and had long, waving gray hair, a beaky nose and dark eyes that were now huge with fright as he held up bound hands to Kirsten.

"Lady! Lady! Don't let them hang poor Maurice! Please, I give new merchandise for what they say is not so good—"

"Not so good!" scoffed the fair-haired man. "That calico you sold my woman was full of moth holes and mouse droppin's! And them shoes fell apart first time they got wet."

"That liniment you get three dollars a bottle for ain't nothin' but creek water, molasses and red pepper," accused a lanky young man in overalls, and added the ultimate grievance. "Don't even have alkyhol in it!"

"That necklace you said was gold turned my wife's neck green," growled brown-haired, stocky Win Kelly, Kirsten's neighbor.

"You switched knives on me and the one you left won't cut hot butter," accused a skinny granger Kirsten had danced with at the Fourth.

"Gentlemen, gentlemen, I will make all right!" swore the pedlar.

"And travel across the Strip cheatin' other honest folks and laughin' over your shoulder at 'em?" demanded Kelman. "We don't want your kind here, you pesky little varmint!"

"If you will let me go," whispered the prisoner, "I will be so very glad to leave this Strip."

"You're stayin' here," grated Kelman, "till your carcass rots and your bones fall off the tree."

"No." Kirsten sprang down from Honey, trailing the reins so she'd stand, and planted herself between the pedlar and the eight men who'd made themselves judge, jury, and executioners. Staring from one face to another, she met anger from most, hatred from Kelman and a bold, calculating grin from the pink-faced man. Only Win Kelly studied the ground.

"Pile back on that horse," advised Kelman. "This ain't a woman's business."

"It is when you break the law."

"We don't need a foreigner tellin' us the law!" Kelman advanced on her. Though she was trembling, Kirsten stood her ground.

"It seems you do. If this man cheated you, let him make it good, but don't kill him."

Kelman was holding a rope. Now his thick, hairy fingers shaped a noose. "Get out of the way!"

Behind her, Maurice whimpered. Kirsten flung her arms around him. "I'd rather you hung me, too, than let you murder a man for a piece of cloth or a pair of shoes."

Kelman's eyes seemed to swell from their fatty sockets. "You think we won't touch you 'cause you're a woman and Ash Bowden's sweet on you, but if you won't keep a woman's place, we might just teach you where that is! Won't we, Jess?"

"Be a pleasure," grinned the man with yellow hair. He moved toward her.

"Hold on." Win Kelly grabbed Jess's arm. "Miss Kirsten's my neighbor. Sewed my wife's bride gown. If you heard her talk, like we did, last Fourth of July, you know she expects Americans to be a whole lot better than we are, but that's no crime."

There was silence, a shifting of boots. Then several of the men grunted approval. Most wore guns, and when they moved toward Win, Kelman and Jess were alone. The granger Kirsten had danced with nodded and looked at the pedlar. "Main thing is to teach this scroungy little liar a lesson. Reckon he won't try cheatin' us again."

"No, indeed," quavered Maurice. "Indeed, I won't! Though I assure you, I sold in good faith—"

"Stop while you're ahead," Win cautioned. He untied the smaller man's wrists and then his arms.

As if dazed, Maurice stood beneath the tree for a moment before he sank to his knees and began to kiss Kirsten's hands. "Kind lady! Maurice Krakowski adores you, he is your slave! Only command—"

"Get up, for heaven's sake! And give these men what they paid for or hand back their money."

He winced but gave a willowy shrug. "At once, dear lady. If you will come with me, gentlemen."

When he had made restitution, for he had quality goods as well as shoddy, the men went their separate ways, except for Win Kelly, who helped Kirsten mount and said with a meaningful glance after Kelman and Jess, "Why don't we ride together, Miss Kirsten?"

"Fine, if you don't mind falling in beside the wagon for a while."

Kelly slanted her an appreciative grin. "Yeah, Gus could still shoot this rascal."

Maurice almost jumped off the wagon seat and his relieved smile faded. "You—you won't let him?"

"He's not likely to try with us along," Kirsten reassured him, and couldn't resist adding, "If you're so nervous, Mr. Krakowski, you'd better be careful about what you sell in the Strip."

"You are right, kind lady." He sighed, smoothing his silky gray moustache. "For many years I have been a merchant in Arkansas, but the frontier called—"

"More like there was a sheriff behind you," Win said.

Maurice smiled unabashedly. "Let us say I was drawn to new horizons. It was my intent to purvey necessities, yes, even luxuries, to women isolated on ranches and homesteads through all this barbarous—I mean, beautiful—plains country, Kansas to Texas, this No Man's Land to New Mexico."

"I don't see how you expected to get customers to buy again if you sold them poor stuff once," said Kirsten.

"Oh, I wouldn't do that anywhere I meant to travel again," he said quickly, and went on to regale them with his adventures. When they stopped to eat and rest their horses, he curried his sleek gray team and gave them grain in nosebags, procedures that raised Kirsten's opinion of him.

To unsaddle Honey, the Family Gem had to be taken off first. When Win helped Kirsten place the heavy bundle on the ground, Maurice eyed it speculatively.

"Madam is also a merchant?"

"That's my sewing machine," Kirsten laughed. She explained her business, then, and he listened with glowing eyes.

"Madam," he said when she finished, "you need a partner, and I am he!" Looking up at the sky, he added piously, "Already God has rewarded you for your compassion."

"Do you sew?" asked Kirsten, bewildered.

"Ah, for that you can hire assistants if need be. No, I will represent you on my travels, obtain for you rich customers, spread your renown!"

"I already have quite a few patrons," said Kirsten. "But even when I've fitted them before and have their measurements, I worry about gowns fitting when I can't actually see people try them on. Thank you, Mr. Krakowski, but I really am afraid—"

He raised a dramatic hand. "Wait!"

Win rolled his eyes as the pedlar vaulted nimbly into the wagon. "Watch him, Miss Kirsten. He's goin' to try to sell you somethin'."

"Sell?" cried Maurice, puffing as he hauled out a cloth-wrapped object as big as he was, set it on the seat, and reverently pulled off the covering. "This is my gift, gracious lady, my thanks for my life. Ah, Providence has indeed brought us together, for here I have precisely what you require to carry on your profession at a distance from your clients."

"Watch him," Win muttered again. "That contraption looks like a dadburned giant mousetrap."

To Kirsten it looked more like a fantastical birdcage. Made of wires fitting over five round centerpieces rigged with puzzling mechanisms, it still had a somewhat familiar shape. "What is it?" she frowned.

"Madam," he breathed ecstatically, "it is a dress form. A model of the female figure, adjustable at all the—er—strategic places." He manipulated the device at the waist. "Behold! In a few minutes you can create the shape of a maiden, a well-endowed matron, or a behemoth. Imported from Paris, this Milady form will never fidget or twitch like real women. It won't chatter till your brains whirl, or keep changing its mind. It won't—"

"Remember," cut in Win, "you ain't a-sellin' it."

Maurice's eloquence stopped in midflow. "You'll like it, madam," he concluded.

After examining it and trying several adjustments, Kirsten grew as excited as he was. The device would tremendously ease her efforts to achieve good fit without the client's presence. She could hardly wait to get it home, fix it to Amanda's measurements, and start the summer dress Amanda had ordered.

"It's exactly what I need, Mr. Krakowski, but I'm sure it costs far too much for me to accept it as a gift. Set a fair price."

"You think Maurice's skin is not worth the Milady?" he said with indignation, and then chuckled. "It is not perhaps, except to me, so you must have your present."

"Take it," Win advised. "He'd be dancin' with those patent leather slippers of his pawin' the breeze if you hadn't got him off."

Maurice's smile ebbed, but he brightened immediately and extended a slender, well-manicured hand. "We are partners, yes?"

"Perhaps." Kirsten didn't take his hand as she looked him sternly in the eyes. "I won't be partners with anyone who cheats anyone, anytime, anywhere. Before we talk business, I'll have to see you get rid of all that shoddy stuff, and if I ever hear that you've played such tricks again—"

He waved his hands in injured protest. "Madam, I can see it is not smart to cheat these clodhop—I mean, worthy farmers. But you will not object if I sell my less serviceable goods at a bargain?"

"From what the men said, you ought to be ashamed to give it away," said Kirsten.

With a tragic expression, he turned to Win. "Sir, you also aided me. I make you a gift. All my wares that are—"

"Not worth carrying home," shrugged Win. "Why not? If they don't cost nothin', we can't be disappointed."

Maurice thrust out his hand again toward Kirsten, but she delayed. "We haven't talked yet about this partnership. What sort of commission will you want for getting new customers?"

He studied her. "Twenty-five percent?"

"Not unless you do part of the sewing. After all, you're going to these places anyway."

"But with my connections I can get very good prices for you on cloth, lace, trimmings, buttons, everything you need."

"When a woman gets a dress of mine, she'll like it so much that she'll buy more from you."

"I'll find you customers—rich ones—you'd never get otherwise."

Kirsten had to laugh. "Fifteen percent."

"Twenty."

"Seventeen and a half."

"Madam, you should have been a pedlar," he beamed. They shook hands. He tucked Milady back in place and pulled on a green velvet coat. "Let us proceed to your dwelling, madam, and while I recuperate from nerves and rough handling, I will make sketches of some of your styles and you must compose a message to your new clients."

As they made ready to travel, Win said, "If I was you, Miss Kirsten, I'd sure count my chickens before that sweet-talkin' little polecat leaves. Ain't he got a tongue in him, though? I'm kind of glad we didn't hang him."

Though they were so different, Blue and Maury, as he asked to be called, took a great liking to each other. Maury had played the violin in his youth and taught Blue what he said were tunes taught him by a Hungarian father and French mother. Born in New York, he had lived in California and even Alaska and had an inexhaustible supply of stories. He filled a pad with sketches taken from Kirsten's pattern books and had her write beside each what the garment was suitable for and what fabrics it would look best in, and he went over Kirsten's letter to customers, changing a word here, a phrase there, till she was exhausted and he proclaimed it a masterpiece.

"This makes you the confidant of each patron," he exclaimed. "You ask a woman to tell you about her life, what occasions she'll need the dress for, her coloring, her preferences in style. For those who seldom see another woman, you will become a friend." He tapped his fountain pen against his teeth. "But do you think it wise to say you don't want payment till after the garment is delivered and the lady is satisfied?"

"I don't think anyone will take advantage of me and keep a dress they won't pay for. But if there is such a person, I don't want her for a client." When he still looked dubious, she said, "I want to try it this way. If it doesn't work, I can change."

Maury departed after five days, perhaps speeded by Blue and Kirsten's beginning to plant corn. To prepare the plowed, harrowed field, Blue drove the team, which pulled a homemade four-runner sled, to make furrows in one direction and they crisscrossed these by pulling the sled the other way. To make the runners dig into the earth, Kirsten stood on the sled, legs braced to keep from falling off at the turns.

Then, with a bag of seed corn slung over her shoulder, Kirsten walked along the furrows. Where the lines of the checkerboard joined, she dropped in three or four kernels. Blue followed to cover the seed with a hoe. There were seeding machines, and though it wouldn't pay to buy one for their small field, Kirsten thought it could be lent to Win Kelly and others in return for the sort of heavy work neither she nor Blue could manage. If Maury got her as many customers as he vowed he could, at the prices they had agreed on, she could gradually invest in a self-raking reaper and binder and in time maybe even a thresher, expensive but labor-saving machines that could be used for miles around.

Meanwhile, she savored the rich, musky odor of the loamy soil and with great enjoyment wriggled her bare toes into it with each step. This lasted for the first few hours. After that, it became a chore, something to finish so they would have those roasting ears Blue spoke of with such relish, and later, cornmeal and chick-enfeed.

By early afternoon, they had planted a little over half of the four acres readied for corn. The soil had lost its earlier moisture and softness and was harsh against Kirsten's feet, no longer receiving them in sensuous yielding, and she began to realize what she had been too young to fully comprehend in Dalarna. Planting and harvest controlled people, people could not control them any more than they could the seasons that marked these times. It was good to feel linked with all those in all ages and places who had dropped seed, nurtured it, and lived from the crop, but it also brought fear that the work could be in vain, that the crop might fail, as it too often had in Sweden, as potatoes had failed in Ireland.

That, at bottom, was why many folk had come to America. Crops could fail here, too, but the nation was so big and there was so much land that surely people would never starve here as they did in other countries. Deep in these thoughts, Kirsten didn't see Ash Bowden till he called from the edge of the field. He was mounted on his black horse and two men were with him.

"Miss Mordal, I got tired of waiting for you to keep your promise. These men will do your planting while you decorate my house."

Kirsten let her skirts down but held them off the earth as she walked to the fence, ready to give him a piece of her mind. How dare he be so high-handed? Before she could open her mouth, he forestalled her, taking off his hat and tipping it toward his companions.

Doffed hats showed the freckled, gangly one to have reddish hair and the sturdy, short one to have a curly black thatch. Both smiled bashfully and mumbled greetings as Ash said, "Thad Perry and Noah Jones grew up on farms. They can plant as well as you can. But neither one can decide what curtains I need, or rugs, or pictures." He smiled in his disarming way. "Please, Miss Mordal! My house is built, the furniture's freighted in, the grounds are landscaped, and I'm eager to wind up the finishing touches."

She said drily, "I can't believe that you, of all people, don't know what you want."

His eyes made her regret the words, but he replied smoothly, "I know the effect I want but not how to get it, and though I could import a decorator, I wouldn't trust any of them not to ruin my house with gewgaws and frippery." His tone changed from coaxing to challenge. "I know you pay your money debts, Miss Mordal, but do you keep your word?"

She had promised; she owed him that much. Slipping the seed bag over her head, she hung it on the fence post. "All right. I'll come."

The two-storied white house, situated on a slope overlooking the flow of Coldwater Creek into the North Fork of the Canadian, dominated the town below. Central City was already as large as Tascosa and reflected careful planning rather than haphazard sprawl. Businesses occupied two broad principal streets and four intersecting ones, with a square in the center, obviously laid out to encompass giant cottonwoods; they were just now budding leaves that would cast welcome shade in summer.

"That's where the courthouse will be," Ash said. "See, there are two churches now and that's the school going up. The brick building on the last block is the library. Later, when the academy's built, it'll serve students as well as the community. I've brought in a doctor from Kansas City. The brick building on the south end is his surgery, and as the population grows, I'll build a hospital. Merchants who're tired of getting burned out in Dodge have moved here, and you'll notice that most of the houses are frame and even the soddies have good shingled roofs. I'll give you the grand tour this evening and take you to dinner at the hotel, but now let me show you my house!"

Turning their horses over to a lanky, bow-legged young man who hurried out of the red-painted stable, Ash set his hand beneath Kirsten's arm and escorted her toward the house, following the paving stones that circled around it to the front. She was glad to see that he hadn't tried to use tame grass for a lawn but had simply mowed the buffalo grass. Nor had he imported exotic trees, but had planted copses of hackberry, ash and cottonwood, with cedars near the house. When they grew, they would form a native parkland, and the only flowers were those that grew on the plains.

"It's beautiful," she said. "And yet you've kept the prairie."

"I thought you'd approve." Stone steps led up the broad porch that ran the length of the southern and western exposures, and there was another verandah opening from the second storey. Wicker chairs, small tables and a cushioned settee showed that the porch was intended for enjoyment, and indeed it pleasured the eye to gaze out across the rolling country or follow the greening bends of river and creek. The porch floor, like the window trim and shutters, was painted sage green, and Kirsten thought, *Ash doesn't need advice on colors, or much of anything else inside, I'll be bound!* To suit his taste would certainly be an exacting test of her own.

If he doesn't like my ideas, he has only himself to blame. Taking courage from that, she paused as they stepped inside, waiting for her eyes to adjust. She felt, rather than saw, Ash at her side and sensed his proud expectancy.

As she was able to look around her, she saw that she could honestly congratulate him. "Ash," she said, "It's—" She reached for the right English word. "It's magnificent!"

And it was, in a simple, masculine way that relied on the burnished grain of fine wood, sweeping space, and huge windows that framed broad sky and prairie into living landscapes that would change with sun, clouds, and seasons. A broad hall, paneled in mellow golden oak, ran the length of the house and demanded paintings. Why not of birds, gray sandhill cranes with maroon caps; the whole plains family of owls, from the small burrowing ones that companied with prairie dogs, to the great horned predators that were the eagles of night; and of course, bald and golden eagles, and the wheeling clan of hawks? And there must be the tribe of larks rising from gayfeather and bluestem; jaunty magpies; gossiping crows, chickadees and winter's perky white-crowned sparrows—oh, somewhere in this great house, there'd be room for them, shown with the trees or areas they favored, at different times of year. Prairie chickens, of course, must be shown at the booming ground, orange sacs puffed out, the hens demure.

When she burst out with this, Bowden's eyes widened for a moment in surprise before he laughed. "Now how did you know that the only pictures I've ever bought are some prints of a painter named Audubon? He's dead many years so I can't engage him to fill in what we're missing, but I daresay I can find a nature artist in St. Louis or Kansas City who'd be delighted to come out and paint whatever we suggest." Bowden tilted his head, watching her and gave an abrupt nod. "You may decide all the paintings save two. In my study, I must have you in your wagon, setting forth to conquer though you wear a mourning dress. That sight will stay in my mind forever, Kirsten."

"I don't know," she began doubtfully. "I—"

"Merciful heavens, girl! Don't act as if I wanted you to pose in the nude. Think of yourself as the spirit of the pioneer or something. Now come meet Mrs. Shelton and have some coffee before I show you around."

When Kirsten exclaimed over the huge iron range with its warming ovens and hot-water reservoir, the gray-haired housekeeper, looking most professional in her black dress and starched white apron, loftily informed her that it used coal, which was much less trouble than wood. Kirsten, who considered wood a luxury and couldn't aspire to any baking she couldn't do in a Dutch oven, met Ash's sardonic eyes and said, "Yes, it must be convenient."

As Mrs. Shelton brought coffee and assorted cakes and muffins to the living room and placed the silver tray on a polished slab of walnut set on three rounded legs, Kirsten saw that even the piano was absolutely unadorned with flutings or knobs or the pineapples and acanthus leaves so beloved by Amanda Allen. Surrounding the fireplace set into a stone wall were easy chairs and a settee, covered with tawny flecked tweed and large enough for a tall man to sleep on. Similar groupings occupied the two bay windows. The floor was oak, waxed to the shade of honey. Long mirrors gave back the vistas from the windows.

"No pictures for this room," said Kirsten, thinking aloud as she enjoyed an unfamiliar but delicious blend of coffee and munched a crisp chocolate nut bar. "Except for one above the piano. Rugs the color of yucca spikes. And your draperies, homespun looking, they must fall straight and be, I think, the shade of summer buffalo grass when the wind ripples it, brown with a hint of rose."

"I was right to trust you," said Ash. "But I suppose you'll prescribe a fancy chandelier?"

Kirsten gave him a look of horror. "That would ruin it! Copper would fit, but black wrought-iron would be better."

"Wrought-iron it is," said Ash, rising as if he couldn't control his eagerness. "Come and let me show you the rest of the place."

Mrs. Shelton's quarters, which they didn't enter, a study furnished with oak, a small dining room in maple, and a large one in mahogany completed the first floor. Up the staircase was another hall with rooms on both sides and again, light streamed through windows that made ornaments and ordinary pictures superfluous, though paintings of wildlife would help bring the outdoors within.

"This is the mistress's private domain," Ash said, stepping into the southwest corner room looking out on creek and river. It had a small rose stone fireplace, a rocking chair and table. At Kirsten's puzzled expression, he said gravely, "Not to make a mystery of it, this will be your room or no one's. I didn't presume to choose your furniture."

"Ash—"

He raised his hand. "Don't say anything. You came to advise and I won't use your kindness to bedevil you." He chuckled. "I did furnish the lady's guestroom next door and hope you'll approve."

Here, again, the poster bed, dresser and armoire were walnut, and Kirsten said at once, "Yellow curtains and coverlet, yellow jute rug, sunflowers and black-eyed Susans on that wall and a pronghorn doe and her fawn on this one."

Two other guestrooms were for couples. Kirsten advised gold mohair plush for the stately mahogany room; and plaid curtains, rag rugs, and a starburst quilt for the maple. On the threshold of what had to be Ash's room, Kirsten hesitated, but he drew her in.

"Cypress won't rot, even under water," he said, indicating the huge bed and dresser, the closets running the length of one wall.

"See, on lazy mornings I can watch the sun rise. I only want one painting in this room, Kirsten. Coyotes sitting on a knoll, singing to the moon, clever and crafty, able to survive when men kill off the other wild things."

"I like coyotes, too," she smiled, "but I keep my chickens shut up at night."

"Prudent Kirsten," he said with a flicker of irony. "Now, what will enhance the cypress?"

She touched the smooth gray-brown dresser. "Let me think about it," she said, wanting to escape from this private chamber.

"Yes," he said, though she had asked no question. "I do dream of you, Kirsten, dream of you here. And there's nothing, I assure you, darling, that either of us can do about that."

30

Kirsten couldn't deny enjoying the three days she spent with Ash, so much so that she felt guilty when she thought of Lorena's aching breasts and that small grave on the slope. Ash gave her little time for such regret, however. They made a list of birds and animals to be painted and of the spots where they would best hang. As if it were as vital as his farflung business ventures, he wrote down colors she advised for curtains, rugs and coverlets, the type of lamps or chandelier for each room.

During Kirsten's stay, Mrs. Shelton occupied the adjoining guestroom, and her initial wariness of Kirsten seemed to abate. Never once did Ash try to make love to Kirsten, but her consciousness of his iron control raised tension between them, Kirsten feeling as if she'd made a brief truce with a lion. It was headily flattering to have such an escort, but she knew the power in him, guessed at his ruthlessness, and knew he forebore to woo her only because he judged this was not the time.

After he took her to dinner at the Central, his hotel, which was even more elegant than the Dodge House, he showed her through a number of small shops located on the first floor, one that sold expensive chocolates, a barber shop, a leathergoods shop, a men's tailor, and a shop for luxury feminine articles such as gloves, handbags, hats and lingerie.

"This space is yours whenever you want it," he said. "Don't you think it would help your business to have several outfits displayed in the window?"

"I may not need more business." When she told him about Maury, Bowden shook his head in annoyance.

"Now why would you prefer a deal with a fraudulent wandering pedlar to prestigious exposure in a hotel that attracts people of means?"

She had to think about that for a minute. "He got rid of his bad merchandise."

"He can get more."

"I don't believe he will."

"That's it, Kirsten," said Ash with a sigh. "Think the best of everyone—except me."

She ignored that. "I suppose his idea appealed to me because he *does* travel, visits women who never go to town and seldom see anyone except their families. I'd rather sew for them than for ladies who live in town and don't get so lonely."

"There's always Sears Roebuck and Montgomery Ward."

"Yes, but that's not the same as having a dress fitted and made for you personally. We can write back and forth about what they want and—"

"I dare say you'll learn a lot more than that," he said acidly. "They'll tell you their troubles, their health problems and woes, complain of husbands and then ask if you can help their daughters find one."

"Fine. That way I'll get to know each one. I'll be sewing for a special person, not just one who orders from a store model."

His disgusted look gradually changed to one of keen interest. "Yes, you will get to know them, women way out in the western part of the Strip, folks from all over; and women can't vote, but they have plenty to do with how their men ballot."

"No one can vote yet in the Strip," frowned Kirsten. "We don't have a government."

"We need one, and faster than Congress will move. I'm going to Washington again, grease all the wheels and palms I can, but if nothing happens, I'm going to work with others of like mind to call a meeting, vote ourselves a territory, send delegates to Washington, who, even if they won't be seated, can exert pressure, and meanwhile elect our own judge and officials." He paused, seeking her eyes. "You hate the Committee, Kirsten. Wouldn't you like to help put elected law officers in its place?"

"Of course I would, but—"

"But what?"

"Why are you so anxious to have law and government?"

"It's much better for business."

"Especially your business?"

"Absolutely. Why not? I've put money and effort into Central City and I intend to get us a railroad and develop the Strip. Naturally, my interests will thrive."

She hadn't told him that Kelman had threatened to "put her in her place" when she'd halted Maury's hanging, and didn't choose to now, for much as she detested the vigilante leader, she didn't want to be the cause of Ash's shooting him, something she considered more than likely if she repeated Kelman's words.

"You've said Kelman had his uses," she ventured. "And he seems inclined to do what you say. Has he run off people you didn't want around Central City? Helped those you approve of protect their claims?"

"Of course he has." Ash raised a silver eyebrow. "I make use of whatever tools I find."

"I won't be your tool."

The pupils of his eyes widened to narrow rims of quicksilver. "I hope you'll be my partner. Can you deny that my town is clean, well ordered, and by far the best place you've seen in all the Triangle for families?"

"It still can't be good to use a man like Kelman."

"My sweet innocent, I intend to be governor of this territory, and to that end I'll employ the necessary means." Her face must have mirrored her revulsion, for he gave a short, vexed laugh. "No one comes to power, my Kirsten, not even in your wonderful America, without some dirt on his hands."

"And blood?"

He shrugged. "You chose the frontier, Kirsten, No Man's Land at that. If you wanted law, order and Sunday school, you should have stayed east of Kansas City."

"I decided to live in No Man's Land—and see law and justice come here—when I found Bob Randall hung."

"You'll get your law a good deal sooner if you'd use your influence for my plans."

"I don't have influence."

"No? I'll bet you've got more than any woman in the Strip. For a start, the Allens and Rawlings think the world of you. You're a legend at road ranches and along the trail for surviving the blizzard and rescuing that little girl. And your Fourth of July speech—"

"It wasn't a speech!"

"Maybe not, but more folks in the Triangle have heard about it and what you said than could tell you what's in the Gettysburg Address or the Declaration of Independence. What you say matters."

"Not much," she said bitterly, "or Kelman wouldn't be riding around with his Committee and claim club."

"He won't be needed long."

"If you need him at all, I can't help you."

"Don't you mean *won't*?"

"It comes to the same thing."

They left the hotel in silence, but as he helped her into the carriage, he said, "Kirsten, I've warned Gus Kelman not to bother you, but if you keep on provoking him, as you did when you rescued that pedlar, there might come a time when he'd get worked up enough to forget what I've said. For God's sake, girl, don't meddle in things that don't concern you."

"Like lynchings?"

"Especially lynchings, you crazy little fool! Your neighbor sided with you to save Krakowski's neck, but he may not be there next time."

Remembering Jess's greedy eyes, she shivered but didn't answer. Bowden escorted her home next day. In parting, he thanked her for her suggestions. "I'm going to St. Louis this week," he said. "I'll find an artist to do those paintings. But the first one he must do is you in your wagon."

"I'm busy," evaded Kirsten. "I can't waste hours posing."

"Oh, I'll send Thad and Noah with him," Bowden returned airily. "They'll work while you sit for your portrait. Can't you see it, with a bronze plate beneath that reads 'Lady of No Man's Land?'"

He grinned at her and rode away before she could summon a retort.

Noah and Thad had worked hard with Blue. All fourteen cultivated acres were sowed and they'd dug irrigation channels from the creek to the garden, which was ready to plant with peas, beans, onions, carrots, squash, pumpkin, cucumbers, cabbage, mustard greens and radishes. Kirsten's back ached from kneeling to plant the seeds she'd bought in Dodge, but she scarcely noticed as she imagined the fresh good food they'd enjoy that summer.

Next came setting out cuttings and saplings on the tree claim.

This was an endless task, but Kirsten worked at it with Blue mornings and sewed in the afternoon. Jackie would be a year old the seventh of April, so she hurried to make him some cool little nightshirts and sent them off with two frilly nightgowns for Lucy and a simple, pretty gingham wrapper for Lorena. When Blue took them to the post office, he returned with four orders from women Maury had told about Kirsten's sewing, so with her regular chores, she was busy indeed and not overly welcoming to Bowden's painter, Seymour Carrington, who arrived early in May riding in a buckboard between Thad and Noah.

Of course it was wonderful to have the men's help; depending on how long the painter took, they might almost finish planting the required ten acres of trees, but they all had to be fed and, she couldn't just let her sewing go completely.

"I'm sorry," she said at once to Carrington, a tall, angular man of middle years with alert green eyes in a hawkish face framed by jet-black hair and beard. "But I can't sit up there for hours on end or you won't get your meals."

"Not necessary at all, ma'am," he assured her, twinkling. "But my meals are. Before I do a portrait, I like to get acquainted with my subject and do some sketches, so if you'd be kind enough to give me some coffee, you can go on about your work. Perhaps tomorrow you'd sit in the wagon and let me do a few quick studies. After that you won't need to pose for more than an hour at a time, and of course I can do the team and wagon without you."

At first it made Kirsten self-conscious to find him studying her and making swift strokes of pencil on pad, whether she was kneading biscuits, sewing, or milking Dolly, but she relaxed as she noticed that Seymour watched everyone and everything with that same critical eagerness. At night, when Blue played the violin, Seymour captured him in a few eloquent lines. He drew Thad and Noah rolling smokes, Dimma on the windowsill, and Chief in the pasture.

So that the light would be the same, Kirsten posed for him awhile each morning, sitting in the wagon with the reins in her hands, though of course the horses were only hitched up for the first time, when she wore her ruffled black dress and Seymour worked out the composition.

"I do portraits for a living," he told her as he worked, "but birds and wildlife are what I'd paint all the time if I could. However, those pictures go slowly, and for the most part, mine lack the

exactness required by the few patrons interested in nature to start
with."

"Why is that?"

"You see plenty of meadowlarks on the wing, but can you imagine trying to paint one accurately from glimpses?" His full lips
curled down in distaste. "I won't follow the example of Audubon
and most wildlife artists, who shoot what they wish to paint. I
have field glasses, but observation is of almost no use with noctur-
nal creatures, or secretive, fast-moving ones." At Kirsten's dismayed look, he said more cheerfully, "I'm delighted with Mr.
Bowden's commission and his attitude. He doesn't mind if some
paintings are more habitat and blurred impression of the subject
than detailed portrayals. Fortunately, some do sit still long
enough. Yesterday I got a whole family of burrowing owls at the
prairie dog village, and I have roughs of a magpie and the shrikes
up in that honey locust. Besides, back in St. Louis I do have access
to some stuffed collections, and I'll use them when I must."

He wouldn't let Kirsten see her likeness till it was finished, but
at the end of a week, he set the canvas on the chest at dinnertime
and stepped back to let them all look. Kirsten stared in amazement.

How strange to see herself, head high, face expectant, black
dress somber against the blue sky, though the sun turned the
yellow-brown of her hair to gold. Seymour had brightened the
green of the wagon, with its crimson and yellow stripings and
curlicues, and the red running gear and wheels, so that the wagon
looked the way it had at the beginning of that long, long journey,
a journey not only of miles but of people, danger and death, the
joy of having Lucy, the grief and growing of giving her up—

Blue gave a soft, drawn-out whistle. "It's you, Miss Kirsty! And
there's Honey and Stockings, nat'ral as life. Ash'll be tickled
pink."

"I like it very much," said Kirsten in response to Seymour's
inquiring glance. "Even when I'm old, even when I'm dead, I'll
still be in your picture, just starting out from Dodge."

Seymour nodded, pleased. "Yes, painting is one of the small
ways we have to conquer time. Perhaps you'd like this pad with
my sketches. It should be quite a family treasure someday."

"Is the one of Blue here?"

"Several of Blue. And one of Chief. Would you like any of them
mounted and framed?"

"Oh, yes, the one of Blue and the violin, and Chief, and maybe this one of me at the sewing machine with Dimma in the window. I can pay you now."

"Call it thanks for your hospitality," he smiled. "I've never had a commission I enjoyed more. Besides, Mr. Bowden's paying so generously that I can afford the rare luxury of making a gift."

The three men had been easy to please and Kirsten missed their lively conversation, but after their departure she was glad to be able to concentrate on her sewing. Seth Collings, returning to prove up on his claim to the west of them, had in neighborly fashion brought their mail: a letter from Bridget and six orders obtained by Maury, four from rancher's wives and two from Beer City women who were almost surely prostitutes, though each requested something "refined and ladylike."

They would get it. Kirsten didn't intend to judge her customers. But she had better order a variety of materials from Sears or Ward's, for the selection she'd brought from Dodge was running low. She had purchased most of Maury's stock, but at this rate, it, too, would be quickly used up. She wished now that she'd bought quantities of cloth at Central City's excellent dry goods store, but she hadn't dreamed that Maury's endeavors would yield so many clients in such a short time. She sent off a sizable catalog order and two completed gowns with Win Kelly when he went to Hardesty.

"Daisy's fine," the stocky, brown-haired young man replied to Kirsten's inquiry. "But this warm weather and the wind a-blowin' all the time's getting her down. She'd sure love a visit if you could get over." He rubbed the white line where his hat shaded his forehead. "I'll be doggone glad when that baby gets here."

"It's good the baby will come before the worst hot weather," she consoled. "Is Daisy's mother coming?"

Win almost groaned. "No. Her ma, Daisy's grandma, has got too poorly to be left alone and there's no one else to take care of her. I recollect your sayin' Miz Steiner is a good midwife, but she's such a long ride away that I'm scared I can't fetch her in time." His brown eyes pleaded. "I know you ain't married, Miss Kirsten, and it maybe ain't proper, but it sure would make Daisy and me both easier in our minds if you'd come."

No! Thinking of Lorena, the golden-haired baby's breaking bones, Kirsten went faint and dizzy. But she was the closest neighbor, the only woman for miles.

"Of course I'll come." She had at least watched Margrit Steiner and had some idea of what to do—which really wasn't much, provided the birth was normal. "After you fetch me, you can go for Mrs. Steiner just in case it takes a long time." No need to add, *or in case something's wrong.*

Relief turned Win's round face boyish. "I'm sure obliged."

"That's what neighbors are for," Kirsten smiled. "Thanks for mailing my packages. And listen, since you'll be away all night, I'll ride over this afternoon and spend the night with Daisy."

"Say, that's mighty sweet of you. Tell you the truth, Miss Kirsten, I don't like leavin' her alone since I got out of the claim club and Committee."

"You quit?"

Shamefacedly, he nodded. "I got to thinkin' after you kept us from hangin' that scroungy little pedlar. What he done was maybe worth a dunk in the river or a good whuppin' but not his neck. Daisy never has liked my havin' anything to do with Kelman, so when I talked it all over with her, we figgered I should quit." He paused. "Gus wasn't real pleased."

"But surely he wouldn't bother you."

Win shook his head. "Don't know, ma'am. Haven't told Daisy, and don't you, either, but I found a pouch with a couple of bullets in it on the threshold of our door the other mornin'. Jess Darnell's said more'n once he likes my claim. I reckon since I quit 'em, they're tryin' to run me out." His young jaw hardened. "I'm not a-runnin', though. Put every dime I had into fixin' the house nice as I could for Daisy, shingled roof and glass windows, and I've broke twenty acres of sod."

Kirsten remembered Bob Randall and went cold with dread. "But Win, there are so many in the claim club. If—"

"Onliest way I'll leave my land is dead," he said in a flat, determined voice. "I keep my shotgun loaded just inside the door and bought a rifle on credit in Central City to carry when I ride." He forced a smile, trying to sound nonchalant. "Likely it'll come to nothin'. They'd rather scare folks than fight. But mind, Miss Kirsten, that you don't drop any of this to Daisy. It's hard enough on her as it is, out here a long way from her family. It means a lot to her to know that you're our neighbor, even if we don't get to visit much." He touched his hat and resumed his journey.

Troubled, Kirsten went back to her sewing but couldn't concentrate. It was her fault that Win had broken with Kelman, and she decided to write to Ash with the details and ask him to use his influence to restrain Kelman. By the time she finished the letter, it was time to fix dinner. As soon as she'd done dishes and put her nightgown in a saddlebag with some mending, she told Dimma to keep Blue company, saddled Honey and followed the deepening trail eastward.

Though they had met only briefly at the Fourth and visited a few times since the Kellys settled here, Daisy greeted Kirsten with a kiss and heartfelt embrace. "You can stay the night? Oh, I'm so glad, Kirsten! Please don't ever tell Win, but I hate being alone even in the daylight, and when he's gone at night I just sit up till it starts turning light and then I sleep a little. Thank goodness he's not gone often!"

"Well, you need your sleep with the baby coming, and after that you won't get lonesome. Till then, Blue can carry any letters you want to send and bring your mail, or I'll come stay with you."

"Oh, that's dear of you, Kirsten. It's silly because I know I'm older than you are, but I guess because you made my beautiful wedding dress I catch myself feeling like you're a lot older and wiser—sort of a fairy godmother." The yellow-haired, rosy-cheeked young woman was far along in pregnancy but carried her burden higher and moved with less difficulty than Lorena had. "Come in and have some beverage while you tell me all the news."

"Beverage" turned out to be water mixed with enough vinegar to give it a tart, rather pleasant flavor. Win had indeed made the two-room soddie as clean and comfortable as he could for his bride. Its walls were whitewashed and it boasted four glass windows in a region where windows were few and often covered with hides oiled to make them somewhat transparent. There were rag rugs on the hard-packed earthen floor, a bright flower quilt on the bed, a wedding picture on the mantel and several vases, small cheap pictures and figurines that Kirsten suspected were the choice of Maury's discards. The house, with its wood ceiling, was far better than most soddies, which again were incomparably better than dugouts, but Kirsten, with a swell of tenderness and gratitude, realized again what a good home O'Brien had built for her.

She regaled Daisy with an account of her trip to Central City, Seymour Carrington's visit, and their progress in planting. "Win's set out some cottonwood cuttings on our tree claim," Daisy said, "but I haven't been much help outside lately. I can't even bend down to tie my shoes." She made a face and her clear hazel eyes probed Kirsten's. "Kirsten, is it true Mrs. Steiner had to tear Lorena O'Brien's baby apart to get it out of her? Someone told Win that."

"It's not true," said Kirsten forcefully. It made her angry for the O'Briens' sake that such stories should spread and foster heaven only knew what other exaggerations. "The baby had very wide shoulders. Mrs. Steiner had to break one to bring him and perhaps he had some broken ribs that pierced his heart or lungs. But he was perfectly shaped and all together."

Daisy shuddered. "It was still awful. Poor Mrs. O'Brien! I haven't let on to Win, but I've been really scared ever since I heard about it."

"Usually nothing like that happens," Kirsten pointed out with more confidence than she felt. "You're bigger than Lorena and have larger bones. Your baby should come easier."

"Win was going to ask you; will you come?"

"Of course. And you'll have a beautiful little boy or girl and wonder why you ever worried." Praying with all her heart that it would be so, Kirsten's gaze wandered to the shotgun by the door.

"Win says we'd better keep it handy in case a claim jumper comes along," said Daisy. She gave a nervous laugh. "He's showed me how to shoot it, but I expect I'd blow my toes off. I'm still glad he got out of that claim club, though, and the Committee. Kirsten, did you really go into business with that pedlar?"

Kirsten explained as she mended. They had a cold supper of leftovers and sat up late talking. When Kirsten left next day, she promised Daisy that she'd try to visit in the next few weeks and would most certainly come for the baby and stay till Daisy was on her feet.

Seth Collings was going to Central City for supplies, so Kirsten sent her letter to Ash by him. It was several weeks before she got his answer:

> *Returned from Washington to find your letter. I'm sorry I can't oblige you, my Kirsten, but the matter you mention is between Kelly and Gus. I'm delighted with your portrait. In it, you smile*

*at me all the time, not just occasionally. Doesn't it please you to
know that in the picture you'll always be young and lovely,
starting out to discover your America? I remain yours faithfully.*

Before dawn on the tenth of June, Win rode up to say Daisy's
pains had started; he wouldn't even drink a cup of coffee before
he rode off for Mrs. Steiner. Kirsten had her gift, flannel blankets
and cool, cotton gowns, ready to go, and tucked these into the
saddlebag with her best scissors. Adding some cottage cheese and
butter, she mounted Honey and was off as the rising sun streaked
the eastern sky with rose and gold and crimson.

Oh, let there be new life this day, blessing and joy, not death.

31

Daisy was frightened and crying when Kirsten arrived, but a cup of tea and soothing words steadied her, and after that, about all Kirsten needed to do was sponge off her face and arms, talk to her and, when the pains intensified, let Daisy grasp her hands while she screamed and bore down. When Kirsten saw the baby's head straining against the dilated opening, she remembered what Mrs. Steiner had done and held her palm lightly against the wet fuzz. It was well she did, for with a rending cry, Daisy pushed, and in the next instant, the little head shoved hard, pushing Kirsten's hand back, and the rest of the body slipped out in a breath, so easily that Kirsten stared blankly for a moment at the tiny spraddled body before she picked it up.

The boy gave an indignant, lusty yell. Laughing with relief, Kirsten tied two bands of cotton around the cord and cut in between, wiped off the worst of his waxy, mucousy coating, cleaned his nose and mouth, and placed him in Daisy's eager arms. "Here he is. Was he worth the trouble?"

"Oh, he's beautiful!"

Kirsten couldn't have said that about the small, flat-faced, mottled red creature, but she did think the way they looked together as Daisy cuddled him to her breast was the most beautiful thing she had ever seen. This was how it was supposed to be, pain forgotten in joy. Poor Lorena. Poor O'Brien.

Gently rubbing Daisy's slack belly as the contractions faded, Kirsten couldn't hold back tears for that futile struggle and the child who had never breathed, but tending Daisy left no time for grief. Saving the afterbirth for Mrs. Steiner's experienced eye, Kirsten cleaned Daisy up as well as she could, putting the stained sheets to soak and spreading fresh ones on the grass-stuffed mattress before she gave the baby a thorough washoff. Maybe it was her imagination, but he already seemed fairer and his nose less flat. She then fixed Daisy a light meal and more tea, and brushed and braided her thick yellow hair into one plait. When Mrs. Steiner arrived with Win, Daisy was sleeping with the baby in her arms and a proud, blissful smile on her face.

"You did as good a job as I could," Mrs. Steiner said as she examined the shriveling navel cord. She gave only a cursory glance at the afterbirth. "It's all here or she'd be hemorrhaging instead of sleeping like a lamb."

It was too late for Mrs. Steiner to start home that day, and she was exhausted from riding horseback, so she rested while Kirsten started supper and Win doted on his wife and son. "Have you seen Lorena O'Brien?" Kirsten asked as she mixed cornbread.

"I stopped off about a month ago after I brought a baby over in their direction." Mrs. Steiner shook her graying blond head. "She sure looks peaked, all big brown eyes and not much else. But she said she was fine and got a mite snappy when I asked if she felt all right in her female parts. If you ask me—"

Not wishing to hear speculation on the O'Briens' private life, Kirsten asked after the children. "Jackie's already walking," said Mrs. Steiner. "I expect that's because his sister toddles him around. She's a regular little mother, but kind of scared of me. Reckon she thinks I had something to do with that other little brother winding up in a coffin."

"I think it's likely his dying made her remember when her parents died, at least a little. Does she still worry when Jackie goes to sleep?"

"Didn't act worried about anything." Mrs. Steiner's blue eyes softened. "She's a corker, that one. Plenty of gumption. Too bad Lorena—"

"It certainly has been a dry spring," Kirsten said, straightening from scraping coals over the Dutch oven.

Mrs. Steiner reddened. After a pause, she changed the subject. "Are you going to the big Fourth of July celebration in Central City? Hear tell there's going to be a parade and band, fireworks, and a big barbecue."

"I hadn't heard, but I doubt I'll go."

"You've got to," said Win, coming out of the bedroom. "Mr. Steiner just got back from Central City and he told me about it. Goin' to be a heap bigger doin's than they'll have even in Dodge.

If Daisy and little Win get along real good, I aim to take 'em. Let Blue hold down the claim and come with us."

"We'll see," Kirsten said and, while Win did his evening chores, went in to see how Daisy was and admire the baby, who looked less scalded by the minute. How could such tiny fingers be so perfect? The diminutive ears were like pink shells, and already his dark eyebrows could furrow in a scowl.

Again, Kirsten grieved for the O'Briens, and since there seemed no way for her to have a child of her own, she ached for herself, too.

Daisy felt so well that she insisted on getting up the third day for a little while, and on the fifth urged Kirsten to go home. "You've been wonderful and I just hope I can do something for you someday," she said, cradling the baby as he nursed. "But you've got your own work and Win will help me." She nuzzled the fine black hair and laughed. "I just can't wait to show him off! Do go to the Fourth with us!"

"I don't think so," said Kirsten, and when Daisy looked disappointed, she suggested, "In spite of the drought, there've been lots of blossoms on the sandhill plums. When they get ripe, why don't we take a lunch and spend a day picking them?"

Daisy brightened at that and Kirsten made her farewell. She didn't want to attend the gala in Ash's town, partly because she was afraid people would expect her to get up on the platform and say something. She had said all she could last summer, and had it done any good? Since then, with the coming of many settlers who wanted protection, any protection, for their claims, Kelman's power had doubled, and Ash tolerated him because the vigilante took care of his dirty work. No, she had no heart to celebrate America until there was law in the Strip.

While she was at the Kellys', a Lazy R cowboy brought an invitation to the Rawlings sisters' wedding. It would be held in the Central, Ash's grand hotel. A cousin of the twins, a Presbyterian minister from Dallas, would perform the ceremony, and Kirsten and Katharine Allen were to be the brides' attendants. "You don't need a special dress," Meg wrote, but the cowboy, stopping at the Allens' first, brought a request from Katharine for "something that will complement the bridal gowns but not make me look ridiculous—please, Kirsten!"

After perusing all her patterns, Kirsten found a simple one that would not make her look prematurely aged, nor Katharine girlish. By good luck, she had a summery cross-bar lawn in misty green for herself and a primrose yellow that would suit Katharine. With the help of Milady, she did Katharine's dress first, dispatching it by Blue, and finished the green gown just in time to drive in for the wedding. She packed bedrolls, since they'd have to overnight. Seth Collings was enlisted to stay at their place and do the chores.

"Aim to be a bridegroom myself purty quick," confided the chunky sometime freighter as he wiped his bald head with a bandanna. "Put an ad in the Kansas City paper, heard from this schoolmarm, and we bin a-correspondin'. She's comin' soon as I get a soddie built and a well dug. If you'll come help me, Blue, I'll trade work."

"Just say when," said Blue.

The wedding, the first held in No Man's Land, was a grand affair, attended by friends from all over the Triangle, including Truman and Persia Hollister, come all the way from their new ranch south of Abilene—but the O'Briens weren't there. Tom Reynolds had somewhat trimmed his bushy yellow handlebar moustache, and both he and Bill Mabry had slicked down their hair and wore suits and starched white shirts.

"You won't get me in this rig again till you bury me," Kirsten heard Tom mutter to Meg, and as soon as the vows were made, he unbuttoned his collar to much laughter before he kissed his bride. Hi Allen was Tom's best man and Ash Bowden served as Bill's.

At the splendid reception in the hotel dining room, Bowden fetched Kirsten and Katharine glasses of champagne. "The brides are indeed lovely," he said with the smile that softened Kirsten even when she was vexed with him. He raised his glass in a sort of toast. "But may I whisper that in my view, the attendants outshine them?"

A tide of crimson rose to Katharine's dark hair, but Kirsten was braced for him and said coolly, "You may whisper what you please, but don't say it out loud."

He lifted an eyebrow in bland amusement. "Have you heard about the Glorious Fourth celebration?"

"Wouldn't miss it," said Hi, strolling up with Amanda. Kirsten slipped off to visit with the Hollisters, who liked their new home though they missed their old neighbors.

Ash joined them, and after a few minutes Persia said, "Oh,

look, Tru, there are the Cators! If you'll excuse us—" She bore her puzzled husband away and Ash turned his back to the crowd, trapping Kirsten in a corner.

"Will you come to the Fourth?" he asked bluntly.

"No. There's nothing to celebrate while August Kelman runs the Strip."

"I've told you he has his uses."

Kirsten shrugged and stood silent. "You ought to come," Bowden pressed. "I'm going to announce a territorial convention. We'll hold it here next spring and elect our own government if Congress won't act before then."

"And you'll be governor."

"Can you think of anyone more qualified? I'd like your support, Kirsten."

"You won't get it, not while you do nothing to check the Committee. In fact," she added hardily though she couldn't guess what he'd do to advance his ambition, "I'll ask my customers *not* to vote for you."

His smile faded. Their eyes dueled and then he stepped aside with a short, hard laugh. "What good will that do, Kirsten mine, if there's no one to run against me?"

She pondered that as summer wore on and the sun baked the prairie dull brown, each day seeming hotter than the last. The Kellys stopped on their way back from the Fourth, and while Kirsten held little Win and marveled at how he could almost support his weight by gripping her finger, Daisy told of the parade with a real if small band in Central City uniforms, the fireworks that *did* go off this time, the barbecue put on by the Central City Merchants' Association, and the dance that lasted till morning.

"Quite some fandango," summed up Win, smothering a yawn. "A senator friend of Bowden's gave the main speech, all about pioneers bein' the spirit of America, but Bowden's talk was the real rip-roarer, about how we're entitled to decent government, and if Washington won't give it to us, we'll set up our own." Win chuckled. "Since he'd just treated everyone to a big party, some wanted to elect him our delegate to Congress then and there, but he said all modest like that he appreciated our confidence but he'd just go on workin' for the Strip in Washington. If he has to give up on 'em, then we'll have elections."

"And vote Gus Kelman sheriff?" demanded Kirsten.

Win's jaw dropped. "You reckon he'd run?"

"You think he won't? Who else rides all over the Strip enforcing his notion of the law?"

Thinking on that, Win narrowed his eyes and his boyish face hardened. "He was at the celebration but not makin' a lot of noise like he did last year. 'Fore I'd see him elected, I reckon I'd have to run myself."

"Win!" protested Daisy. "You don't need to get mixed up in something like that! There's plenty to do at the claim and little Win and I need you!"

"Honey, if Kelman was elected sheriff, how long do you think he'd leave us on our claim? If there's goin' to be a government, folks who don't like Kelman's ways better get together and elect men who'll be fair."

Daisy still looked worried, so Kirsten said nothing, but as they drove away, she determined that should an election come, she'd do all she could to make sure Kelman wasn't empowered by the will of the voters to do what he now did because there was no other law.

The O'Briens hadn't been at the Fourth, and by August, Kirsten grew so concerned about them and hungry for the sight of Lucy and, yes, O'Brien, too—simply to behold him—that after the plumming excursion with the Kellys, she took a bag of the reddish-orange fruit and some clothing she'd made for the children and set off on Honey one morning before light.

To earn some cash, O'Brien was freighting for the summer between Camp Supply and Dodge. Jackie could not only walk now, he could run, and had a few intelligible words. Lucy still lugged him around but with great puffing, for at a little over three, she was small for her age, and he was almost as big as she was.

Lucy's joyful hug and "Aunt Kir'sn! Aunt Kirs'n!" were reward enough for the long ride, though Kirsten was surprised at how her heart sank when Lorena explained O'Brien's absence. As Mrs. Steiner had observed, Lorena's eyes were huge and somewhat hollowed in her heart-shaped face, but her cheeks were pink and she was more cheerful than Kirsten had dared hope. The reason emerged after supper when the dishes were done and they sat outside to catch the breeze and enjoy the respite from the sun.

Lorena faced the slope where a white stone marked the baby's grave. "Kirsten," she said, smiling at the children, who were tumbling on the sparse grass with Patchy. "I'm going to have another baby. And this time I feel so well that I'm just sure the baby will be fine."

It was a moment before Kirsten could answer. When she could, she said, "That's wonderful, Lorena. I—I hope everything goes exactly as it should."

"Pat wanted to wait," Lorena confided. "He was afraid I wasn't strong enough. He—he's always been so kind that way, Kirsten, in fact, I have to admit that I've had to—well, lure him. But I was so upset over losing the baby that I couldn't eat and cried and got so rundown that I guess Pat decided I wouldn't get any better till I knew his baby was on the way."

"Lorrie, Pat loves Lucy and Jackie as if they were his own. I'm sure he doesn't want you to run risks so he can see that red hair of his on some innocent youngster's head."

"Of course he doesn't." Lorena's face set in surprisingly stubborn lines and Kirsten had a flash of how wilful she could be, how unable a man like O'Brien would be to oppose her. "But that's all the more reason. He's given me so much that I have to give him a child of his own. I want that more than anything on earth."

A chill shot down Kirsten's spine, and she was glad that Lucy plunged into her arms at that moment, panting and laughing, so that she didn't have to think of anything to say.

The two acres of winter wheat they'd planted the previous fall had yielded thirty bushels of grain, threshed out by riding the horses around a hard earthen threshing floor, and then winnowed, grain from chaff, by fanning in a sheet. This was enough for their needs even after the settler who'd built a mill on the Canadian took his share. Kirsten's sewing was bringing in substantial sums, so Blue traveled to Dodge and bought a mower and rake for the haying. In return for its use and Blue's help, Win would do their fall plowing and Seth would help as he was needed.

Meanwhile, Kirsten used all the strategies she'd heard of for preserving their garden's bounty: drying corn, green beans and shelled peas; putting tomatoes in kegs of brine; submerging plums in plain water; and pickling cucumbers. In September, they harvested oats and maize, saving stalks for fuel and storing the animals' feed in a shed Blue had built on to the stable, where fodder, leaves stripped from the corn while still green, was already bundled. As they laboriously threshed and winnowed the oats, sweating and itching with the chaff that burrowed everywhere, Kirsten suggested to Blue that next year, as well as a reaper-binder, they might buy a threshing machine that could be used all over the settled parts of the Strip.

"I like living on a farm," she said, rubbing at the chaff that prickled maddeningly beneath her clothes. "But some work, like this, I'd a lot rather let neighbors do in return for using our machinery."

"I won't argufy with that," grinned Blue. "That's why I turned cowboy, to get shut of farm chores." At her contrite look, he said, "This is different, Miss Kirsty. It's our place. On top of that, I'm a dang sight older and wiser."

In October, as geese and cranes flew south, Blue and Kirsten broke the ears of corn, still in their shucks, from the stripped stalks and dumped the ears in a railed crib in the feed shed. Shucking and shelling the corn would be a winter job. Now it was time to dig the potatoes, and thanks to water from the river, there was a good crop. These went in a large bin in the root cellar, another of the summer's achievements, like the well house with its troughs for keeping milk, butter and cream fresh. There were onions in the root cellar, pumpkins, Hubbard squash, and kegs and tubs of preserved foods.

They'd eat much better this winter than last, and in three or four years, the carefully tended fruit trees should begin to bear apples and peaches. Kirsten's mouth watered at the thought, and she smiled, thinking that she now understood much better Ash Bowden's insistence on fresh fruit than when she had waited on him in Minnie's dining room.

She hadn't seen or heard from him in months. Most likely he was off on business or lobbying in Washington; or perhaps he had simply lost interest in her, though Kirsten, knowing him, couldn't quite believe that. But feelings did change. She loved O'Brien more than ever, but since the baby's death she seldom had to check those guilty but thrilling dreams of him when she relived that first dance in America, the kisses that had never touched her lips, the lightning fire that flashed between them so wildly and sweetly. She thought of him with almost unbearable sadness, for Lorena was as dependent on him as Lucy or Jackie, and her fierce resolve to give him a child bound him even tighter. From longing for him, rebelling against his marriage, Kirsten was forced to admit that it *was* a marriage and the needs of his wife and family left nothing for her beyond the friendship that would endure, even if she never saw him again.

Her love was hopeless and yet it was her love. She couldn't marry Ash, attracted as she was to him, pleasurable as his company could be, so there was no use in subjecting herself to suitors eager to find any woman to bring comfort to their farms or ranches. Again, she insisted that Blue go to play the violin at the Allens' Christmas ball while she took care of the chores, and this time neither Ash nor O'Brien appeared. She read the Christmas story from the old Bible and went to bed early with Dimma at her feet.

Blue returned with news that dwarfed his report that Bat Masterson was closing down saloons in Dodge and that a proud Seth had been at the ball with his bride, a plump, pretty woman who had sent the gathering into fits of hilarity when she referred to calves as "cowlets." "Ma'am," Tom Reynolds had replied, straightfaced, "them ain't cowlets, they're bull-lets."

"Ash Bowden wasn't there," Blue continued. "But he'd sent Hi a letter from Washington—asked him to read it at the ball and tell everybody to spread the word. Seems like Ash's got a few congressmen on his side, but he figgers it'll be several years at least before the Strip's made a territory or tacked on to Indian Territory or a state." Blue cleared his throat and gave his momentous news. "Ash is callin' a convention next month in Central City to declare the Strip a territory, elect delegates to Washington, and set up a slate for electin' a passel of officials. With all the new folks comin' in, seems like we got to do somethin'."

"I suppose so," frowned Kirsten. "What worries me is who'll be on Ash's ballot. Were Bridget and Zeke at the ball?"

"You bet they were, with a baby boy the spittin' image of Zeke. Baby was duded up in that fancy sweater you sent. And young Annie sure danced a lot with Monty Hall. Soon's she's a mite older, you can start her bride dress."

That child? A wave of the increasingly familiar left-behind feeling swept over Kirsten but was swiftly supplanted by worry about the slate.

She spent most of the next few days writing letters to all her customers in the Strip about the importance of the convention and the slate. "If you know of a good man for sheriff or judge," she wrote over and over till her fingers cramped, "his consent should be obtained and his name offered at the meeting."

It was still no surprise to hear what had happened at the convention from a stammeringly angry Win Kelly. He had gone horseback, leaving Daisy at home, for at that time of year, a storm could rage in at any hour.

"It all went slick as a greased hog. Cimarron Territory was organized with Bowden and Ollie Fergus, the manager for that big ranch his syndicate's put together, elected delegates. I don't quarrel with that. But Kelman on the slate for judge! Darnell for sheriff!"

Kirsten's heart plunged. "Weren't any other names put up?"

"A few, but they weren't anything as well known as Kelman, and of course he's got plenty of folks beholden to him for protectin' their claims and property and was buyin' drinks free and easy. It was a shoo-in." Win brooded for a moment. "When I was leavin', Jess Darnell caught up with me. Said it was too bad my claim wasn't recognized by the club and if I didn't join up again the club would support any member who wanted it. I said that'd be over my dead body. He just grinned."

What a terrible situation! Kirsten felt more than a little guilt for being protected by Bowden. Win had put everything he had into the home he'd built for Daisy and proving up the claim. He couldn't meekly give it up. Yet what chance did he have if Kelman went after him?

"I'm still a fair shot," said Blue. "If Miss Kirsty don't mind, I can come stay at your place a while."

"I sure do appreciate that." Straightening, Win looked heartened by the offer even as he refused. "But if someone's set on shootin' me from cover or at night, they'll sooner or later get it done. No, what I want to do is run for sheriff, if Daisy agrees. I'm hopin' you'll back me, Miss Kirsten, though maybe I hadn't ought to ask 'cause it could cause you bad trouble."

"I'll do everything I can." Kirsten didn't hesitate, though her heart was pounding and she seemed to taste blood. From the moment she'd seen Bob Randall swinging from that tree she had burned to see an end to Kelman's mockery of justice, longed to see her dream of America come true in No Man's Land. Bowden had warned her she might provoke Kelman to a point where nothing could restrain him, but if Win, with his family, chose to run that risk, why so must she.

Win shook her hand. "The election's set for March. I won't have any chance with the folks backin' Kelman, but I'm goin' to ride all over the Strip meetin' people and tellin' 'em how I see things, ask 'em to sign a petition for puttin' me on the ballot."

Blue shook his head. "Son, that'll sure make you a target."

"Rather get killed doin' somethin' than hidin' in the house."

"Daisy's welcome to stay with us when you're gone," offered Kirsten.

"That's mighty nice of you. I'll tell her."

When he was gone, Kirsten and Blue looked at each other. "Honey-girl, what would you say if'n I was to ride along with that young fella?"

Kirsten caught his hands. She'd never thought about her feelings for Blue before, they had just deepened into love as he came to fill the place of her family as well as being her steady, ever-present friend. "Blue, they might kill you—"

"I wouldn't be much loss."

"You would to me."

His wrinkled face glowed and his eyes glistened. "Doggone, honey-girl, it's worth gettin' shot to know you mean that! Look, I was a bum when you came to Dodge, a wore-out crippled old has-been. You started my life all over, you with your eyes a-shinin' for all you expected to find in America. I don't have any dreams. How can I after what's happened to my folks, the Kiowas? But enough of you's rubbed off that I want to have a decent sheriff, and if there's chance I can keep that boy safe for his wife and baby— well, I'd be proud to trade my beat-up ole hide for his'n."

"If you really want to go, God bless you," she said, embracing him as tears blurred her eyes. "But, oh Blue, be careful!"

"Don't worry, honey-girl." He patted her shoulder. "I'll use ever trick I learned dodgin' sheriffs and that's a bunch. Guess now I'd ought to ride after young Win."

32

Daisy did bring little Win over to stay while her husband and Blue set out on their journey. "I'd rather lose the claim than have Win hurt," said Daisy tearfully. "But I know how that'd eat at him and like he says, I guess it's better to do something than just wait for that gang to shoot him in our own home." Cuddling the baby to her breast, she gave a heavy sigh. "It's awful, Kirsten. I love Win because he *is* a man, but what makes him that way could get him in trouble. I've told him as long as we have each other, we can always start over, but that's not how he feels."

Little Win, who had his father's brown hair, though his eyes promised to be the hazel of Daisy's, was seven months old now and spent long periods pushing to his knees and rocking on his blanket spread over a rug. He was doing this one chill, bright afternoon in late January, about two weeks after his father had left, while his mother sewed on the Family Gem and encouraged him with loving pride.

"He'll soon be crawling," said Kirsten, who was sewing, too.

"Yes, I'll have a time keeping up with him this summer when he's old enough to run but not to stay out of things." From Daisy's smile, she anticipated more than dreaded it.

Kirsten glanced out the window toward the skeleton trees and her feet stopped on the treadle. She sprang up and ran toward the door, snatching her cloak from its peg. Bent so low his face almost touched Stockings' mane, Blue was riding in. He led Win's sorrel with a blanket-wrapped form tied across the saddle.

* * *

Daisy wept over her young husband, but she must have prepared herself, for after her first violent grief, she was eerily calm. "We'll bury him on that ledge up the creek from the house," she said. "That was his favorite place to stand and look over our claim."

"When you're ready to move back to your folks, I can drive you, Miz Kelly," said Blue, arm bandaged against his chest to keep it from wrenching his wounded shoulder. In the flurry of shots that had killed Win at their campfire two nights ago, Blue was knocked down by a bullet but, grabbing the Winchester, crawled out of the light into some plum bushes and made things so lively that the ambushers had faded away. It was Win they wanted, and with the back of his head blown away, he was plainly dead. Of course there was no way to prove Kelman had done it or had had it done, but who else would?

Blue, weak from loss of blood, had bandaged the shattered skull, and plugged his own wound, lying all night beside his dead friend before he revived enough to make his painful way home.

"Thank you, Blue," said Daisy, "but I'm not leaving."

Knowing Daisy's timidity, her fear of being alone, Kirsten stared. "But Daisy—"

"It's our claim. I'm going to stay there, keep it for little Win, and when he's old enough, I'll tell him how brave his daddy was, how precious the land is." Holding the baby on her hip, she turned and started for the house. "Please, Kirsten, help me get my things. I want to take Win home."

Because of Blue's shoulder, Kirsten couldn't stay with Daisy after the burial, but though pressed, Daisy insisted on staying in her own house. "Win built it for me," she said. "I feel close to him here. Go home, Kirsten. I've got to get used to this. And thank you for lending me your Family Gem to sew for little Win." Her face contorted. "I guess I don't have to say 'little Win' anymore, do I? There's only one."

Daisy had learned to use the sewing machine so quickly that Kirsten had already thought of asking her to help with the simpler tasks like seaming. That would pay her enough to hire a man to do the heavy work. When a little time had passed, Kirsten would ride over and ask her. It was unlikely that even Kelman or Jess Darnell would terrorize a widow, but as they rode homeward, Kirsten and Blue agreed that one or the other of them would visit Daisy weekly for a while and see if she needed anything. Anything that they could bring her.

Could she have done something to change what had happened? During the next days, Kirsten agonized over that, but she'd been careful not to encourage Win, had only written letters of support for him after he'd made up his mind. No, unless she blamed herself for interrupting Maurice's hanging, she didn't see what she could have done differently.

What would happen now? Was Win to have died for nothing? Kirsten burned to spread the horror of Win's murder from one end of the Strip to the other, but what good would that do if there was no one to take his place, to run against the Kelman slate? Of course she thought of O'Brien but went sick at the thought of him ending as Win had. Besides, Lorena must be nearing her time.

If he wouldn't be pitted against killers, though, O'Brien would have been a natural candidate. Known and well liked all over the Strip, friendly with both grangers and ranchers, he could mediate quarrels and often prevent trouble rather than arrest men after the damage was done. Though Kelman's influence was strong in this part of the Strip, O'Brien had friends over the whole Triangle. If he ran for any office, he'd have a good chance of winning—if he lived.

Certainly Kirsten couldn't ask him to run, or really urge anyone to put himself in that kind of danger. If only women could! But even in America, they were not allowed to vote, much less hold office. Strange, wasn't it, when England had a queen?

Blue must have been musing along the same lines, for a week after the burying, as Kirsten was changing his bandage, he looked up at her and said, "I think maybe I'll run for sheriff, Miss Kirsty."

"What?"

He looked a bit offended. "I'm a good shot. And what's more important, if I get killed, I won't be leavin' a family."

"I'm your family!"

He caught her hand, held it to his weathered cheek for just a second. "Sure, and that's the proudest, best thing ever happened in my life. But you know what I mean. I wouldn't be all that much loss but if you'd write letters for me, tell what happened to Win, even if I did get bushwhacked it might rile enough good men up to make 'em put an end to the Committee. 'Course if you'd rather, I could go huntin' Kelman."

For a flash, that seemed the best way. Kelman had earned killing a dozen times over. Bob Randall, Win—She shuddered away from what she had almost consented to. In judging, she had done as Kelman did, decided who was worthy of death. That was exactly what must end.

Blue grinned at her. "You know, Miss Kirsty, I reckon it'd be fun to be the one wearin' the badge for a change."

"Let's wait a little while," Kirsten temporized. "I've written a lot of letters, before and after Win decided to run, and I'm writing again to tell what happened to him. Maybe somebody'll get stirred up enough to put together a slate and push it."

"Somebody?" derided Blue. "Family men like Zeke, who're scratchin' to make a go of it? Ranchers like Hi Allen or Sheldon Rawlings who figger they can take care of their own range and what happens off 'em is bickerin' amongst squatters they'd rather weren't in the country to start with? That's the reason lawmen are most always hired from outside, honey-girl. No one local wants the job."

Kirsten sighed. "I guess you're right. But someone who lives in the Strip and knows people could do a lot more good with less shooting than one of those famous sheriffs that seem about as bad as the outlaws they kill. Let's wait till the first of February. If no one else moves by then, we can start campaigning if you're still willing." She arranged the dress she was making on Milady and began pinning up the hem. "As soon as I finish this dress, I'm going to see Daisy and then ride on over to the O'Briens'. I wrote last month offering to stay with Lorena about the time she expects her baby but they haven't answered. I'm getting a little worried."

"Want I should ride over to their place?" asked Blue. "This time of year, I don't like the notion of you ridin' that far alone."

"I want to see Lucy," Kirsten said, and Blue argued no further.

Daisy had dark circles beneath her eyes and was so thin that her husky little son seemed too big for her to hold. But she did hold him, and spoke and moved with an assurance Kirsten would not have believed possible in Win Kelly's sweet, compliant wife. It was as if, without him, she'd had to develop the traits he had supplied in their marriage. Daisy was young and very pretty. On this woman-starved frontier she would almost surely marry again, but for the time being she seemed intent simply on proving up on the claim and holding it for small Win as a heritage from his father.

"I'd love to sew for you," she said eagerly and, when Kirsten named a sum, protested, "Oh, that's too much! Really, I'll be glad to have something to keep me busy till I can start working outside."

"I'm only paying you what I reckon I'd be paid for that part of the sewing," Kirsten said. "I'm getting so many orders that I can't handle them all. If you still like the work after you've helped me for a while, maybe we can get you a treadle machine and you could start your own business."

"I'll never have your knack for style and figuring out what color and fashion look best on someone," Daisy said. "I'd a lot rather work with you."

"We'll see how it goes." Kirsten spread the cut-out garments she'd brought and explained what was needed, assigning to Daisy only the easy, straight seams. With practice, of course, she could do most of the basic sewing, leaving the intricate parts to Kirsten.

Kirsten was spending the night in order to reach the O'Briens' in one short winter day. As they were preparing for bed she glanced at the shotgun. It was still by the door but placed behind a trunk where the baby couldn't reach it.

"Can you shoot that now, Daisy?"

"Win showed me before he left. I didn't actually shoot it because it has such a kick that it'd bruise my shoulder. But it's loaded and I'll use it on anyone who tries to make me leave."

Kirsten believed her.

Smoke curled from the O'Briens' chimney, but though it was a brisk, sunny day, no one was moving around outside. That was strange, for there were invariably plenty of tasks for a nice winter afternoon—mucking out the barn, fixing fences, even getting an early start on spring plowing. Kirsten could make out the white stone on the slope, but—was that another one? By the patch of raw, upturned earth?

It was, and Kirsten's heart tightened with fear as she urged Honey on. One of the children? Oh please, not Lucy! But not Jackie, either. Had Lorena's new baby come early and died or, perhaps, like the last, never even breathed?

Mrs. Steiner met Kirsten as she was turning Honey into the corral. "It's good you've come. I was goin' to send my man for you because I can't do a thing with O'Brien—"

"Lorena?"

Mrs. Steiner shook her head. "The baby's fine though a tad small. I'd reckon he's a few weeks early. But Lorrie—she started bleedin'. Nothin' I could do. Blood poured out of her till she was whiter than the pillow." The big woman snuffled into her apron. "At least she got to hold her baby and after all that pain, dyin' came easy. She was huggin' her baby and smilin'. She said—she said, 'Pat, here's our son.'"

"Yes." Kirsten swallowed, scarcely able to speak through the aching knot in her throat. "She wanted that more than anything."

"That's what it cost her. Go on in. I'll grain your horse."

Dazed, Kirsten approached the cabin with the bag of clothing she'd made for the children and a pretty wrapper for Lorena. How could she be dead? So young, with three children! In spite of herself, a deep, protective affection had grown in Kirsten for the woman she had at first nearly hated for marrying O'Brien. Now Kirsten almost hated herself for the inevitable realization that O'Brien was free, but most of this guilt ebbed quickly, for she knew, absolutely, that she would have given everything she had to bring Lorena back. Though they'd had opportunities, she and O'Brien had never done anything Lorena couldn't have watched with utter peace of mind. Probably the strain of managing that was why O'Brien hadn't visited in close to a year.

How glad now Kirsten was of his honor, for she didn't delude herself. If he had come to her in need and love and longing, she couldn't have refused him. And had that happened, how poisoned their love would be now, how cursed and guilty. She wouldn't let herself really think ahead, but surely, after a while . . .

O'Brien lay on the disordered bed, breathing heavily, the golden growth on his face so long it was almost curling. A whiskey bottle was on the floor. Curled up against his father's back, Jackie slept, too. Lucy was rocking the cradle, but when she saw Kirsten, she jumped up and came running, leaping into Kirsten's arms, hugging and kissing her as she wept.

"Oh, Aunt Kirs'n, Mama's dead! Like the other little baby boy!" Sobbing, she pointed to the small shape in the cradle with its reddish fuzz of hair. "Mama gave us this baby, though. We have to take care of him 'cause Mama can't. She called him Pat like Daddy's name." Lucy's ringlets bounced as she shook her head worriedly. "Daddy won't get dead, will he? He—he sleeps a lot and I can't wake him up."

"He's sad about your mother, honey. He'll get better." O'Brien, in his stupor, could wait a moment. Right now, Lucy needed reassurance. "Pat's a nice baby, isn't he? May I pick him up?"

"Course you can," said Lucy in a proprietorial manner. "Bet you can hold him good as I can. Jackie can't, though. Jackie's still a baby. Isn't he?" Apparently this was the crux of some dispute, and Kirsten, carefully picking up the baby Lorena had held so briefly, answered with all the diplomacy she could summon.

"Jackie's two in April, so I don't think you can call him a baby, but you'll be four this summer, and that's really a big girl."

Lucy nodded. "That's what I tell him. I'm a big girl so he has to mind."

Apparently a streak of tyranny went with Lucy's mothering instinct. Even in her shocked grief, Kirsten had to repress a smile. Before she could better explain the uses of sisterly authority, Lucy rushed to O'Brien and shook him. "Daddy! Daddy! Aunt Kirs'n's here!"

As if escaping a pestiferous insect, O'Brien mumbled thickly and turned over. This dislodged Jackie who gave a yelp and began to cry. "Hush up, Jackie!" admonished his sister. She clambered behind O'Brien and hauled on his shoulder.

"Lucy," said Kirsten, "can you take Jackie to the rocking chair and sing to him?"

"He needs the potty," said the older child and hustled him off the bed and into the other room.

Meanwhile, at Kirsten's voice, O'Brien's eyes opened. He stared at her blankly, blinked, frowned, and only as the children vanished did he seem to understand she was actually there. "Kirsty!"

Swinging his feet to the floor he started to rise, before, wincing as if he'd been sledged, he sank back down and buried his face in his hands. Reared in a strict Lutheran community, Kirsten had seen little drunkenness till she came to Dodge, and it both disgusted and frightened her. In spite of O'Brien's sour reek, however, he looked so beaten and lost that she had to fight the impulse to cradle him against her, soothe him like a child. Something warned her that at this moment that wasn't what he needed.

"If you drank all that, it's no wonder your head hurts," she said, pouring him a cup of coffee. "You can't act like this, O'Brien. You've got three children to think about."

He gulped the coffee, pushed his hair out of his bleary eyes, glanced toward his sleeping child, and shook his head. "Sure and I don't think I can stand the sight of him."

That touched off such fury in Kirsten that she grabbed O'Brien and shook him hard. "How can you say that when Lorena wanted him so much, wanted to give you your very own child? It was her way to thank you, she died to do it, and all you can do is get drunk and blame that poor motherless baby!"

His flushed face turned even redder and he caught her wrists. "Now, damn it, Kirsty, hold on a minute. I know it's not the little guy's fault. It's mine." The dark-green eyes were full of despair. "I shouldn't have let her have that baby, not this soon anyway. I shouldn't—"

"Who do you think you are?" she asked brutally. "God?"

As O'Brien stared, she held his gaze and continued in a grim voice, though her anger had faded and again she yearned to console him. "Lorena talked to me when I was here last summer, O'Brien. She was so happy about the baby, so sure he'd be born healthy. She—she told me she was so distraught over losing the other one that you finally gave in. She was determined, she made her choice, and she gave you the son she felt she owed you."

"She didn't. Lucy and Jackie were enough."

"That's not how she felt."

Staring at the floor, he said beneath his breath, "Was that because she knew I didn't love her, not at the first? Later I did in a way. Who wouldn't? She was pretty and sweet and soft and always tried to please me. We never talked about it, but I think she guessed—" He swallowed hard. "I think she knew how I felt about you, Kirsty. But now all I can think of is the way she died."

Kirsten's heart twisted. Did he mean he'd discovered, too late, that it was Lorena he'd come to truly love? Small wonder if Lorena's adoration had evoked a response. In any case, it was too soon for Kirsten and O'Brien to bare their feelings for each other, if indeed they ever could.

Bringing him more coffee, she said, "O'Brien, do you remember what you told me after Lucia died? Of course you have to grieve. Of course you'll wonder if you should have done some things differently. But you did the best you could for Lorena, you wrapped her and your friend's baby in your love and got her a white dress—"

"We buried her in that."

A bridal gown for a shroud? That struck through Kirsten's defenses. She turned away, weeping bitterly, as Mrs. Steiner came in.

A fine comforter you are, Kirsten told herself, but O'Brien stood up, straightened the bed, and went in the other room. When he came back, he had combed his hair and wore a clean shirt.

Approaching the cradle as if his feet stuck to the floor with each step, he stood looking down at the baby who was squirming, waving tiny clenched fists, and opening his mouth as if working up to a howl. When it came, it was no whiny complaint but a battle cry of outrage.

O'Brien dropped to one knee and a grin spread over his face as he picked up the infant. "Goin' to be a preacher, son? Maybe a lawyer? You got the lungs for it. Hey, son, hey! Have mercy on your old man's splittin' head!"

When Mrs. Steiner started to take her leave, Kirsten told her about Win Kelly. It was important to spread the word, make people see that Kelman was a murderer, not a protector of settlers' rights.

"You don't have proof," the graying woman pointed out after her first shocked revulsion. "Anybody could've killed Win."

"Who else had a reason?"

"I don't know," said Mrs. Steiner, "and neither do you, Kirsten Mordal. If I was you, I'd be careful about accusin' a good man like Gus Kelman. He's run several claim jumpers off our place and got us back a good horse that was stolen. My man's goin' to vote for him and so's everyone else I know of." She glanced from Kirsten to O'Brien. "What're you goin' to do about the children? Lucy's a bright little gal, but she can't take care of the baby when you start your field and cow work."

Kirsten longed to say she'd come to stay and the thought of scandal didn't deter her. What did was the inner knowledge that it was too soon for her to be much with O'Brien. He had to mourn his wife, come to terms with his feelings of guilt; and Kirsten, too, had tangled emotions to sort out. Her glance touched the bed, flicked to his eyes, and what she found there sent a jolt through her entire body, made her knees threaten to go out from under her.

If she stayed, they'd wind up in that bed he had shared with Lorena, where Lorena had died, and his young wife's memory would make a barrier between them that might never be overcome. Just as O'Brien had owed Lorena faithfulness, he owed her now a time of mourning.

"I can take the children home with me," said Kirsten. She saw no other way, though she hated to deprive him of the healing company of the little ones.

O'Brien looked at her and she knew he'd been thinking and feeling a good deal as she had. "Sure and that'd be mighty kind of you, and probably the best thing for a while."

"If you want to go back to freightin', we can take care of your milk cows and kind of keep an eye on your claim," offered Margrit Steiner.

"I'd be obliged, Miss Margrit, though you may want to back out when you hear what I'm thinkin' on."

"What would that be?"

"I'm goin' to run for sheriff."

In the same breath, Mrs. Steiner and Kirsten cried out in protest, but O'Brien's face showed a hint of his old zest and recklessness. "Someone needs to and I reckon I've got enough friends to beat out Jess Darnell."

"You could be killed, just like Win," Kirsten argued. "What about the children?"

He gave her a steady, even look. "You've always loved Lucy, and now you've got a home for her. I know you well enough to believe you'd love the boys. And my stock and property should fetch somethin' to help with their keep."

"I don't care about that," said Kirsten. "Of course I'd love them and bring them up. But they need *you.*"

"So did Win's boy need him." O'Brien's jaw set, and though he was haggard, he had never looked more masculine and handsome. She had never loved him more than now, when he planned an action that might bring his death and could mean they would never share a life.

He took Kirsten's hands, compelling her to meet his gaze. "Listen, colleen, ever since you found Bob Randall hanged, you've wanted justice in the Strip, all those rights you talked about your first Fourth of July. I couldn't run for sheriff while Lorena depended on me, but I can now."

"Blue's said he would."

"He's got guts and I'd reckon he's a better shot than me. But Kirsty, even with your backin', do you think folks would elect a man who used to be a cattle thief and who's mostly black and Indian?"

She had no answer to that, but stood with bowed head, tears brimming her eyes. She had loved him for so long, and when it at last seemed she had only to wait till he had mourned his wife, he was bound on defying a gang of murderers. How could she bear it if she lost him now?

He said gently, "I'm responsible for the kids. You're the only one I'd trust them with, Kirsty. It's not fair to leave them with you if you don't want me to run. I guess it's up to you."

There really was no choice. "I don't want you to run," she said, "but I'll do everything I can to help you win."

"And we'll look after your stock," said Margrit grudgingly. "My man'll still vote for Gus and his slate, but it's American to have another ticket. Can't say I'm thrilled to see elections here, though. Back in Ohio, folks got so mad at each other over politics that they wouldn't speak for months."

"Well," said O'Brien with a fleeting grin, "that's the American way, too."

That night after Lucy and Jackie were asleep, Kirsten fed the baby while O'Brien packed the children's things. In the morning, he'd drive them to her place in the wagon and then return to get ready for his campaign. He thought he could persuade a lawyer friend recently come from Dodge to run for judge and Zeke would make a trustworthy clerk of the court. Kirsten, of course, would write to her far-flung patrons and ask Maury to promote the new slate on his journeying.

Fearful as she was for O'Brien and his friends, the chance of ending Kelman's reign was exhilarating. And if the candidates rode together on their campaign, it would cut down on chances of ambush. Kirsten, smiling at the way little Pat's eyebrows knit in concentration as he tugged at the bottle, dared hope that some day she'd hold a baby just as clearly O'Brien's, and nurse him at her breast. She glanced up to find O'Brien watching them.

"Pat's a beautiful baby," she said. "I'm glad Lorena got to see him. She had a right to be proud."

"Sure and she did." O'Brien pushed a trunk over and sat on it, frowning in a manner echoed by his tiny son. "Kirsty, there are things I can't tell you now, part because of Lorrie, part because I may not live through this election. But one thing I've wanted to say since that night at the Dodge House when we drank our champagne punch. I love you. Nothing ever changed that. Nothing ever will."

Though she had known it, hearing his words made up for all the denial and pain. Feeling as if a light sparked glowing within her, she let her eyes speak. *Yours and only yours . . .*

"I love you, O'Brien. I have since you made yourself my first friend."

"I can't give you what Ash Bowden can."

"You can give me what he can't—you."

O'Brien caught a deep breath. "Reckon that's all we can say for now. But Kirsty, you can bet I'll sure try not to get shot."

"You'd better stay healthy, O'Brien. You've got to help me raise these children."

"Lord willin', I'll do just that." Rising, he caressed the curve of her cheek, just for a moment, before he said good night. Kirsten sat holding the baby close, wondering how she could be at the same time so happy and so sad.

33

Kirsten's plans to ride around the Strip and personally urge her customers to vote for O'Brien's slate crumbled as she found how deeply Lucy and Jackie were affected by Lorena's death and their father's absence, Lucy the most. Her fears about sleeping people being dead caused her to disturb the baby even after she'd spent an hour patiently rocking him to slumber, and in order for Jackie to get the afternoon nap he still needed, Kirsten had to forbid Lucy to go in the bedroom and had to keep her diverted.

The child was so frightened of going to bed that Kirsten adopted the strategy of putting Jackie down first and then washing Lucy and slipping on her nightgown before wrapping her in a blanket and rocking her, while Blue played Lucy's favorite tunes on the violin. Or he might hold Lucy and Jackie while Kirsten sewed, and tell them about the Star Girls and a holy person called Grandmother Spider and her lament for her husband, Old Man Snake: "Stony Road, your beautiful spotted body. Stony Road . . ."

When Lucy fell asleep, Kirsten put her beside Jackie in Kirsten's bed, which she shared with the children. Their restlessness disturbed her own sleep, but for now they needed the comfort of a motherly body. The baby slept in his cradle beside Blue and the fireplace, and Blue fed him when he woke up hungry in the middle of the night.

"I can give him that bottle just as good as you can," Blue told Kirsty. "And change him, too. You got your hands full with the others."

Gradually, Lucy became less fearful. She and Jackie still romped with Patchy, who had with great difficulty been taught that

Dimma was not for chasing, but Lucy found the gray cat a much better size than the dog for carrying around and dressing in the scraps Kirsten gave her.

Dimma tried to evade her relentless adorer, but once captured went limp as a rag doll and allowed handling that would have earned Kirsten a scratch. When she'd had enough, however, Dimma vanished beneath the bed where neither Patches nor children could pursue her.

The children's toys had been brought with them, but Blue whittled out more buffalo to go with the one Jim Cator had made, because Lucy and Jackie were so impressed by Chief. Kirsten got out the Dala horse that she and Lucia had played with, and though the children could hardly understand Kirsten's story of how far the scuffed red steed had traveled, they had great fun trotting him after the buffalo.

One quiet game Kirsten invented to occupy Lucy while she was sewing was to put a heap of scraps on the rug and let Lucy, eyes squeezed shut, smooth a bit of fabric with her fingers and identify it. Velvet, silk, chenille, ottoman and marquisette were easy, but it amazed Kirsten how after only a few handlings Lucy could distinguish between bombazine and cassimere, each with a twilled weave, or tell sheer nun's veiling from mousseline de soie, a gauzy silk muslin. The little girl reveled in dressing up in scraps that were big enough somehow to be draped or wrapped around her, and though her chubby fingers couldn't control the biggest of Kirsten's needles yet, she sat at a box with fabric across it, treadled her feet, and sewed away for fairly long periods of blessed peace.

Kirsten loved having the children, but even with Blue's help and virtual adoption of baby Pat, she found much of the day went in wiping noses, washing hands, getting drinks and "somefin to eat." If Daisy hadn't relieved her of much of the plain sewing, Kirsten would have dropped far behind on orders. As it was, she kept up by working as she could in the day and sewing several hours by lamplight after the children were asleep.

She still wept for Lorena, but work and the constant needs of the children drained her emotions. O'Brien was always in her thoughts—where he was, his safety, and if he had gotten others to be on his slate. The first task Kirsten set herself on returning home was to write again to the women she'd come to know through sewing for them, summing up Kelman's record and her conviction that though there was no evidence, he was behind Win Kelly's death. She told these women why O'Brien was running and, for those who might not know him, cited his experience in the Strip and his reputation.

Daisy Kelly's determined to stay on her claim so her son will one day inherit what his father died for. Make your husband see he must not empower August Kelman to do by the will of the voters what he now does by force. Don't let Patrick O'Brien's children grow up without either a mother or father. Let us have law in the Strip, and justice, and an end to Kelman's hangings and cowardly shots in the night.

She wrote twenty-nine such letters, and special ones to the Allens and Rawlings, urging Hi and Sheldon to realize this was not simply a squatters' quarrel but a matter of condoning the murder of a young husband and father who had most certainly not been a cattle thief. She also pointed out to them that should Kelman win, he might well push measures they had scornfully rejected, insisting that they interrogate strangers and cowboys riding the grubline and forbid them to cross their land.

"You say it real good," said Blue when she read the message to him. "But if Kelman gets wind of it he may be too mad to care about Ash Bowden, 'specially since Ash is off in Washington delegatin'."

"It's the least I can do." Kirsten sealed one letter and started on the next. "What I'd like to do is run for sheriff myself, or at least travel around to all my friends and convince them that O'Brien has to be elected."

Blue laughed and picked up the letter as if it might explode. "Reckon this is purty near as good, honey-girl. I've showed you how to shoot the Winchester and shotgun. Till things settle down, we better keep them loaded."

"Then put them where the children can't reach them," warned Kirsten. "Maybe in the stable."

"Too far from the house if we get night visitors." Blue thought a moment. "I'll hide 'em in the fuel shed behind the logs."

A blizzard gusted out of the north in mid-February, heaping drifts to the rooftops, and again Blue and Kirsten groped their way between stable and house by clinging to a stretched rope. Kirsten could only hope that O'Brien wasn't caught far from shelter, and she worried, too, about Daisy. When travel was possible, Blue rode to Daisy's with butter, cheese, and eggs, and returned with carefully rolled sewing and the report that she had made a sort of blanket tent around the fireplace that enclosed her sewing machine and little Win's cradle. Leaving that warmth only to get more fuel, she and the baby stayed there while snow sifted in up to the windowsills and doorlatch and underneath the roof. Daisy had seen the black clouds in time to bring in plenty of fuel, so she and the baby were all right, but she was mightily glad to see Blue.

"Soon's the snow melts, I'll go caulk around those windows and seal up cracks," Blue said. "Win did a good job when he built, but the clay's shrunk and cracked and needs daubing over."

As snow melted, the sodden grass once again half hid the bodies of birds and animals, though Chief, rugged old survivor that he was, had sheltered as usual in the hay stacked behind the stable. It was dead meadowlarks and pronghorns that made Kirsten the saddest.

"Is this going to happen every winter?" she asked Blue. "And will there always be a drought the rest of the year? This must have hit cattle hard. I don't see how there can be any left. And I doubt O'Brien was close enough to home to do anything about his herd."

"Maybe Steiner fed 'em some of that hay O'Brien put up last fall," Blue suggested. "This has been a run of mean weather and no mistake, Miss Kirsty, but it seems like there's always enough critters left to start over."

He was right, of course. Pussytoes, vetches and hairy peppergrass were peeping through remnants of snow, and Kirsten took the children to see the cluster of pink anemones blooming in the rocks by the spring. From there, she could point out to them the hollow in the big cottonwood where the great horned owls were making their nest. Death and winter. Spring and new life.

On a bright day in early March, Blue, carrying several cut-out garments, rode to Daisy's to caulk the windows and cracks in the walls. As usual after his lunch, Jackie was sleepy, and Lucy and the household peace still profited from her having a nap, though she resisted lying down till Kirsten struck on the idea of putting it to her that Jackie needed watching so he wouldn't roll off the bed.

They were both asleep with Dimma curled at Lucy's back, and little Pat was smiling in long infant dreams in the cradle, Kirsten started to sit down to her work. But the blue sky called irresistibly, and it was easy to convince herself that she'd sew better if she got some fresh air and stretched her cramped muscles.

While the ground was soaked would be a good time to replace any dead saplings or cuttings on the tree claim. She'd go see how many were needed. Slipping on her cloak, she stepped outside and smiled to see Chief feeding on the slope while Dolly grazed below. It was too bad the brave old warrior would not leave progeny, but at least he should live out his years in peaceful contentment.

Passing the plowed-over garden and potato patch, Kirsten reflected that as soon as the ground dried enough, it would be time to plant potatoes, and then time to plow out weeds from between the rows of wheat that were just starting to sprout. Next came planting garden and row crops—yes, and time for the election.

She thought of O'Brien with a surge of fierce pride and love. For a few days after Lorena's death, he'd sought oblivion in drink, but from that, he'd ridden out to put an end to vigilante rule, to dedicate himself to bringing law to the Strip. He'd planned to cover the east part first and then zigzag to the west and had promised to stop by to see the children when he was fairly close. She wished that he'd come or she'd hear about him in some way, for until she did, she'd worry that he might have been caught in the blizzard.

The fruit trees that were the hopeful beginning of an orchard all seemed to be alive. So were most of the saplings, but the cottonwood cuttings had fared less well. Walking through the acres planted with such labor and watered all summer with buckets carried from the creek—for it would have been too wasteful of water to irrigate—she sighed as she knelt to examine blackened, rotting stick after stick.

At least half would have to replaced. But she supposed that after the drought and freezing storm, it was lucky that any of them had rooted and lived. Fortunately, all the cuttings cost was work, unlike the expensive peach and apple trees especially ordered and brought with care from Dodge City.

Straightening, Kirsten drew in a deep breath of clean, sparkling air. These few fruit trees would become an orchard. The saplings and cuttings might have to be replanted time and again but by the time those children sleeping in the house were grown, this would be a cooling, shady grove, and how it would be loved by nesting birds and animals, wild or tame, craving relief from summer's pitiless heat.

In her, too, fresh energy coursed strongly, making her blood tingle. O'Brien loved her and he was free. Together, they would raise Lucy, her heart's child, Jackie, the son of his friend, little Pat, bought gladly by Lorena at the price of her life, and though these made a family, she hoped she and O'Brien might make in their loving at least one child, one child to firmly root the Mordals in America.

She was pausing to caress a young apple tree's gray bark, when a scatter of horsemen appeared on the dirt cliff to the north, saw her and came spurring down the bank and across the creek. Heart stopping, Kirsten recognized Gus Kelman in the lead and Jess Darnell beside him.

Blue had taken the Winchester, but the shotgun was in the fuel shed. It might as well have been ten miles away. There wasn't even a club close at hand and running was useless. *If only they'll not hurt or scare the children!*

Hauling his gaunt, jug-headed horse to a stop with a cruel sawing of the bit, Kelman stared down at her with mingled rage and satisfaction in his small coal-chunk eyes. He fished a crumpled page out of his pocket and threw it in her face.

"Been damned busy, ain't you? Spreadin' these lies all over the Strip, tryin' to turn folks agin me! When I'm through with you, you'll be glad to mind your own business, providin' I don't smash your hands to pieces to make sure you can't write any more such stuff!"

"Have—have you hurt O'Brien?"

"Not yet, but I hear he's headed to see you and his bunch of little bastards." He grinned, showing square yellow teeth. "We'll just settle in and wait for him while you cook us a good dinner."

"Ash Bowden—" she began.

"He gave me this letter you wrote to all your friends," Kelman jeered. "Said it looked like you were hell-bent on messin' up the election."

Kirsten gasped in disbelief, but the letter was genuine, and she couldn't imagine any of her clients turning it over to her enemy. She had some idea of Bowden's ambition and ruthlessness. Apparently returned from Washington, he'd heard that Lorena was dead, and with her his chance of ever winning Kirsten. Hadn't he even said that was one of the circumstances under which he'd abandon his hopes?

Yet she couldn't believe he'd do this . . . "Ray," barked Kelman, "you and Sam go up to the house. Keep an eye peeled for that damn redbone and kill him. Don't let his limpin' fool you, he's a dead shot."

"Blue's not here," Kirsten choked. "The children are asleep. Please, please don't bother them."

Kelman jerked his head toward the house. "Go ahead, men. If the Injun-nigger ain't around, we'll get him when he comes. Tie the kids up if you have to, we don't want 'em bawlin' and gettin' underfoot."

"Let me take care of them," Kirsten pleaded. "I'll keep them quiet."

"They'll be quiet one way or another," Kelman said. "You just stay here a minute. I'm goin' to teach you a lesson, and if you learn it you may get off with a good floggin' seein' that you're a female. Jess, get ahold of her. Boys, let's trample that wheat and drag up any trees too big to ride over. Don't leave a thing standin'."

Kirsten stifled a scream. It might frighten the children and would only gratify Kelman, but when Jess Darnell started to close his arms around her, she kicked him viciously and, remembering something Blue had told her, struck his Adam's apple as hard as she could with her doubled fist. He staggered backward. She grabbed for the rifle in his saddle scabbard, but Kelman made his rope into a quirt, and slashed her across the face and arms. He swung it again, striking her head with stunning force, and again and again in weltering, stinging blows that beat her to her knees as blood dripped into her eyes and left salt in her mouth.

"I've got her, Gus!" yelled Darnell. In her ear, he warned, "Behave yourself and I'll try to get you off easy. But you make Gus any madder than he is and there'll be hell to pay."

"Make her watch," said Kelman. "Wipe that blood out of her eyes."

Darnell smeared his bandanna across her face, then clamped her tight against him, one hand on her breast. Kirsten scarcely felt it, or the hurts left by the rope. Her loathing and pain joined with a fresh wave of physical agony as Kelman gloated over her while five men rode up and down the lines of trees, trampling them into the ground. Then, with whoops of glee, they tossed nooses over the fruit trees and larger saplings, hauled them up by the roots, and galloped over them till the young trunks and limbs were crushed and scattered.

Kirsten wept in outrage and helplessness as they obliterated the tender wheat sprouts, and with them all the work of plowing and planting and the hope of a bountiful harvest.

"Let's go," said Darnell, squeezing her breasts. "Remember, don't make Gus any madder'n he is and I'll try to see you ain't hurt bad."

"The children—"

"Like I say, do as you're told and I'll do my best. But don't try anything with me again, sweetheart, or I'll make you wish it was old Gus after you 'stead of me."

"You can let go of me. I've got to see about the children so I can't run away."

"Reckon you can't at that." Releasing her, he lounged several steps behind as Kirsten hurried to the house.

She froze at what she saw. The hay around the stable was ablaze, men were twirling chickens in the air, wringing their necks; as shots rang out, Chief pawed upward, ran a distance and fell, Honey sped wildly down the creek, and Dolly collapsed as if poleaxed.

It was like war, except these men weren't fighting men. If they'd shoot harmless animals—she had to get to the children. She thought of the shotgun in the shed, but it would be no use against nine men, all heavily armed. She thought of Blue with a stir of hope. If she could think of some way to warn him. Honey had run that way. If the horse was wounded, if Blue saw her—But that couldn't be counted on.

"That red nigger ain't here, Gus," called the swarthy man named Ray. Kelman awkwardly discharged his bulk from the saddle and flung his reins to Sam, ordering, "Couple of you take all the horses up the creek a ways and keep 'em out of sight. Don't want either O'Brien or the redbone to get a whiff of us till they hit the dirt."

Kirsten's mind flailed back and forth. O'Brien. Blue. If they rode in unsuspectingly—If they came in daylight, they'd see the burned hay and charred stable, of course, but O'Brien might think Kirsten had dropped a lantern while doing chores after dark, and Blue probably wouldn't get home till night.

How to warn them? "Aunt Kirs'n!" Lucy ran up and grabbed her skirts. "Don't like these men! They killed Chief and Dolly and our chickies! Make them go home!"

Kneeling, Kirsten held the trembling child close and fought to make her tone steady and calming. "They'll go after a while, honey, but for now you must keep Jackie and Patchy and Dimma in the bedroom. You go in there and don't come out till I tell you to, understand?"

Lucy's mouth quivered. "Baby boy?"

"I'll see to him." Surely not even Kelman would hurt an infant, but she could well imagine his shooting the dog and cat, perhaps hitting the older children if they annoyed him. She gave Lucy a firm push. "Go along now, dear. This is when you need to be a really big girl and take care of Jackie."

The baby, who'd been fretting, gave a few preliminary sobs and emitted the howl that meant he was wet, soiled, hungry, or all three. "You'd better let me tend to him," said Kirsten, "Or he'll get angry and scream for hours."

"Go ahead," grunted Kelman, sinking into her rocker. "We've got plenty of time. Just goin' to take life easy and let you cater to us while we wait for O'Brien and your pet nigger. Don't try anything or you'll get a worse whippin'."

Bruised and sore, Kirsten changed little Pat and warmed his bottle in the teakettle. Someone had built up the fire and set on the coffee. Carrying the baby to her sewing chair, she cuddled and fed him, grateful for once that his milk didn't come from her breast, for it would surely carry the growing fear that had absorbed her anger. She glanced around the room, trying to think of some signal.

She always drew the curtains at night. Blue knew this, and she'd remarked to O'Brien how nervous it made her to be in a curtainless house after dark. But Kelman, having shot men through windows, wouldn't risk being seen through one. He'd make her pull the curtains.

While doing that, was there some warning she could display? She was racking her brain when the door opened. Ash Bowden stepped inside.

"Kelman," he said, drawing his gun. Amazement changed to fury in Kelman's face. He let out a roar, knocking over the rocker as he pushed up and leaped forward.

The bullet stopped him like a giant fist and spun his heavy body halfway around so that he fell with the wound between his eyes showing while his brains leaked out behind.

"You double-crossing bastard!"

Jess Darnell had his revolver out, but Bowden's shot ripped

through one china-blue eye. Darnell flung up his arms, flopped like a headless chicken, and fell at Kirsten's feet, legs and arms twitching till they stiffened. A foul odor came from him and a damp stain spread on the stones.

The swarthy man, Ray, had his gun out and fired wildly. Bowden dropped him before he could squeeze off a second shot.

Surveying the other four men, Bowden said, "As I understand it, Miss Mordal is so esteemed that, excepting for Darnell, Gus couldn't get his Committee to ride with him on this escapade. He recruited you out of Indian Territory, with what lies and promises I don't know or care. I see your horses are being held up the creek by a couple of your friends. They're being watched by some of my friends, as is this house. If you want to see another day dawn, I suggest you do it across the territorial line." He indicated the corpses. "Take this garbage with you. Darnell has a wife. Leave him with a neighbor so they can clean him up and break the news a little gentler—though from what I hear, she may be glad he's gone."

The men didn't argue. They dragged the bodies outside, and cleaned up the mess on the floor, though one man vomited and had to stumble outside. It took all of them to get Kelman's bulk through the door.

At the shots, little Pat had screamed with fright. Kirsten soothed him till he was ready again for his milk and was glad she wasn't standing, for there was no strength in her legs and she shook as if with palsy. The executions, for they had been that, had happened so fast she still couldn't believe Kelman, who had beaten her, was dead, as was Darnell, who had pawed her.

"I'm sorry I had to kill them in front of you." Ash gazed down at her, only the spasm of a muscle in his jaw betraying that he had just walked in on seven men and killed three of them. He got soap and a basin of water and gently washed her face, though his tone grew savage. "Goddamn Kelman, I didn't dream even he would whip you with that rope. I couldn't shoot him without risking hitting you while you were bunched up so close by the trees—and I don't have any friends out there, so I had to wait for the best time."

"You gave Kelman my letter. That's why he thought you were turning him loose."

"Why do you think I did it, my sweet innocent?" Ash turned his back, gripping his hands behind him. "When the Allens wrote me that Lorena O'Brien was dead, I knew I could never win you, and at that point I lost all interest in developing the Strip. My partners can take over. But I couldn't leave you to Kelman or let him bushwhack your bridegroom, so I figured a way to kill him in the middle of a raid that would discredit him and vigilante law for good."

"Ash—"

"Call it my parting contribution to the Strip. I've formed a company to finance mines in the Klondike and I'm going there with Katharine Allen as soon as we can be married."

Dazed, Kirsten echoed, "Katharine? Married?"

"Yes, my love. I admire her, we enjoy each other's company, and we both want children. She knows what she can have of me and is content." Swinging around, he smiled. "It might be more romantic to persist in yearning for my heart's desire, as you did with O'Brien, but I'm a realist. I never will forget you, but I won't waste one moment in futile regrets."

What was it she felt for this man who had shown her the prairie's broad horizons, inspired her to be bold? She didn't love him but the bond was deep. "I'll miss you," she said. "I wish you were my brother."

"I don't. I've enjoyed the dream of you more than I have the body of any other woman."

"But your house—"

"My partner's buying it. For a wedding present, you may take any of the paintings you'd like. The only thing I want out of that place is the picture of you, Kirsten, starting out to discover your America. That's how I'll always see you."

They both knew his real gift had been to shoot Kelman before he could ambush O'Brien. "Aunt Kirs'n!" called Lucy from behind the partition. "Aunt Kirs'n! Can we come out?"

Ash laughed softly. "Won't be calling you that much longer, will she?" Crossing to the partition, he said kindly, "Come in, honey. It's all right now."

Two hens had evidently cowered far enough back in the coop to be missed by the spoilers. They pecked unconcernedly around the dead ones. The sod of the stable still smoked on the outside but the hay within was all right. While Lucy watched her younger brothers, Ash walked with Kirsten to examine Dolly and Chief.

Dolly was dead, pierced by five bullets. Patting the black muzzle, Kirsten couldn't hold back tears.

"Why did they kill her? She hadn't hurt them."

Ash helped her to her feet, wiping her eyes with his linen handkerchief. "If I knew that, I'd be a wise man. Some men build. Some destroy. Some do both."

Like you. But his shooting of Kelman and Darnell was in its way a building, for it cleared the way for good men to establish order in the Strip.

Chief stirred as they approached the shaggy brown heap of his body. Blood had dried along his hump and still oozed from a wound in the hair above, but he scented them, bellowed, and shakily began to paw his way to his feet.

Ash caught Kirsten and rushed her upwind where the dull-sighted bull couldn't smell them. "Only creased enough to knock him out for a while," Bowden said. "He's a tough old brute."

"I'm glad he's alive. Blue's awfully fond of him."

"Blue?" teased Ash.

"All of us. He'll miss Dolly, but he's gotten used to the horses, and someday we'll get another cow."

Ash glanced toward the ruined wheat, the broken, trampled young trees. "If you'll allow it, Kirsten, I'll send Thad and Noah out to replant your trees. I've got a load of fruit trees that I won't have planted now. It would please me for you to have them." When she hesitated, he grinned. "You know how I love fresh fruit. One of these days when we're back to visit Katharine's family, you can give me a luscious apple or pear or peach."

"I'll take the trees, then, and thank you. But we'll do the planting ourselves."

"You and O'Brien?"

"I hope so."

"Yes. From now on, you will do things together. That's how it should be, but I couldn't stand to be around to see it." Outside the door, he turned her to him, slowly traced the welts across her forehead before his lips followed his fingers and at last found her mouth.

He didn't take his kiss. She gave it. When at last he drew away, pulses throbbed in his temples at the edges of that thick silver hair. "Good-bye, my love," he said. "Fare well, my Kirsten." He bent to kiss her hands. When he straightened, he wore his familiar mocking smile. "I left without breakfast and I'm a hungry man. Aren't you going to feed me?"

Blue came in while they were eating, and only after he was sure that Ash's presence was benign did he stow his Winchester in the shed and join them at the table. Honey had fled down the creek till she found Stockings, and Blue had looked up from caulking beneath the eaves of Daisy's soddie to see Honey standing by the other mare, blood staining her shoulder. It wasn't much of a wound, but it could only mean trouble and Blue had left at once. The devastation around the stable deepened his fear. Stealing up to a window, he'd watched Ash till he was sure he'd had no part in the havoc.

"Good riddance," he said when Ash, in a few words, sketched what had happened. "Daisy'll be right glad to hear that, and since she's worried about what's gone on here, I reckon I'll go right back to tell her." Rising, he shook hands with Bowden. "Good luck in Alaska. Guess you know how to make your own."

"In some things." When Blue was gone, Bowden straightened his tie with the black diamond and shrugged into his perfectly tailored coat.

"Don't take it as a reflection on your skill, but Katharine feels she's a bit past the traditional white gown, and rather than delay, for we'll be married Sunday, for the wedding she's going to wear that gold brocade you finished recently. She'd be honored if you would be her bridesmaid. Hi will stand up with me. Luckily, a minister's just moved to Central City and he'll perform the ceremony. Our honeymoon will be the trip to Alaska."

Kirsten shook her head, between awe and a certain pique. It didn't seem quite decent for him to have arranged this marriage before making sure that she was definitely pledged to O'Brien. Lurking amusement in those crystalline eyes told her Ash read her thoughts and she immediately rallied.

"I'd love to be Katharine's bridesmaid. But will it be all right if I bring the children? They're still upset over Lorena, and today won't have helped."

"There'll be room. And of course O'Brien's invited."

"Do you know," said Kirsten, bursting into laughter, "I think he'll be very glad to come."

Ash laughed, too, and that was how they parted.

O'Brien rode in late that night after Blue was sound asleep by the fireplace. When O'Brien saw Kirsten's battered face and heard what had happened, he paced up and down, swearing every oath he'd learned as a freighter, before he took her in his arms, kissed the welts and bruises, slipped her dress from her shoulders and kissed those hurts, too.

"Colleen, colleen! I've no mind to be thankin' Bowden for this. I should have been the one to kill those spalpeens!"

"No, you shouldn't. You're going to be sheriff, not a gun-fighter."

"If they didn't kill me first, I'd have won the election," he said and hugged her to him. How wonderful that they could love each other now with their bodies, not only with their eyes. "Do you know what happened, Kirsty?" he asked proudly. "Zeke and my friend who's running for judge sashayed around with me, and folks who'd read your letters were rarin' to get shut of Kelman, even most of those who'd been on the Committee. Men with Winchesters rode along with us. Only trouble we had was runnin' a little short of rations when we holed up in a barn durin' the blizzard. The men are waitin' for me at Zeke's because I said I had to come see the kids before we headed west. I'll have to ride down tomorrow and tell 'em we've campaigned enough."

This time as he caressed her, slow fire spread through her, and when he made her look at him, the dark green of his eyes smoldered. "Kirsty, if I'd lost you—"

She knew then that Lorena was no longer between them. "You haven't lost me," she said. "You never will."

" 'Scuse me, folks," mumbled Blue, rising from his bunk. "It's a mild night out there. I've got a hankerin' to sleep in the stable." He pulled on his boots and went out, draped in blankets.

"Shall I go with him?" asked O'Brien.

Kirsten drew him down to her and let that be her answer.

A week later as they drove home from Katharine's wedding, Blue riding alongside the wagon, Lucy and Jackie in back, Kirsten glanced up from little Pat, asleep in her arms, and slowly gazed over the plains in all directions, north toward Dodge, west toward New Mexico, south toward Texas, east toward Indian Territory. Bowden was a restless spirit, always drawn to new challenges, but this country, so strange when she'd first beheld it, had become her home.

Hers and O'Brien's. Blue's. And it would belong to these children. Her heart swelled with thanksgiving, deeper because it was tinged with sorrow for the dead. Lorena, Win, Bob Randall; yes, and Lucia.

As if he sensed her mood, O'Brien gathered the reins in one hand and closed the other over hers. "Colleen, how long do you reckon it'll take to make your bride dress?"

A meadowlark rose from the grass before them and her heart sang with it. "Not so very long," she said. "And do you know, your bridegroom's shirt's already finished? I made it years ago, but I had to come to America to find the man to fit it." ·

He stopped the team and kissed her before they traveled on.

Afterword

The road ranches, background characters, droughts and blizzards are presented as accurately as possible. There was vigilante justice in the early settlement of the Neutral Strip, and claim clubs that enforced their members' sometimes dubious rights with tactics similar to those fictionalized in my book.

Ash Bowden and his Central City are fictitious, but at a convention held in Beaver (now in the Oklahoma Panhandle) early in 1887, the Cimarron Territory actually was declared and officials were elected from two opposing slates.

The Organic Act of May 2, 1890, established Oklahoma Territory and attached No Man's Land to it as Beaver County, so legal government at last came to the Strip. Congress passed a law that settlers already on their land for at least three years, as Blue and Kirsten had been, needed to wait only two more years to receive patents on their homesteads.